THE MISSING ONES

EDWIN HILL

KENSINGTON BOOKS
www.kensingtonbooks.com

KENSINGTON BOOKS are published by

Kensington Publishing Corp.
119 West 40th Street
New York, NY 10018

ISBN-13: 978-1-4967-1934-8
ISBN-10: 1-4967-1934-4
First Trade Paperback Printing: September 2019
First Mass Market Printing: August 2020

ISBN-13: 978-1-4967-1935-5 (ebook)
ISBN-10: 1-4967-1935-2 (ebook)

10 9 8 7 6 5 4 3 2 1

Printed in the United States of America

To Jennifer

Books by Edwin Hill

LITTLE COMFORT

THE MISSING ONES

WATCH HER

Published by Kensington Publishing Corporation

The Fourth of July
Finisterre Island, Maine

Lydia wolfs down a lobster roll she picked up at The Dock. She rips at it as though she hasn't eaten since Sunday, as though she'd rather spend her precious free time with him rather than savoring the taste.

At least that's what Rory imagines.

Since they've known each other, since before Rory can remember—certainly since before Lydia surprised everyone and eloped with Trey, an off-islander—Rory's wondered what it would be like for Lydia to want him the way he needs her. He's fantasized about her touch, her breath on his neck, a whisper in his ear. He's pictured waking up and watching her sleep beside him. And he's practiced confessing his love for her, and hearing her say she knows, that she's always known, and that she loves him—adores him—too.

But, in his heart, he understands. She relegated him to the friend category years ago. Or worse, brother.

"This thing cost me eighteen bucks," Lydia says. "You'd think Maggie would cut me a deal. But I'm treating myself. It's a holiday, right? Everyone but the locals gets the day off. I get ten minutes, if I'm lucky."

They both take a tentative step away from the weathered clam shack. Sweat drips from their bodies. Mingling. Reacting.

This is part of their daily ritual. First, Rory comes to the bakery where Lydia works. He stands in the long line until she notices him and brings him his coffee— iced, black, one sugar.

"You're the only person I know who drinks iced coffee black," she says.

He pats his flat stomach. "Watching my figure," he says.

The same conversation. Every day. Followed by this stroll as Lydia picks up an early lunch. She starts work at four a.m., so by ten o'clock her day is mostly over.

"What a scene," she says.

So many visitors crowd the narrow dirt paths on tiny Finisterre Island, eight miles off the coast of Maine. People wander into the General Store, over to the hotel, tearing at cotton candy, waving flags, celebrating summer. Strangers moving shoulder to shoulder. Rory is the only cop patrolling the festivities, so he has to be especially alert, but he watches as Lydia's eyes move from the mob on the path in front of them to the marina beyond. Her eyes match the color of the water and the sky and everything that's beautiful. He wonders if she's ever once seen him as desirable. He's tall and fit, a handsome man he likes to think could sneak up on her.

"Here, have some," Lydia says, holding the lobster roll toward him, her hand cupped beneath the red-striped paper boat.

Rory shouldn't take a bite, because it means something to share food, but they've shared food—they've shared everything—for their whole lives. He chews the meat, his mouth so dry he barely tastes the sweetness. She sees him—really sees him—in a way no one else does, and in a way no one else ever has.

"That's about four dollars' worth," she says. "Pay up."

He reaches for his wallet, exaggerating in time to show he's in on the joke. She laughs. A laugh right from the gut. God, he wants to touch her. He wants to take her in his arms and kiss her in front of these people.

"Look at that," Lydia says, nodding toward the General Store. A woman with greasy red hair and hollow eyes backs out through the screen door, a package of Hostess CupCakes in one hand. "I paid," she shouts. "So, go to hell."

Rory is instantly on alert. He steps toward the store, his hand at his waist, placing himself between the building and Lydia. Merritt, the proprietor, comes to the door with a broom in hand and waves Rory off. "All set," he says. Terse. To the point.

"Yeah, all set," the woman with red hair says, glaring toward Rory as she tears open the cellophane packaging and eats one of the cupcakes in two bites. She flips him the bird before noticing Lydia and trying to transform the gesture into a wave.

"Hi," Lydia says, with a weak wave back.

"I'll stop by. Tomorrow?" the woman asks.

"Great," Lydia says, watching as the woman hurries away.

"You know her?" Rory asks.

"She's been around," Lydia says. "She's out at the Victorian with the rest of them. She comes by the bakery every few days. Pays for coffee with change she probably scrounged up, then loads it with cream and sugar and begs for a job. If I was a better person, I'd give her a chance."

"Never give a junkie a chance," Rory says. "Things start disappearing."

The summer may bring tourists to the island, but it also brings people from away looking to disappear. For a tiny place, Finisterre offers plenty of hiding spots, including an old, dilapidated Victorian on the other side of the island where, last fall, Rory found a junkie who'd OD'd, the body gnawed at by raccoons. "What's her name?" he asks.

"I don't remember. Anabelle, maybe? Or Annie?" Lydia says. "That house should be torn down anyway."

"Talk to your husband about that."

Rory has already reported the Victorian and what goes on there to the state police—he reported it to Trey, Lydia's husband, a state detective—but nothing happened. Rory plans to take the state exam next month, and maybe once he passes it, he can start making a difference.

"I should get back," Lydia says.

At the bakery, the line still stretches out the door, but Rory ducks into the shade of a maple tree to keep their time together from ending. Even here, the heat pummels them. A bead of sweat runs down Lydia's chest and soaks into her pink t-shirt. Rory closes his eyes to keep from staring, but anyone who saw them now would know how much he loves her. She must know too. He focuses on a bevy of teenage girls in tight t-shirts and short-shorts.

"Eyes," Lydia says. "I don't want anyone thinking you're a perv."

Rory mumbles an apology.

"We never dressed like that, did we?" Lydia asks.

They're both north of thirty, only just but still on the wrong side of the number, and those memories of being young and moving forward have begun to fade behind regrets. "I never did," he says.

"I'd have paid money if you had!"

She laughs again, and so does he because he'd never get away with short-shorts, but maybe he'd try. For her.

She takes out the brown paper bag she brought with her lobster roll.

"No containers," he says. "Not on the Fourth of July."

She bites her lower lip and pouts. Or is that his imagination?

He glances away as she holds the green beer bottle to her forehead, takes a long swig, and hands the bottle to him. Surely she can't keep this up. She can't pretend that the connection between them doesn't lacerate her heart or that she doesn't go home and stand paralyzed in the middle of her kitchen for five minutes or five hours, thinking about him, only looking up when she realizes the frozen pizza she'd put in the oven has burned to a char and that the smoke alarm is scream-ing. But then, if she felt that pain, why would she go on break with him? Why would she punish herself that way? She touches his arm. It's like a burn, another scar to join the imaginary wounds of many years, remem-brances of every touch of skin on skin. She brushes dark hair from her face. None of this should matter, but it does, to him at least, because if it didn't, then he'd have no reason to be here anymore. She adjusts the apron around her waist and sweeps a stray hair into her ponytail. "Do I look okay?"

Much better than okay.

"Passable," he says.

"Shut up. These summer people . . ." she says. "Massholes. But they're good for business. Only two months to go, right?"

She takes a few steps and turns, walking backward on her way to leave, her hair catching in the breeze. "Look for Oliver," she says.

He smiles at the sound of her son's name.

"Bring him a worm. He's into bugs these days. And he likes you. He thinks you're cool."

"It's the uniform," Rory says.

"It's more than that."

"Where is he?"

"With Trey."

Then she's gone, waving over her shoulder as the crowd swallows her whole, and the mention of Trey lingers like a bad smell. Rory watches after her for too long. Then he wanders. Feeling empty. People part for him, as though these strangers know not to get too close. Happy faces falter momentarily, warily, at his expression. People try to hide their illicit beers. But he's used to this, to being on the outside. Watching. Getting the feel for who's here, who needs observing, who's dangerous. He softens his expression. He reminds himself that he—Deputy Rory Dunbar, Island Patrol— can blend into the background. His radio blares. The ferry is on its way. He'll need to be on the dock to meet it.

Bang!

He jumps. Some brat set off a firecracker behind him, and before he can stop himself, he has the kid by the shoulders, shaking him and telling him that he'll spend the night in jail if he ever, *ever* does anything like that again. He can feel his face, flushed and hotter than the sun. Spittle sprays from his mouth. And the kid starts to cry, snot and everything, and what Rory really wants is for the kid to never know how hard life will be or how many disappointments he'll face. "Don't do it again," Rory says.

The kid dashes off.

A few faces have turned away, people afraid to meet his gaze. A couple of phones capture video. Who cares?

The parade will start soon, winding through the narrow paths of the island. Boy Scouts and the local jazz band and the Over the Hill hikers. And tonight, after the boat show, fireworks out over the harbor will light up the water with flashes of red, white, blue, and gold; the crowd lining the piers; and the lucky few, in their boats, drifting on the water. He has a boat. And he'll be working tonight, even though all he wants is to be with Lydia, lying on the deck, too warm to touch each other on the hot summer night but too in love not to. If they were out there, they'd watch the fireworks cutting through the dark, sizzling to embers. He'd feel her breath, and hear her voice, and stroke her wavy hair. And then he'd slip her clothes off and she'd want him the way he wants her. They'd stay out on the water all night, rocking with the tide long after the fireworks ended.

"Where's the bathroom?"

Rory shakes the image away. A man wearing Nantucket red shorts and a gingham shirt stands in front of him holding a little girl. Why do investment bankers insist on pink shorts? The girl tugs at the man's sleeve. But as the only deputy assigned to the island, it's Rory's job to deal with this.

"Up the path here, on your left."

That's when he sees Oliver, Lydia's son, standing on the side of the path by the schoolhouse. The boy looks toward the sky at a red balloon drifting out over the Atlantic. People on the island think it's safe. Somehow, they believe they've created a world that's held off time, one where bad things don't happen to good people. Rory wishes that were true. Even in Maine, even on a tiny dot in the middle of a vast ocean, seeing a four-year-old boy on his own is odd.

"Oliver!" Rory says.

The boy beams in recognition. He holds out a palm, and they high five.

"What are you looking at, buddy?"

"Ba-goon," Oliver says, pointing up, delighted and on the verge of tears all at the same time.

"Where's your dad?"

Oliver shrugs.

Rory looks around the crowd for Trey, who should be here, with his son, protecting him. Rory's seen Trey leave Oliver alone before, but not on a day like this one, not with so many strangers around, not with so many opportunities to lose him. Lydia should know about this. She should learn.

"Why don't we find you another balloon?" Rory says. "Let's find your dad too. When did you see him last?"

"Do-know," Oliver says, dashing ahead.

Rory jogs after him. Out in the harbor, the ferry chugs around tiny, uninhabited Bowman Island. Rory needs to be at the pier to meet it. It's part of his job. He catches Oliver and lifts him up. "We'll watch the boat come in," he says. "Together. Maybe Pete will let you up on deck."

Rory's brother, Pete, is the ferry boat captain. The two of them live together in a house just outside of town. Rory holds Oliver's hand and stands right at the edge of the pier, facing the water. People crowd around them. The ferry from Boothbay Harbor comes twice a day, unleashing a new mob and taking away the old one. Today, even from here, Rory can see a mass of people jammed onto the upper decks for the day trip. They'll take the return ferry at four o'clock, or else they'll be stuck here for the evening. And they'll be Rory's to deal with.

"What the hell?"

Rory turns to see Trey standing behind them. Trey is tall and preppy with thick, dark hair falling in his eyes, and like a hundred other men on the island, he looks as if he came in straight from the regatta, not like a stereotypical state cop. "Are you kidnapping my son now?" Trey says, putting an arm out for Oliver, though the boy presses himself into Rory's leg.

"You left him," Rory says.

"Yeah, I was in the bathroom. Nice surprise, coming out and having him gone. I've been in a panic for the last five minutes."

Trey talks to Rory like the help, or worse, like they've never met. And somehow he's made Rory feel as if he did something wrong. Trey's the one who left a four-year-old alone, Rory reminds himself. He wouldn't have been doing his job if he hadn't intervened.

"And don't go blabbing to Lydia," Trey adds. "It won't get you what you want."

"What would I want?" Rory asks.

A grin starts at the edge of Trey's mouth. "We both know the answer to that one. Everyone on the island does. Lydia too."

Rory can feel his face burning red. It takes all his strength to match Trey's gaze. But he doesn't dare speak, knowing his voice will betray him.

"And I heard you signed up for the state exam," Trey says. "Again. Third time, right? Here's a tip: One thing you need as a state cop is good judgment. You can't be someone who wanders off with someone else's kid."

Oliver points toward the sky.

"What?" Trey snaps at the boy.

"Ba-goon," Oliver says.

"No baby talk," Trey says. "And you let the balloon go, didn't you? I told you to hang on to it."

Someone on the pier yells, "Run!"

Rory turns on alert. Out in the harbor, the ferry is barreling toward them, no sign of slowing down. On the boat, he can see one of the deckhands, a teenager, fighting her way across the crowded deck to get to the bridge. A solid wall of people come at him, and in the chaos, Rory loses Trey but manages to grab Oliver's hand and lift him onto his shoulders. He carries the boy to a post by The Dock, away from the crowd and away from the pier. "Hold on to this with both hands," he says. "Don't move. Not one inch."

Then he waves his hands over his head, dashing forward, straight into the crowd. "Get back," he shouts. "Run!"

All around him, people scream. He sees panicked faces, strangers from away mixed in with friends he's known his whole life. And the ferry chugs toward them, sixty yards, then fifty, then forty, till, at the last moment the engines reverse, and the boat slows. It drifts in excruciatingly slow motion toward the pilings on the pier, reversing course seconds before a crash.

Rory closes his eyes and breathes for what feels like the first time in five minutes. He turns to the crowd. "Everything's fine," he shouts. "You can calm down."

Trey appears at his side. "Isn't your brother the captain of that boat?" he asks.

"You know he is."

Rory takes the radio from his belt and calls the ferry. One of the deckhands, probably that teenager, picks up. "Give me Pete," Rory shouts into the radio.

"I can't," she says.

"Why not?" Rory says.

"He's passed out."

"From what?"

"Not a clue."

Rory lets the radio fall to his side and avoids looking at Trey. Right then, someone grabs Rory's arm. It's Lydia. Her eyes are wild. "Where's Oliver?" she says.

Word of the near accident must have already spread to the bakery. "Everything's fine," Rory says. "Nothing happened. He's right here."

"Where?" Lydia says.

"Over there," Rory says, pointing toward The Dock, to where he'd left Oliver, to where he'd told him not to move.

But the boy is gone.

MONDAY, SEPTEMBER 23

CHAPTER 1

Hester Thursby stuffed a plastic bag filled with Goldfish crackers into her niece Kate's princess backpack. *Today will be different,* Hester thought.

"Today will be different," she said to her reflection in the mirror by the front door of the apartment in Somerville, Massachusetts. Then she said it nine more times, to make sure it was true.

Kate shoved her bowl of Cheerios off the placemat at the kitchen island and into the sink; then she jumped from the bar stool to the floor, a move that still had Hester convinced would crack open the girl's skull. But Kate had turned four in August, learned to use pronouns (finally!), and now insisted on sitting in a big-girl chair. She'd also learned to count to a hundred; changed favorite colors, swapping pink for green; and lost her baby softness. She was wiry and taller now, in a way Hester wasn't sure she liked, but time marched forward.

Somehow, today had to go well. It was Hester's more-than-boyfriend-not-quite-husband Morgan's thirty-seventh birthday, and Hester had invited a few friends over for dinner. If it was Morgan's birthday, it was also his twin sister Daphne's birthday. Daphne was Kate's mother and Hester's best friend. Exactly one year earlier, Hester and Morgan had come home from celebrating his thirty-sixth birthday to find that Daphne, who'd left the party early, had skipped town, leaving Kate behind with a Post-it taped to her pajamas that read *Back in an hour. Tops!* Since then, Daphne had sent a few e-mail updates, but besides that, hadn't been seen or heard from, which had left Hester and Morgan—but mostly Hester—responsible for looking after Kate. A year into raising Kate, Hester had realized that she'd do anything for the girl and had begun to dread the day Daphne would return and upset the lives they'd settled into. Most of the time, Hester tried to convince herself that none of this was a big deal.

Even though it was.

She turned off the radio. All week, a storm that had devastated the western Caribbean had dominated the news. Now, the remnants of the hurricane were due to pass over New England sometime later this evening.

She surveyed the kitchen and living room for anything she might have missed. Breakfast dishes spilled from the sink. Toys, both dog and child, covered the floor. All of that could wait till later. Since Morgan had taken the truck that morning, Hester and Kate needed to catch the public bus from Union Square to Porter Square to get to Kate's preschool. Then Hester would jump on the Red Line into Harvard Square where, if she was lucky, she'd be at her desk at Widener Library in exactly—she checked her phone again—twenty-one minutes. She swung her own bag over her shoulder and held the door open for Kate to duck out onto the landing.

"Where are we going?" the four-year-old asked.

"School," Hester said, keeping her voice cheerful and mentally preparing herself for what was to come.

As if on cue, Kate crumpled, starting with her face, which turned raisin-like, followed quickly by her body, which collapsed to the floor. "No school," she screamed, fingers locked on the banister.

"Oh, come on," Hester said. "Where did you think we were going? Please, please, please."

The bus would be at the corner in three minutes, and the next one wouldn't come for twenty more.

Hester's niece had found her voice, and that voice meant that no matter how much pleading or cajoling Hester tried, when Kate got an idea stuck in her head, in the end Hester had to resort to brute force. She hauled the screaming, crying child from the floor, prying her fingers from the banister (on every step) while balancing her own bag and Kate's princess bag on one shoulder. At the front door, Kate used all four limbs to keep them from getting through to the porch. Once on the sidewalk, Hester ran toward the bottom of the street, the bags slipping from one arm, her glasses sliding down her nose and her hair spilling from her ponytail. At the bus stop, she stood with the other commuters, staring straight ahead while Kate shrieked, and her neighbors tried not to look away from their phones. Most of these people Hester knew by sight, if not by name. After this, they'd probably call child services.

But when the bus finally turned the corner, and the bus driver said, "Hello, little missy," Kate beamed at him as though the last five minutes had never happened and, despite it all, Hester's heart swelled with love for the kid. "Perfect child," the driver added, while Hester found her bus pass. "Wish mine had been like that."

"Me too," Hester said, making her way toward the back of the crowded bus, where the two of them stood and clung to a pole and Kate talked. And talked, her voice penetrating every cubic inch of the bus. She yammered about her favorite foods ("CHICKEN FINGERS AND ARUGULA"), her least favorite foods ("MEATBALLS AND ORANGE MARMALADE"), her stuffed animals, her plans to be a princess and a doctor and a teacher and a veterinarian and a gas station attendant ("GAS SMELLS GOOD") and a police officer and a chef.

"How about a librarian?" Hester asked.

Kate shook her head. "Nope," she said.

"Figures," Hester said.

A moment later, the bus pulled into Porter Square and emptied out. Hester took Kate's hand and hurried across the median, through a parking lot, past Porter Square Books, and down Mass Ave. With all the rush and drama at the apartment, Hester hadn't had a spare second to think, or to dwell, but now, as they ran past a Dunkin', she tried her best to push her thoughts down, to ignore what was happening, what had already begun: the thumping in her chest, the shortness of breath, the idea that had begun to germinate in her mind, tiny at first and then growing, swirling, till it roared through her imagination and swept away anything—any reason—in its path.

The storm.

It was coming.

Tonight.

And the forecast called for up to five inches of rain. Flooding on the coasts. High winds that would cut power. Stay at home, the newscasters said. Leave work early. Avoid driving. Don't make trouble.

Storms could change track. They could veer off course. They could speed up. What if the storm came early? What if it flooded Cambridge and Somerville and Hester couldn't get from the library to the preschool? She remembered coverage of Hurricane Harvey in Houston, the images of people trudging through the streets, children and animals piled in canoes. Desperate. She didn't own a fucking canoe.

Stop!

She tried to shut off her brain.

How could this be happening? Again.

She slowed her pace. Ahead, the preschool announced itself with a daunting sign, brightly colored, letters built from wooden blocks. Other parents kissed their children goodbye before hurrying off to their own busy lives. Though, of course, Hester wasn't a parent. She was an aunt. Not even an aunt, since she and Morgan weren't married. An interloper. Would the police even speak to her if Kate went missing?

That was a new worry to obsess over.

Ahead, one of the teachers stood at the gate scanning the sidewalk for latecomers. She was the head of the school, middle aged, thick, competent, with a voice that had been scarred into a childlike pitch from years of teaching four-year-olds. What was her name again? Miss Michelle?

"Ms. Michaela!" Kate said, trying to run toward the woman, but Hester didn't want to let her go.

She had to. She had to get to work.

Ms. Michaela crouched down, and it was all Hester could do not to grab Kate and flee. But she released the girl's hand and watched as she ran, arms and legs pumping. Already, Hester couldn't breathe.

"I don't think we can stay," she said.

Inside, the other students had taken their places at their little tables in their little chairs, with their little craft projects lined up in front of them. The corps of preschool teachers marched among them, keeping the peace, protecting. But Hester couldn't trust anyone else to protect. Or to run, or to hide, or to fight. Too many dangers lurked. The world was a scary, frightening place, where terrible, terrible things happened. Anywhere. And everywhere. She reached for Kate, and she could already see the tears beginning to form in Kate's eyes.

"She has a cold," Hester said.

Kate grabbed at Ms. Michaela's leg.

"It's okay," Ms. Michaela said. "Why don't you come inside and stay for the day?"

Hester reached out for the girl, lifting her from the ground.

"You don't have to keep doing this," Ms. Michaela said.

"Don't be silly," Hester said. "We'll be back tomorrow. After the storm."

She hurried away as Kate sobbed into her shoulder. When she turned the corner, she found a bench and collapsed on it. She pulled out her phone and dialed

Kevin at the library to tell him she couldn't make it to work.

"Tomorrow?" Kevin asked.

"Absolutely," Hester said.

Kevin sighed, and in the silence that followed, Hester almost hoped that he'd reached the end of his patience and would fire her. But Kevin had proven over the past weeks that his well of generosity was bottomless. "See you then," he said.

She clicked off her phone and immediately felt a flood of shame wash over her as Kate sucked her thumb and cried quietly beside her, the silent tears that broke Hester's heart. She could see herself from the outside, and what this, all of this, looked like to others. And of course Kate hadn't wanted to go through this charade again. Of course she hadn't wanted to get on that bus and come here, only to have to turn around and leave. Who would?

All of this—every bit of it—was irrational and had nothing to do with the storm and everything to do with last winter, the kidnapping, the cold, the sound of a trunk door slamming, the darkness, the tingling from frostbite in Hester's pinky that wouldn't go away. All of this had to do with the risks Hester had taken, and the danger she'd made Kate face.

"Want a Goldfish?" Hester asked.

"No!" Kate said.

"I'll buy you an ice-cream cone if you stop crying." The tears shut off like a faucet. "For breakfast?"

"I could use one too. We'll go to Christina's."

What Hester could really have used right then was a shot of whiskey.

"You have to promise me one thing," Hester said.

"Don't tell Uncle Morgan," Kate said.

The kid was getting too smart for her own good, but she was right, Morgan had no idea what was happening. Somehow Hester had managed to hide that she hadn't been to work since early August and that Kate hadn't attended school either. She'd given him old reports from school, from when Kate was three years old, and passed them off as new. She'd made up stories about annoying Harvard students researching the history of *Diff'rent Strokes*. It surprised her how easy it was to deceive, to keep these tiny little lies going. And she knew that when it all came tumbling down, it would be spectacular and ugly and messy.

How on earth had she morphed into this complete lunatic?

"Tomorrow will be different," she said to Kate. "I promise."

"I want a sundae."

"Sure."

"With marshmallow?"

At least the kid was learning how to work a bad situation. "Anything you want."

CHAPTER 2

"**D**on't run off!" Lydia shouted to Oliver, the sound of her voice cutting right through Rory.

The four-year-old boy dashed through the crowds of people waiting to catch the last ferry off Finisterre Island as the storm bore down on them. No matter what had happened, it was still Rory's job to keep the calm.

And he could feel Lydia watching him.

She walked through the thick, unseasonably warm air with trays of iced coffee and doughnuts, her dark hair in a messy knot, an apron tied around her waist. The two of them had existed in an uncomfortable silence these past two and a half months, ever since the Fourth of July, ever since Rory had pulled a sleeping Oliver from the hull of a yacht in the marina and ended the desperate, hours-long search for the missing boy. Rory should have been a hero. He should have been *her* hero. But rumors had started within hours of finding Oliver, that *Rory* had taken the boy because he wanted to impress Trey and join the state police, or because he worshipped Lydia—anyone who'd ever seen them together knew—or simply because Rory, like his brother, Pete, who'd nearly killed half the town by crashing the ferry while high on Oxy, was pathetic. And the people of the island, the people he'd known his whole life, had taken those rumors and turned them into truth.

Rory hadn't spoken to Lydia since that day. He didn't know what she believed, and as much as he'd tried to ferret out the source of the rumors, they'd persisted all summer long.

He kept his gaze forward as he walked within two feet of her. She gave him a half-hearted wave, which he ignored. Why offer up that power? There was nothing there, and as much as he'd yearned for her these many years, maybe there never had been.

He glanced at his watch. The ferry would dock in forty-five minutes. He still had time to do one last loop around the island and be in place to meet the boat. Besides, he should check to see if anyone was running late. As he went to leave, Lydia stopped him. "I've hardly seen you all summer," she said.

"Summer's busy," Rory said, shifting from one foot to the other, feeling like he had when he was a kid, when he and Lydia spent summer days exploring every inch of the island. "Busy for both of us," he added.

"Season's over," Lydia said. "And the crowds are leaving. Maybe we can slow down and fix a few things around here. Maybe you can help me out."

"If you need help fixing something, ask your husband," Rory said.

He slammed the door to the Jeep and sped off, passing small groups of people pushing wheelbarrows and pulling suitcases toward the pier as he drove through "town." Finisterre's town consisted of a dirt road lined with a few shops and a handful of hotels and restaurants, all of which, except for the General Store, would close after Columbus Day. Finisterre Island fell under the jurisdiction of the Boothbay Harbor Police but had its own island-based police force, which employed Rory. Rory worked twenty-four hours on, twenty-four off, twenty-four on, and then he had five days off. Most of the other deputies on the island force traveled in for their shifts, but Rory had grown up on the island and had left only for the two years he'd attended community college. Today, four hours into this shift, he'd spent most of his time on station chores and responding to two calls—one about a free-ranging dog, Bosco, who spent more time off leash than on, and the other about an unattended bonfire, which had been doused by the time he arrived. If the storm hadn't been on its way, this would have been a typical day.

Now he pulled out of town, stepping on the gas as he sped by Lydia's B and B, with its perennial garden and tiny bakery, Doughnuts and Pie. He drove up a hill to where the Atlantic opened in front of him and down the hill, past the brewery, to the swing bridge, which connected Big Finisterre (Big Ef) to Little Finisterre (Little Ef). The bridge opened and closed using a manual crank. Open meant it swung parallel to the ravine to allow boats to pass through, and it was open now, meaning anyone stuck on Little Ef wouldn't be able to cross to get to the ferry. Rory slammed on the brakes and leaped from the Jeep. "Gus!" he shouted, searching for the gnarled old man who operated the bridge.

When he didn't appear, Rory jogged to a tiny red hut, where he found Gus listening to the weather forecast on an ancient boom box.

"Come on, Gus," Rory said. "People are trying to leave before the storm."

"Ain't no storm coming," Gus said.

"I wouldn't bet on it," Rory said. "And the ferry'll be here in a half hour."

"I can feel it when a storm's coming. In the knee."

The knee. Like every prehistoric former lobsterman roaming this island, Gus had a joint that he claimed forecast the weather, but Rory couldn't count on a feeling to overrule a national weather alert.

"They're already lining up at the pier."

"Mainlanders," Gus said. "Can't live with 'em. And I'd be fine without 'em."

"Close the bridge! And keep it closed."

"Close it yourself," Gus grunted as he turned up the radio. "And you should talk to Lydia, anyway," he added. "She doesn't believe what people say about Oliver. Or about you."

"Could have fooled me."

No matter what people said, Rory knew the truth. He remembered that night clearly. He'd clambered onto that yacht after the sun had gone down and found a loose tarp covering the hull. He pulled at the fabric, the remaining snaps releasing, and saw Oliver's feet. The worst case possible flashed through Rory's imagination as he clawed his way into the hull and lifted Oliver to his chest and listened. Was he even alive? The boy's gentle breathing filled his ears. "I got you, kid," Rory whispered, knowing that he'd done good. "You're safe."

He called Lydia right away so that he could be the one to deliver the news. He heard her cell phone clatter to the ground and her feet pounding the earth as she ran. Toward him. Then he radioed to headquarters, listening as people in the background cheered at the news. He waited, the boat rising and falling on gentle waves. He held Oliver. Hoping for the rewards of being a hero, for Lydia to see him the way he saw her.

She ran along the pier, emerging from the dark, taking Oliver, kissing Rory, hugging him close, tears of joy streaming down her face. He kissed her back, holding her tight, not ever wanting to let go. And the words came out, before Rory knew he'd even said them. *I love you. More than anyone I've ever known. I love you so much.* Those words you can't take back.

Her face collapsed. "Not now," she said, as other people began to arrive, and the celebrating began. They lit off the fireworks, the same fireworks that had been cancelled for the search. The jazz band played. People danced all along the pier.

Even Trey had congratulated Rory that night, into a bullhorn, no less. "Let's give a round of applause to the deputy," he'd said, Lydia on his arm, Oliver asleep against his shoulder, "our local hero!"

The crowd had cheered, but Lydia, at least in Rory's memory, hadn't even been able to look at him. And the next day, the whispering began. Quiet at first. Rory, they said, had given Oliver a sleeping pill. He'd used the distraction from the near ferry accident to sneak the boy onto the yacht. He'd purposefully searched the boat on his own so that people would call him a hero. By the time the rumors got to Rory, they were whole and indisputable even though Rory had been on the pier waving people to safety. He'd been doing his job, for all the world to see. Trey had been there with him. But time lines warped, and memories changed. Someone saw him scurrying away, Oliver's hand in his.

"That didn't happen," Rory said, the first time he heard the rumors.

But the denial had only made him sound guiltier.

"Mind your own business, Gus," Rory said. "And don't open that bridge again."

Back up on the road, Rory turned the crank till the green metal bridge slammed into place. The bridge, which was barely wide enough for the Jeep, connected two steep cliffs that ran down to a fast-moving channel below. Rory almost flipped off Gus as he sped across the bridge.

About a square mile in area, half the size of Big Ef, Little Ef was nearly a perfect circle of wooded granite with nothing on it but trails, cottages, and coastline. "Town" hadn't yet extended here. Since Finisterre didn't allow cars besides a handful of service vehicles, the little road that did exist on this island rarely saw anything larger than a wheelbarrow. Rory drove with caution as he wove along the shoreline, into the trees, and back out to the water. Most visitors to the island, especially this late in the season, understood how things worked, so Rory waved to the people he passed as they cheerfully headed to the ferry on their own.

About halfway around, on the leeward side of the island, the trees opened to a coastline dotted with seaweed and tidal pools. A red and white lighthouse perched on a circle of stone about a quarter of a mile from the path, and the low tide had exposed a sandy spit connecting the lighthouse to the shore that would soon be swallowed by the sea. The lighthouse had been built at the turn of the eighteenth century and almost immediately had become a popular subject for landscape painters, appearing in hundreds if not thousands of paintings, from masterpieces to decidedly amateurish renderings. Like nearly all lighthouses, this one had been automated decades ago, and the structure, along with the keeper's house attached to it, had been unoccupied ever since.

Today, despite the storm, no fewer than six painters stood at easels as they captured the darkening sky and boiling sea. Rory stepped from the Jeep and watched for a moment. Then he spoke into the handheld on his dash, his voice booming from a speaker as he announced that the ferry would leave in exactly twenty-five minutes. "It's the last one before the storm," he added, watching as the painters packed up and scurried off to their homes.

Some people never learned. It was the same thing every day, even without the storm. The ferry came, the ferry left. Most people made it, a few didn't. And no matter what, Rory had to clean up their mess. He watched the sea for a moment, trying to push away thoughts of Lydia. He and Lydia had grown up next door to each other, roaming the woods and the rocky shores and attending the one-room schoolhouse through eighth grade with the few other children on the island. Afterward, they'd taken the ferry to the mainland every Monday to attend high school during the week, where they'd been "islanders." Weird and inbred and outcast.

Inseparable.

There had never been a time in Rory's life that he didn't remember yearning for Lydia, but it wasn't as though he hadn't tried to escape her pull. He'd gone to college in Portland, sharing an apartment with four other guys, living the big-city life, and dreaming of making it work far away from this place. But circumstances had pulled him back in. His parents had died, and Pete, still a teenager, had needed him. Then Lydia, who'd gone to Orono to college, had moved home one day, surprising everyone with a new husband. An off-islander. Trey.

Someone tapped on the window of the Jeep. Pounded really, and Rory came out of his reverie half expecting to see one of the painters on the road demanding a ride to the ferry. Indeed, a woman danced from foot to foot, a suitcase beside her, its contents sprawled across the path. She was frantic.

Everything on this island ran on ferry time.

"You have twenty minutes," Rory said, rolling down the window and summoning a smile from somewhere. "Plenty of time to make it."

The woman gasped. She pointed up the path and finally found her words. "There's a man," she said.

"Yep," Rory said. "Does he need a ride?"

"In the road. Around the bend. He has a knife."

Rory's training kicked in. Call for backup (scrap that, what backup?), clear the area, isolate the problem. "Run," he said, his voice a whisper of a growl. "To the bridge. Tell anyone you see to clear out. And keep moving, whatever you do."

The woman stared at him, frozen.

"Now!"

She stumbled over her own suitcase and fled. Rory

radioed into dispatch on the mainland as he swerved around the corner on the path, and nearly collided with a man swinging a cleaver over his head at something only he could see. He was bleary-eyed, stumbling, naked as the day he was born. Rory slammed on the brakes and jumped from the Jeep.

"Dammit, Pete," he shouted. "Put that knife down."

Rory's younger brother had once been muscular and handsome, but now he barely had an extra ounce to him, and his body—on full display—was covered with track marks and scars. "Faggot, faggot, faggot, queer, faggot," Pete said, swinging the knife as he spoke.

"Jesus Christ, what are you on this time?" Rory said, which focused Pete's rage.

He lunged, knife slashing, his wiry frame flailing in every direction. But Rory had spent a lifetime tussling with his younger brother, a lifetime making the kid feel small. He regretted that now. He stepped aside, avoiding the cleaver, and Pete sprawled onto the ground into a puddle, his naked ass shining toward the sky.

Rory tossed the cleaver into the bushes, dug his knee into his brother's back, and slapped a set of cuffs on his wrists. "Sorry, guy," he said.

Pete was six years younger. Unlike Rory, Pete had barely made it through high school and had only been a kid when first their mother and then their father died. While Rory had left for college and joined the police force, Pete had taken a job running the ferry to the mainland, a job their father used to have. Pete had liked the job. He liked being in charge and feeling the comfort of the familiar. He liked the girls and the beer that crossed on the ferry every day. And most days, especially during the summer, the job was easy. But drugs had crept onto the island and into Rory's family, taking each person he loved one by one. It had started with his mother, who'd taken Oxy as cancer had spread through her body. It moved to his father, who'd slipped pills from her prescription to deal with pain from an old injury. The two of them had found doctors to keep the prescriptions going. Rory's mother died from cancer seven years ago. His father overdosed a year later. And now Pete.

Pete started stealing pills from both his parents and selling them in high school. Rory knew but didn't know, turning a blind eye to what he didn't want to see, which was something he'd live with for the rest of his life. Since the ferry incident, since Pete had lost his job and been given a suspended sentence for using, things had gotten worse. Rory wondered now when, not if, he'd have to use one of the vials of Narcan he carried everywhere to save his own brother. He'd certainly had to use them plenty of other times on the island.

He hauled Pete to his feet, who snarled and tried to bite his hand as Rory shoved his brother into the back of the Jeep and tossed him a blanket. "Cover yourself up," he said. "That shriveled little thing won't help your reputation."

This, being high and naked and waving a knife out in the woods, was a clear violation of Pete's probation. Maybe the time had come for Rory to report his brother. Rory couldn't protect him forever. But jail, where it was easy enough to get drugs, wouldn't solve any of their problems. It would make them worse.

Rory suddenly felt exhausted. The ferry left in ten minutes, and he should be there to see it off. He should do one more sweep of Little Ef to catch any stragglers.

He should also get his brother dressed, take him to the mainland, and turn him in to the local sheriff. As an officer of the law, that's what he'd do if he was doing his job. But what was his duty to family? Besides, he needed to be here tonight. He needed to ride out the storm with the rest of the islanders and make sure they made it through safely.

"Faggot, faggot, faggot," Pete said, banging at the windows in the Jeep.

"Stop," Rory said. "Please," he added, his voice faltering. But it seemed to connect somewhere in Pete's mind. His brother smiled, softly, and closed his eyes. "Hey, bro," he mumbled.

Triage.

What was most important?

Family came first. That's what his mother had always said. It was what Lydia said too.

Rory started the engine. Eight minutes till the ferry left. The last ferry till morning. Eight minutes to decide.

Up the road, a few hundred yards away, Rory saw another woman running toward him. He nearly drove off. Anyone late for the ferry would usually be on their own now, but something about the way she ran made him stop. She stumbled, sprawling into the dust, scrambling on all fours. She didn't have a bag or a cart, and her blond hair flew around her face in greasy tendrils. He recognized her as one of the squatters from the run-down Victorian, though she'd been on the island only for a week or two. The house sat in the woods around the bend. Rory didn't doubt that whatever Pete had taken, he'd scored it there, and he wished, not for the first time, that he'd taken a match to the old house. Too many strangers on the island. Too many people from away trying to take advantage of anyone they could.

He turned to Pete. "Do you know her?" he asked. His brother just stared ahead, eyes vacant.

The woman screamed, but Rory couldn't make out the words.

He waited. Assessing. Checking for weapons. And he could see now the panic in her face. The tears. The sweat. And Rory remembered. The boy. Dark hair. Sad eyes. The morning they arrived, a crisp, fall day. He clung to his mother's leg as they departed the ferry and trudged up the road with nothing but a dirty green duffel bag between them. Rory had nearly followed them that day, knowing they'd wind up at the house, a place no child should ever see.

A moment later, Rory sped toward the pier. Four minutes. Gus had better have left that bridge in place.

"This is your lucky day," Rory said to Pete.

Because the thing with being the only deputy on duty was that sometimes Rory had to choose. He switched on the siren and lights. Somehow, he had to stop that ferry from leaving.

CHAPTER 3

Morgan Maguire ran his hands over the cocker spaniel's belly. Rufus. Rufus was fifteen years old. His black fur had begun to mat and fall out in places, and he was covered with benign moles, but besides that, he was healthy. His owner, a man named Ervin, clutched at the arms of a chair as Morgan went through a routine exam.

"I brought in a fecal sample," Ervin said.

"We can test it," Morgan said. "But I don't know what for. Nothing's wrong with Rufus besides the indignities of age."

In a year or two, the conversation would be a different one, a much more difficult one. One that Morgan wondered whether Ervin would be able to handle. Ervin brought the dog into the vet office in Cambridge's Central Square practically every week and had for the past two years, ever since his wife had died. He had to be in his late seventies and had begun to look like the dog, with his own moles and thin hair. Morgan imagined the two of them, at home alone, on the sofa, watching *Jeopardy!*. He imagined their walks around a neighborhood that had transitioned as friends moved away. He lifted the dog to the ground. Rufus found his footing and walked gingerly over to Ervin, who scratched him behind the ears.

"I worry," Ervin said.

"I know," Morgan said. "Come in whenever you want."

Morgan had months worrying, even since he'd walked into that hospital room in New Hampshire and seen Hester's broken body. They hadn't been the same since, not the two of them. They couldn't be, really, not with Kate living with them or with Daphne off doing whatever she was doing. A part of him had wondered if Daphne would contact him today—it was their birthday after all, something they'd hated sharing as kids but had grown to love—but most of him dreaded hearing from his sister too. Morgan and Hester needed to find a way to heal, and Daphne would only make that more difficult.

"You take really good care of Rufus," Morgan said, hating the platitude even as he said it. What Ervin wanted, and what Morgan couldn't give him, was to go back to a time when his wife was healthy, his children were young, and Rufus's belly was pink and translucent. He wanted a time when life was happier.

It was the same thing Morgan wanted.

Now, as he walked Ervin and Rufus to reception, his phone rang. He took the call, and when he was done, he made another call.

"I need your help," he said. "Tonight."

Annie grasped the lobster boat's washboard, waiting for the next trap to emerge from the roiling Gulf of

Maine. She wore yellow oilskins and thick rubber gloves to keep the lobsters from snapping at her fingers as she worked the lines off the coast of Finisterre Island, with nothing but gray water between her and Ireland.

"Hey, Red. Keep moving."

Annie turned to the boat captain, Vaughn Roberts, who had an eye toward the dark western sky. His black lab, Mindy, wound her way across the deck, nosing at Annie's gloves. Annie hated being called "Red," a name that brought up memories of playgrounds and mean girls who mocked her red hair and fair skin, but she reminded herself that Vaughn was the boss for the day and being nearly homeless meant even worse humiliations. Besides, Lydia Pelletier had gone out on a limb to get her the job, and Annie couldn't afford to lose the money she'd earn, or the sole friend she'd made all summer living on the island.

"Got it, Boss!" she said.

As the hauler lifted the next trap from the water, Vaughn cut seaweed off, using a six-inch knife with a blue hilt. While he moved down the line, Annie worked methodically, reaching into the trap to pluck out one of the writhing creatures. Its claws snapped helplessly as she measured the carapace at three and a quarter inches, the smallest length possible for a legal catch. A fraction of an inch shorter and the lobster would have gone back into the gray waters for another day, but luck wasn't on its side. Annie tossed it into a waiting tank and flipped through nine more lobsters, discarding six, including one female, whose tail she notched. When they finished the line, Annie banded the claws on the catch while Vaughn maneuvered the boat through the waves, Mindy standing on the bow, her black ears blowing in the wind. "Think that storm's coming?" he asked. "We need to clear these traps in case it does."

"Who knows?" Annie said.

"You never do," said Vaughn, who was salty and windblown, what Annie expected in a lobsterman, even one as young as he was. But Vaughn also had a soft mouth made for talking and a Down East accent he worked hard to tame. "How do you know Lydia, anyway?" he asked.

All day, he'd peppered Annie with questions that she'd managed to parry away. "I don't really," she said. "How about you?"

"You know everyone when you've spent your life on an island like this one," Vaughn said. "Everyone except who you don't. But Lydia and I, we grew up here. Took the boat to the mainland to go to high school during the week. Even went to the same college. Now we both wound up back on the island, for better or worse. We can't seem to get away from each other. You must know Trey, too, her husband."

"Why would I?" Annie asked, realizing too late that she sounded defensive.

"Why wouldn't you?" Vaughn said after a pause. "When everyone knows everyone? Where are you from, anyway?"

"By Dog Cove," Annie said. "On Little Finisterre. There's an old Victorian out there."

"That dump by the lighthouse?" Vaughn said. "Most of the people who squat there have BO worse than five-day-old fish guts. I'm glad you don't. You living off the grid for a while?"

Most everyone who lived in the house was off the grid. They didn't have a phone there, let alone Internet service. Let alone anything else.

"Only the two of us out here," Vaughn said when Annie didn't respond. He steered the boat through the choppy surf. "How about trying? You know, I ask where you're from, you tell me. You ask me the same question, and I tell you I'm from here, that I got away for a few years and moved to Portland, but now I live on the island because my ex-wife banished me from our house two months ago, and you say, how can a handsome guy like you possibly be single, and I say I'm not handsome, and you say, yes you are, you really, really are. You know, that kind of thing."

In truth, Vaughn wasn't bad on the eyes. He was thirty. Maybe thirty-five. Definitely a few years younger than Annie. He had premature salt-and-pepper hair and blue eyes that peered out from under the hood on his slicker. Annie was thirty-seven, maybe too old for Vaughn, but perspectives changed, right? Beds got lonely and cold. How long had it been since his divorce? How long had he gone without sharing a bed with a woman? She'd have to play his game, for a bit at least. She got ready to track her answers, to remember her truth. "I'm off the grid," she said. "But it's temporary."

"I'm surprised anyone's still at that house," Vaughn said. "It usually clears with the summer crowd."

When Annie had moved in that June, every room but one in the house had been full. Since Labor Day, though, it had emptied till she'd been the only person left. Then, two weeks earlier, a woman named Frankie and her four-year-old son, Ethan, had set up camp.

"Are you planning to stick around?" Vaughn asked.

"Brave the winter? Only the hearty do. Or the stupid. That place gets cold once the snow comes. Take my advice and move into town. Rents get cheaper real quick around here. And winters are long enough, even with heat and running water, but you'll always be from away if you can't handle a Maine winter. What brought you here anyway?"

Annie thought for a moment before answering. "Luck," she said.

The boat lurched in a swell. Annie gripped the washboard with one hand, and Mindy's collar with the other. A sheet of frigid seawater swept over her, sucking the air from her lungs. She swiped water from her face, the salt lingering on her lips.

"You okay?" Vaughn asked.

The summer had taught Annie not to complain. She nodded and told him to keep going.

"You have good sea legs," he said.

"I don't know anything about boats."

"Could have fooled me."

He cut the engine back to idle speed, scanned the horizon with a pair of binoculars, and caught a purple and blue buoy with the gaff. "One more stop," he said, hooking the line to the hauler.

Annie scanned the horizon, too, as Mindy leaned into her leg with her whole body. The buoys they'd spent the day pulling had all been yellow and orange, and Annie knew enough about lobstering to know what not to do—especially when it came to molesting other lobstermen's gear. She also knew enough to keep her mouth shut and took her place behind Vaughn, ignoring the feeling of dread in her stomach, or that the easygoing man she'd spent most of the day with had grown tense and aware. What other choice did she have? She was on the water with him, alone. And at the end of the day, Vaughn would pay her with seventy-five bucks and a pair of chicken lobsters, more money than she'd had in months.

The first trap emerged, and Vaughn examined it. Then he let it fall back into the sea without taking the lobsters out. He did that at the second trap, and the third. Only at the last trap did he pause. "Hot dog!" he said. "Look at that baby!"

The lobster barely fit in the trap. Vaughn pulled it out, glancing across the choppy sea as if to check that they were still alone, before dangling the lobster in front of himself while Mindy snapped at its tail. It must have weighed more than twenty pounds with claws twice the size of Annie's hands.

"Jesus, this'll get me on *Chronicle* if it doesn't swallow the two of us whole!" Vaughn said.

"She's beautiful," Annie said, watching the lobster struggle against Vaughn's celebration. "How old do you think she is?"

"Got to be forty, fifty years old," Vaughn said. "Imagine, outsmarting us for all these years! Hold her. She's strong. She might rip apart the rest of the catch."

Annie held the lobster beneath its claws. This was a creature someone would pay good money for, the kind of illicit catch that would make it onto a centerpiece and into the trash. And it wasn't fair to her. Not after all this time. Not after surviving.

Annie tossed the lobster overboard.

Vaughn clutched at the empty air. "Oh, fuck!" he said,

kicking at the side of the boat and spinning around. He seemed as if he might jump in after it. "Fuck. Jesus! Oh, you fucking . . . that was a huge fuckup!" he shouted.

Annie glanced toward the island, perched on the horizon. She had no idea what Vaughn was capable of, but she did know that he was angry. She remembered Lydia, who'd insisted Annie was worth a chance. "I'm sorry," she said.

It was all she could manage.

"That's what I get for hiring a flatlander," Vaughn said. "I'll think better of it next time. Fifty bucks. That's what that lobster was worth, and that's what your little stunt cost me."

"That lobster was too big," Annie said. *And poached from someone else's trap*, she nearly added.

"And she was female," Vaughn said. "Already notched. Didn't you see? She would have gone back into the water anyway, if you'd given me a minute. Biggest lobster of the year gets first prize from the lobster pound and a fifty-dollar payout, but I need a photo to prove it. Now no one will believe me. I'm taking the money out of your wage."

Fifty dollars. Oh, how Annie needed that money. How could Vaughn possibly know that Annie was down to her last five-dollar bill, that she was desperate, more desperate than she'd ever been in a life of desperation. But Vaughn must have seen it in her threadbare clothes and yellowed nails. He must have known he could do anything he wanted with her here, that she was powerless. She took in a deep breath to keep from begging or losing her last scraps of pride.

Vaughn punched at the air. "Great cap to the day."

"It wasn't yours," Annie said, softly.

"Say that again."

"It wasn't yours to claim," Annie said. "That fifty dollars belongs to someone else."

Vaughn turned the boat and revved the engine as they headed toward the island. The waves had grown higher as the weather had turned, but Vaughn steered the prow of the boat into the surf with the light touch of someone who'd seen worse, focusing on the task at hand and treating Annie like the hired help she was. She'd hoped he might ask her to work for him again. Now, she'd ruined any chance of that happening.

A swell smashed the starboard side, lurching them off course and filling the hull with water. "Youza," Vaughn said as he struggled at the helm. "Hold on to the dog! We should have gone in an hour ago."

Annie gripped Mindy's collar and struggled across the deck, tying down anything loose, happy for the diversion. As the boat arced around Bowman Island and toward the harbor, the water calmed a bit. Vaughn cut the engine back and cruised at headway speed, keeping to the channel. Ahead, blue lights from the island's sole police Jeep flashed, and for a moment Annie wondered if a search party had launched to find them. She wondered what it would feel like to be missed, but more than that, she wished they were still out at sea. At times during the day, she'd forgotten about the world away from the boat, away from two people working in tandem, and now she wanted more than anything to be far from what those flashing blue lights would bring.

"Ferry's still here," Vaughn said, checking his watch. "It's after four. It should have left twenty minutes ago."

He pulled the boat along the dock, and Annie jumped to the planks with a line. It would take another half hour to unload and weigh the catch, but Vaughn leaped after her, tied off the boat, and headed up the gangway without looking back, Mindy at his heels. Annie ran after him. "Let's unload," she said.

"There's something wrong," he said. "The ferry runs like a clock."

Annie stopped short at the top of the gangway, right as the skies opened and huge drops of warm rain filled the air. Rory Dunbar, the local deputy, leaned against his Jeep. A man wrapped in a blanket sat in the Jeep's back seat and stared out the window like an abandoned dog. Annie recognized him from his visits to the Victorian.

"I saw your boat in the harbor and came to meet you," Rory said as Mindy tried to jump on him. "You been out all afternoon?"

"Yep," Vaughn said, glancing at the man in the back of the Jeep. "He okay?"

"He's fine," Rory said, his voice short, shoving the dog away. "See anyone else out there?"

"Not really. And if they are still on the water, they'll be in trouble soon. What's going on? Why didn't the ferry leave?"

Rory crossed to where Annie waited, looking her over like a piece of trash. She felt her stomach clench. Had he come for her?

"The island's on lockdown till the state cops get here," Rory said. "Another boy is missing."

CHAPTER 4

When Oliver disappeared earlier in the summer, the whole town, including Annie, had mobilized, but Rory had been the one to find him. Annie remembered watching from the crowd as the deputy handed the sleeping boy to Lydia and raised his arms over his head in triumph. "You're a hero!" someone in the crowd shouted, and Rory waved a hand and said, "Just doing my job," with a false modesty that had lingered with Annie ever since.

The whole incident had cast a pall over the summer, but to Annie, the missing boy had almost been a relief. It had given her something to talk about. Something to bond over. Something to connect her to these small people on this small island. Best of all, it had led to a friendship with Lydia.

Now, Vaughn turned to Rory. "Who is it this time?"

"Another four-year-old. His name's Ethan, mother's name is Frankie. From away," Rory added, as if that mattered. He nodded at Annie. "You know them, right?"

Ethan and Frankie lived at the Victorian, too, though

she hardly *knew* them. They'd shown up right after Labor Day when most people were leaving the island for the season.

"Tell me about them," Rory said.

Annie stalled by gripping a rusted metal railing, and she must have looked on the verge of fainting, because Vaughn stepped to her side, one hand under her arm. A part of her wanted to fold into Vaughn. To give in. She also wanted to run. But to where? There was no place to hide. Not on this tiny island. "I'm okay," she said, waving off the assistance. "Ethan's a good kid."

"And his mother?" Rory asked.

Annie pictured Frankie, with her stringy blond hair and bleeding gums. She could have been pretty after a bath and a roll of floss. What Annie wouldn't tell Rory was how often she'd seen Frankie wipe powder from her nose while Ethan screamed and smelled of shit. In another life, Annie would have called family services. Here, alone, she said, "She seems okay."

"When was the last time you saw Ethan?" Rory asked.

"Last night. When I went to bed. How do you know he didn't wander anyway? There are plenty of places to get lost here."

"I don't," Rory said. "But even if he did, he's four years old and on his own. We better find him before this storm hits, especially if he's hurt. Besides, he's been gone for a few hours now. You didn't see him since last night? Not at all?"

"We headed out in the boat early this morning," Annie said. "Long before he'd have gotten up."

"It's true," Vaughn said. "We left at seven."

Rory took a step forward. He was tall, even taller

than Annie. And he used it to take up her space. To intimidate. "I hear it's just the three of you out there now," he said. "That all those other losers left for the winter. You know that everyone's a suspect till we pin this on someone."

"Fuck you," Annie said, which, even as it passed her lips, sounded extreme. Ever since she'd come to town, Rory had treated her the way she looked, dirty and worthless.

Rory's face turned red. A vein throbbed in his neck. "Oliver went missing in July," he said. "Right after you moved to town. And two is a trend."

Vaughn stepped between them. "Take it down a notch," he said. "You too, Rory-boy."

Rory shoved him away.

"We all know there are summer people coming and going all the time," Vaughn said.

Rory smoothed his shirt and adjusted his badge. "Fine," he said. "The state cops will be here within the hour, then we'll get the ferry off. Till then, I'll need your help. Unload that catch, then go to the community center. That's where everyone's meeting. See if you can get people organized and out there searching on Little Ef. That's where Ethan will be if he wandered off. I have to stay here with the ferry."

"I can do that," Vaughn said. "This'll take me ten minutes."

Rory climbed into the Jeep, slamming the door hard enough to make the man sitting in the back jump.

"Wait," Annie said, calling after him. "Where's Frankie now?"

"She's at the house," Rory said through the open window. "Hoping her son comes home."

Vaughn watched Rory speeding down the gravel path and said, "Don't mind him. He's just being a dick."

The kindness in his voice surprised Annie. She hadn't forgotten the lobster or the fifty dollars she owed him.

"He's my sister's husband's cousin's nephew," Vaughn added. "If you can follow that. We went to high school together. Lydia too. The three of us used to ride the ferry over every Monday, and Rory would stay with me at my aunt and uncle's house during the week. I know him well enough to know that he's pissed off because the state police are here again. The same thing happened in July when Oliver went missing, just like whenever something interesting happens around here. Rory doesn't like outsiders on his turf."

"You and Rory are the same age?" Annie said.

"Is it the hair?" Vaughn asked, touching his white head.

It wasn't the hair, but to Annie, Vaughn seemed more solid, more fully formed and adult than the deputy. "I wish he'd leave me alone," she said.

"New things, new people, scare him. And he takes it out on anyone he can. Besides, he has some family things going on, and he's had a tough summer. He wants to be a state cop but failed his exam for the third time. And his brother. Pete. You saw him in the back of the Jeep there. Rory's whole family . . . well, you don't have anything to do with him being sad and dumb, so don't beat yourself up."

Vaughn pulled two fifty-dollar bills from his wallet. They flapped in the wind, and it was all Annie could do not to snatch them away. "I thought you were docking me," she said.

"I don't stay angry too long," Vaughn said. "And

missing kids put things in perspective. Besides, it's good to have a soft heart. Even on the water. And anyone who can get under Rory's skin can't be all bad."

"You owe me seventy-five dollars. I don't have change."

"Keep it. And keep the story about the lobster and where it came from between us, okay? I don't need any more rumors flying. Maybe you can come out with me again in a few days. After the storm."

Annie's fingertips itched to take the money, even with strings attached. She understood secrets, what they meant, what they could carry with them. But she remembered the five-dollar bill, folded up and tucked into her knapsack to keep herself from spending it. She remembered how much hunger hurt. She took the two bills and stuffed them into her pocket.

"We have a deal," Vaughn said.

"We do," Annie said.

A hundred bucks! She nearly said thank you.

"You go," Vaughn said. "I'll see you at the community center when I'm done."

Vaughn headed down the gangway to the boat. He looked up at her from under the hood on his oilskins, pausing. "Go," he shouted.

"I'll find you later," Annie said, walking toward the harbor.

The harbor had three sections. On the commercial side, fishermen docked to unload catches and weigh them at the lobster pound. On the public side, yachts and other pleasure boats pulled up all summer long to refuel. Now, with the storm coming, the team at Finisterre Boats was working overtime pulling the few remaining vessels from the water and loading them into drydock. The third section was the pier, where ferries from the mainland docked. Two ferry lines ran to the island, one from Bar Harbor, in the north, and the other from Boothbay Harbor, to the west.

Annie headed to town, where wooden signs hanging above the doors of the few establishments swung precariously in the wind. Halfway up the road, Lydia's bed-and-breakfast sat nestled behind two beech trees. The house was a small, shingled cottage painted blue and white. The garden, in the last throes of fall, sat behind a white picket fence. In summer, guests sat in the white rocking chairs that filled the inn's front porch, and people from all over town spilled out of the modest bakery attached to the side of the house.

Annie stopped at the gate, hesitating before going in, as she always did. Lydia was her friend. Her best friend. It was because of Lydia that Annie had a hundred dollars burning a hole in her pocket. And yet, a part of her still felt like an outsider, like an interloper. Part of her wondered why someone like Lydia would even give her the time of the day.

"Aunt Annie!" said a little voice, followed by the squelch-squelch of tiny feet moving through mud.

Annie spun around to greet the source of her joy, Oliver, who ran toward her through the rain. He ran the way four-year-olds do, putting everything into it, too innocent to hold back. She lifted him, his raincoat slick with water.

"I had lunch today," he whispered in her ear.

If only he knew how lucky he was to say that, and to believe that it might always be true. "I bet it was delicious," she said.

Lydia followed him, decked out in head-to-toe blue

Patagonia to match her eyes, her dark hair tied in two happy knots on the sides of her head. Lydia managed to bring brightness wherever she went, even on a search for a missing child. "Just who I needed!" Lydia said. "I have to get the horses for the search. It'll take me about fifteen minutes to get over there and back. Take Oliver to the community center, would you? There'll be someone there to watch kids." She stepped in close and kissed Annie's cheek. "How was the job?"

"Good," Annie said. "Till Rory met the boat and told us what was going on. He tried to pin this on me."

"Good ol' Rory," Lydia said. "My bet is he wants this pinned on anyone but himself, which I get. I've known Rory my whole life. He wouldn't do anything, ever, to hurt Oliver or me. So whatever people are saying, don't pay attention. And if there's some mystery connection between Oliver and Ethan, it has nothing to do with him. Got it?"

The intensity in Lydia's voice surprised Annie, but small towns ran on rumors that could be more destructive than the coming storm. To truly know what people believed, you had to become part of the fiber of the place. "You went to high school with him?" she said.

"Yeah, did Vaughn tell you that?" Lydia said. "Vaughn's got one big mouth on him. Practically impossible to get him to shut up. What else did he tell you?"

"Not much," Annie said. "He said he's divorced and moved back here this summer."

"Vaughn split with his wife Sophie a few months ago. I don't think he's too happy about being here, but that's life. And I'm glad he's here." Lydia's phone beeped, and she glanced at a text. "That's Trey. He's on his way. They're in the boat from the mainland now, so things should get going soon. And he wants to talk to you." She ruffled Oliver's hair. "Be a good boy. Do what Annie tells you."

"We'll have a blast," Annie said.

"A blaft," Oliver said, in a way that Annie suspected he did it on purpose, to melt her heart.

As Lydia turned to leave, Annie asked, "Do you know who uses purple and blue buoys for their traps?"

"Yeah," Lydia said. "Me."

"You have traps?"

"Just a few. They're not commercial. Most people on the island have some for themselves. Why do you ask?"

"I found one. On the beach. I wanted to return it."

"Lucky. It wouldn't have lasted the night," Lydia said, then hurried off through town.

Annie waited till she'd turned the corner to pull Oliver in close. He was too old to smell of talc, but Annie loved the way he babbled, his words just tipping over the line of forming coherent sentences. She loved him, more than he knew, more than his parents could ever understand.

"I'm an inch worm!" she said, holding her arms at her side and pretending to slither along the ground.

"I'm a bee!" Oliver ran from flower to flower, sticking his nose deep into each one.

"I'm a bear! And I want honey!" Annie said, standing tall and looming over Oliver till he shrieked and darted away. She chased after him, catching up and offering a hand.

He took it, without question.

The community center was an old multipurpose

building that served as police headquarters, the volunteer fire department, space for community gatherings, a summertime church, and the jail, when needed. Today, as the afternoon turned toward evening and wind and rain increased in intensity, people spilled from the building and huddled under awnings. A group of young men in flannel poured beer from growlers into red plastic cups. From inside the building, the strum of a guitar and the wistful notes of a local folk singer floated on the wind. The whole scene felt more like a celebration than a search for a missing child. Annie hung back, bracing herself against the gusts of thick, warm air. One of the men offered her a beer, and she took it while a band of children chased one another, weaving in and out of the crowd. Oliver joined them, melting into a sea of faces. Annie ran after him, forcing her way through a wall of bodies till she saw that he'd joined a circle of other children in the one-room schoolhouse while the local teacher watched over them. Annie told the teacher that Oliver had joined the kids, and the young woman raised a gentle hand. "I've got it," she said.

Back outside in the rain, Annie saw Vaughn stride up the hill, like her, still in his oilskins. He lit a cigarette as he began conferring with some of the people. A moment later, he went inside and came back out with a bullhorn. "No luck finding this kid yet," he said to the group. "The state police are on their way, but in the meantime we'll need every one of you to do the best you can in the time we have left. The storm'll be raging soon." He waited for the murmurs to stop as people in the crowd whispered to one another. "There's an Amber Alert out, and they're working that on the mainland. But here, tonight, we'll assume that Ethan is still local. He may be lost. He may be confused. He may be injured. Understood?"

Vaughn spent the next few minutes organizing people into small groups, which then set out on foot or piled into the few trucks on the island. When he caught Annie staring, he waved her over. She pretended not to see and retreated inside the community center, but a moment later, he found her again. "Are you avoiding me?" he asked as he held a cup of coffee toward her. "Cream and sugar, right? Friends remember those details."

Annie took the coffee and let the friend comment wash away.

"We're nearly organized," Vaughn said. "There's only another hour of light, though, and it's a moon tide tonight on top of everything else, which means flooding. Half the island lost power about ten minutes ago. The other half should follow, at least for anyone who doesn't have a generator."

Vaughn bit into a sandwich, which was all Annie needed to feel her hunger at last. Her stomach rumbled, and Vaughn pointed to a corner of the room where a group of women had set up tables and seemed to celebrate each time another platter arrived. "Gotta grab some sustenance before you head out."

Annie pushed her way to the table, where she wolfed down a sandwich, barely taking the time to chew. A smorgasbord of food stretched out across the surface, and Annie ignored the way the women attending the setup looked at her as she refilled her coffee cup. One of them, with steely gray hair, approached with a smile. Annie suspected that she was the type who took her dahlias seriously. "Can I help you, dear?" she asked.

Annie wiped a hand on her oilskins. "I'm a volunteer. Like everyone else."

These women, with their boats and their L.L.Bean fashion, had never had to fight for anything in their lives. They wouldn't survive a day of Annie's life. And they wanted her to leave. She felt her resolve washing away right as a hand slipped around her waist. It was Lydia, who dropped two boxes from the bakery on the table.

"Thanks for rallying the troops," Lydia said to the older woman. "It'll be a long night. You've met Annie, right?"

"Of course," the woman said.

"She's my friend, so be nice," Lydia said, steering Annie away from the table.

They stopped by the schoolhouse to check on Oliver and then went outside and crossed the muddy path to where Lydia had tied two draft horses to a tree. Annie stood back as her friend ran a hand through the horses' manes. The horses were huge, one black and the other a mottled dun color, the kind bred to work a farm, not for riding in the countryside. Lydia waved Annie over and handed her the reins. The horse whinnied, and Annie couldn't help but take a step away.

"Nothing to worry about with these two," Lydia said. "They're both about twenty-five years old and tuckered out, but they've always been gentle. The black one is Lenny." Lydia took Annie's hand and rested it on the horse's mane. Her fingers ran through the rough hair. "This one is Squiggy," Lydia said. "Don't tell Lenny, but Squiggy is my favorite."

Annie reached toward Squiggy but withdrew her hand when he brayed and showed his yellowed teeth.

"They don't bite."

Vaughn appeared at Lydia's side, taking Lenny's reins from her. Annie stepped away, grateful for the distance. Lydia swung under Squiggy's neck and held him by the muzzle. "There you are," she said to Vaughn as she leaned against the horse's shoulder.

Vaughn pulled an apple from his pocket and offered it to Lenny. "You ready?" he asked.

"Should we wait for Trey?" Lydia asked.

"We should get going," Vaughn said. "There's a missing kid."

Lydia nodded, and Vaughn cupped his hands to give her a leg up. She leaned into him. "Have you been smoking?" she asked.

"No."

"Liar."

Lydia swung into the saddle and fixed her boots in the stirrups. The horse took a step backward, then steadied himself with a snort. Vaughn lifted himself onto Lenny. Annie watched them in silence till Lydia seemed to remember she was there.

"Is that woman at your house by herself?" Lydia asked. "The mother? You should go be with her."

"We're not friends," Annie said.

"Still, you know she's worried sick. And you're the only other person who lives there."

"Why do you care?" Annie asked.

"Because I've been there. I know what it's like to feel completely alone. Promise me you'll go."

"Okay," Annie said. Lydia was right. No one should be alone in their worst moments, not even Frankie.

Lydia turned the horse and began walking it down the path with Vaughn following. The sound of hooves clopping on mud floated beneath the roar of the wind. Annie walked after them, down the hill and away from the crowd, watching till Lydia and Vaughn disappeared into the rain.

All summer long, Annie had done anything she could to learn more about Lydia, to learn the things a best friend should know. Lydia liked mountain biking and spaghetti carbonara and listening to Phil Collins without irony. She seemed to tolerate her husband, Trey, and definitely loved her son. But in three months, Lydia hadn't mentioned Vaughn Roberts once, not till yesterday when she'd told Annie that a friend from high school needed a sternman on his boat. "He comes to the bakery all the time," she said, with a dismissive wave of her hand. "We used to be friends, but now I barely know him."

Now, Annie reached the swing bridge and glanced at the raging water below. As she crossed, clinging to the metal railing, a smile slowly crept across her face. Before that very moment at the community center, she hadn't ever been alone with Lydia and Vaughn. Not once. But she'd experienced enough in her life to know what she'd seen. Those two were in love. And knowing that truth made everything, all of it, so much easier.

CHAPTER 5

Somehow, Hester's whole day had melted away till, well into the afternoon, she and Kate wound up in the Union Square Market Basket, wandering up and down the narrow, crowded aisles of the supermarket, the heels of Hester's sneakers slipping on the sawdust-covered floor. *Flowers*, she told herself. *Don't forget the flowers*. What would a birthday party be without them? And a cake. And candles, of course. In truth, Hester was thrilled that Morgan's birthday party would coincide with tonight's storm. It would be fun to ride it out with friends, and she hoped the storm would provide enough of a distraction from Daphne's absence so that she and Morgan wouldn't actually *talk* about it. That would be too hard.

"What should we have for dinner?" Hester asked Kate.

They'd been here for over a half hour, and Hester hadn't managed to put a single item in her cart. Maybe she'd make a roast or a stew, something that fit the stormy weather. But she stood with her feet rooted to the ground in front of the long cases filled with meat of every cut and couldn't decide. Couldn't commit.

"Arugula!" Kate said.

Arugula. Always arugula. At least Kate was consistent. "And chicken fingers?"

Kate raised both hands over her head. Score! But you couldn't feed adults with chicken fingers and ketchup.

"Will Mommy come to the party?" Kate asked.

Hester touched the girl's curly, honey-colored hair. Daphne came up in conversation less and less these days, though Hester still made a point of taking out a photo of her from time to time. Still, Kate picked up on things that surprised Hester, making connections on her own. "Mommy has the same birthday as Uncle Morgan. They're twins, right?" Hester said.

"Like Isabel and Aiden."

Hester resisted asking who Isabel and Aiden might be. It had been over a month since Kate had been to school, let alone had a playdate. Best case, they were stuffed animals. Worst case had Kate reverting to creepy imaginary friends, and twins no less.

"I don't think your mother will make it tonight," Hester said. "Though I'd love it if she did."

Kate took the news in stride, humming to herself, her face tied in thought as Hester pushed the empty cart forward.

Flowers.

That would be easy.

Get the cart there. Choose a bouquet. Move on.

But when Hester maneuvered to the front of the store, the choices—the roses and the carnations and the dahlias and the tulips—overwhelmed her. None of this was hard, she reminded herself. She'd chosen flowers dozens of times in her life. How about roses? Who didn't like roses? And they came in red and pink and white and some strange shade of orange.

"Blue!" Kate said, pointing with her entire body to a bouquet of daisies, dyed electric blue and dusted with glitter.

"Blue?" Hester said.

"Yes!" Kate said.

There was a choice. An easy one. Give in to blue daisies, no matter how ugly. "Pretty, right?" Hester said, tossing the bouquet into the cart. Not too hard!

"Orange!" Kate said, this time pointing to the orange roses.

"Orange!" Hester said, and she tossed those into the cart too.

"Pink!" Kate said, and Hester grabbed two bouquets of pink tulips. Pink would lighten up the evening on a fall night. Besides, giving in was easier than choosing on her own.

"Red!" Kate said.

Maybe choosing meant buying *everything*. Maybe Hester would fill the cart with nothing but flowers, and she could fill the house with long-lost cheer. That's something Hester's mother would have done, unfettered, blissful, tossing fistfuls of petals while Hester scurried behind her, trying to create a sense of order. And that thought stopped Hester, her hand hovering over the red roses. Whatever happened, she couldn't become her mother.

"Red!" Kate said, her face turning a similar shade.

It used to be that Hester could distract Kate with princesses or with a raspberry. For the longest time,

Kate called raspberries "rubles" and she'd come in for sneak attacks, covering Hester's ear or cheek with spray. Hester could use numbers now for an even longer distraction, but she missed the rubles. She missed the surprise. She missed that she'd missed the last one, that she'd probably wiped it off with the back of her hand instead of leaving it there to dry.

"How many flowers do we already have?" she asked. "Count them."

It worked. Kate's face softened as she moved from the precipice of a tantrum to contemplating the flowers in the cart. She began to count right as Hester's phone rang. Hester glanced at the display, which told her it was someone calling from Scituate, on the South Shore, near where she'd grown up. Near her mother.

These days, Hester usually ignored calls from numbers she didn't recognize, preferring to stick to her small, close-knit group of friends. But she needed a distraction from the flowers. She needed to keep herself from buying the store out. And when she answered, the resulting conversation was what she'd expected: a potential client; a man (be wary); looking for a woman (very wary); one he'd dated (alert!) as a teenager. His voice was steady with a touch of the South Shore in his long vowels. He talked about the Iraq War, about leaving town, and a baby that might have been his. "I wasn't ready then," he said. "But I guess I am now. I guess I want to see if I can make up for lost time."

Until last winter, Hester had run a side business finding missing people—adopted children, long-lost prom dates, friends from elementary school. And until last winter, it had all seemed so innocuous, innocent even. She'd believed that she provided a service, one where everyone she touched benefited. She hadn't realized how much danger lurked in secrets, or that some things—some people—were better left lost.

The man kept talking, and she should have stopped him right away, but there was something in his story, something in his voice that made her want him to continue. She used to pride herself on being able to weed out the crazies in the first few sentences, something about the tenor of their voices or the words they chose gave them away. This guy's voice sounded genuine—and his name was Charlie! How could you get more genuine than Charlie? She imagined him, the straight back and close-cropped hair of a youth in the military. He was probably close to her age, staring down forty and trying to undo his few (or many) regrets.

"What else can I tell you?" the man asked.

"I'm sorry," Hester said.

"What else do you need to know about the case."

"Nothing," Hester said.

"I didn't tell you much."

Kate tugged on Hester's sleeve. "Forty-eight," she whispered. "Forty-eight flowers."

"Good job," Hester whispered back. "I don't do that anymore," she added into the phone. "Find people. I gave it up."

"But I read about you," the man said. "Online."

Hester wished she could find every website that mentioned her name, that told a version of her story, and delete it, but there were too many of them. And what did she really know about Charlie anyway? No matter how nice he sounded, he probably had a wife, a family, people who didn't want the unpleasant truths

Hester might bring to their lives. Who was she to decide anyone's fate?

And maybe he was bullshitting her. Maybe he wanted to find his long-lost ex and her new husband. Maybe he'd already bought a shotgun and a hundred rounds and drove around at night in a rusted-out Chevy Nova hoping to hunt them down.

"If you're serious about finding this woman," Hester said, "I'd hire a real private detective. I'm just a librarian. Good luck."

She clicked the phone off before he could protest. Then she returned all the flowers but the blue daisies, paid for them, and left the store, ignoring Kate's protests the whole way.

Triage, Rory reminded himself. He could only do so much. And he had to choose. He forced his way through the crowd on the pier. It was well past five o'clock now, over an hour since the ferry should have left. More than one voice shouted his name. Someone called him an asshole.

He pressed to the gate and down the gangway to where the ferry's captain, Zoe, waited, looking toward the darkening sky. Zoe had taken over the ferry when Pete had been fired, and it still seemed to surprise a lot of passengers to have a captain who was young, pretty, and female. But she knew how to take charge.

"If we wait much longer," she said, "it won't be safe to go."

"Pete's in the Jeep," Rory said. "He's high."

"What's new?" Zoe said.

She used to date Pete, before, and she'd faced his

addiction by retreating as far from him as she could. Rory knew enough not to ask her for help. He walked to the end of the pier and held up a hand to block the rain and spray. Off in the distance, a water taxi chugged into the channel, a wake streaming out behind it. State cops didn't bother with headway speed, no matter the regulations. As the boat came closer, Rory could see Trey standing at the prow like a figurehead, decked out in head-to-toe raingear that looked brand new. Trey hated Rory. But Rory needed Trey, especially if he ever wanted to take the state police exam again, and tonight, Rory reminded himself, could be an opportunity. Trey would need to rely on Rory's knowledge of the island and the people who lived here, because even though Trey had married Lydia, he was still an outsider. And he always would be.

The driver cut the engine just shy of the pilings. Trey, another detective, and a state trooper jumped to the pier. Trey barely acknowledged Rory as he marched toward the gangway. The second detective followed—a woman with yellowish hair that fell in soft curls to her shoulders, jeans with an elastic waistband, and sensible shoes. She'd also come to the island when Oliver disappeared. "Barb Kelley," she said, sticking a hand toward him. "You're the local deputy. Denton, right?"

"Dunbar," Rory said.

"Faces, those I remember," Barb said, studying his. "Names, not so much."

Rory went to shake her hand, but she doubled over and threw up. "Lived on the coast my whole life," she said, wiping bile from her chin with the back of her sleeve. "But I've never managed to find my sea legs. Man, I hope we don't have to go out again tonight."

"I'll find you some saltines," Rory said.

"I remember that about you," Barb said. "Helpful. Competent. My two favorite qualities. Should we catch up with the lieutenant?"

Rory wasn't used to hearing people compliment him. She took a few steps toward the gangway. "Come on," she said. "You can't do much standing there."

On the pier, Trey and the state trooper had waded into the crowd. The trooper was short, maybe five foot six, with thick, sandy hair. Trey, on the other hand, towered over everyone. He had the build of a college soccer player, and his dark hair looked like it had been styled since he got off the boat. He'd grown up in Bar Harbor, a coastal town of country clubs and yachts, and though he looked preppy enough, he'd spent his summers caddying rather than actually swinging a golf club.

"I kept the ferry from leaving," Rory reported, and instantly felt the authority that the island imbued in him melt away. "I thought you'd want to talk to the passengers before they left."

"Have you searched the boat?" Trey asked.

"I thought you'd want to." Even as the words slipped from his mouth, Rory wanted to pull them back and stop apologizing. How could he keep order, watch his brother, get the search parties going, and search the ferry all on his own? In fact, wasn't part of his job to call in the state cops when things got out of hand?

Trey shot him a glare as he whispered in Barb's ear. She glanced at Rory and then led the state trooper across the gangplank and onto the ferry.

"People in town are gathered at the community center," Rory said. "Some people are out searching already. Anything you need, I'm here to lend a hand." He paused a beat. "Sir."

"Where's the mother?" Trey asked. He glanced at a notepad. "Frankie Sullivan. That's her name, right? Didn't I hear she's the one who raised the alarm?"

"I told her to stay put at the house in case the boy wanders home. I told her that we'd come find her."

Trey paused and smiled at the people waiting to leave. "We'll have you underway in a few moments," he said to them before touching Rory's arm and leading him a few feet away. "You kept these people on the island with a hurricane bearing down, even though any idiot could see there's no missing kid waiting to get on that boat. And you left the kid's mother on her own in a drug den to do whatever the hell she wants. Shouldn't you have called family services about this woman weeks ago? Most kids who wind up dead are killed by their own parents. You know that, right?"

Before Rory could defend himself, Trey cut him off. "Shut up. Don't say a word. It'll only make it worse. I'll go pick up the mother."

Rory stood still. Trey could make anyone feel small, but how much of this had to do with Lydia and the love Rory had confessed for her? How much of Rory's humiliation had Lydia shared with her husband?

Trey leaned in and whispered. "Don't do any more thinking. You aren't good at it. Lydia's right," he added, tapping his temple. "You're touched. Maybe I *should* feel sorry for you. Make sure the ferry gets off, then come to the community center and follow orders for the rest of the night. And let me give you a little warning: If by some miracle you wind up being the one to find this kid later tonight, I'll come for you. No matter what Lydia wants. Got it?"

Rory's mouth went dry. He'd had enough, tonight and every night. "I didn't take your son," he whispered back, grabbing Trey's arm. "You know that. You were right there with me on the pier. There was no opportunity at all. All that bull people are saying about me, none of it's true. *You* are the one who left Oliver on his own that day. Remember? *I* was the one doing my job."

"Get your hands off me."

Rory held his hand exactly where it was. If he moved it, he worried he might punch Trey and have a much bigger problem.

"Dunbar."

It was Barb Kelley.

"Take a step back," she said, glancing over her shoulder to be sure no one had noticed the altercation. When Rory still didn't move, she added, "That's an order."

Rory released Trey's arm. Trey straightened his jacket and smoothed his hair. "Don't ever touch me again," he said. "You'll regret it if you do. And stay away from my wife and son."

Barb smiled and waved to a woman staring at them from the line. "Get out of here, Trey," she whispered through gritted teeth. "You're making this worse."

Trey turned and raised his voice. "Great job," he said for all the world to hear. And then he headed up the hill toward town.

"Now I need *you* to cool off," Barb said to Rory. "And help me find this kid."

Pete chose that moment to get out of the Jeep, walking like a zombie toward the line of people and letting the blanket fall into the mud and reveal his nakedness. A group of children screamed and ran. Someone yelled for Pete to cover it up. Barb retrieved the blanket from the mud and wrapped it around Pete's shoulders. Then she turned to Rory and shot him a glare. "Who the hell is this?"

Rory stared at her, rain pouring from his visor. He couldn't answer. How had any of this happened? How could he be the only one in his family still standing?

"Faggot, faggot, queer, faggot," Pete muttered.

"Would you shut up?" Rory said, turning on his brother. "Please shut up."

Pete stumbled forward, his eyes barely open. The blanket flapped around him, and all Rory wanted right then was to make this better in some small way. He wanted to go back in time, before the summer, long before the Fourth of July, to when he could still go home.

"I'll take care of it," he said.

"Does he need to go to the hospital?" Barb asked.

"He needs to sleep it off."

"He's not drunk."

"Yeah, he is," Rory said.

Pete couldn't go to the hospital. He was on parole.

"Listen," Barb said. "Do you know what he took? There's a shipment of Oxy that hit the area last week that's laced with fentanyl. It's already killed nearly a dozen people in Portland."

"This is nothing," Rory said, leading Pete to the Jeep. "Nothing new at least."

"I hope not," Barb said. "For both of your sakes."

CHAPTER 6

Hester put the daisies into a glass vase, blue dye leaching into the water almost instantly. Then she set the vase in the middle of Morgan's dining room table. Then she moved it. To the kitchen counter, to the front table, to the windowsill. Finally, she stashed it in the fridge, out of sight. Away.

Kate sat in front of the TV, watching something insufferably cheerful, and Hester stared at her phone. She craved a mess, a metaphorical one at least, and what could possibly be the harm in calling the man she'd spoken to earlier? She pulled up his number, her finger hovering over it, ready to hit Send. Surely, getting out of the house, meeting people, digging into this new mystery, would help her heal. Maybe it would take her on the road, take her someplace she'd never been. But then Kate giggled at something on the TV, and Hester could feel the cold. Seeping in. Enveloping her. Instead of calling Charlie, she texted Morgan.

Left work early and picked up the kid. You're off the hook! See you at home.

Another lie.

The lies had grown easier to tell.

She lay the phone on the kitchen counter, facedown. Even then, it called to her as it usually did. She could google her own name, read the blogs that had popped up about the story from last year, the ones that tracked the killings from state to state. But hadn't people moved on? Hadn't they realized that Hester Thursby was nothing more than a four-foot-nine-and-three-quarter-inch, thirty-seven-year-old librarian who was afraid to face the world? She hadn't worked since that day in August when she'd lost Kate at the dog park, when she'd heard the slam of a car trunk and run into the street shrieking at a man driving away in a teal-colored Saturn, a man who'd locked his doors in panic while she pounded on his windows and hurled rocks at his back window. Then Hester had dialed 911 and screamed at the dispatcher till she heard a siren off in the distance.

It turned out that Kate had wandered to the community garden, where she sat cross-legged in a bed of daisies. Waffles found her, nosing at the girl's cheek while she pushed the basset hound away. And the whole incident couldn't have lasted more than five minutes. Ten, tops. Though it had seemed an eternity. It had made everything that happened, everything Hester managed to push away, very, very real.

She gave in and typed "Hester" into the search box and saw that her name still beat out "Hester Prynne" in popularity. That wouldn't last much longer. Hester wasn't famous. She could walk down the street or shout her name in public without much notice, but within a tiny microcosm—a very vocal, very anonymous online microcosm—she held interest. Members of that world wrote about what she'd done and what she hadn't done. They called her a bad mother, and Hester wanted to remind each and every one of them that she wasn't a mother at all. They made her a hero, a victim, and a whore. Here's what was true: Last December, when Hester still found missing people, a woman had hired her to find her brother, Sam, and Sam had turned out to be more dangerous than Hester ever could have imagined. Now Sam was dead, and his friend Gabe was serving a life sentence in a federal prison in central Massachusetts. And Hester placed all the blame—every last bit of it—on herself. She'd been bored and had wanted to fill her life with other people's stories. Women out there wanted Gabe; they wanted to save him, to protect him, to help him heal, and some of these women thought Hester could connect them to him. And they wrote her. And Gabe wrote her. Letters in plain white envelopes with postmarks from Devens, Mass., that she left unopened and shoved into a shoebox hidden at the back of a closet. She kept those from Morgan too. Would she ever have the courage to open them, or to visit Gabe in prison, to look him in the eye and fully forgive him for what he'd done? Right now, she didn't have the courage to leave Kate out of her sight or to choose dinner at the grocery store. Baby steps, right?

She pulled up a group text and wrote:

Potluck tonight! Jamie, you're in charge of the cake!

She silenced the phone and shoved it into her pocket. Out of sight, out of mind.

"Come with Aunt Hester," she said to Kate, who

managed to look away from the TV long enough to shoot her a glare. "Haven't you seen that show before? Come."

"I am *not* Waffles," Kate said.

"No, you're not a dog," Hester said, hitting pause on the TV and holding out a hand. "But you still need to come."

Upstairs, through a door at the back of Morgan's walk-in closet, they headed into the new room. The room used to be Hester's own apartment, her private aerie high above Somerville that she'd clung to even after Kate came to live with them. With its slanted ceilings and tiny kitchen, with its love seat and ancient television and VCR, with its dust and grime, Hester used to come here and lock the door whenever she needed to escape. The apartment used to be her sanctuary.

But Morgan had taken a sledgehammer to the wall between the apartments in December.

Afterward.

And Hester . . . Hester had told him to do it. She'd insisted that she didn't need the space—the escape— anymore. When he finished, she cleaned out everything that had made it hers: She left the VHS tapes in a box on the side of the road. She pried the cabinets from the kitchen walls and hauled the red-and-green-plaid love seat to the sidewalk where, despite a Craigslist posting, it sat for two days in the rain till a garbage truck hauled it away. She painted the walls white and installed beige carpets. The final swipe of the eraser came when she hung blinds from Home Depot. Now the space felt huge and airy and as generic as she could make it. Anything to forget.

She opened the closet and took out the shoebox filled with Gabe's letters. And then she sat at the top of the narrow staircase that led to the landing below and dared herself to open one. The carpet here still smelled new. She wished Morgan hadn't taken Waffles to work today, that the dog was there to waddle after her and force herself onto Hester's lap. "Why you cry?" Kate asked, sitting beside her and touching a tear on her cheek.

Hester forced a smile. "I have something in my eye."

Kate went to touch one of the envelopes, and Hester snatched it away, as though it might scar the little girl, as though Gabe could reach through the paper from his prison cell and harm her. She slammed the lid on the shoebox, shoved it away, and texted Charlie.

Send me her full name, Social Security number, and birthday. And a photo of both of you. I'll see what I can do.

Once Charlie sent the information, it took ten minutes in databases for Hester to find his ex-girlfriend. She'd moved to Maine two years earlier, changed her name, and taken out a restraining order on someone named Daryl, who bore a remarkable resemblance to "Charlie."

Fuck off, Hester texted. Then she powered down her phone for the rest of the afternoon.

The sun had nearly set by the time Annie turned the bend on Little Ef to where the lighthouse flashed on the point. Rain lashed at her oilskins. Here, where the trees opened, winds raged along the coast. With the surf pounding on the granite shore, seawater had begun to sweep into the bay and cover the jetty out to the lighthouse. Soon enough, it, along with most of the coastline, would be isolated and unsafe to search till morning. Soon it would be too late.

She stopped, remembering a day much hotter that this one, when the tide had pulled all but a trickle of the thick, salty water from the bay. Sailboats tied to their moorings had sunk into the wet sand, their masts leaning at forty-five degrees. Midafternoon sun had beaten down on the rocky sand as Annie had picked her way into the silt wearing shorts and an old pair of sneakers. The mud swallowed her feet whole, each step releasing a belch of sulfurous gas. About fifty yards from shore, she dug into a clam bed with a pitch-fork and filled a wire basket with a bushel of quahogs. She worked fast. The fine for digging clams without a permit was thirty-five dollars, and it might have been a million as far as Annie was concerned.

Once she'd filled her basket with the large clams, she waded to shore only to see a flash of blue lights that made her heart sink. How could he have come so quickly? How could he have known? She stashed the basket of clams behind a clump of beach grass as Rory lumbered toward her, his heavy uniform in sharp con-trast to the sweltering day. He took a moment to size her up, assessing the muddy shoes and the pitchfork lying in the sand. "Have you been out here all after-noon?" he asked.

"An hour, maybe," Annie said, and knew enough to smile.

Even though she had at least five years on Rory, pretty had always been a tool in her toolbox, and at the time she'd still believed she'd maintained enough of her former self to emit health and middle-class prosperity.

"I thought I saw you in town," Rory said. "At the Fourth of July festivities. Right before the ferry almost crashed."

"I left," Annie said. "Crowds aren't my thing. Did anyone get hurt?"

"Not from the crash." Rory rested his thumbs in his belt and pushed back his cap. A trickle of sweat ran down his temple. "Anyone else been out here?"

"Me and the seagulls."

He scanned the horizon. "At least these boats are out of commission," he said, adding, "We have a missing kid in town. Fireworks are cancelled, so is the light parade. The state police are searching every boat in and out. And we need all hands-on-deck to help. Toss the clams, get changed, and come with me. You're lucky I'm not writing you a ticket."

Relief surged through Annie's body. Rory waited till she'd surrendered the clams back to the sea, before driving them off in the Jeep, lights flashing, telling Annie that the missing boy was Oliver, Lydia's son.

"From the bakery?" Annie asked.

"Yeah. Do you know them?"

"Not really. Is her husband on the island?"

"Trey? He's here. And kids wander off all the time. There are plenty of places to get lost. Right?" Rory said, but the lines on his face betrayed his true concern.

"I bet it's nothing," Annie had said. "But I'm here to help."

* * *

"Ethan!"

Annie shook away the memory. She heard someone shouting the boy's name over the wind as, first, flashlight beams cut through the dusk, then a small group of four people turned the bend. As they approached, Annie recognized most of the faces poking out from beneath raingear, though she didn't know their names.

"Any luck?" she asked.

"None," one of the women said. "What are you doing out here, anyway?"

"I have to go to the house," Annie said.

The woman glanced at one of the men in her party.

"Where he lives," Annie added, quickly, too quickly. "Where I live."

"Right, you're one of them," the woman said, already walking away.

Annie wanted to shout, to make the woman know that she was real. But she watched instead as the group disappeared into the trees. How had she become one of "them"? How had she become the other? It hadn't started on the island, but coming here hadn't helped either. She thought about that day again, the Fourth of July. There hadn't been a storm then. There hadn't been so much danger.

That day, as the search parties had mobilized, Lydia had placed herself at the very center of the action, her voice steady as she stood beside Trey outside the community center and described Oliver while holding up a photo of him on her phone. To Annie, he looked like thousands of other children who wound up on missing posters, with Lydia's freckles and eyes.

"He has curly hair," Lydia said, her voice strong, determined. "Much thicker than a four-year-old's should be. He insisted on wearing red, white, and blue today. He likes bugs."

Annie had made sure to join Lydia's search party, and the two women had walked together for the rest of the day, shoulder to shoulder, shouting Oliver's name. They searched for hours, plodding over sand and stone and beach grass, long enough for the tide to sweep in and fill the bay to bursting and then drain all over again. As the summer sun began to set, as they trudged over this same ragged coast, and as the desperation that came with darkness began to grow, a man in the group shouted from a rocky crag in the distance. "It's him! I found him!"

Lydia took off, her arms pumping, her sneakers slipping on wet stone. It was all Annie could do to keep up, but by the time they'd arrived, the man had realized his terrible mistake. "I'm sorry," he said, tossing a discarded American flag out from where it had caught on the cliff.

For a moment, Annie thought Lydia might break. She walked away from the group toward the sea. A breeze caught her hair and blew it around her face. Annie left the others and stood at her side till she dared speak. "I know," Annie said. "I know what this is like."

Lydia grimaced. "You don't," she said. "How could you?"

Annie straightened herself and turned to look over the water. A crescent of a moon hovered on the horizon. "Because I lost my daughter," she said, her voice barely a whisper. She hadn't meant to say it, and she tried to pull it back. "I'm sorry," she said. "I shouldn't make this about me."

Lydia's eyes shone in the moonlight, and Annie

wondered if she'd erupt in rage at the intrusion or break into sobs as unasked questions hung between them: *What happened? When? Was she found?* Annie preferred to let the questions answer themselves.

Lydia took her hand, like an old friend bonding over a shared loss, her nails digging into Annie's palm. "You're right. You shouldn't."

Lydia's phone rang.

And the moment between them ended. So did the search.

Rory called with the good news, telling Lydia that he'd discovered the boy asleep in the hull of a boat in the marina. Once awake, Oliver told a story of balloons and gorillas and being chased along the docks by an enormous spider. No matter how they probed, he couldn't describe who, if anyone, had taken him. And later, when Lydia had probed on Annie's story, asking what had happened to her daughter, Annie had been able to fend off the conversation. "Feel lucky," she'd said. "Don't ever forget that your story had a happy ending."

A gust of wind swirled in off the ocean, nearly knocking Annie to the rocky ground. That had been weeks and weeks ago. Over and done, right?

She pulled up the hood on her oilskins and left the lighthouse behind. Around the next bend, she came to an overgrown gravel path that led into the trees. The Victorian, her home—if she could use that word—for the past three months, sat a hundred yards from the path, nestled among overgrown rhododendrons. Most of the windows had been boarded up with plywood. A few chips of pink paint remained on the shingled exterior, and the outlines of gardens filled in what must have once been a lush lawn. She edged up the front steps, keeping to the sides to avoid crashing through the rotten planks. The wraparound porch groaned under her weight. She heaved open the heavy oak door and stepped into the shadow of the foyer. "Hello?" she shouted into the silence.

Inside the front parlor, with its ten-foot ceilings, stone fireplace, and trash-strewn floors, rain dripped from ceilings onto wide-planked floorboards and brought out the house's secrets. Damp air smelled of ash from the chimney and mildew and dogs long gone. Wallpaper lining the parlor—someone had once loved this house enough to choose those pink and gold flowers—lifted a bit more from the horsehair plaster, where oil lamps, long burned dry, hung. The house had rooms running into rooms, and wardrobes with rusted keys, and toilets that once flushed with the pull of a chain. Now the inhabitants carried buckets of water from the old well in the yard.

Annie passed through the dining room and into the kitchen. She'd taken a few steps across the black-and-white tiled floor when she sensed someone in the room with her. She swallowed and turned. A man sat in the fading light at the long kitchen table, a box of Nutter Butters open, the cookies strewn across the dark maple.

Annie could have panicked at the sight of him, but at this house, people came and people went. They did what they wanted, with one another or on their own. So even if Annie wanted to heed every instinct life had taught her and run, she played it cool. Even if the man had lank hair that fell to his shoulders and tattoos running up each arm. Even if he shoved the cookies into his mouth and chewed like a wild animal.

"Hey," she said, as though they'd met a thousand times.

She kept moving, though, hoping to get through the kitchen to the backstairs. To escape.

"Red!" the man said, standing, half-chewed cookies spewing from his mouth. And he moved quickly, more quickly than she'd have guessed he could. "How'd you wind up here?" he asked, blocking her way.

He was tall and thin and wore an old concert t-shirt. In the dim light, she couldn't tell if his hair was gray or blond.

"Portland," he said, close enough for her to smell the peanut butter on his breath. "I remember you. You hung with Emily!"

Emily was from another lifetime. Before Annie came to the island, she'd lived in Portland for a few months. Existed would be a better word. Emily dealt and used, and eventually Annie had needed to get away. So she'd come here. Now she remembered this man too. She'd seen him loitering on street corners and crawling out of abandoned houses on the outskirts of town. She'd watched him lug a microwave across an intersection on his way to return it to Walmart. She'd heard things about him—he sold guns or ran a prostitution ring or dealt drugs—and she'd stayed away from him. She'd heard similar stories about other people, and God knew what they'd heard about her. A lot could take on the strength of truth in a world without power or trust. Here, on the island, in this house, your truth was what you wanted it to be.

"Small world," Annie said. "The cops'll be here soon. You know that, right? They'll be all over this house and anyone here."

"Right-o," the man said, saluting with two fingers. "Thanks for the warning. Gotta find my nephew. I'm Frankie's brother, Seth. I came in on the ferry this afternoon. Must have thrown up ten times."

"Where is she?" Annie asked.

"In the storm," Seth said. "Freaking out. Like, really freaking out."

"Wouldn't you be? If it was your kid?"

"I am," Seth said. "I'll go out too once I finish my dinner. Now that you mention the cops, maybe sooner rather than later." He stacked three cookies and ate them in two bites. "Hungry?" he asked.

Annie shook her head.

"I have other stuff, too, if you need it."

"Not my thing," Annie said. "And good luck tonight," she added, heading up the back staircase to her room, a narrow closet with a single window, where she slammed the door and stood with her back against it, trying to slow her breathing. She dug her heels into the floorboards, bracing herself against the solid wood, as the last light of the day faded. No matter what his reasons for being here, no matter how much power Annie had ceded to life, that man—Seth or whatever his name was—was not someone she wanted to be alone with.

Ever.

Only once she heard the back door open and Seth head into the storm did she let her guard down. She slid to the floor and crawled toward her mattress. In June, when the house had been packed, this room, filled with chests of drawers, had been the only empty space to claim. Annie had formed a wall with the tallest of the chests and dragged a water-stained mattress from the attic to sleep on. Now she took a black knapsack from one of the drawers, stuffed the money Vaughn had given her into one of the pockets, and took out a burner phone. She sat on the mattress, knees pressed into her chest and her back to the wall. The phone was nearly dead, but she typed a text to the one number she still had memorized.

It's me. I'm on Finisterre Island in Maine. Come find me.

She nearly hit Send, as she had so many other times, hoping that the person on the other end might be the one person on earth missing her. And as she had every other time, she deleted the message. It was for the best. She wasn't ready. Not yet. And she didn't know if she ever would be.

The bedroom door opened.

In the darkness, Annie gasped. She hadn't heard anyone coming, but she fumbled for a stick that she'd left on the floor beside the mattress. When she peered around the wall of bureaus, the dim light from the burner phone showed Frankie edging through the door.

"You scared me to death," Annie said.

Frankie took another tentative step into the room, sniffled, and flicked on a flashlight. She must have been in her midtwenties, and was short and fleshy, like the girls from college who partied all night. She wore the same pair of jeans she'd worn since the day she moved into the house. Her hair, the color of dishwater, dripped from the rain, and she smelled damp and un-bathed. "Your brother's here," Annie said.

"My brother?" Frankie said, her voice raw.

"Seth."

"Oh," Frankie said. "I saw him already."

"I'm so sorry, sweetie," Annie said. Even though she barely knew Frankie, even though they'd hardly spoken a word to each other in the time they'd lived together, the "sweetie" felt like something Annie would say. "I bet this will all work out."

Frankie wiped her nose with the back of her fist. Annie would have offered a tissue if the best thing they had wasn't already a sleeve.

"He's an asshole sometimes," Frankie said. "Ethan is. He probably wandered off. Or he's hiding and thought this would be funny. I checked the well. . . ." Her voice trailed off, and she dug in her pocket for something, crushing two pills with a spoon, dividing the powder into lines, and snorting one of them up. "It's Oxy," she said with the hint of an offer, the sadness in her eyes already dulled.

When Annie shook her head, Frankie hoovered up the second line. She slid onto the mattress next to Annie without asking. "That cop told me to stay here and wait."

"Trey?" Annie asked.

"Trey," Frankie said softly, smiling at the sound of the name.

"Do you know him?"

"We all know Trey."

"Was he here?"

"Not him. The other one."

"You mean Rory."

"He was kind," Frankie said, though Annie couldn't imagine Rory being kind. Rory had harassed her since the day she'd come to the island, and she suspected he wished that everyone who lived in the Victorian would leave. She'd have wished it too in his position.

"He told me that he used to wander all over the island," Frankie continued, "and come home long after dark. He made it sound like I shouldn't worry. But he doesn't understand."

"Well, there's a whole search started in town," Annie said, suddenly feeling terrible and seeing Frankie as the mother she was. "If he didn't understand then, I think he does now."

Outside, the storm had grown in intensity, swirling around the house, rain pounding at the roof. Downstairs, over it all, Annie heard something fall over. She ran a hand through Frankie's dirty hair. "I bet that's the cops now," she said. "Stay here. I'll go see. And get rid of anything you don't want them to find. But whatever you do, tell them anything you know. Secrets only hurt."

"I don't have secrets," Frankie mumbled.

"We all have secrets. And they find them out anyway."

Annie took the stick with her. Downstairs, she walked through the darkened house. "Who's here?" she shouted into the silence.

In the front parlor, a bright light shined in her face. She held up a hand to shield her eyes, refusing to betray her own fear. "Who is it?" she asked before recognizing Trey's familiar silhouette.

She nearly swore at him. She hadn't seen him, not since he'd come in from the mainland. He flicked off his headlamp and plunged them into complete darkness. "You're in a rush," he whispered, his voice closer than she'd expected it to be. "You going somewhere?"

He prodded her coat with his fingers, finding pockets, patting her down. He was the type who got off on power, on having it and wielding it.

"I heard someone in the house," Annie said. "I came to see who it was."

"Where's the mother?" Trey asked.

"Upstairs. You should give her some time," Annie said, thinking of the pill Frankie had snorted and wanting to offer the woman the smallest of kindnesses. "She's in no state to talk to anyone. Not now."

"While her son's missing?"

"You have no idea what it's like to lose a child," Annie said, and even in the darkness, she could feel Trey stare her down. He did know. Oliver was his too.

"I'll tell you this much," he said. "Taking a hit and passing out isn't how most parents react to this type of situation." He flipped the headlamp back on, sweeping the beam around the trash-strewn room. "Honestly, I don't know how you live like this."

Annie let the silence hang between them. She wouldn't let him shame her into agreeing.

"Fine," he said a moment later. "Tell me, do you know Frankie? From before, in Portland?"

"I may have seen her around, but we didn't know each other."

"How did she find this house then?"

"Same way I did. Someone in town told her about it. It's not like it's a mystery."

"I guess not," Trey said. He leaned his back against a wall and slid to the floor, patting the ground beside him.

Annie understood the invitation, and here, in this house, maybe she'd have been smart to give in to it. But it wasn't right. Not now. "We're not alone," she said.

"Hasn't she passed out?"

Trey reached toward her. Even his near touch was electric. Annie forced herself to move, to go up the stairs. "I'll get her," she said over her shoulder.

She ran through the hallway and down the back stairs to the kitchen, where she edged open the water-logged back door. She slipped through the narrow opening and into the night. Her eyes had adjusted to the dark enough for her to find her way through the trees. Behind her, Trey called her name, his voice swept up in the wind. And she ran. Down the path. Toward the beach. Toward the lighthouse. She might still have time.

The coast opened in front of her. Rocky crags and a sharp cliff. The water in the bay churned as waves crashed against the jagged granite that dropped steeply into the sea. The lamp from the lighthouse burned into the storm. She was too late. The jetty had disappeared beneath the dark water. Behind her, Annie heard the engine of Trey's truck roar to life. His headlights swept the landscape. She dashed forward, onto the rocks. Rain soaked beneath her oilskins. She heard the truck skid to a stop and the door slam closed.

A blast of wind nearly knocked her over.

A small light flashed from shore, and Annie could see Trey running, his headlamp bouncing with every step. She turned and fled. She leapt from one barnacle-covered boulder to the next till she reached a beach. Here, five- and six-foot waves crashed on the shore. Surf stretched across the sand and pulled at Annie's feet, trying to suck her out to sea. She could sense Trey somewhere in the darkness.

She knew this place. She'd come here on nights when her empty stomach had kept her awake, searching tidal pools for mussels and clams. Now, she leapt from stone to stone. She imagined Frankie here with Ethan, on a sunny day, building sandcastles while the tide crept higher.

A wave knocked her over. Water pounded around her as she dug her fists into cold sand that melted away like caramel. Seawater flooded under her slicker. She struggled forward, forcing herself to stand and retreat right as Trey appeared.

"Annie!" he shouted, and she could almost smell him—sandalwood, tobacco, a touch of cinnamon.

They shouldn't be here. Not together. Not now.

When he passed by her hiding place, she ran up the path. She scrambled to the edge of the cliff, lowering herself halfway, and finding a foothold. Frigid water roared into a chasm beneath her. She clung to the stone, barnacles cutting at her fingertips. When the surge subsided, she found another foothold and lowered herself a few feet farther. Another wave struck. The frigid Atlantic engulfed her till her lungs nearly burst. She inhaled, sucking in saltwater. The lighthouse flashed behind her. Images of letting go, of being swept to sea or smashed against rocks, flooded through her. Would a world of silence finally bring relief? She imagined a day without regret. But she'd never given up a fight. Through despair, she'd clung to hope.

A hand gripped her wrist. It gave her enough strength to pull herself up the rock wall, inch by inch, till she slipped over the lip and onto level ground. Trey fell back and pulled her onto him. She coughed and expelled water from her lungs. She crawled onto her hands and knees and coughed till she couldn't cough anymore, and then she collapsed onto her back. Rainwater rinsed the salt down her cheeks, onto her lips, and into her mouth. She sucked at it, so grateful for the taste. So grateful to be more than surviving. To be alive.

"Annie, Annie, are you all right?"

Annie looked into Trey's eyes. He was laughing. That's what you said to a CPR dummy.

"Shut up," she said.

He fell beside her, turning so that he faced the sky as well. "What the hell were you doing? Why did you run like that?"

"I didn't want Frankie to see us. And I was thinking about Lydia. She's my best friend."

"Best?" he said, rolling toward her.

The light from his headlamp blinded her, but the touch of his fingertips on her cheek was unmistakable. Now she could give herself over to that version of herself, of the Annie who, at least in her imagination, was open and kind and funny. Who was someone she'd always wanted to be. Unlike Lydia and Vaughn, Annie understood that no matter where you lived, people watched and drew conclusions. She knew that you could lose the thread of your story and lose track of your lies if you gave away too much. But out here, in the storm, under the cover of night, she felt safe. Finally. And the lighthouse would still be there tomorrow.

She turned off Trey's headlamp. She kissed him. Deeply. It felt like the first time all over again. With him. With anyone.

It wasn't. On either count.

CHAPTER 7

"**D**arling," Prachi said to Hester when she took the vase of blue daisies from the refrigerator, "these flowers! They're hideous!"

"Shut up," Hester said, as Prachi quietly lifted the flowers from the blue-tinted water and trimmed the stems, every snip of the scissors an indictment. The woman, who could make sweatpants and a Burger King t-shirt look refined, couldn't help herself.

"Put them someplace you'll appreciate them," Hester said, right as her phone beeped with a text from Wendy Richards, bowing out of the evening: **Something came up! So sorry!**

Hester had met Wendy when she'd been hired to find Sam Blaine. Wendy was rich, from a prominent Beacon Hill family, and she'd helped guide Hester through the confusing media frenzy that had followed Sam's death. Recently, though, Wendy had opted out of most of their plans, and it seemed that the season of their friendship may have passed. How many times could they talk about what it felt like to date a serial killer? Besides, Wendy's prominence had grown since last winter, and she likely had something better to do on a Friday night than eat potluck in Morgan's second-floor apartment. Hester flashed the display at Prachi, who finished trimming the flowers. "She's moving on," Prachi said. "And forgetting."

"It's not that easy for everyone," Hester said.

"Let me know how I can help," Prachi said, filling the vase with fresh water and letting the silence of the unsaid hang between them.

Hester yanked open the silverware drawer and grabbed a fistful of cutlery.

Out in the open-style living room, the rest of the party guests chatted away. Besides Wendy Richards, all of Hester and Morgan's friends had shown up for the celebration—all five of them. There was Prachi, who'd gone to Wellesley with Hester and Daphne, and Prachi's partner, Jane. Jane was tall and blond and taught yoga a few hours a week, and the less Hester spoke to the two of them about money, the better they got along. Of course, Angela White had come too. Last winter, Angela, a detective with the Boston police department, had headed up the murder investigation involving Sam and Gabe, and she'd befriended Morgan. Now, the two of them spent most Sundays camped out in front of the TV watching sports. Her wife, Cary, was a quiet, thoughtful African American woman who worked as a social worker at the YWCA in the South End, and their six-year-old son, Isaiah, managed to tolerate Kate constantly following him around. Prachi's greyhound, O'Keefe, snaked from the living room and into the kitchen, with Waffles at her heels.

The last guest to arrive was Jamie Williams, who strode into the apartment as though he lived there, his enormous hands dwarfing a pink bakery box he'd picked up from Lyndell's in Ball Square and a little white dog named Butch at his feet. Jamie had moved into the first-floor apartment—Daphne's apartment—in the spring, right after being released from the hospital for a gunshot wound, a wound Hester still blamed herself for. Now, on most nights, he came upstairs and joined them for dinner, usually staying into the evening.

Hester took the bakery box and stood on her toes to kiss his cheek. "Thank you," she said.

Jamie paused. He always paused before speaking, the words taking a while to form. "It was . . . nothing," he said.

"Is it raining?"

"Not really."

"So much for the storm," Hester said. The hurricane had changed course and headed out to sea toward Maine with only a few scattered showers and gusts of wind to mark all the preparations and panic.

"Jamie, my man!" Morgan said. "How about a beer!"

Jamie grabbed two Jack's Abby lagers from the fridge. "Nice . . . flowers," he said, before joining Morgan in the living room.

"It's a bigger crowd than last year," Prachi said. "Any word from The Post-it?"

"Where do you think she is?" Hester asked.

"Who knows? Daphne is just being Daphne," Prachi said, giving Hester's shoulder a gentle squeeze.

In the fifteen years since they'd graduated from Wellesley, Prachi and Daphne had held an unstable truce, their sole connection being their friendship with Hester. Hester often wondered if Prachi was glad Daphne had left. She stacked a pile of paper plates on the breakfast counter. "Soup's on," she shouted.

Everyone had come through on Hester's call for a potluck, bringing pizza, roast chicken and vegetables, pad Thai, and a pupu platter—enough to feed twenty. Prachi was first in line, unable to resist taking the lead, as ever. Once they'd moved to the farmer's table, pouring wine and water, passing a salad, Hester dug into a mound of macaroni and cheese, watching across the table as elegant Prachi and gentle Jane tore into slabs of meat and sawed at chicken legs. They'd gone from vegetarian to vegan to paleo over the summer, and Hester could feel Prachi judging her for the pepperoni pizza on her own plate, but she shoved those feelings aside. Kate and Isaiah finished their meals and asked to be excused. Angela raised a glass and toasted to Morgan, and once the warmth of being together settled in, Hester closed her eyes and let the feelings of love and friendship envelop her. These people, every one of them, cared for her. Somehow, she had to remember that. Why had she spent these past weeks feeling terrified and alone? Why had she spent even today feeling that way, when she could have called anyone here? Could she confess? Could she treat this party like an AA meeting and admit she had a problem?

She opened her eyes. The room had grown quiet. All faces had turned to her.

"Maybe you need a change," Prachi said.

"We could meditate together," Jane said.

"Or go to the shooting range," Angela said, wrapping an arm around Hester's waist. "You haven't been yourself," she added. "What happened, anyway?"

"We want to talk to you," Morgan said. "About work. About Kate's school."

"What's happening?" Hester asked.

Behind her, in the living room, something fell over, and Angela shouted to the kids to stop horsing around.

"I think it was O'Keefe," Jane said.

"We're doing this because we care about you," Angela's wife, Cary, said.

And she used her therapist voice, which was what set Hester off. They *were* treating this like an AA meeting, and it would have been okay if it had been *her* idea, if she'd been able to maintain control, but it was not okay for them to ambush her like this. She held out an arm so that Kate ran to her. It was all she could do not to swear in front of the kids, and then she thought, *Fuck it.* "Is this a fucking intervention?" she asked.

Kate smiled. "Fucking intervention," she said.

"Fucking intervention!" Isaiah said.

"Thanks a lot," Angela said.

Hester stood, her napkin falling to the floor. Kate clung to her leg. Waffles snatched the paper napkin, and O'Keefe and Butch chased her around the table, into the living room, and across to the kitchen.

"Honey," Morgan said.

"It's just that . . ." Angela began.

"Darling," Prachi said. "You have to admit you've been acting mad!"

Jamie didn't say a word, and for once his silence sent Hester over the edge.

"You can all go to hell," she said. "Party's over. The storm never came anyway, so who cares."

She stepped over the bench and headed to the stairs. As she passed the buffet, she stacked two slices of pizza on top of each other and glared at Prachi. "I love carbs," she said, as she tore at the crust.

She carried Kate up the stairs, and it took all her strength not to turn and face the silence, to take in the stares from the people in the world who cared about her most. Minus one. Daphne. The only one who could truly understand.

Rory and Pete still lived in the same house where they'd grown up, a sprawling farmhouse right outside of town that had been one of the first structures built on the island. Every year, Rory painted one side of the house red and by the time he came around four years later, the wind and elements on the island had worn the paint away. The house had a barn, where Lydia kept her horses, and a meadow where they'd played as children. He pulled the Jeep up to the back door and helped Pete inside. Walking into the kitchen still felt like home, though most nights he ate dinner at the counter, something straight from the microwave. In the years since his parents had passed away, Rory hadn't changed a thing. The same photos hung on the walls, the same carpets covered the floor, the same furniture filled the rooms. Even Rory's own bedroom, with its single twin bed and *Lord of the Rings* posters, hadn't changed. When he'd left this house at eighteen, he hadn't ever imagined moving back.

He led his brother up the narrow stairs to Pete's room and helped him lie down. Pete seemed to be coming down from his high. He closed his eyes as his head hit the pillow and mumbled, "Thanks for having my back."

He sighed, his chest rising and falling with each breath.

Rory sat in a chair and watched for a few moments. "What's in the house?" he asked.

"Nothing," Pete said.

"Are you sure?" Rory asked.

"It was a one-time thing."

"Okay," Rory said as he waited for Pete to fall asleep. When he did, Rory began the search, in the bathroom they still shared, in the medicine cabinet, then the toilet tank, and then the linen closet. When he didn't find anything, he moved on, through the house, from room to room, till finally he found a stash of blue pills at the back of his parents' closet, in the pocket of his mother's down parka. Rory flushed them down the toilet.

Pete had been sixteen when their father had died. Like Rory, Pete went to high school on the mainland, so it had been easy enough for Rory to leave Portland on the weekends—to leave the friends he'd made there—to come home. He'd needed to keep family services at bay. Rory's dreams certainly hadn't included being responsible for a sixteen-year-old kid, but family came first. Still, it had been easy to ignore the warning signs, the missing cash and Pete's failing grades. How could any teacher expect a kid who'd lost both parents in the space of a year to learn algebra? But the ferry had been a wake-up call. Pete could have killed someone that day. Today was another wake-up call. It was time for things to change.

Back in the room, Rory tossed the empty vial on the bed. "I found them," he said. "And they're gone."

Pete sat up. "Where?" he asked.

"You know where," Rory said.

"Those must have been Mom's," Pete said. "See, the prescription's from years ago."

Rory was used to bargaining. He'd bargained with his mother first, who'd wanted the pain to end. Afterwards, he'd bargained with his father, who'd wanted to forget. "Next time," Rory said, "you're going to the hospital, and you'll take the consequences."

"There won't be a next time," Pete said.

There always was. "Let's hope," Rory said, pausing as a thought flashed through his mind. "You don't know the missing boy, do you? He's four years old, and he lives at the Victorian. That's where you were today, wasn't it?"

Pete shook his head and closed his eyes.

"Are you sure?"

"I was taking a walk."

The thing with drug addiction was that everyone had to lie. Pete lied about what he took, and Rory lied about what he saw and knew. It was a hard habit to break.

"Be careful tonight," Rory said as he left.

At the community center, he found Barb Kelley studying a map of the island with the state trooper who'd made the crossing with her. "This is Nate. Nate, this is Rory. And Rory, we need your island expertise," she said, her vowels long and her accent unapologetically Down East.

Law enforcement in Maine was enough of a tight-knit community that Rory knew Barb had a husband who taught high school math and two children under the age of five. He knew that she could come off as an easy-to-dismiss housewife. But he also knew that Detective Kelley had an unparalleled close-case record, much better than Trey's. The only thing holding her career back was herself—she refused to take the lieutenant exam.

"You gonna stand there like a trout, or are you gonna help us out?" she asked.

"Sorry," Rory said.

"No apologies," Barb said. "Not on my command. Everything all set at home?"

Rory nodded.

"I hope so," Barb said. "It's heading toward seven o'clock. How long has the boy been missing?"

"Since about three forty-five," Rory said. "At least, that's when his mother found me."

"We probably have two, maybe three hours before the storm really hits. The island may be small, but we can't cover all this terrain tonight, even with everyone in town searching."

Rory stepped up to the map. "We're still two hours from high tide, but it'll be as high as it gets. I asked Vaughn Roberts to send people to Little Ef, where the boy lives. That's assuming he wandered off."

"And if someone took him?" Barb asked.

"Then he could be anywhere. But let's assume the best, at least with civilians involved."

"Good instincts," she said, turning toward Nate to confer. He nodded and headed outside.

"Where'd Trey drive off to in such a hurry, anyway?" Barb asked as soon as Nate was out of earshot.

Rory still smarted from the way Trey had belittled him on the pier, but in his heart, he knew the lieutenant had been right. Rory should have brought Frankie Sullivan in. He should have isolated her and questioned her till she told him everything she could about her son, about her life and her secrets, and by not doing so, Rory had jeopardized the case and Ethan Sullivan's safety. He had no excuse. If the child had done anything but wander off on his own, then his mother would be at the very center of that story. Rory didn't want to admit any of that to Barb, even as she smiled patiently. But the detective could probably wait out the most stubborn of suspects, and until Rory answered her, that's exactly what he'd be to her. "Trey went to pick up Frankie Sullivan for questioning."

"He went by himself?" she asked.

"As far as I know."

"He's been gone for over an hour. How long does it take to get there, five minutes? And that wife of his, where is she?"

"I don't know," Rory said. "I just got here."

"She's pretty," Barb said. "His wife."

Rory caught himself. He'd started trusting the detective, letting her draw him in too close, but now she was hinting at something he didn't want to touch. "People say that, but I don't really see it," he said. "I've known her too long."

"Since when?"

"Since forever. We grew up next door to each other. We used to play in the field between our houses."

"Have you been a hothead since forever?" Barb asked, and when Rory went to defend himself she put a hand on his arm. "Look, you're one person. And one person can't be in more than one place at a time. Seems to me that maybe the pier was the place to be this afternoon, with everything else going on. And I'd have left the mother alone at the house too. What if Ethan had wandered home and we'd dragged her here for questioning. That's not a scenario I'd have liked. And I'm sorry about your brother. That must be hard."

Rory knew enough not to respond, keeping his mouth shut till Barb turned her attention to the bulletin board. "What about houses?" she asked. "Most people are gone for the season. And boats. You found the first boy on a boat."

"Most boats are in drydock, and most houses are empty," Rory said. "We should search outside while we still can and turn to structures later. If he wandered into an empty cabin, at least he's out of the elements."

"Exactly what I was thinking," Barb said. "You'll stay here with me and manage the command center."

"What?" Rory said. This was *his* home. He wanted to be out in the storm, to take charge and make something happen, not be stuck here minding the store. And, once and for all, he wanted to prove to the people of the island that their gossip about what had happened with Oliver was just that. "Did someone say something to you about me and that boy?" he asked. "Did Trey?"

"Hold on," Barb said. "You know the terrain. You know the people. If an emergency comes up, I need someone who can help me respond, and respond quickly."

"Whatever," Rory said.

Barb raised an eyebrow and swept her blond hair behind an ear. "I'll say this exactly one time," she said. "Listen or not, it's up to you. I don't know what's going on between you and Trey, and I don't care. I've heard good things about you, and don't forget, I was here on the Fourth of July when you found the other boy. You did exactly what you were supposed to do, no matter what people say."

So the whispers had traveled across the water too. How much of the story had become truth with the state cops? "What do they say?" Rory asked.

"Who cares?" Barb said. "Is any of it true? Did you take that boy and sneak him away all while making sure a ferry didn't crash into the pier? While half the town was watching? How would that even be possible? Forget motive and means, where was your opportunity? Half the state police force came out here to search for Trey's kid that day. If any of those rumors were true, you'd think one of us would have figured it out. You know who would have definitely figured it out? *Me*, because I'm damn good at my job. All this talk sounds like a bunch of nothing to me, and if you forget about it, it'll forget about you. Today, you and I are going to handle this situation, but I need you to stop acting like an idiot. That's Trey's job. Got it? I need you to cowboy up, especially once the mother comes in for questioning."

"Trey won't let me anywhere near Frankie," Rory said.

"If Trey treats you like a jerk, then give it right back. It's the only way to make it, and it's the only way to earn his respect. Plus, you can practice with me. I always play good cop. I'll need you to be an asshole tonight. A real fucking asshole."

Rory laughed.

"You like hearing me swear?" Barb said. "Guess what? I know all the swear words. Even the really bad ones. And if Frankie Sullivan has any secrets, they need to come out. Tonight. Even if I have to say the c-word.

You've been living on the island with her. What do you know?"

"Nothing, really. She showed up a few weeks ago."

"Out of nowhere?"

"People come here to escape."

"Any idea what she wanted to escape?"

"Not really. It's just an impression I got from Annie."

"Who's Annie?"

"She's another one who just appeared one day, but earlier in the summer."

"What about the drugs? The ones your brother took. Do either of these women have anything to do with it?"

"There have been drugs on the island for years now," Rory said. "That's your job. State cops work drug cases. I'm local."

"Point taken," Barb said. "And this Annie. What's she escaping?"

In truth, the only thing Rory knew about Annie or Frankie was that he wished they'd leave and take all their troubles with them.

The doors to the community center slammed open, and Nate rushed in. "Tree down! By the brewery. It landed on a truck. People are trapped."

"Jesus Christ," Barb mumbled. "We shouldn't be out in this. We don't have any equipment for this type of situation." She looked to Rory, who waved a hand her way.

"Go," he said. "I'll hold down the fort."

She nodded, lifted her hood, and dashed into the storm.

After she left, Rory sat in the silence, listening to

the wind and rain lashing at the building and losing himself in his own thoughts while the radio crackled every now and then with an update from the field. He crossed over to the one-room schoolhouse and checked in on the children. Oliver sat in a circle while the teacher read a story. He lifted a hand to give Rory a high five. Rory had barely seen the boy all summer. Even now, he wanted to lift him up and fly him through the room, but he knew enough not to get close. Not again. He remembered Pete as a kid. He remembered him at Oliver's age, such a pain in the ass, following him around the island, always wanting to be included. "Meet him halfway," Rory's mother used to say.

He wished he had, more often at least.

The phone rang in the community center. Rory ran through the rain and picked it up. "Dunbar here," he said.

At first, he couldn't understand the voice on the other end. And then he did. And he forgot everything: his training, the need for backup, his role here in the community center. He dropped the phone and ran.

Storm clouds churned across the darkened sky. Cool rain slapped at Annie's naked skin. Despite the gusts of wind and the raging sea, she heard only Trey's heavy breathing. And she was happy.

More than happy.

Complete. Content. Worthwhile. She felt strong and healthy. Solid. Like she mattered for the first time in a long time. And a part of her hated herself for placing so much of her own worth in someone else's desire, but boy, did it feel good to be wanted! And knowing that Lydia, the one person she had no desire to destroy, could claim Vaughn as her own meant the world to her. In the few short weeks since the affair with Trey had begun, Annie had been torn by guilt. Lydia was her best friend! How could she sleep with her best friend's husband? How could she be *that* woman? But now they could all go forward. They could be friends! Ones who got together on Saturday night and grilled burgers and played Hearts. Lydia and Vaughn; Annie and Trey.

Trey rolled toward her.

"I love you," she whispered.

Or maybe she thought it.

It was something she barely dared to think, let alone to say out loud, but it was something she'd believed in her heart since his first touch.

She rested in the crook of his arm and imagined a mattress instead of cold granite. She imagined the soft touch of sheets, the feel of a pillow under her head. She could hear the patter of Oliver's little feet and smell fresh-brewed coffee.

Coffee.

This, the tangled lives, the mess, Lydia and Trey and Annie—and now Vaughn—this story had all begun with a cup of coffee. Or many, really.

From the day Annie had arrived on the island, she'd gone to the bakery each morning for coffee, sometimes counting out exact change from what she'd scrounged the day before—the change she found on the paths of the island, near picnic benches, or on the beach. She hadn't known what a difference a single dollar could make in her life, not till this year. On days when Trey wasn't on the mainland working, he visited the bakery in the morning too, and one sunny day in July, he said, "Morning," to Annie, his eyes feasting on her.

Trey was beyond her reach. She understood that. And by then—this was after Oliver had disappeared—Lydia was her friend, but that didn't keep Annie from timing her arrivals to coincide with his, which was at 7:45, not quite on the dot. She could slow or quicken her pace so that she arrived right behind him. She could let her hand nearly brush his. Some mornings, she nodded hello. Others, she pretended they'd never met. It was fantasy, that's all.

Then, in late August, she found Trey by the schoolhouse with Oliver. He texted while the boy slid down the slide on his own.

"You'll lose him that way," Annie said, sweeping the boy up and carrying him to his father.

Oliver squirmed in her arms and demanded to be put down. Annie lifted him high, toward the sky. He gave up struggling and shrieked in delight. He shrieked in a way that made Trey look away from his phone. Annie released the boy, but the downy soft feel of his cheek, of being needed, lingered like the most delicate perfume.

"Work," Trey said. "It's relentless. I'd give anything for a free afternoon. To not be needed all the time."

Annie couldn't remember the last time anyone had needed her. "Life," she said, waving a hand around the playground. "It gets in the way."

She kept her actions flat, avoiding the toss of hair or the bat of an eye. Nothing tells a man to run quicker than obvious flirtation, especially at a playground. And besides, Trey was the type who needed to make the first move. That was part of the attraction.

"Do I know you?" he asked, in a way that sounded menacing, though Annie suspected that was how he asked all questions. And that he knew to listen for lies. It's what kept her from saying, *I'm only your wife's best friend!*

Instead, she said, "I've been here since Memorial Day."

He paused, assessing. It *was* the truth. He didn't take his eyes away from her till his phone beeped. "Lydia wants me home," he said.

"Lydia!" Annie said. "From the bakery. That's how I know you. Coffee, black."

"Trey Pelletier," he said, lifting Oliver and swinging him over his shoulder. "If I see you tomorrow, coffee's on me."

"No," Annie said too quickly.

Coffee would connect them and send Lydia an alert. They'd already begun to collude. Trey seemed to understand that, too.

A week later, on Labor Day, he found her as she walked along the path toward home. He stood in the trees, perched on a rock, waiting. "You've been watching me," he said.

Trey was impossible not to see. She'd watched him with Lydia, with Oliver. She'd watched him sweep his thick hair out of his eyes as he'd stood on the deck of the ferry on his way to the mainland. And she watched him then, as she followed his voice into the woods, into the darkness, and let him run his hands along her arms, under her shirt, over her breasts. She didn't worry about her stale breath or dirty nails. She didn't ever remember Lydia, not till later. She didn't ask why. She'd given herself over to him. Completely.

"Are you awake?" Annie whispered.

"Sort of," Trey said. "One more minute. Sixty seconds."

"We need to go," Annie said. They shouldn't have done this. There was a child missing.

From under their sodden pile of clothing, Trey's radio crackled to life. He groaned and kissed Annie's cheek. "The world calls," he said. "Pelletier here."

While Annie couldn't quite make out the words, she recognized the panic in the voice on the other end. When Trey flicked off the radio, he said, "Get dressed," with a brisk efficiency that made her feel herself fading away. He could do that. He could turn in an instant. And it made her want him even more.

"There's been an accident," he said.

"Who?"

"Come or stay," Trey said, as he struggled into his wet clothes. "Lydia's in trouble."

He didn't need to say anything else. Annie's place in his hierarchy was suddenly painfully clear. And it made her feel worthless and ashamed all over again.

CHAPTER 8

Gus had called it in. Lydia and Vaughn had been swept into the ravine beneath the swing bridge.

Rory ran, shouting an update into his radio. It took a full minute for Barb to respond. "We have a mess up here, too," she said. "Three people trapped under a tree, one unconscious."

"I'll handle it," Rory said.

He signed off and tried Trey, who picked up after a minute. Rory updated him before driving through the storm at full speed, mud spinning from his tires, his wipers sloshing away buckets of rain. A plastic deck chair whipped across the path and ricocheted off his windshield. By now, anything not tied down was fair game. At the bridge, Gus clung to the railing, his frail body pummeled by the wind as he peered into the dark, raging water in the ravine below. Rory could see Lydia's horses tied to a tree. Gus pointed toward the ravine and shouted, the wind whipping away his thin voice. Rory motioned him to the Jeep, and once inside, Gus said, "Vaughn climbed down the ravine and got swept into the water."

"Is Lydia in the house?"

"She went in after him."

Rory considered Gus's wrecked knees and hobbled frame, realizing he'd be more of a hindrance than a help. "Go make sure nothing happens to those horses," Rory said to him.

"I've ridden out worse storms than this," Gus began to argue, but Rory held up a hand, and Gus had the good sense to stop.

"Make tea," Rory said. "Get blankets. Find some brandy. They'll be hypothermic when they get out of the water. And send anyone who shows up down to the ravine."

From the back of the Jeep, Rory dug out a flood-light, which he attached to the railing on the bridge. It lit up the churning water, where he could see Lydia and Vaughn clinging to the branches of a fallen tree. Lydia waved both hands over her head. She wouldn't be able to see that it was Rory who'd come to save her, but he hoped that she knew. Vaughn held up a hand to block the bright light. They both had too much Maine in them to panic.

So did Rory.

Like all cops who served coastline communities, Rory had been trained in water rescue. His Jeep was equipped with nylon rope, life vests, a helmet, and a rescue can. He scaled down the side of the ravine, using the rough granite as hand- and footholds. Water in the ravine swept from the bay to the Atlantic and back again, depending on the tides, but no matter what the source, it would be too cold to stay in too long. He waved his arms over his head till Vaughn saw him. Rory looped the line around his arm and hurled the rescue can into the water. It fell short, and the current picked it up and swept it away. He reeled in the line, and tried again, with the same result.

Above, headlights flashed across the bridge. A moment later, Rory heard scrambling above him, and Trey slid down the embankment toward him.

"They're too far from shore," Rory shouted. "We need to wait for backup, for the right equipment."

"We can make a human chain," Trey said.

"Not with that current," Rory said. "Or with just two of us."

Annie stepped out of the darkness. "Three of us," she said.

Rory shined his headlamp toward her. Her face was covered in scratches, and even with her oilskins, every inch of her looked drenched in water.

"Is Frankie with you?" Rory asked.

"We haven't picked her up yet," Trey said.

"You left over an hour ago."

"We got stuck," Trey said.

"Three won't be enough to get to them either," Annie said. "I can go in. I'm a strong swimmer."

"Good," Trey said. "There's a deep spot upstream where kids jump in during the summer. You can get in there."

Annie's eyes flashed toward him, a momentary emotion Rory couldn't quite place. "Not a chance," he said. Rory knew the power of the sea, and that sometimes it didn't matter how strong of a swimmer you might be. "That water has a mind of its own."

Annie turned away and headed upstream along a stony ledge. Rory grabbed her shoulder, and she shrugged him off.

"The water isn't even fifty degrees," he said. "If anyone's going, it's me."

Annie began to object. Trey caught up with them. "Once you're in," he said to Annie, as though Rory weren't there, "ride the current right to them."

"She's not trained," Rory shouted. "And she has no wet suit."

Trey stepped toward him, raising his fist, and Rory hated himself for flinching.

"Lydia doesn't have a wet suit either," Trey said. "I'd think you'd be more worried about her."

"And I'd think you'd be most worried about Frankie," Rory said. "Where the hell is she?"

Trey cocked his fist again. This time Rory stood firm.

"Stop," Annie said. "Let me do this."

Something in her voice—the plea, maybe, or the offer—took the fight out of Rory. It was two against one, and he knew he'd already lost. Besides, Trey was right: Rory would choose Lydia over this strange woman any day. He turned to survey the ravine. Dark water swept past them as Annie stripped off her oilskins and secured a life vest while Trey looped the line through it and tested the knots. The yellow plastic helmet was too big and nearly covered her eyes.

"Go down feet first," Rory said. "And let the current do the work for you."

Trey advised Annie too, speaking softly, close to her ear, and she seemed to hang on each word, taking the scraps of kindness thrown her way. "You can do this," Trey said. "You're strong. If you're in trouble, pull on the rope three times. Got it? One, two, three. We'll get you out of there. And whatever you do, don't try standing. The current could break your legs."

Rory stared at her, willing her to pull out.

"I owe this to Lydia," Annie said. "We're best friends. And I know she'd do the same for me. Besides, I've survived much worse."

Her words hung around Rory, resistant to the wind and chaos. He remembered seeing Annie on the Fourth of July, the way she'd backed out of the General Store clutching those Hostess CupCakes. He doubted Lydia would brave this water for Annie. In fact, he wondered whether Lydia even remembered Annie existed.

"Jump!" Trey said.

And she did.

Annie hugged the rescue can to her chest as she seemed to hover in midair. She'd have done anything for Trey, anything to keep him. The drive here had been excruciating. She'd tried to talk to him, tried to say those words, *I love you,* even as he'd gripped the steering wheel, his knuckles white, the accelerator pressed to the floor. She thought about the way he looked at Lydia on those mornings in the bakery, his hips, his elbows, even his lips, all drawn toward her like lead shavings to a magnet. Everything about them—from the outside—perfect. And she thought about how much she wanted even the tiniest piece of that for herself. She still believed he could be hers. Or at least a part of him.

You've been watching me.

Annie gasped. She plunged into the frigid seawater.

The cold forced the oxygen from her lungs. Water rushed over her head and up her nose at the same time. The ravine's current swept her forward, her body spinning with the force, and the line tangling around her limbs. She'd grown up two blocks from the beach in South Boston and had spent her summers working as a lifeguard, training, doing sprints. But none of that mattered. Her limbs barely responded to the impulse to flail. The only thing that kept her from tugging at the rope was that she didn't want to test Trey's loyalty.

She gasped and inhaled water. She tried to orient herself as the floodlight from the bridge surged closer and careened over her. She'd missed the mark. She hadn't even managed to catch a glimpse of Lydia or Vaughn.

The rope grew taut. Water surged down her throat and into her ears. She struggled until someone's hand grabbed her and hauled her to shore.

She gasped for air, crawling across stone, coughing.

"You almost did it," Rory said, squatting beside her. "A few more yards and you'd have made it."

"I'll make it this time."

"Not a chance," Rory whispered, but she pushed past him and stumbled to where Trey still gripped the end of the line. One of the horses, tied to a tree by the red hut, whinnied in terror, a sound that muted the storm.

"Trey, please," she said.

"Shut up," he whispered.

She heard Rory approaching. She looked across the water to where Lydia still clung to the tree. Lydia had everything Annie had ever wanted—a child, a husband, a business, success—and when Trey had finally seen her, it had made Annie believe that she could have those things too. It had made her believe that she might have found a home.

"This is too dangerous," Rory said. "We'll figure out another way."

"Don't let go of the line," Annie said to Trey. She leapt into the water again.

It was as cold as before, but this time she surfaced without fighting the current, lifting her knees to her chest and holding her nose and mouth above the water's surface. Ahead, she could see the fallen tree against the floodlight. She maneuvered herself to the center of the ravine, hurtling forward till she felt a hand clutching her arm and another grabbing at her leg. Lydia and Vaughn pulled her toward them till she could grasp at one of the tree limbs with her numb fingers.

"What the hell are you doing?" Lydia managed to shout, her lips blue, her teeth chattering.

"Saving your butts," Annie said.

"Idiotic," Lydia said.

"So was going in after Vaughn."

"When we left on the boat this morning," Vaughn said, exhaustion in his voice. "Who'd have guessed we'd wind up here?"

"You forgive me for the lobster? For wrecking your chance at fame?"

"Done and done."

On shore, Rory and Trey had lashed the other end of the line to a tree. "We need to get you out of the water," Annie said.

Lydia rested her head on Vaughn's chest. He whispered something and kissed her forehead tenderly, and Annie wanted to shout at them both to stop. They'd ruin everything! They'd show Trey what he'd lost.

Without Lydia, without the danger of discovery, Annie wouldn't have a chance with Trey.

The tree shifted in the current.

"We have to go," Annie said. "Now."

Thankfully, Lydia pushed herself away from Vaughn. Above them, lights flashed from the bridge as backup finally arrived. Annie tied the rescue can to Lydia's chest, and Lydia pulled herself hand over hand the thirty yards to shore. Vaughn went next, and Annie waited till Rory had hauled him to shore before following. By then, she barely felt the line in her numb fingers as she edged forward. The current ripped at her as water swept around her shoulders and over her head. She'd never imagined that ninety feet could feel so far. When her feet finally found a rock, she tried to stand. The current shoved her upper body forward while her sneaker stuck in the rocks. She fumbled for the line, losing it in the spray and darkness. Which way was up? How could she have survived this much and let this be her end, stupid enough to stand in a flooded ravine?

Again, it was Rory who reached for her, lifting her out of the current with his strong arms while Lydia and Vaughn gripped a line hastily tied around his waist. He tossed her onto the shore and collapsed beside her, his body wet and warm. "I told you not to stand," he whispered. "You almost killed us both."

Annie shoved him away. "Don't tell me ten seconds in that water had you beat."

"Ten seconds in that cold would have anyone beat."

Just then, the tree in the ravine lifted. With a groan, it swept away, snapping the line.

"A few more seconds out there and we'd all have been beat," Vaughn said.

Rory held a plastic bottle to Annie's chapped lips. She sucked at the sweet water.

"Gus is making tea," he said, offering a hand. She took it, though her legs still felt like jelly.

"Thanks, man," Vaughn said to Rory.

"Doing my job," Rory said. "Nothing else. And it's Annie who took all the risk."

"Well, I'm thanking you anyway," Vaughn said. "And you," he said to Annie, "you saved our lives."

Above, Annie heard someone slipping down the embankment. They only had a moment before the rest of the world descended on them. "Where did Trey go?" she asked.

"He took off," Rory said.

"What?" Lydia said. "Why?"

"I'll give you one guess," Rory said.

Lydia glanced at Vaughn, her expression defiant. "I don't know what you think you saw . . ."

"I know exactly what I saw," Rory said. "We all do."

Annie felt numb. And she was horrified as a sob started in her chest. The more she tried to push it down, the more her face crumpled in despair.

Rory glanced away.

"It's okay," Vaughn mumbled. "We're all safe."

But it was Lydia who came to her side. "You are a hero!" Lydia said. "Really. We owe you so much. We owe you everything!"

"I'm fine. I'm fine," Annie said, wiping tears away with a fist. "It's so embarrassing."

Somehow, she'd still hoped that if she brought Lydia to shore, Trey would be here for her, waiting. She'd thought they'd go back to the way it had been, and she'd have been happy to keep secrets. But he'd seen too much. He knew too much. The fantasies she'd clung to, the ones that had kept her moving forward, swept away in a single instant.

"The search is over for the night," Barb shouted as she descended the final few yards to join them.

Annie wiped away the last of the tears and stepped out of Lydia's embrace. "You found Ethan?" she asked. "Is he okay?"

"We haven't found anyone," Barb said. "But it's too dangerous to keep going. We've already had a tree land on a truck, and now this. It's time to bring people in."

"But you haven't found him!" Lydia said. "He's out in this storm."

"It's over," Barb said. "At least till morning." She seemed to take in the motley crew for the first time. "What happened here anyway?"

Rory briefed her quickly.

"You're Annie, huh?" Barb said. "You're a tough cookie if you took on this mess. But come on. We need to get everyone out of this storm and inside. Dunbar, get everyone up on the bridge and checked for injuries. Then do a sweep around the island to send people in."

A moment later, the group had climbed the embankment to the bridge. Lydia took Annie by the arm and led her to the side of the road. "I know what you're thinking," she whispered. "And I know what you saw out there. But things happen. And you don't mean them to, then people who've been there your whole life . . . they suddenly mean more than you realize. If you don't do something about it, then life passes you by."

Rory unhooked the floodlight from the bridge, plunging them into darkness. Annie reached for Lydia. Her skin was cold to the touch. After Oliver had disappeared, after he'd been found, Annie had believed that having Lydia was enough. They were best friends. And from the outside, Lydia's marriage to Trey had seemed mostly good. Then, one night, Annie had heard them fight as she went through the bakery's trash searching for day-old muffins. She found two and her hunger almost kept her from catching the fierce whisper that floated through an open window. "Get out!" Lydia spat at Trey.

"I can't," Trey said.

"Do it. While you still can."

"What about Trey?" Annie asked Lydia. "What will you tell him?"

"I'll face that later," Lydia said. "Right now, I'm bringing my horses home and picking up my son from the community center."

Lydia walked to where she'd tied Lenny and Squiggy to a tree. Vaughn joined her, but she shrugged him off as she stroked the horses' manes and kissed their noses.

Annie shivered, the events of the evening finally catching up with her. She watched as Rory came out of the red hut and walked toward her. "Look at those two," he said, glaring toward Lydia and Vaughn as he draped a blanket over her shoulders and handed her a mug filled with hot tea. "You okay?"

"I'm fine."

But even as she sucked the warm liquid down, it didn't help. She allowed herself to feel everything that had happened so far. Trey wouldn't choose her. Not now. Not over Lydia. Not even to replace Lydia. It was as easy as that. But why, she wondered, had he chosen her at all? She remembered that first time. The way he'd lurked in the trees. "You've been watching me," he said, drawing her in.

And she followed. She'd have gone anywhere he wanted.

"You," he breathed into her ear, "you'll be a good one to get to know. I bet you can do things for me."

And for the first time, Annie asked herself what he'd meant.

CHAPTER 9

"**Y**ou must be freezing," Rory said to Annie. "Get in the Jeep and I'll give you a ride. Detective Kelley wants me to pick up your roommate for questioning."

Annie hadn't had a "roommate" in years, and Frankie hadn't begun to earn the intimacy that the term implied, but she let Rory lead her to the Jeep. Even with his help, it took every ounce of her energy to get into the vehicle.

"Listen," Rory said, after they'd driven a few moments. "You were a rock star back there. Can you and I call a truce? At least till we find Ethan?"

This was a tactic, Annie was sure of it, something Rory had read in a textbook as he prepped to fail his state trooper exam, but she didn't have the strength—emotional or physical—to combat him. Not tonight. "My dad was a cop," she said, the truth bursting from her in a single gasp of relief. "I know you're not all bad."

Rory glanced at her. The Jeep's console lit up his

angular face, his hair buzzed nearly to the scalp, pockmarks from teenage acne dotting his skin. He could have been handsome had his features not tipped from strong to rat-like. "Where?" he asked.

"In Boston," Annie said, tempting fate. Adding pieces to the puzzle. Though Rory would be hardpressed to do much with that simple fact. Besides, Annie's crimes were of the heart and head, nothing that made it onto a permanent record. Nothing he could find by searching on a name. Most of the people she'd grown up with had moved away anyway, including her own mother. The last time she'd gone to L Street in South Boston, she'd barely recognized the neighborhood, with its condos and coffee shops and traffic. She'd expected to find kids playing stickball and instead found only boys with beards and strollers.

"I should have guessed! Irish, right?" Rory said. "But you don't have an accent."

"Some of us have it. Some of us don't. Like here."

"Do I have one?"

"Not like Vaughn does," Annie lied. "He tries to hide it. You sound more sophisticated."

Rory swallowed, his Adam's apple bobbing in his stringy neck. "I'd love to live in Boston," he said. "I'd love to live anywhere but here."

"Why don't you, then?"

"Because things happen, that's why. Have you seen *The Town*?"

"Seen 'em all," Annie said. "*Gone Baby Gone. The Departed.* But those movies aren't my story. Have you been to Boston? Most of the city is nothing like that. Most people aren't gangsters."

"I've been to Portland," Rory said, a touch of pride

in his voice, pride that he'd taken a ferry off this rock and driven a few miles to the big, bad city.

Annie kept herself from laughing but then gave into it. "Have you left Maine? Ever?"

"Shut up," Rory said, surprising her with a smile. She hadn't meant to draw him in. But he was in on his own joke. "I've been to New Hampshire," he said. "We go hunting there sometimes. And I did go to college. Best two years of my life. I may not have a rich ex-wife like Vaughn, but I'm not a total redneck."

Ahead, a wave crashed across the path.

"Eyes forward," Annie said.

"Yes, ma'am."

"You're better looking when you smile."

"I could say the same of you, but that would be sexist," Rory said. "Besides, I've never seen it happen."

Annie punched him in the arm. "I laughed," she said. "Right now. Here. With you in the car. We laughed together."

"Yeah, you laughed *at* me. But that's not smiling. That's being you."

The Jeep jolted as it hit a rut. Rory turned the steering wheel with the skid and managed to keep them from spinning out. When they glided to a stop, Annie was surprised to find that she held Rory's arm.

"No one should be out in this," Rory said, staring into the dark. "Least of all a four-year-old."

"Let's hope he found his way into someone's house. We'll find him tomorrow, right?"

"Yeah, maybe."

In the path in front of them, the headlights caught a group of people trudging toward them. Rory rolled down the window. "Any luck?" he asked.

"Nothing," one of the men said. "Just got that call that the search is off."

"Yep," Rory said, and as he continued the conversation, Annie turned away, an image of Trey flashing through her mind.

What had he seen in her?

She turned the rearview mirror her way. Recently, she'd avoided her reflection, whether in the mirror or when it surprised her in a window or on the water. When she had caught it, she dismissed what she saw. Annie thought of herself as healthy, a few pounds past slim, athletic. She'd played field hockey in high school and used that to get herself to college. Men looked at her, took her in, and she liked that their desire gave her power. So it hadn't surprised her when Trey saw her too. That's what she was used to.

But Rory's mirror reflected something different, something she'd been too afraid to admit. She saw greasy hair hanging around a wan face, yellowing teeth from too many nights without a toothbrush, hollow eyes. How much weight had she lost since she'd come here? She held her hand to her mouth and breathed in the breath of someone unhealthy.

She was homeless. A vagrant. Worthless. She was someone Rory wished would move along and become someone else's problem. She wasn't someone Trey Pelletier should seek out. Rory signed off with the search party and pulled back onto the road. Annie stared out the window, her breath fogging up the glass. Men like Trey didn't sleep with women like her. Not without a reason. How had it taken her so long to see this?

"Hey," Rory said. "I asked you something."

Annie turned to him. "Would you have sex with me?" she asked, and the look on his face gave her the answer. "Just curious," she said. "Sorry, I was off somewhere. What did you ask?"

After a pause, Rory said, "What can you tell me about Ethan and Frankie?"

"I barely know them," Annie said, shaking the thoughts of Trey away.

"Is she into drugs?"

"She seems like a good mother," Annie said.

"That's not an answer."

"It's the only one I have," Annie said, even as she remembered a day not a week earlier when she'd come home to find Ethan sitting in a mud puddle digging with a stick. It had been a cool day, the first that felt like autumn. Annie had known instinctively that Frankie had left the boy on his own.

Ethan slapped a ball of mud onto the grass, and Annie pretended to eat it. "Delicious," she said.

"That are mud," Ethan said.

Above them, wind rustled the changing leaves.

"Thomas here," Ethan said.

"Thomas?" Annie said, glancing into the trees.

"The Tank Engine," Ethan said.

"That Thomas! Let's find him. I think he's inside."

She lifted Ethan from the puddle, surprised when he curled into her and rested his head on her shoulder. His hair was thick and dark, like Oliver's. She ran her fingers through it, burying her nose in his shirt and breathing in the scents of childhood. Inside, she wrapped him in a blanket while she filled a lobster pot with water from the well and put it on the stove to warm—she knew what was warm enough for a four-year-old. She turned the burner off and lifted the boy into the water.

"You cook me?" Ethan said.

"I'll cook you," Annie said, squeezing his nose.

He was small for his age. Small enough to sit in the pot while Annie ran a bar of soap over him. She used dish soap to wash his hair and told him to close his eyes tight while she rinsed suds away with water from a mug. She didn't hear the front door open, or the footsteps in the foyer, or the bag hitting the floor till Frankie shoved her away. "You're sick," Frankie said.

Annie pressed her back into the wall. She'd done terrible things in her life. Shameful things. Who was she to judge?

Frankie lifted the boy from the pot and wrapped him in a towel. "You crazy bitch," she shouted.

"I'm taking care of your kid," Annie said.

Softly.

Or maybe she'd only thought it to herself, like she did with Trey.

By then, Frankie, hugging Ethan to her body, had already retreated up the back stairs to her room.

"Frankie keeps to herself," Annie said to Rory. "We all do. She said that Ethan was probably hiding somewhere, like this had all happened before. She said he could be an asshole."

"She said that about her own kid?"

"You don't have kids, do you?"

"No, maybe someday, though."

Annie could hear in his answer that Rory had imagined tossing a ball to a son and playing house with his daughter, and he didn't know that girls sometimes turned out to be tomboys and boys danced ballet, no matter what you wanted as a parent. He didn't know about the sleepless nights or the boredom or the endless poop.

"Well, don't give up," Annie said. "Not yet. You might think that you're over the hill, or that you've missed out on too much, but you're a baby. You'll pass that test. You'll meet a girl, especially if you stop acting like a jerk all the time. And when you do have kids of your own, you'll learn that parents have all sorts of evil thoughts. Sometimes saying them out loud is the only way to survive."

Annie heard a catch in Rory's breathing. To her surprise, his face had broken with sadness; he was about to cry. She wanted to shake him, to tell him he'd never know true regret till he'd ticked through a parenting schedule—the up-all-nights and early mornings, the day care on Tuesday and gymnastics on Wednesday, the relentless planning. He would never know despair until he watched the details of his own life disappear and become someone else's. She couldn't explain this to him. Instead, she faced forward, in silence, and pretended not to hear him struggle to regain control. She could offer that small dignity.

A moment later, Rory pulled up to the path that led to the Victorian.

"How long have you loved Lydia?" Annie asked.

"Forever," Rory said. "As long as I can remember. How did you know?"

"Anyone who saw the two of you together for one second would figure that one out. Did you know about her and Vaughn?"

Rory sighed. "I saw that, didn't I? In the water.

Maybe it's been there, and I've tried not to see it, but I don't think anyone knew, and secrets don't stay secret on this island."

Annie opened the door to leave but stopped herself and kissed Rory on the cheek, like an older sister. Or at least that's how she'd meant it. "Thanks for the truce," she said. "I'll send Frankie out."

She ran through the rain. Inside, she edged through the foyer, stubbing her toe on one of Ethan's toys. Then she followed laughter to the kitchen. When Annie walked in, Frankie covered her mouth and tried to squelch a grin. She wore a blue t-shirt that read *Mama's Hangry*. A few candles dotted the counters, and even in the dim light, Annie could see that Frankie's pupils were like saucers. An open box of Tuna Helper spilled across the counter. Seth hovered in the corner juggling three cans.

"Red!" he said. "Yeah, baby! Have dinner with us. Tuna Helper. It'll be awesome."

He caught the cans, cranked one open, and dumped the tuna into a ceramic bowl along with a full bottle of mayonnaise. The kitchen reeked of oily fish.

"I almost drowned looking for your son tonight," Annie said to Frankie. "And you're higher than a kite."

The joy drained from Frankie's face.

"There's no news," Annie said quickly. "Good or bad."

She shouldn't have judged. She didn't have the right. No one did. Frankie could approach her grief however she liked, because when it was over, she'd have to find a way to cope. "So many people came out to help," Annie added. "Practically everyone on the island. We searched for as long as we could. Till it was too dangerous."

Frankie put her hands to her face as she was wracked with sobs.

"Oh, man," Seth said, wrapping his gangling arms around her. "Bummer!"

Frankie pushed him away.

"Rory's outside waiting," Annie said. "He's here to bring you in for questioning. And I'm taking the morning ferry," she added, realizing it was time to leave. No one would miss her. And whatever Trey had wanted from her wasn't important now. If she stayed, she'd only hurt herself and others. "Good luck. I'm sorry this happened to you."

Frankie sobbed. "Where are you going?" she asked.

"Anywhere but here," Annie said.

Upstairs, she listened as their muffled voices echoed through the empty house. A few moments later, the front door opened and shut as Frankie left to meet Rory. Annie lay down on her damp mattress. A tree groaned in the wind, and something hard and plastic whipped through the trees. She imagined the people of the island huddled in their houses, waiting out the wind and rain as they had for centuries.

She was no better than Frankie.

She'd been no better than Frankie. That's why she'd left.

But she'd changed. She really had. And she had to leave here before the cops came for her in the morning. Before the questioning began. Before she had to face Trey again. Or Lydia. Before she had to face her own truth.

She rummaged through her knapsack till she found the burner phone. It had one bar and 5 percent power. She typed out the message first and added in that one phone number she knew by heart. Then she stared at the screen, her thumb hovering over Send. It was good to be remembered, to be missed. It was even better knowing someone out there might care enough to respond. And if she was in danger, someone should know.

She hit Send and almost immediately regretted it.

But some things you cannot undo.

CHAPTER 10

Frankie Sullivan felt light enough to blow away as Rory led her across the muddy ground from the Jeep toward the community center, where a generator buzzed to allow lights to blaze. Frankie hadn't said a word to him during the drive here, not even asking about Ethan. Inside the old building, Barb stood by the map of Finisterre Island studying the grid.

"Whatever you're on," Rory whispered in Frankie's ear, "you won't be able to get any more. Not here. Not with everything that's going on."

Frankie's eyes were blank. How many hours a day did she spend on a high? And what would she do a few hours from now when she begged for a hit and none came? Would she trade her secrets for a thumbnail of heroin?

"Come," he said, surprised by the sudden weight of the woman. Her feet remained planted to the carpet, but Barb seemed to sense Frankie's fear. She flashed her a welcoming smile and gave her the softest of hugs. "Honey," she said. "It feels like it took all night to get you here. I thought you'd have come yourself. You know, taken charge. Ripped the bullhorn out of my hands and started issuing orders."

Frankie squinted, processing Barb's words and everything they implied. "Where's Trey?" she asked.

"Off somewhere," Barb said. "We were focused on the search, but that's over, so now we can focus on other things, like talking to you and finding out what's going on. Come. Sit. You want some tea?"

Frankie nodded.

"I'll get it," Barb said. "You try to relax."

Frankie waited for Barb to cross the room before asking, "Do you know him? Trey?"

"Do you?" Rory asked.

"What's he like?"

"I couldn't say."

Frankie brushed hair behind her ear. "Is he good to his son? Does he love him?"

"Is there any reason he wouldn't?" Rory asked.

"He *has* to care."

Rory leaned in. Barb wanted him to play bad cop. Why not start right now? "The only person who doesn't seem to care is you," he said.

Frankie covered her face with her hands. Barb returned as if on cue and set a mug on the desk. "Looks like we've already started," she said, waiting for Frankie's tears to subside. "You must be exhausted. And it's late. What do you need? We have tons of food out there. People bring food when there's a crisis. It gives them something to do! Someone made Rice Krispies treats out of Froot Loops. You want one of those?"

"I need to find Ethan," Frankie said, and this time her voice had an edge to it, one Rory hadn't heard from her yet.

Barb leaned forward and spoke softly. "I'm a mother too," she said. "Though you don't need to be a detective to know that. If you looked up *Mother of Two* in the dictionary, it would say, *See Barb Kelley*. I mean, look at me! I *know* you want to find your son more than anything in the world. And that's exactly what we're trying to do. Find your son. And you're going to help, right?"

"I am," Frankie said.

"So, tell me when you saw him last."

"This afternoon. We had lunch."

"What did you have?"

"Peanut butter. It's the only thing we ever have."

"Why?"

"Because we don't have a refrigerator."

Barb wrote something on her pad and handed Frankie a tissue.

"I thought it would be better out here," Frankie said. "On the island."

"Has it been?"

"It's more of the same. What's that saying? *Wherever you are . . .*"

"*Wherever you go, there you are*," Barb said, waiting a moment before speaking again. "You had lunch, right. And then?"

"Seth came."

Barb glanced at Rory. "Who's Seth?"

"My . . . brother. Or he's like a brother. He watches out for me."

"But he's not your brother," Rory said. "You have to tell the truth here."

Barb held up a hand, signaling Rory to back off. "Your brother came to the island this morning," she said. "Before Ethan went missing. Why would he come? With the storm and everything. I mean, he must have known this wasn't the best day to choose."

"He showed up," Frankie said. "Out of the blue."

"He showed up and your son went missing." Barb glanced at Rory. "Have you talked to this guy?" she asked, her voice no longer gentle.

Rory shook his head. This was the first he'd heard of him.

"Take me through this again," Barb said. "I want to be sure I have the details right." She flipped a few pages back in her notepad and read through what she'd written. "From what I hear, you found Deputy Dunbar earlier today, and you were panicked. Right? You were *in* a panic, I should say. And you should have been, because Ethan was missing. He is missing. And that's what good parents do. You were panicked because you have a four-year-old son, and you should have known where he was, right?"

"I was panicked," Frankie said.

"How long was it?" Barb asked. "From the time you started looking for Ethan till the *panic* set in. Like the full-on 'I can't control this, I'm going to run into the streets and flag down a cop and start screaming' panic. I mean, that's what you did, right? You screamed in the road."

Rory nodded to confirm. "It's what I saw," he said.

"How long?" Barb asked.

"Right away," Frankie said. "He should have been in bed. I put him down for a nap, and when I came back, he was gone."

"That was after lunch?"

"Yes, after lunch."

"And you had . . . ?"

"Peanut butter! I already told you that."

Barb flipped through her notes. "Yep," she said. "Peanut butter. Because you don't have a refrigerator. And your brother. Or whoever. Where was he during all of this?"

"I don't know."

"Was he in the house?"

"The house is big. It has lots of rooms. He could have been anywhere."

"And Ethan could have been anywhere too, right? He's four years old. He knows how to get into mischief. He could have been in one of those rooms. Did you look in the rooms first, or did you run out to find Deputy Dunbar first?"

"I don't know," Frankie said. "I couldn't find him."

"Who's 'him'?"

"Ethan!"

"See, I have kids," Barb said, pulling out her phone and flashing a photo of a girl and a boy on a beach. "They're three and four years old. Irish twins. And they make me panic all the time. Like this day, at the beach, when I took this photo. Used to be I loved the beach, but now when we go, I spend the whole day hoping, no, *praying*, that they don't get swept out to sea or eaten by a shark or pecked to death by seagulls. That last one isn't even rational, and I know it, but I still worry about it. And we live in Portland, kind of a big city. It has some crime here and there, but it's mostly safe, these days. My daughter is the same age as Ethan. Her name is Chloe. And this is the thing: when Chloe disappears, which is not an infrequent occurrence by the way, my first instinct is usually annoyance. Or frustration. Or amusement. Because usually, she's off at the neighbor's or in the pantry sneaking cookies, or down in my office banging away on my work computer. It's only when none of these things are true that the *panic* sets in. For the *panic* to set in, I have to not know something. Or, I have to know something. So, what didn't you know? Or know?"

Frankie stared at Barb.

"Let me ask a different way," Barb said. "What are your secrets?"

"I want to find my son," Frankie said.

"I hope that's not a secret," Barb said. "And so do we. It's the *only* thing we want to do."

Rory leaned toward Frankie. "Do you remember when you found me today? When I was on the path by your house? You said Ethan was missing, right? And then, what did I say?"

"I don't remember," Frankie said.

"I bet you do."

"Okay. You said that people on the island let their kids run wild. They think it's safe. They think bad things don't happen to good people. And you said that I shouldn't worry."

"And then you said the same thing to Annie," Rory said. "You told her that you thought Ethan might have wandered off. That he'd done this before. You called him an asshole."

"Did you say that?" Barb asked.

Frankie's shoulders and head fell forward.

"My kids are assholes too," Barb said.

Frankie began to sob. A single tear, leading into full, body-aching sobs. When they finally passed, she sat up and seemed spent.

"Your tea is cold," Barb said. "Do you want another cup?"

Frankie nodded.

"We'll put sugar in it. And milk. Tea fixes just about anything, right?" Barb's smile had only grown more wolfish. Frankie seemed to retreat.

"We'll be back in a minute. You sit tight." Barb led Rory across the room. "Get out to that house. Find this guy Seth and bring him in."

"What about her?" Rory asked.

"Leave her to me," Barb said.

Back out in the storm, Rory drove as fast as he could to the Victorian. He headed into the trees where, unlike at the community center with its generator, the darkness was so complete he couldn't see a hand an inch from his face. Once inside the house, he flipped on his headlamp and swore he saw the glow of eyes as something scampered away. The storm swirled around the house, pressing on the walls as rain poured from the ceilings. He hadn't been inside here in months, and in that time the smells had grown worse. The place should have been condemned years ago. After tonight, he wondered if they'd have a choice. "Who's home?" he shouted.

In the kitchen, the remnants of a makeshift dinner littered a huge wooden table. Upstairs he tapped open each of the bedroom doors along the long hallway. In one of the rooms a suitcase sat open with women's and children's clothing spilling out of it. The last room was filled with chests of drawers. He peered over the furniture, where Annie slept on a single mattress. He tapped her with the end of his flashlight, and she woke with a start, sitting up and scrambling away from him.

"It's me," Rory said.

"Fuck you," Annie said, sweeping her greasy hair out of her eyes. "What happened to the truce?"

"Why didn't you tell me about Seth?" Rory asked, flipping off the flashlight. "Frankie's brother. He showed up today, on the day Ethan disappeared. At least that's what she told us. That would have been good information to have."

"Well I just met him," Annie said.

"Has anyone come to see Frankie besides her brother? Anyone from town? Strangers?" Rory paused. "Any men?"

"Like a boyfriend?"

"Or not."

"You think she might be a hooker?"

"I don't think anything," Rory said. "But I've seen plenty of shit go down in this house. I'm just asking questions."

"What would you think if I had a man come by?"

"I wouldn't care, unless he was here last night or today. Your kid isn't the one missing." Rory paused for a beat. "*Have* you had any men come by?"

"No," Annie said. "And neither has Frankie. We've been out here by ourselves since Labor Day."

"Well, where is Seth? He's not here, and I need to talk to him. Now."

"I don't know. He was here when I went to bed."

"If he shows up," Rory said, "tell him to come find me."

Out in the Jeep, he called Barb on his phone. "The guy's not here. Seth. Did you get anything else out of the mother?" he asked.

"Not much," Barb said. "Though she's definitely dealt drugs before, which is hardly a surprise."

"Did she deal here?"

"She says no."

"Do you believe her?"

"I don't believe anything she says. Get back here. I need my bad cop."

Rory was glad she couldn't see him grin. "I'll do one more loop around the island."

"See if you can find Trey too. He hasn't answered his phone or his radio in an hour."

"He may be out of cell range," Rory said.

"That's why we have CBs. Call it in if you find anyone. No one should be out in this storm, and that includes you, so come in afterward."

"Roger that," Rory said.

He drove around Little Ef, stopping by the lighthouse, its reliable beam flashing out to sea. The tide had begun to recede, and soon the lighthouse would be connected to the land again. Here, alone, Rory finally let himself think about Pete. When the first wave of opioids had hit the island, Rory had fantasized about rooting them out, finding the source, marching the culprit to the docks for everyone in town to see. It was part of the reason he'd joined the police force, and why he'd agreed to island patrol. That was before he realized how many leaks there were in the supply chain, and that finding a way to plug up one only made the others flow more freely. But he did know one thing: He wouldn't think twice about killing whoever had supplied Pete with this latest hit. And he suspected this guy Seth had something to do with it.

He pulled away from the beach, over the swing bridge and toward town. Rain lashed at the windshield. It was past one a.m. When the sun came up, and the storm had finally swept north, there'd be miles of beach to search, hundreds of cliffs and ravines and caves to check. They would have all day to come to terms with moving from search-and-rescue mode to search-and-recovery. He passed the community center, where the generator buzzed and the lights blazed. He could stop there like Barb had asked. Barb would still be questioning Frankie, because she was the type who never gave up. But he drove on.

He wanted to go home. He wanted to talk to Pete, to tell him how much things needed to change. They could do this, together. He knew they could, but first they had to stop lying, to each other and to themselves. Rory parked the Jeep and ran through the rain. Inside, the house was silent. He listened as the wind shook the structure to its very foundation. In the hallway, he averted his eyes from family photos of bonfires and clambakes and reunions. Of happier times. Upstairs, he tapped open the door to Pete's room. Pete lay on his side, facing the wall. Rory said his name. And he listened. To the silence.

Later, he drove into town, dazed and exhausted, turning the headlights out and drifting the last hundred yards. He knew Lydia's inn by heart—the garden paths, the gates, the best vantage points. He stepped over the fence to keep the squeaky gate from giving him away, then he walked up the path and through the spent perennials to the bow window in the back. He'd come here before, to watch and feel a part of what could be. Inside the inn, Lydia sat on the sofa, still awake, with Oliver asleep across her chest. Like Rory, she probably churned over the incidents of the evening. A kerosene lantern burned beside her. And Rory worried. That the lantern would fall. That the house would catch fire. That Lydia wouldn't be able to make it out in time.

He worried about Trey. Trey, who'd stood on the banks of the ravine and watched Vaughn touching Lydia. Touching his wife. Stroking her. Caressing her. Those touches had cut Rory to the heart. They'd made him want to leap into the water and hold Vaughn's head under long enough so that he'd beg when he gasped for air.

"Cunt," Trey had said, not even bothering to whisper.

Rory turned on him.

"She's a slut," Trey said. "And always has been."

They'd secured the lifeline to a tree. Trey took out a knife to cut through the fibers. Rory didn't think. He moved, his fist plunging into Trey's gut. Trey doubled over and charged him. Rory slammed to the ground, his head cracking on stone. He held his arms over his face, absorbing blows as Trey pounded at him. Finally, Trey rolled off. "You're done," he said. "You're stuck. Here. On this island. Forever. I'll make sure of it."

Trey sheathed the knife and stood. He jerked a thumb toward the water, where Lydia had begun to pull herself toward shore. "You can have her," he said, before scaling the bank to the bridge above. A moment later, headlights had swept through the darkness as Trey sped off toward Little Ef.

At the B & B, Rory leaned against the dripping shingles of the cottage. There was too much going on. The storm and the missing boy. The strangers and their drugs. The state police.

And Pete.

Pete, who lay tangled in a nest of blankets, a spoon and a lighter on the bedside table. Pete, who had foam drying at the corners of his mouth. Pete, whose body had already begun to cool.

Triage.

This choice was easy: Rory would stay right here as long as he was needed. He'd didn't mind the rain. He'd stay till he knew Lydia was safe.

CHAPTER 11

Hester lay in bed with Waffles snoring beside her. Downstairs, the TV blared, and Hester sandwiched her head between two pillows to drown out the sound, but the buzz of NASCAR wormed right through, one of Morgan's awful habits that he'd agreed to indulge on his own, in his own space, when they each still had their own spaces.

Earlier, soon after Hester had spoiled the intervention, she'd heard her friends leave one by one and had waited for Morgan to man up and to face her. But he'd stayed downstairs watching TV with Jamie, and now, it was well past midnight and Hester had to get to work tomorrow. Right? She'd make it this time. She didn't have much of a choice after what had happened. And Kate probably hadn't slept, so she'd be exhausted and cranky in the morning. And God forbid that Morgan help by taking her to school.

The bedroom door opened, and Morgan slipped in. Waffles sat up to greet him, but by now, Hester no longer had the energy for a confrontation and was happy that she'd clicked the light off and could pretend to be asleep. She even threw in a fake snore.

"Don't bother," Morgan said, getting into bed beside her.

She punched at a pillow and rolled away from him. He shimmied up behind her, draping an arm over her, and even that simple touch made her want to shove him out of the bed.

"You didn't need to be such an asshole tonight," he said.

"Was that supposed to be a joke?"

"Sort of. We could use a little levity."

"It's not working," Hester said, flicking on the light. "I don't want to be touched right now. And you were the asshole. All of you were a bunch of assholes." She jabbed a finger toward him. "But most of all, you."

He reached toward her, stroking her leg.

"You're drunk," she said, moving away from him. "Stop."

And he did. She'd give him that much.

"You've known all along, haven't you?" she said. "Do you have any idea how difficult it is to construct a whole world of lies? I've been walking around lying to every single person I know, and you all knew it the whole time."

"You lie to me for weeks on end and it's my fault?" Morgan said. "You do that all the time. You lied to me last winter too. You never, ever take the blame for your own actions. You never own it."

The rage that Hester had suppressed for months erupted. Rage at Sam and Gabe and Daphne. At all of them. And she aimed it right at Morgan. "Why did you make me give up my apartment?"

He stood and paced across the room, into his walk-in closet, and through the door at the back of it into what used to be Hester's apartment. She scurried after him with Waffles at her heels, and when he flipped on the overhead lights, the white walls nearly blinded her.

"It's right here," Morgan said, arms out, spinning around. "Maybe you forgot. It isn't covered in dust and scotch stains anymore. It's not piled high with useless crap. And it doesn't smell like garbage. But it's right here for you to do whatever you want with it."

Waffles raised her snout in the air and howled.

"You should stop shouting," Hester said.

"You stop shouting," Morgan said. "But while we're at it, why are all of our friends lesbians?"

Hester swiped hair out of her eyes and shoved her glasses up her nose. She pointed at the dog and said, "Stop," so that Waffles stopped mid-howl and sat. "Really," she said. "Is that who you want to be? Those are our friends. We have five friends, and they all came over tonight to be with you. And you decided to make them talk to me about a problem because you were too scared to do it yourself. If you want other friends, go make them. And FYI, Jamie isn't a lesbian. He's a full-fledged, testosterone-fueled, NASCAR-loving boy, just like you."

Hester stomped back into the bedroom, slammed her glasses down so hard on the bedside table, she was lucky they didn't break, and flipped the light off. When Waffles leapt onto the bed beside her, she positioned the dog to make a barrier between her and Morgan's side. A few moments later, Morgan got into bed too, and she could almost see him on his back, eyes open, staring at the ceiling. Waffles shifted onto her own back, and Morgan scratched at her belly.

Traitor.

He sighed, and Hester wanted him to say something, anything, so that she could tell him to shut up. He'd already messed up so, so badly. Even when he said, "You're right. I should have spoken to you first. I'm sorry and I was a jerk tonight. We all were."

"Don't say anything else," she said.

"I don't know what to do anymore. I don't know what to say.

"I mean it. Don't talk. I fully intend to go to bed angry tonight and head to work tomorrow without speaking to you. And you are doing drop off and pick up for the next three months. You're grounded! You really, really, really fucked up."

She got out of bed and walked across the hall to Kate's room, and couldn't have been more satisfied when she heard the thump of Waffles's paws on the wooden floor as the dog padded after her. Kate had fallen asleep in a sea of stuffed animals, seemingly unmoved by the shouting from the other room. And tonight, unlike most nights, Hester wouldn't have to pretend. She wouldn't have to wait for Morgan to sleep before sneaking out of their bedroom to watch over Kate. Hester didn't dare leave the girl to sleep alone, despite the bolts on the windows. Kids needed independence and time to be themselves. Hester both knew that and understood that she had the potential of making Kate into a case study in some future early-childhood development textbook. She also knew that her relationship with Morgan was in serious jeopardy, but she didn't even know how to begin fixing all the problems that stretched out in front of her. Maybe she could start tomorrow.

Tonight, she lay down, jostling Kate enough to wake her. She read a story, more to herself than to the dozing child. Afterward, she stretched out on the knotted rug, Waffles curled up beside her. She used a teddy bear as a pillow because a real pillow would have made the decision permanent and planned, rather than something she decided on a whim. She wrapped herself in a quilt. She'd stay here, on the floor, like she had every night since August. . .

Still, she couldn't sleep.

She rolled over and pulled her phone from where she'd left it in her pocket. Maybe she'd watch something on Netflix to get her brain to stop racing, but when she powered up the phone, a whole stream of texts from Charlie or Daryl or whatever his name was, the one with the estranged girlfriend who'd run away to Maine, downloaded, each message angrier than the next. One called her a celebrity-chasing bitch, another accused her of murder. If only Charlie had been the first to level those same accusations. She forwarded the whole chain to Angela, adding,

In case I wind up dead in the morning. 😊 **(And I'm still angry, BTW.)**

She nearly replied to Charlie, too, before reminding herself not to engage.

Phone aside and done with technology for the night, she'd nearly fallen asleep when she heard a beep. She fully expected detailed apologies from every single person who'd attended the "intervention," and thought this might be the first. Probably Jane. She was the weakest. Or maybe it was Angela, chewing her out for texting with someone dan-gerous.

She glanced at the screen.

Then she sat up and read the message again.

After the third time, she was up and out of bed, getting ready to leave. She planned her note to Morgan.

And she planned her lies.

Annie hadn't even known she'd fallen asleep again after Rory had left the house, but she woke with a start, the hurricane still raging. For a moment, she lay still, her mind washed clean of worry. Then, one by one, the regrets ticked in. She remembered being with Trey, out on the beach, rough granite digging into her back and rain pounding at her skin. She remembered his lips at her ear, the way he panted with every thrust.

Next, she moved on to Lydia and Vaughn, and imagined giving in to her own secrets and the relief that must come with releasing the truth to the world. Had Lydia ended her marriage tonight? Was she lying in bed with Vaughn, curled into him, happier than she'd ever be again?

Most of Annie's regrets had to do with this past year, with another life. She remembered grinding up a Benadryl with two spoons and mixing it with ginger ale in a sippy cup. She remembered piling pillows up to create a moat of safety. Children should be safe. They should be protected. She remembered fleeing, too frightened of herself and what she might do. Too frightened not to act.

She remembered the lighthouse. The tide would be out by now.

It was time to go.

She crawled from the mattress, pulling on a ratty sweater and struggling into her damp jeans. Frankie's room was empty, with children's clothes littering the floor in small, ghostly piles. Downstairs, Annie put on her oilskins. And she ran. Outside, into the thick, tropical air that felt nothing like Maine. Wind blasted her with sheets of water, and the night, right before dawn, was darker than she'd ever known. She ran like she hadn't run in years, not since college, on those hockey fields.

At the shore, the tide had receded enough to bring the stench of sulfur and to expose the spit connecting the shore to the lighthouse. Annie charged across the sand and over the rocks, her feet splashing through tidal pools. The lighthouse rose a hundred feet in the air. The keeper's house was built from thick stone and had tiny windows designed to fend off the elements. Annie yanked at the door. It had swelled with the rain and wouldn't budge. She circled the perimeter, searching for another way in. Rain pelted her face. Her hair whipped into her eyes. She peered into one of the windows. Even in the dark, she could see the child. Cowering. Afraid.

"I'm here!" she shouted.

She shoved her shoulder into the heavy oak door. She kicked it. And she kicked it again. This time it cracked. With a third kick, the door flew open.

Annie ran into the darkness. Here, the air was close, the walls thick enough to mute the loudest of noises.

Something moved. And whimpered. Annie rushed forward, hands flailing.

A child screamed.

"Shh, shh, shh, it's okay."

Annie crouched and touched the child's face. She ran her fingers through thick hair. Ethan's hair.

She pulled him to her.

He rested his head against her shoulder and stuck a thumb in his mouth. She turned slowly in the small space, the darkness impenetrable. She balanced the child on her hip and backed into the storm. When the wind and rain engulfed her, she slung the boy over her shoulder and ran. She could make amends for everything—all of it. She could make things good again. She could be a hero.

Wet sand swirled and eddied around her ankles, sucking her down. She struggled forward, across the sandy spit. And she swore she heard someone behind her. She spun around.

Nothing.

Fifty yards.

Thirty.

Ten.

She plunged forward into silty mud, losing her grip on Ethan. He landed a few feet in front of her, and she crawled to him. A wave crashed against the rocks. Ahead, Annie could see the outline of the path to the house. She swore she saw a flash of blue lights. She almost felt safe, as though good could come from bad, and maybe, just maybe, she'd found a way to redeem herself.

The blow came from behind. At first, she didn't feel it, not till she'd fallen forward, her chin slamming into granite. She tasted a tinny explosion of blood. Pain screamed from her wrists and neck. She pushed forward, crawling on all fours. Someone caught her by the hair, snapping back her head. "Ethan!" she shouted, blood spewing from her mouth. "Run!"

"It was you. All along. You took him!"

She pivoted on her hip. To defend.

On the horizon, gray light had begun to seep through the clouds. Trey loomed over her. She saw a flash of steel.

"Who sent you?" Trey said. "Who put you up to it? How much are they paying you?"

She grasped a rock, turning and swinging blindly.

And she imagined going back in time, a day, a week, a month, a year. She imagined undoing it all, every regret, and facing her own truth. She imagined calling herself Daphne again. "I'm Daphne," she'd say. "Daphne Maguire. Kate's mother. Morgan's sister. Hester's best friend."

She imagined going home.

Trey came at her. Something crashed into her skull. She skidded forward. And the world went black.

TUESDAY, SEPTEMBER 24

CHAPTER 12

Hester felt as though she'd been awake for days. She and Kate joined the end of the line for the ferry to Finisterre Island and, as they waited, all Hester could think was, *Bringing Kate to Maine was a mistake. A massive, I-probably-won't-ever-recover-from-this mistake.* Or, at the very least, that it didn't show her in the best light or exercising the best parental judgment.

Again.

In Hester's defense, she *had* tried leaving Kate behind. She'd left the house by herself, climbed into the truck, and even driven two blocks before turning around. Even then, she'd sat with the engine running for over a half hour before sneaking inside, wrapping Kate in a blanket, packing a tote bag of toys, and putting the sleeping girl in her car seat as they'd headed toward Maine. She knew that all of this put her on the wrong side of lunacy, but knowing that and doing something about it, making the sane, logical decision, were two different things. It also *almost* convinced her that the intervention the night before had been justified.

Almost, but not quite.

Now, the autumn sun shone brightly, and the air hung with unseasonable humidity from the hurricane. The ferry, which should have left at nine a.m., sat in the harbor tied to the dock. Noon had come and gone, the daily schedule disrupted by rough seas, though from what Hester could see, the crew had finally begun to prep the boat to leave.

The storm had ended around dawn, and people seemed to be picking themselves up and assessing damage. Despite driving through the night to get here, despite listening to the local NPR station and banging her head against the headrest to stay awake, Hester hadn't quite realized the destruction that the storm had wrought on the area till she'd seen it. Houses were flooded. The roar of chainsaws filled the air. Even here in downtown Boothbay Harbor, a group of men dismantled an ancient elm tree that had fallen across the street.

"It's a shame," the man in front of her in line said. "Not too many of those trees left."

"We had a few showers and gusts of wind in Boston," Hester said.

"Lucky," the man said. "But you'll barely notice it by tomorrow. People around here are used to digging out from storms. We're all survivors."

Hester glanced at her phone. Again. Not at the texts from Morgan that repeatedly popped in demanding that she let him know where she'd gone, why she'd left in the middle of the night, and where Kate was, but at the texts that had come last night from a number she hadn't recognized. The first one had read:

Finisterre Island. In Maine. I need you.

Followed moments later by a second one:

It's Daphne. I'm sorry. For everything.

Hester's first instinct had been to ignore the messages and to go on with the life she'd built over the past year. Now was not the time for Daphne to return. When Hester overlooked the fight with Morgan or the failed intervention or the lies about work or that Kate hadn't been to school in weeks or her inability to make decisions, she realized that, lately, things had been easy. Not easy, exactly. But manageable. All she had to do to move forward was solve her own craziness. She could do that, even if it might take a while, even if it meant swallowing her pride and asking for help from the same people who'd tried to offer it to her. But she couldn't solve Daphne's crazy, and no matter how much Hester loved Daphne, no matter how much she worried about her, Daphne made everything more difficult. Even now, here in Maine standing in this line, Hester still had an opportunity to turn back, to go home, and to push off the inevitable for a while longer. But Daphne was—she existed—and in that existence, she was Kate's mother and Morgan's sister and Hester's best friend, in that order. So, instead of ignoring the text, Hester had come here. She'd even left a note for Morgan that read *Running errands. See you tonight!*

Another angry message popped up on her phone.

WHERE ARE YOU?!!!

She silenced her phone and dropped it into her pocket. That would teach him.

Ahead, the captain, a solid young woman with a ponytail poking out from under her cap, waved from the bridge toward the dock. Two deckhands opened the gate, and the line started to move. "Hold my hand," Hester said to Kate, who dashed across the gangway and leapt onto the ferry.

"Wait up," she called after the girl, who ignored her and ran toward the bow of the boat. Hester pushed away the anxiety that filled her as Kate left her sight. What was the worst that could happen, anyway, besides Kate falling off the boat and drowning, right?

Wait, that was real, not paranoia.

Hester shoved forward, past the man she'd been speaking to, and waved her ticket at the deckhand. On the ferry, she found Kate standing at the front of the boat, leaning over the railing. "Don't leave me again," Hester said, pulling her back.

"Where we going?" Kate asked.

"To an island," Hester said, as the ferry's engine clicked into gear and the captain backed into the harbor.

Another deckhand came around. "All set?" he asked.

"Is there cell service on the island?" Hester asked.

"In most places," he said.

Damn.

She glanced at her phone again and relented, typing in a response to Morgan.

All okay. Needed to cool off after last night. Not angry anymore. Call in a bit!

That should hold him off. For a while at least. She powered the phone down and almost immediately felt a wave of relief at being disconnected.

She took Sebastian the stuffed rabbit out of the tote bag. "Be careful with him," she said to Kate. "Don't let him fall overboard," which was code for, *Don't go near the rail or stand up or move, because if you do, I'm sure you'll trip and fall overboard and drown*.

Kate danced Sebastian across her lap. "Don't tell Uncle Morgan," she said in a singsong voice.

"We'll call Uncle Morgan when we get to the island," Hester said.

"He come too?" Kate asked.

"Probably not. We'll only be here for the afternoon."

"What about Waffles?"

"Not without Uncle Morgan."

As the ferry picked up speed and headed out of the harbor, the captain read through safety procedures over the loudspeaker. "Once we hit the gulf, expect a rough ride," she added.

Soon, as promised, the temperature dropped, and the surf began to roll. The bow of the boat rocked over huge waves, sending waves of frigid water across them. Hester pulled Kate in close as the girl shrieked with delight. "It's like a roller coaster," Hester said.

"Sebastian's wet!" Kate said.

"So are we," Hester said.

On the drive here, Kate had slept most of the way and then accepted without comment when she woke in a strange town. So far, Hester had managed to keep from her that they might see Daphne today. Now, she swooped honey-colored curls from Kate's eyes and kissed the girl on the cheek.

The boat slammed over another wave. Water drenched them both from head to foot. A deckhand appeared, handing out white paper bags. "You may need these," he said.

Hester had already begun to feel nauseated. "Any tips?" she asked.

"Stay above deck."

"Even in this surf?"

"We've had much worse," he said. "But hang on to the rails if you move around."

"Do you think she could meet the captain?" Hester asked, nodding toward Kate.

The deckhand led them up to the bridge, where the captain scanned the horizon. She was in her mid- to late twenties, pretty and rugged. "It's not too late in the season to see a pilot whale," she said into a microphone. "We'll let you know if any make an appearance."

When she noticed Kate, she introduced herself. "I'm Captain Zoe," she said. "Do you want to try steering the boat?"

Kate turned her face into Hester's waist and hugged Sebastian close.

"I'll steer it myself, then," Zoe said. "No need for help here."

Kate managed to pry her face from Hester's sweater. "I can steer," she said.

"I don't think so."

"I can."

"How about a please in there?" Hester said, and like usual, she couldn't quite believe the words that came out of her mouth. But Captain Zoe didn't know that Kate wasn't hers, or that any of Kate's bad habits could be blamed on someone else.

"Please," Kate said, glumly.

Zoe lifted the girl up and rested her hands over hers as they guided the ferry forward for the next few minutes. The captain showed her the compass and walked her through some of the other instruments on the panel. She pointed toward the horizon where a small mass of land began to emerge from the mist. "See that," she said. "That's Finisterre Island. Where we're headed."

"The storm hit pretty hard out here," Hester said. "I didn't know if we'd be able to leave."

"The ferry's a lifeline to the island," Zoe said. "Especially on days like today. I have cases of supplies below for first aid and the cleanup, but we've survived much worse than last night. From what I hear, a few boats ran aground, some lobster pots are missing, and there was flooding on the coasts, but nothing more. It's all you can hope for in the end."

"Are you from the island?"

"Grew up there, but I have a place on the mainland now. The island can get claustrophobic, especially during the winter. But I'm there twice a day during the summer. Back and forth. And once a day over the winter. There's another ferry that goes out of Bar Harbor up north. It runs twice a day too."

Hester scrolled through her phone till she found a photo of Daphne. "Any chance you've seen this woman?"

Zoe barely glanced at the photo. "Where are you from?" she asked.

Hester nodded toward Kate, who seemed sufficiently distracted with the steering wheel. "I've been watching my friend's daughter," she said. "We're supposed to meet up, but she hasn't answered her phone."

"Phone's probably dead. Power's been out all over

the island, so unless she has a generator, she'll be out of luck. And I doubt that woman has a generator."

"You have seen her?"

Zoe nodded. "I've seen her, but I don't know her. She came to the island at the beginning of the summer. I don't even know her name. But someone'll point you in the right direction. Try Rory. He's the local cop."

Hester took Kate from the captain. "Thanks for the tour," she said.

Out on the deck, Hester gripped the iron railing and tried to calm the rising nausea. Beside her, Kate seemed unfazed by the waves as she pirouetted and then stumbled in a way that nearly had Hester diving to the slick deck to keep the girl from spinning right off the boat and into the choppy gray water. But nothing happened, and Hester managed to keep her cool long enough to hear Kate sing out, "Mommy's here!" at the top of her lungs.

Damn! The kid heard every word she said these days. She heard and processed and made those words into her own truth, and right now that truth was something that would lead to disappointment, and Hester had no one to blame but herself. Hester should have found Daphne on her own! Why hadn't she been able to see that last night, sitting in that truck, trying to leave?

"Kate," Hester said, her voice level. "I don't know if your mother will be here or not. She sent me a note this morning and asked me to come, so here we are."

Kate spun again, and this time Hester grabbed her by the arm to stop her. She let go at once, stunned by her own intensity, by her desire to shake the girl and to tell her to stop celebrating, that none of this was good news. Kate rubbed her arm and seemed to be considering whether to go into tantrum mode. But she hugged Sebastian close. "It's Sebastian's birthday," she said.

Most days, it was Sebastian's birthday. "We'll get cupcakes to celebrate," Hester said, which seemed to cheer Kate up right away.

The ferry rounded a small, uninhabited island. On a larger island that looked as though it had been carved from solid stone, a small town rose, and a set of piers stretched into the gray sea to greet them. Hester took Kate's hand as the shore grew closer. She wanted to hold on to this moment, this time between what was and what would be, and make it last. She wanted to remember it as special and untouched, something that was only theirs. The girl glanced up at her and smiled. "You know I love you, right?" Hester said. "More than anyone."

"More than Sebastian?" Kate asked.

"More than Sebastian."

"More than Waffles?"

"Even more than Waffles."

More than Daphne. And more than Morgan, though Kate seemed to know enough not to ask.

A few people milled about the pier. Hester squinted, scanning for Daphne's telltale red hair and imagined her there, calm and smiling. She'd say something simple like, "Hey," in that tough-girl voice she'd perfected on the streets of South Boston. She'd act as though she'd been gone for the morning and that the past year had never happened. And she'd lift Kate into the air in a way that would make Hester feel Kate melting away.

But as they pulled along the pier, Daphne was nowhere to be seen. Kate skipped forward and threw her arms in the air. "I'm so happy I have to let it out!"

"I'm happy too," Hester said.

I need you.

If Hester had written those same words these last twelve months, would Daphne have been at her door within hours? But now, even though she wanted to stay on this boat and go home, she couldn't. She had to face whatever came next. "Ready?" she said to Kate.

Kate dashed to the stairs.

"Not without me," Hester said, as she followed the girl across the gangway to the pier, beyond which sat a weather-worn hotel and a café bearing an enormous bulletin board. Sodden leaflets—for AA meetings, spaghetti suppers, a gathering of the Over the Hill hikers—covered every inch of the bulletin board, and over all of them hung at least a dozen flyers featuring a photo of a missing child, a blurry image of a boy about Kate's age, and a handwritten phone number to call with leads. During her drive to Maine, Hester had heard on the radio about the Amber Alert for the boy, but seeing his photo on these wet posters made it feel more real. She pulled Kate close without realizing it till the girl squirmed free and ran after the other passengers.

"Watch for cars!" Hester said as the girl passed a parked police Jeep, a deputy perched on its hood, the brim of his hat down.

A few passengers greeted him, but most walked by as if he wasn't there. His skin was brown from the summer sun, and his body toned in a way that told Hester he took care of himself. She caught up with Kate.

"Ain't too many cars around here," he said, from behind half-closed eyes.

"You have one," Hester said.

"One of the few," he said, sitting up and lifting his hat.

"You're the cop, right?" Hester said. "Zoe told me to ask you about my friend. I think she lives here."

"Aren't too many who do. Who's your friend?"

Hester showed him the photo of Daphne.

"That's Annie," he said.

Annie.

Hester kept her expression still. Daphne's middle name was Ann. "Have you seen her?"

"I see her practically every day. This place isn't that big." The deputy tipped his hat forward and closed his eyes again. "But we were all up late last night. A kid went missing. I bet you heard about it on the news. I don't think anyone in town got more than a couple of hours of sleep, so if I was her and I had a choice, I'd be in bed." He rubbed his eyes and yawned. "I should be so lucky."

"I take it that you found the missing boy?" Hester asked.

"More like he found us. He showed up at dawn. God knows what he got into or where he'd gone, but he seems mostly unhurt except for a few cuts and bruises. He keeps talking about Thomas the Tank Engine and not much else. I don't know if we'll ever know what happened, but I said it from the start: Kids wander off all the time on this island, and it's not like they can go very far. What do you want with Annie anyway?"

Hester took a split second too long to answer. The

deputy sat up, alert, and leapt off the Jeep, rising to his full height. He was tall enough so that Hester had to crane her neck even to read his name tag, RORY DUN-BAR. He reminded her of the police officers she'd grown up with, the local boys who never left, the ones who still drank beer in the town forest as though they were in high school but who had shown up when she'd needed them. Boys who lived small and dreamed big and found power in carrying a gun. Boys who did their jobs.

"Visiting," Hester said. "She told me she'd moved out here."

"Annie doesn't strike me as someone who'd have visitors. Or friends. Don't bullshit me, okay? I had just about the worst night of my life last night."

Instinctively, Hester put a protective hand around Kate. "We went to college together," she said.

"Annie went to college?"

"Wellesley," Hester said.

Rory seemed to take that in for a moment. "Not the story I'd have guessed, but what do I know? She lives in an old Victorian over on Little Finisterre," he added, giving Hester directions. "It's sort of in the middle of nowhere, so if you can't find it, keep looking. And you might also stop by the bakery in town and talk to Lydia Pelletier. They're best friends, at least according to Annie."

Rory stopped talking as a pickup truck drove over the hill and pulled up to the pier. A group of men lifted a gurney from the back with what looked like a body bag on it and wheeled it onto the ferry.

"Who died?" Hester asked, and almost immediately regretted how callous she sounded. It could have been

easy to miss, too, but Rory's tanned face fell for an instant as he stared at the empty space where the body
had been.

"Sorry," Hester said. "I know this is a small place."

Rory took a moment to answer. "A drug addict," he
said, without looking at Hester. "He OD'd last night.
Unattended death. Off to the morgue. Good riddance,
right?" He glanced at his watch. "And unless you're
planning on staying the night, be back here at three
forty-five sharp. The ferry leaves at four on the dot,
and it doesn't wait for anyone."

Hester gave a half-hearted salute. "Yes, sir," she
said, watching as he got into the Jeep and drove away.
"Ready?" she said to Kate, offering a hand. But Kate ignored the hand and skipped ahead, and Hester had to remind herself that they were in the middle of nowhere, in
a place without cars. Kate would be fine.

"Who's Annie?" Kate asked, running back toward her.

"You know, I'm not sure," Hester said, and for once
she felt as though she wasn't lying. Annie could be
anyone.

The path led down a hill lined with weather-worn
summer cottages to a row of businesses typical of a
summer colony—a fudge shop, an ice-cream parlor, a
handful of craft stores, restaurants, and hotels. At the
end of a row, Hester found the inn, a small Cape-style
house set back among beech trees and hemmed in by a
picket fence. The storm had flattened most of the flowers in the perennial garden. The smells of baking that
wafted across the garden made Hester forget her queasy
stomach. Inside Doughnuts and Pie Bakery, there was
barely enough room for two sets of café tables and customers. Hester made her way to the counter, where a

woman with dark hair worked behind a glass case piled high with baked goods. "What do you want?" Hester asked Kate, who pursed her lips together and shook her head.

"I thought it was Sebastian's birthday," she said. "Doesn't he want a whoopie pie?"

"Yuck."

"Suit yourself. I'll have yours. How about a blueberry muffin?"

"No way!" Kate said.

"Four years old?" asked the woman behind the counter.

"Is it that obvious?" Hester asked.

"I have one of my own," the woman said, pushing one of her dark braids over her shoulder. "He's in the kitchen. He's into insects and peeing on trees these days. Luckily there's plenty of both around here. And he only eats bologna. Won't even do mac and cheese."

"She'll eat hot dogs."

"I'm right here!" Kate said.

"I know you are," Hester said, ruffling the girl's hair. "Can I get a hot dog around here?"

"Up the road by the water. Try The Dock."

It still surprised Hester how easy it was to bond with other parents, how much commonality she found in their experiences and challenges. She spent so much time feeling alone, but usually as soon as she opened her mouth, she learned that nothing Kate did was even original. "I'll take two doughnuts, a blueberry turnover, and a pumpkin whoopie pie. You can't come to Maine and not have a whoopie pie."

"You gonna share any of that?" the woman asked as she put the baked goods in a white paper bag.

"We'll see," Hester said, taking out her phone. "Are you Lydia? The deputy told me you knew my sister-in-law."

"Rory?"

"Yeah, I think that was his name. Tall guy."

"That's Rory. How's he doing?"

"Fine, I guess. He said he was up late, but then so was I."

"It was a rough night, in a lot of ways," Lydia said, glancing at Daphne's photo on the phone. "What do you want with Annie?"

"Have you seen her today?"

"Barely anyone's been around today. I only opened to take my mind off things."

"You mean the missing boy?" Hester asked. "Rory told me that he came home this morning."

"That was the good news."

"Was there bad news?"

"You mind chatting in the back?" Lydia asked.

Hester followed Lydia around a counter to a tiny kitchen with racks to hold trays, a wall-mounted oven, a Hobart mixer, and a stainless-steel refrigerator. A boy with dark curly hair sat on a stool playing on an iPad. "This is Oliver," Lydia said, kissing the boy's cheek and then dumping a block of butter into the Hobart. "Coffee?"

"Why not?" Hester said.

"Help yourself."

Hester found a paper cup and filled it, then added cream and seven sugars. In the kitchen, Kate eyed Oliver warily, as if she'd forgotten how to play with other children. "What's on the iPad?" Hester asked.

"*Angry Birds*," Oliver said.

"Could you show Kate how to play?"

The boy scowled but agreed, and soon the two of them were leaning in over the screen, laughing, while Lydia stood at the Hobart, her forehead resting on the machine as she watched the blade spin.

"What was the bad news last night?" Hester asked.

"A friend died," Lydia said, as she scooped powdered sugar from a white plastic bin and added it to the creamed butter. "From an overdose, I guess. At least that's what they're saying." She stopped midscoop, as if hearing her own words for the first time. "He was Rory's brother, Pete."

"But Rory's at work."

"If I know Rory, he'll stay busy. Keep his mind off things." Lydia paused.

Hester didn't know what to say and mumbled something about being sorry, but Lydia rescued her from the awkwardness. "Could I see that photo again?" she asked, taking the phone from Hester. "I barely recognize Annie here," she said a moment later. "She's so . . . happy. Healthy too." She handed the phone back. "She never mentioned you. She didn't say much about a family at all. Just a . . ." Lydia glanced at Kate and Oliver and stopped herself. "Something about a child that went missing."

"I haven't seen her for a year. Family stuff. I'm sure you understand."

"Not really. Less than two hundred people live on this island year-round, and most of them I've known my whole life. When we fight, we fight, and everyone knows it, and everyone takes a side. Strangers stick out, till we let them in."

"Does Annie stick out?"

"Anyone from off island does."

Lydia pulled a sheet of whoopie pies from the oven, each a perfect dome of chocolate cake. "Look, one broke," she said, testing a piece. "Damn, that's good," she said.

Oliver put the iPad aside and snatched up a piece too. Kate edged to the counter and touched a piece with her index finger.

"It's hot," Hester said.

Kate gobbled it up anyway. "Damn, that's good," she said, taking the rest of it and splitting it with Oliver.

"Oops," Lydia said.

"She knows all the swear words," Hester said. "Courtesy of me. She can teach them to Oliver, if you like. And now she likes whoopie pies!"

"It's a win!" Lydia said as she slid the tray onto a rack to cool and lifted a second from the oven.

"Rory told me you're friends with Annie," Hester said.

"Rory said that? I mean, I owe her, I guess, especially after last night. I almost drowned during the search. She was brave, but *friends* might be a stretch."

"That's not a ringing endorsement."

"Patented Down East honesty." Lydia turned the Hobart off and added a jar of marshmallow Fluff to the icing. "I'm glad you're here, because when I look at Annie, I can't really imagine anyone liking her. It's good to know someone cares about her."

"Do you like her?" Hester asked.

"Do you?"

"Of course I do," Hester said quickly. She didn't dare give herself the time to think through the answer.

CHAPTER 13

After leaving the bag of toys—and Sebastian—with Lydia for safekeeping, Hester and Kate made a pit stop at The Dock, where Hester ordered fried clams for herself and a hot dog for Kate, and carried them to a picnic bench. Kate gobbled hers up while Hester dunked the fat, battered clams into tartar sauce. Afterward, they headed out of town, over a bridge to Little Finisterre. Despite the damage from the storm, the island was beautiful, all granite crags and rugged coastlines and trees already turning for the season. Kate dashed along, and Hester wished she'd brought Waffles with them. When they got to the leeward side, the line of trees opened to a protected harbor with a lighthouse sitting at the end of a jetty. Hester barely caught the view, prepping herself the whole way for meeting whoever "Annie" might be and reflecting on Lydia's question. Did she like Daphne? She knew that she loved Daphne, but she liked her too, didn't she? And she always had, ever since college, ever since they'd met during that self-defense course. They'd roomed together after their first year, where Daphne would wake in the middle of the night, unbridled energy flowing through her, and they'd run into the dark around the shores of Lake Waban, hand in hand, the whole world theirs and theirs alone. Hester remembered cold spring air, ferns unfurling, trees budding, a moon so full it seemed like daylight. The ground, only recently thawed, had nipped at her bare feet, but she couldn't imagine turning back. She couldn't imagine being anywhere else in the whole world.

"If we run fast enough," Daphne had said. "We can free ourselves. We can leap into the wind and take flight."

And for a moment, Hester got caught up in Daphne's magic.

Later, after Kate had come along, there'd been new magic. Hester remembered lolling on the sofa in that first-floor apartment as toddler Kate made animal noises and Daphne crawled on the floor and used the *moo* to transform into a cow. Kate clapped her hands together in delight. Any sound, *quack, bark, meow,* and Daphne was up for the challenge.

Now, lost in thought, she managed to pass by the overgrown path to Daphne's house twice before she finally found it. It disappeared into the trees, the autumn light barely penetrating the thick tree cover.

This was it. Her choice.

She could either walk into these trees and face Daphne and whatever came with her, or turn back, find a beach, absorb the sun, and leave. She could create a new path and marry Morgan. He'd say yes, of course. He'd asked plenty of times, and she'd deferred, telling him she liked things the way they were, even if she couldn't imagine a life without him. He'd

even understand her true motivations—to protect Kate—
motivations they'd never talk through. She could establish her right to shelter Kate from the world.

Or—better choice—she could establish her right to
help Kate face life, and everything that came with it.
Warts and all.

"You ready?" Hester asked.

Kate smiled in a way that started with her mouth
and spread through her entire body, till she couldn't
help but dance. It was a smile Hester lived for. And
right now, this time, it wasn't for her.

"Let's find Mommy," Hester said.

They stepped into the shadows. Under the thicket of
evergreens, the temperature dropped by at least ten degrees and sent a chill down Hester's back. They turned
a corner, and the Victorian rose up in front of them,
though when Hester had heard that Daphne lived in
"an old Victorian," she'd imagined towers and turrets
and painted trim, not a near ruin. This house must have
been a majestic summer escape once, with panoramic
views of the Atlantic, before nature and decay began to
take over. A giant beech tree grew on each side of the
structure, and rhododendrons, long unpruned, threatened to swallow it whole.

"Scary," Kate said.

Hester couldn't have agreed more. This wasn't a
place where anyone should live. "We'll be here for
only a few minutes."

She pushed her way through the rhododendrons and
edged around the perimeter of the wraparound porch.
She imagined a swing and rocking chairs, long skirts
and croquet mallets. This was a house from another
era, when whole families took the train from Boston or

New York to spend the summer lounging (and sweating) by the sea. She pictured dinners with bright red lobsters, corn, and blueberry pie; long card games; and reading by lamplight.

She pressed her face to the grungy glass of one of the few remaining windows. A large, sticky-looking table bore remnants of a partly eaten meal. She tapped on the glass. When no one answered, she retraced her steps to the front door, where she rapped on the heavy oak. The door swung open on its own to a thick stench of rot, mildew, garbage, and the unmistakable odor of unwashed bodies, a foulness that seemed as desperate to escape the house as Hester was to escape it. Beneath it all, she smelled something skunky and assuredly illicit. "Daphne?" she shouted. "It's me. Hester. I got your text."

When no one answered, she shouted Daphne's name again. "Can you stand the smell?"

Kate shrugged and said, "Sure."

Inside, children's toys littered the floor in the front room. So did trash. "Stay very close to me," she said to Kate. They edged along the wall like rodents. In the kitchen, a ceramic bowl covered in flies sat in the middle of a table. The room reeked of rotten tuna fish and spoiled mayonnaise. Hester opened the back door and tossed the bowl into the trees.

They retraced their steps to the foyer and took a mahogany staircase to the second floor. A long hallway with many doors led down the length of the house. This was a house designed to pack in as many guests as possible. Hester opened each door and found varying degrees of discord from room to room. Behind the fourth door, she found a mattress and clothing belonging to a woman and a child. The very last door led to a tiny room with a single window at the far end. Someone had dragged together a wall of bureaus, and when Hester pushed her way through, she found a single mattress lined with yellowing sheets and an old sweater she recognized as belonging to Daphne. She touched the pilled knitting. Daphne, her friend, her sister, lived here, in this house, in this room, on this mattress, wearing this sweater.

Daphne's life had come to this.

"Is Mommy here?" Kate asked.

"I bet she'll show up."

"When?"

"Soon, I hope."

Hester glanced at her phone. It was almost two o'clock. She could stand the smell in the house for another ninety minutes, till they needed to leave to catch the ferry. Morgan had left three more texts and a voice mail since she'd last checked. He probably hadn't panicked yet and wouldn't till later tonight when he got home from work and neither Hester nor Kate was there. Hester could call him from the road, tell him that she'd gone for a ride and kept on driving. That would work if Daphne didn't appear but not if Hester came home with Daphne sitting in the passenger's seat. Then she'd have to tell him the truth.

Kate jumped on the mattress, and Hester distracted herself by searching the bureaus. The first was empty. In the second, she found a few pieces of clothing, stretched and discolored from hand washing; an ancient, half-eaten granola bar; and a menu from Lydia's bakery. In another drawer, she found a black knapsack and more clothing, enough to tell her that Daphne hadn't left.

A noise echoed down the hallway. Hester put a finger to her lips and left the knapsack leaning against a wall. "Stay here," she whispered to Kate.

Kate nodded, but as soon as Hester had crept into the hallway, the girl said, "Where are you going?" in anything but an inside voice.

"Back in one minute," Hester whispered. "Count to sixty, okay, so that I can hear you and know where you are."

They'd worked on counting all month instead of going to school, and the girl's tiny voice rang out as Hester edged along the wall. "One, two, three . . ."

The door to one of the bedrooms was ajar, light filtering into the hallway.

"Four, five, six . . ."

Hester focused in on hearing Kate's voice. A man knelt at a suitcase tossing clothes aside and ripping at the lining with a box cutter. He had gray shoulder-length hair and managed to overpower the stench of the house with his own body odor. When he heard Hester, he spun, slashing at the air with the box cutter. Hester took a step back, hands up. She calculated the distance from where she was to Kate. She listened to the girl's voice, "Twenty-five, twenty-six, twenty-seven . . ."

She'd seen a back staircase. An escape.

"Checking the place out," she said, her voice as cool as she could make it. "Heard there might be a free room."

It seemed to take a moment for the man to process what she'd said, but he eventually glared at her and took a step forward. She mirrored his movements, stepping into the hallway.

"It's cool," he said.

"If it's cool, then put that thing away?"

The man held the box cutter horizontally and ran his finger along it as though seeing it for the first time. He retracted the blade and slid the knife into his pocket. "Where'd you fly in from?" he asked. "You're like a little fairy."

Hester stared him down.

"Yeah, it's cool. Cold, really. Frigid. Yeah, frigid, man. Are you frigid, tiny lady?"

Hester sighed and waved a fly away from her face. "Do you live here?"

"I don't know."

"You have to live somewhere. How long have you been here?"

"A week, maybe? A day?"

"I heard a boy went missing last night."

"Ethan! My little dude!"

"And he's okay now?"

"Dude. Buddy!"

Hester took out her phone and shoved the photo of Daphne into the man's face. "Have you seen her?"

The man grinned again. "Red!" he shouted. "Tuna Helper!"

"Annie, right?" Hester said. "You know her?"

"Do you have anything to eat?"

Hester jabbed a finger at the photo. "When did you see her last?"

He touched the phone gently, caressing the screen with his fingertips. "For real," he said. "How much does this thing cost?"

"I don't really know. A hundred bucks maybe?"

"She doesn't know!" he said, his eyes angry. "Why would you know? You probably spent a hundred bucks on lunch today. I could use a hundred bucks."

"Let's start with twenty. Tell me what you know about her and I'll give you twenty bucks."

He shook his head and zipped his lips closed.

Down the hallway, Kate hit sixty. "Aunt Hester," she shouted. "It's been one minute."

"One more," Hester shouted back. "Count again so that I can hear you."

"One, two, three . . ."

"Spill," she said to the man. "Or you won't get a dime."

His hand went to the pocket holding the box cutter, and his eyes lost the glazed-over look. He stopped smiling. "Last night, or maybe the night before. Who knows? She was here. Your friend." He took his hand from his pocket, and Hester almost started to run, but it was empty. He held an imaginary phone to his ear. "Frankie says that one there, the one on your phone, Red, that she told the cops that Frankie dealt drugs and abandoned her kid. I bet Red took Ethan. Wanted the attention. She likes that cop, the one with the acne. Wanted to fuck him, from what I hear. And there aren't any drugs here anyway. Only bitches. One real bitch."

"Ethan showed up this morning, right?" she said. "That's what I hear."

"Little pisser," the man said, though he smiled. "I asked him what happened, but he couldn't tell me. This island is one big little place. Lots of spots to get lost and forgotten. Killed even. Half the kids on this island spend their school days out pulling traps," The man kicked at something invisible and nearly fell backward, the smile gone. "The kid's a retard, is my guess. Not that Frankie'll do anything about it."

"Where are Ethan and Frankie?"

"Down by the lighthouse. On the beach." The man pointed in one direction, and then the other. He put a hand to his face and laughed, showing the gaps where his teeth had fallen out. "More lighthouses in Maine than seagulls," he added. "Good luck finding it." A shadow fell across the man's face. "I need some stuff," he said. "Or I'll have the runs. Like, runny runs."

"Is that what you were looking for in the suitcase?"

"Or money," he said, holding out a hand.

"Name."

"Seth," he said.

Hester tossed a twenty into the suitcase. "There. You found some."

Kate's voice rang out from down the hallway. "Fifty-nine, sixty!"

"Be there in a sec," Hester shouted over her shoulder.

"How many?" Kate asked.

"Exactly one."

Fresh air had never smelled this clean. As soon as Hester tripped out of the house and onto the wraparound porch, she took Kate's hand and ran, shoving rhododendron branches from her face and stumbling through the dark forest till she scrambled out of the trees and into the light. She bent over and took deep breaths, feeling the methane that house exuded sweep from her lungs. She never should have brought Kate in there, or to this island. Everyone who lived in that house probably spent most of their day high. What had Daphne gotten herself into? How could she have fallen this far?

Daphne had always been the tough one, the one who took women's studies and wrote poems about her clit that she read during poetry slams at the The Hoop. One of the things that brought them together was their complete disinterest in the past. For Hester, it had felt as though they'd both appeared, fully formed, with ideas and interests and passions, with none of the baggage that she normally associated with new friends. It was as if Daphne cared enough not to ask about Hester's parents or where she grew up or went to school, which freed Hester from tracking her story. Eventually, little truths slipped in: Daphne's father, a cop, had been shot and killed when she was eleven; Hester had worked at the A&P in her small town, where the produce manager had copped a feel while she labeled bananas. When those truths appeared, they caught them and nurtured them and tucked them away for later, all while treating them like no big deal.

After graduation, Hester and Daphne moved into a dumpy apartment in Allston. Daphne drifted from one job to the next, never quite satisfied with where life was taking her, while Hester enrolled in a master's program in library science and took an internship at a suburban data-processing center that was more than two hours away using public transportation and where she spent her days wading through stacks of reports from a dot-matrix printer.

Daphne showed up at the office one day. She smelled of smoke and bus fumes and said something about going to lunch. "Not for another hour," Hester whispered. "Wait for me in the lobby."

Daphne wore a black leather jacket and skin-tight jeans. She snapped on a pair of headphones and gave Hester the thumbs-up, then backed away. Twenty minutes later, the receptionist scurried toward Hester's desk. "Is that your friend?" she asked. "The one with the red hair? She's TP-ing the bathroom."

Hester ran to where Daphne sang "Girls Just Want to Have Fun" while tossing a roll of toilet paper across the stalls. Hester pulled the streams of paper down in armfuls, flushing it and destroying the evidence. "You want this!" Daphne said, lifting the headphones from her ears.

"Get out," Hester said. "Now. And don't come home tonight either. I don't even want to look at you."

Daphne's face froze in a smile. She left, but by then the damage had been done. Even though Hester cleaned the bathroom, Security had been called and waited in the lobby to escort her out of the building. When she trudged to the bus shelter for the commute home, she found Daphne waiting. It was a fall day, crisp, with a promise of winter. The leaves in the office park had begun to turn. It was the kind of day that demanded hot cider and hayrides, though at that time in her life, Hester would have been lucky enough to have afforded an apple.

"You got me fired," she said.

"Come on!" Daphne said. "I saved you. You hated that place. What did that job even have to do with being a librarian anyway? You're so much better than data printouts."

"Who's better than data printouts?" Hester shouted.

"You," Daphne said. "You're better than this bus and a two-hour commute and the $8.50 an hour they were paying you. You're better than me."

"I'm not."

"You are."

Daphne took Hester's hand. And even though Hester hadn't wanted to admit it then—she almost didn't want to admit it now—she *had* hated that job and the commute, and she'd settled for it only because she wanted to feel grounded and permanent. She wanted to live a life where nothing ever changed, one where she could feel normal. Daphne made that impossible. She refused to settle, and she refused to give in.

A week later, Hester found another internship, this one at Harvard, and the one thing that almost kept her from accepting it was that by doing so, she had to admit Daphne had been right all along.

There was an hour and forty-five minutes before the ferry left—just over ninety minutes to figure out where Daphne was hiding. But Seth was right, this was a big small place with lots of nooks and crannies.

"Why wasn't Mommy at the house?" Kate asked.

"I'm not sure," Hester said.

"Does she want to see us?"

The questions broke Hester's heart. "I hope so," she said. "We'll keep looking."

Why the hell was Daphne hiding from her after texting so urgently for help? Why would she have such a sudden change of heart?

They rounded a corner and the water opened out in front of them. Small waves lapped at the shore of a tiny harbor, with the lighthouse perched at the end of a jetty. A seagull cried as it swept across the sky, dropping a clam to the stones below and diving in to gobble up the meat that had broken free. Debris from the storm littered the rocky beach—buoys, driftwood, seaweed, stranded fish, now expired. Hester scanned the horizon for a woman and a small boy but didn't see anyone. She stepped over the beach and onto the shore, where the tide had receded, leaving shallow pools filled with shellfish. Hester had grown up in a beach town, and the smells and sounds of the sea pulled her to those lonely times. Now she watched as Kate dashed from one tidal pool to the next. Kate had never been to the beach. Not once in her short little life. Hester joined Kate at the edge of a tidal pool, crouching beside her and lifting a spiky anemone from the water, the sun reflecting from its rainbow-hued shell. Kate touched the spikes and quickly withdrew her fingers.

"The spikes keep them safe," Hester said, letting the shellfish drift into the water.

Kate ran ahead as they crossed an outcropping of granite. Hester scanned the horizon again, but they seemed to be the only ones out here. A gentle wave swept up the sand and lapped at Kate's sneakers. "Please don't die," Hester mumbled to herself, the same mantra she'd repeated since the day Kate came to live with her. Even before that. Since the day she'd met her as a newborn.

Kate kicked off her sneakers and waded into the surf. No fear.

No fear!

It was a good thing.

Kate's hand shot into the water. She pulled out a horseshoe crab by its spiny tail, its legs clawing at the air. Hester nearly said to be careful, to watch her fingers, but she reminded herself that there was nothing to be afraid of, no risk. Hester had spent a childhood lifting hundreds of horseshoe crabs from the sea, a childhood wandering along the water on her own, and she was still here, with all her fingers and toes. She kicked her shoes off too and waded into the frigid water. "He's probably scared," she said.

Kate released the horseshoe crab. It floated down, swaying back and forth, till it hit the seafloor and scurried off to join the others. Together Hester and Kate examined stones and shells and whatever else they could find, till finally Hester said, "I can barely feel my toes," and turned toward shore.

The sun shone beyond the lighthouse, and for a moment Hester swore she saw a person silhouetted against the light. She nearly called Daphne's name, but resisted. It wouldn't do any good to give Kate false hope. Soon it would be time to go. Time to get to the ferry. Hester had done her best. Really, she had. She'd come to find Daphne, but maybe Daphne didn't want to be found anymore.

As Hester took Kate's hand, a black lab with a red collar ran from behind a boulder. It was wet and covered in sand and waited till it stood right next to Hester to shake seawater from its coat.

"Doggie!" Kate shouted.

Hester let the dog lick her hand. "Where did you come from?" she said. "You lost, pup?"

Morgan had a habit of collecting strays—dogs, cats, rabbits. This dog looked healthy and well loved, but maybe with the storm she'd lost her owner. Maybe Hester would be the one to bring home a rescue, and they'd have something to talk about tonight besides her disappearance. Besides Daphne.

"Everyone's wondering who the woman asking questions might be."

At the sound of a deep voice, Hester spun around. A man stood behind her, his hip leaning into a boulder, a half-dozen lobster buoys lashed together with twine and balanced on his shoulder. "Sorry to scare you," he said. "We're cleaning up after the storm."

"Who's been wondering about me?" Hester asked.

"Oh, it's a small place. When you show up asking about people, it gets around." The man wiped his hands on his jeans and extended a hand. "Vaughn Roberts," he said.

He wore knee-high rubber boots and a gray t-shirt. Sweat from the warm day poured down his handsome face. Kate pressed herself into Hester's leg, shy at seeing the stranger. He whistled, and the dog ran to his side and sat. "This is Mindy," he said. "Best swimmer in Maine." He gave her a treat. "But she doesn't do anything for free."

Kate moved toward the dog, who shook again, and this time Kate squealed and petted her nose.

"She okay with dogs?" Vaughn asked.

"Her uncle's a vet," Hester said. "Our house is full of all creatures, great and small."

"That's a good way to be. You're looking for Annie, right? We went fishing yesterday. Had a blast."

Of the people Hester had met so far, Vaughn was the first to have anything nice to say about "Annie." "Have you seen her today?"

"Not since last night," Vaughn said. "She helped me out of a jam."

"She sent me a text. I drove all the way from Boston to find her."

"Well, there's nowhere to go unless she slipped out on the ferry," Vaughn said, clucking his tongue. The dog returned to his side. "You staying the night?" he asked.

"I hope not."

"We all run on ferry time out here. You'll need to get to the pier soon."

"We're heading out to the lighthouse. It'll only be a minute."

"Careful out there too. The tide's about to turn, and when it does the land disappears. You could be stuck there for hours. You definitely won't make the ferry then!"

"Thanks for the tip," Hester said. "If you see Annie, tell her Hester is looking for her."

"Will do," Vaughn said.

Hester watched him till he reached shore and turned down the path toward town. She could feel the time till the ferry's departure ticking away, but she had to keep trying. "Let's check out the lighthouse," she said to Kate.

Their feet slid through thick, damp sand as they crossed the jetty, a strip that couldn't have been more than ten feet wide. The lighthouse sat on a disk of solid stone that beach roses had colonized. A few seagulls strutted across the ground, but besides that, the island was desolate. "No one here," Kate said, sounding sad.

"Let's keep looking," Hester said.

They walked around the perimeter of the lighthouse rock. The remnants of a teenage gathering—cigarette butts and beer cans—had managed to survive the storm. Someone had written "Anson sucks balls" with spray paint. Hester's eyes swept the lighthouse keeper's house and she noticed that the front door was ajar. She nudged the door, and it squeaked open on rusty hinges. "Anyone here?" Hester's words caught in her throat as they echoed back to her.

"We should probably leave," she said to Kate.

They should *definitely* leave.

But she edged over the threshold while Kate clung to her leg. The little light that filtered through the small windows revealed a cold, hard room with stone walls and a dirt floor. Hester imagined a narrow cot and a gas light, and the lonely suppers of salt cod and potatoes. Otherwise, the room was empty.

"I guess we're out of luck," she said to Kate, and for the first time since she'd arrived a real seed of worry planted itself in the back of her mind. Where *was* Daphne? She tapped out a text to the number Daphne had used the night before.

We came. We'll be on the 4 pm ferry unless I hear from you.

She hit Send and added a second text.

Kate wants to see you.

"Come on, kiddo," she said, walking into the sun. "If we get back to town with time to spare, we'll grab an ice-cream cone. Okay?"

Even ice cream didn't cheer up Kate, who kicked at stones and dragged her feet as they headed over the jetty. Finally, the girl fell onto the sand and refused to move. Hester gave into it and sat beside her. "I shouldn't have brought you with me today," she said. "It was stupid."

Kate balled up a fistful of sand and tossed it into the water. "Stupid," she said.

"So now, here's the deal. We'll have ice cream, get on the ferry, go home, and I'll tell your uncle that I made a big mistake. And guess who'll be in big trouble? It's one of the two of us, and it's not you."

A tiny grin started to form at the corners of Kate's mouth.

"Who's in trouble?" Hester asked.

"You are."

"You got it. I'm in massive trouble. Probably the worst trouble I've ever been in, and I deserve it. Honestly, I do. I mean, I have totally f-ed up. Do you know what f-ed up means?"

"Fucked up," Kate said.

"Yep. And I'll be in even more trouble if we stay out here for the night. So, why don't we get going. Tomorrow, Uncle Morgan will take you to school, and I'll go to work, and maybe we'll be able to take a step forward finally." *Maybe*, Hester thought, *I'll stop acting like a lunatic*. "Do we have a deal?"

"I guess so."

"Come on."

As they stood, Kate walked toward the water, then pointed.

Hester squinted into the sun. "What is it?"

At first, she thought Kate was pointing at a pile of discarded clothing that had washed up on the beach. A wave swept the clothing toward them. It rippled and caught, and a hand fell to the sand. Then she saw a head of hair and a rain jacket.

And the blue hilt of a knife.

"Fuck," Hester mumbled under her breath.

"Fuck," Kate said.

Hester put a hand to the girl's curly head of hair and

led her away. Then she dialed Morgan's number. He picked up after three rings. She imagined him in his exam room, prodding a furry abdomen, coaxing symptoms from a patient that couldn't speak. Morgan was gentle and kind. He deserved someone better than Hester. Someone who didn't lie to him.

"You're going to kill me," she said.

"Maybe," he said.

"I'm in Maine."

"Right now?"

"On an island. Looking for your sister. She sent me a text last night, and I left without telling you."

Hester could hear the need for control in Morgan's sharp inhale. He whispered that he'd be right back, and she imagined him running a hand through his red hair and resting his back against the wall. Then he finally exhaled. "Okay," he said.

"And I brought Kate with me."

"Remember when you said I was going to kill you? You're getting closer to homicide."

"Not as close as I am," Hester said, squeezing Kate's hand. "I can't find Daphne. But I did find a dead body."

CHAPTER 14

Rory sucked on his cigarette one last time and ground it out with his heel. He stood at Lydia's front gate. Lydia Pelletier was the last person in the world he wanted to see, but Barb was being kind. She was trying to keep him busy and trying to keep him from thinking about Pete. So he followed the flagstone path to the bakery. Inside there were no customers, but he could hear Lydia at work in the back. He took his hat off and listened for the bells as he let himself in through the screen door. She popped her head around the corner, and when she saw him she nodded and filled a cup with iced coffee. She seemed to know enough not to smile yet. It was too soon for that. "You're the only person I know who drinks iced coffee black," she said, rubbing her neck as she suppressed a yawn.

She looked as tired as Rory felt. And he was tired enough to give in to their old repartee. "Watching my figure," he said.

It fit like a glove.

Lydia took a tentative step toward him and put a hand to his shoulder, halfway to a hug. They stood like that for a moment, till Lydia broke the silence. "That woman came by. The short one with the girl. She told me you were on duty."

"The state cops are still here," Rory said, "and Andy asked me to take his shift. His house got hit pretty bad by the storm."

"Rory . . ."

"It's fine." He cut her off.

Work kept him at the center of things. And it helped him forget. He didn't want to think about Pete. He didn't want to think about any of it. He drifted toward the door. The bakery was tiny and cramped on the happiest of days, and today it felt miserable. "Is your husband here?" he asked.

Finding Trey. That was the only reason he was here. He had to play the part. He yanked at the screen door and stepped outside, where he tossed back the coffee, letting the bitter liquid burn like acid.

"I haven't seen him," Lydia said. "Not since last night."

"Tell him the detective is looking for him at the community center. She wants to leave the island and can't go till he signs off."

"Talk to me, Rory," Lydia said.

"What was that all about last night?" Rory said, anger erupting in his voice. "At the ravine. What were you thinking?"

He had meant to come here and make Lydia feel small, but he'd already betrayed his feelings. He'd given her the power all over again. "You and Vaughn . . . why?"

"Quiet," Lydia said, glancing toward the road, her eyes flashing with anger. "Trey could be anywhere. So could Oliver. And by the way, mind your own god-damn business."

Rory kicked at a drift of daisies, uprooting a few and sending them flying. Lydia winced as though he'd hit her, and suddenly Rory was the one feeling small. He didn't do those types of things, not to people he cared about, at least. Behind him, he heard footsteps followed by the opening and closing of the garden gate. But he couldn't take his eyes off Lydia's face.

"Things okay here?"

It was Vaughn, standing there in the gate, a bundle of buoys balanced on his shoulder. Like a model on the cover of a romance novel. "I was just out by the lighthouse," he said. "I saw the woman looking for Annie. She's asking a lot of questions."

"Who cares?" Rory said. "This whole island knows about you two anyway."

"Go away," Lydia said quietly. She shouted over the perennials to Vaughn. "You too. Just leave me alone."

She stormed into the bakery. From outside, Rory heard the slamming of pans and dishes into the sink.

Vaughn still hovered at the gate, one foot on the path, the other in the garden. Rory moved forward, and Vaughn backed away. "Hey, come on, man," Vaughn said.

But Rory charged. Vaughn's feet caught on the flagstones as he tried to retreat, and the buoys fell around him. Rory snatched at his sleeve, tearing the fabric on his t-shirt, and Vaughn spun, fists up. Rory imagined one well-placed jab. The satisfying crunch of bones and teeth. The end of Vaughn's pretty, smug face. "I am going to kill you," Rory said, lunging forward.

"Dunbar!"

The voice barely registered.

"Stand down."

And then there were hands on his collar, a knee in his back, and dirt up his nose.

"Are you okay, sir?"

It was Barb, with her practical clothes and her practical hair. Rory tried to throw her off, and she dug her knee in further.

"It's fine," Rory heard Vaughn say, which only made everything worse. "It's nothing. A little misunderstanding, right, Rory?"

Of course it was. They'd known each other for years. They used to be friends.

"Head off, then," Barb said.

Rory heard Vaughn shuffle down the dirt path, and a moment later Barb released the pressure on his back and sat on the ground beside him. "That's not what I meant when I told you to find your spine," she said. "That's the kind of thing that'll keep you exactly where you are, or worse."

"It's not a big deal," Rory said.

"You had your hand on your gun. One more move and I'd be writing up a report right now."

Rory rested his forehead on his fists and stared into the dirt. His heart pounded. He remembered charging at Vaughn, and he remembered wanting to hurt him, to maim him, but he hadn't reached for his gun, had he? He wouldn't have done something like that.

Barb touched his shoulder. "I am so sorry about your brother," she said, and the words struck Rory harder than he knew they could. In his rage, he'd forgotten about Pete for a moment.

"Nate and I'll be out of your hair soon," she said, getting to her feet. "Maybe we'll work together again sometime. Till then, okay?"

He listened as she left, not quite ready to move. He heard the ferry in the harbor, blowing its horn. He should get up. He should get to the pier. He should find a way to keep moving forward, but somehow, right then, it all seemed too hard. He wanted to lie on the ground and look at dirt.

He heard the gate open and footsteps approach.

"Here, eat this."

Lydia slid to the ground beside him holding a whoopie pie. Plain chocolate.

"I'm watching my figure," he said.

"Eat it anyway."

Rory rolled over and sat beside her. He split the whoopie pie in half, like an Oreo, though he barely tasted the sweetness of the icing.

"I'll go with you to the mainland," Lydia said. "To do whatever you need to do."

"I'm on duty."

"Get someone to replace you."

"I'll be off in the morning," Rory said. "I'll deal with Pete, with things on the mainland, tomorrow."

"You should have let me know," Lydia said. "You should have let me know it had gotten so bad."

Rory stood, dusting the dirt from his pants. "What would you have done?" he asked, and when Lydia didn't answer, he added, "You'd have done the same thing I did. Nothing. Now at least I'm the only one who needs to feel guilty about it."

He walked to the pier. The ferry had already come into port, and the few afternoon passengers had disembarked. Zoe waved from the deck and made a heart with her hands and held it over her chest. He tried to smile and be gracious, but Zoe, like so many people in town, hadn't cared enough in the end.

It didn't take long for the ferry to load up and depart. *Good riddance*, Rory thought as he watched it pull out of the harbor. Barb would be gone soon, and the island would mostly be back to normal. Whatever normal might be.

Someone tugged at his sleeve. He glanced down to see the little girl, the one who'd come in on the ferry earlier that day, next to him. "Ice cream," she said.

After a quick scan of the area, he saw the girl's mother talking on the phone and watching them from fifteen yards away. This, at least, he could handle. He offered the girl a hand and walked toward the woman. Oh, and look at that. Now she'd started to run toward him, as if running would do her any good. She had the exact same look in her eyes that he'd seen practically every day of his professional career. People from away never *quite* understood that when the ferry left, it was gone till it came back. And now she'd be the one who'd pitch a fit. "Don't look so panicked," he said.

The woman leaned over her knees, gasping for air. She looked like she'd run a marathon.

"Did you find Annie?" he asked.

She shook her head.

"She'll turn up," Rory said.

The woman said something he barely understood. "What was that?" he asked.

"I found a body," she said.

Rory swallowed. He tapped a pack of cigarettes, knocked one out, and lit it. Lydia used to get on him to quit, but that hardly mattered anymore. "What's your name again?" he asked.

"Hester," she said. "I was out at the lighthouse. By the Victorian. There was a knife."

"That lighthouse is private property," Rory said. "You aren't supposed to go there. If they see you, they wind up calling me. Then it's my problem to deal with. The owners are summer folk. Most of the time they don't care. But when they do, they do."

"I found a body," Hester said.

This wasn't what Rory needed, not now. "Yep, you said that already."

"Do you care?"

"Doesn't matter if I care," Rory said, which was true. "I have to deal with it now no matter what you saw. It's like chest pain. Never go to the doctor and claim to have chest pain unless you really, *really* mean it. They take it seriously."

"This is serious."

Rory held up his hands in surrender. This would be a distraction. And it would be good to be first on the scene. People would notice. "What you probably found is a junkie in the middle of OD'ing," he said. A vision of Pete flashed through Rory's mind, of frothing at the mouth, gasping for air. He pushed the image away. "One who won't have the decency to die before I get there, which'll mean I'll have to radio to shore for a medevac. But I'll go take care of it and you won't. Understand? Don't follow me. Don't go anywhere near that lighthouse." He pointed up the hill to Lydia's inn. "Check in there, and I'll come find you if I need anything."

"The body's in the water, and the tide's coming in," Hester said.

"If it washes away, then good riddance," Rory said.

He ambled to the Jeep and drove away slowly, even tossing in a casual wave. It wasn't till he'd crested the hill and headed down the other side toward Little Ef that he stepped on the gas.

Hester had expected a different reaction from Rory. A decidedly different reaction. She had to stop herself from asking Kate if they'd actually seen a dead body. She had. She knew that she had, and that she'd approached it and touched the rubbery skin to check for a pulse, which she'd have to remember to tell the police. Anyone who'd ever watched one minute of TV knew not to touch the body.

She thought about calling Morgan one more time but opted against it. He'd told her that he would rent a car and drive to Maine as soon as he finished work, and that he'd take the ferry to the island first thing in the morning. Hester had listened to his clipped words and ended the call as quickly as she could. In their years together, she'd learned to let him stew in his anger. Besides, she'd pushed him pretty far this time.

"Ready for an adventure?" she said to Kate. "We're staying in a hotel tonight. But let's pick up supplies first."

A handwritten sign in the window of the General Store read, LIVE BAIT AND AMMO. A man with steely gray hair sat at the register in the dimly lit room, signaling that he knew Hester and Kate had entered the store, in the way he silently watched their every move. This store had aisles too narrow for a cart, and floor-to-ceiling shelves stacked with everything from canned chicken to Saran wrap to fishhooks. Hester found two toothbrushes, some toothpaste, and bags of snacks. As she piled the goods by the register to pay, a blond woman with a small boy in tow walked through the door and lingered in one of the far aisles.

"A fifth of Johnnie Walker," Hester said.

The man reached for the bottle from the shelf behind him and added it to the bag without taking his eyes off the new woman, or carding Hester, which almost never happened. After Hester paid, he stepped from behind the register and into the store. Hester had grown up in a small town in Massachusetts with a mother who could barely get out of bed. The two of them had subsisted on a government check that arrived once a month. When the money ran out, Hester had done what she'd needed to. Even all these years later, she could spot fellow shoplifters, the way their hands darted from pockets, the way, like a magician, they distracted with the tiniest of movements. This woman wouldn't have success today though.

Outside, Hester lingered till the woman backed out of the store, the boy clinging to her leg. "Well, fuck you too," she shouted.

Hester caught Kate's eye. "Don't do it," she warned.

"Well, fuck you too," Kate said softly, which, Hester supposed, beat yelling it.

After the store owner had slammed the door, the woman crumpled to a picnic bench, her head cradled in her arms. He opened the door again and waved a broom at her, pointing at a sign that said "SEATING FOR CUSTOMERS AND SEAGULLS ONLY."

"Move on," he said.

"She's with me," Hester said.

The man harrumphed. "Don't stick around," he said, and went back inside.

Here, out in the sun, Hester could get a better look at the pair, and what she saw concerned her. The boy was rail thin, too thin, and wore clothes that hadn't been washed in days. The woman's skin was sallow and pockmarked. "What do you need?" Hester asked.

The woman glared. In that glare was a woman who knew exactly what had been asked and now teetered on the narrow edge between pride and necessity. Hester had been there.

"Dinner," the woman said. "Anything they have. Ethan likes Dinty Moore."

"Back in a few."

In the store, Hester filled a basket with anything remotely healthy—beef jerky, canned green beans, mandarin oranges. She added four ice-cream sandwiches from the top-load freezer and ignored the *tsk-tsk* from the man at the register while she paid and slipped a twenty into the bag too. Outside, she handed out the ice-cream sandwiches and watched as both Kate and the boy gobbled theirs up. When they'd finished, she split hers in two and gave each of them half. "You live out at that house," she said to the woman. "The Victorian. I recognize your son's name. He's the boy who went missing last night."

The woman swept greasy hair from her eyes and wiped her hands on her jeans. She crumpled the ice-cream sandwich wrapper into a ball. "What's it to you?" she asked.

"I'm looking for Annie," Hester said.

The woman scratched at her cheek. "Annie left this morning," she said. "Early. Really early. Right into the storm. Woke me up, slamming doors."

"She left the house?"

"The island. She told me last night that it was time for her to go."

"But the ferries weren't running this morning."

The woman shrugged. "She told me she was leaving. She left. I haven't seen her since. Seems pretty simple to me."

"You're Frankie, right?"

The woman looked Hester over suspiciously before nodding.

"This is all for you," Hester said, leaving the bag of food on the table. "I'm staying at the inn over there. Or at least I hope I am."

Frankie seemed as though she might pass on the groceries but relented, reaching into the bag and holding up each of the cans. When she found the twenty, she folded it into a wad and stuffed it into her pocket. "Mandarin oranges?" she said.

"We can hit the bakery too," Hester said. "Whatever you need."

"We don't *need* anything," Frankie said.

"I do," Hester said. "Five minutes?"

Frankie moved over on the picnic bench.

"I heard you got lost!" Hester said to Ethan, who pushed his face into his mother's side.

"He wandered out to the lighthouse," Frankie said, ruffling his hair.

"The lighthouse," Hester said, stopping herself from mentioning what she'd found there.

"Thomas with me," Ethan said, peeking from his mother's side.

"Like the train," Frankie said. "Thomas goes everywhere. At least in his imagination."

"Not train," Ethan said. "Tank engine!"

"Tank engine," Hester said. "Thomas the Tank Engine was with you. How about anyone else?"

Ethan thought about the question. "Maybe Gordon too?"

"Another train," Frankie said. "There are a lot of them, and he'll keep going. They were probably all there."

"Go play," Hester said to Kate and Ethan. "Stay where we can see you."

Kate took Ethan's hand and led him toward a patch of grass. "Can you count to sixty?" she asked, and when he shook his head, she said, "How about a hundred?"

"What happened this morning?" Hester asked.

Frankie shrugged. "I found him sitting on the back stoop, soaked to the bone. He must have gotten trapped when the tide came in. I'm lucky a wave didn't sweep him out to sea."

"He's seen a doctor, right?" Hester asked.

"Of course he did," Frankie snapped. "And if you want to give me the third degree, I'll get going."

"Got it. Sorry to be nosy. Tell me how you know Annie. Then we're done."

"From the house. I saw her around Portland, too, before she left."

"She lived in Portland? Do you know for how long? Or what she did there?"

"Not a clue. She probably did what I did, which was get high and steal things."

Hester suddenly felt all the sleepless nights of the last year at once, and the drive to Maine in particular. She felt every favor she'd ever done for Daphne. But she also remembered the boat coming into the harbor earlier and scanning the line of people waiting to leave. She couldn't have missed Daphne's bright red hair. And even Daphne couldn't have watched Kate getting off that ferry without coming forward.

"Did she say anything at all that might be helpful?" Hester asked.

"I'm telling you," Frankie said. "You're wasting your time. Annie left the island as soon as she could this morning."

"You're back," Lydia Pelletier said, from where she counted cash at the bakery counter. She took Hester's tote bag from behind the counter. "I thought you might have left without this. I'm about to close, though."

"I don't need a whoopie pie as much as I need a room," Hester said, glancing into the kitchen. She took Sebastian from the bag and handed him to Kate. "Where's the kiddo?"

"He still takes naps, thank God," Lydia said. "Missed the ferry? I can't tell you how many times I've missed that damn ferry by ten seconds! Follow me!"

Lydia led Hester and Kate through a connecting door to the inn on the other side, an ancient house with low ceilings, creaking floorboards, and a fireplace in every room. A narrow staircase off the front foyer led up to a second-floor landing.

"This house is over two hundred years old," Lydia said as she opened a door to a cozy room with sloped ceilings, flowered wallpaper, a rocking chair in the corner, and a window looking out over the water. "It was built when people were much smaller," she added.

"Not smaller than me," Hester said.

"Maybe not," Lydia said. "The bathroom's in the hallway. You're the only ones here tonight, so you won't need to share."

Kate climbed up onto the bed and jumped on it.

"Can I help you with your bags?" Lydia asked.

Hester tossed the paper bag from the general store onto the bed along with the tote bag filled with Kate's toys. "That about covers it," she said. "How about a drink?"

"Let me get Oliver and I'll meet you downstairs," Lydia said, and a moment later Hester and Lydia sat on the inn's front porch drinking beer from the bottle, while Oliver led Kate from flower to flower in the garden, arms spread wide. "What are you two doing?" Hester asked.

"We're butterflies!" Oliver shouted.

"Bugs," Lydia said. "Can't get enough of them. How'd you miss the ferry anyway?"

Hester considered unburdening all of it, telling Lydia Daphne's real name. Telling her about the texts and why she'd really come to this island. But she held back. "Who do I talk to about family services out here?"

"That's all run from the mainland," Lydia said. "On the island, we mostly watch out for one another."

"Is anyone watching out for Frankie Sullivan?" Hester asked.

Lydia drank down a gulp of her beer. "You can only help people who want it," she said.

"Even when they're four years old?"

"We spent the night searching for him because he didn't pay attention to the tide."

"Four-year-olds don't usually know how to read tides," Hester said, sitting back in the rocking chair and holding the beer bottle to her forehead. She'd been up for almost thirty-six hours now, and, honestly, Lydia's island wasn't sitting well with her.

"You're right," Lydia said. "Sorry. None of us got much sleep last night, you included, it seems. You hungry?"

"I could be," Hester said.

"Wait here."

Lydia disappeared and returned a moment later with two more beers and a charcuterie platter. Instinctively, Hester went to block Waffles from snagging anything from the tray.

"I can spot a dog owner from a mile away," Lydia said.

"Guilty," Hester said.

Lydia held up her beer and clinked it against Hester's.

"Could Annie have left this morning?" Hester asked. "On the ferry to Bar Harbor?"

Lydia shook her head. "That boat was canceled. The water was too rough to sail."

Right then, Rory Dunbar let himself in to the garden and took his hat off. He waved to them, then carefully closed the gate behind him in a way that made Hester's heart sink as she realized he was here with bad news, news that she'd helped uncover. Oliver ran to the deputy and gave him a high five.

"Could I talk to you?" he said to Lydia.

"I'll leave you two," Hester said. "We'll get ourselves sorted out upstairs." She stood and called to Kate. "Oliver, you come too."

"What's going on?" Lydia asked.

"Let me know what you need," Hester said.

She left as Rory sat in the rocking chair beside Lydia and took her hand.

CHAPTER 15

Hester waited at the top of the staircase for Lydia's sobs to begin. When they didn't, she turned to Kate and Oliver. "Play on your own," she said, as the children barely looked up from a coloring book. "And don't get into anything," she added, which only made Kate glare at her.

A few steps out of the room, Hester found that she couldn't go any farther. "This is pathetic," she mumbled, taking the children's hands—Kate tried to pull away—and dragging them along after her, but she had no idea what was in that bedroom, what dangers lurked. Whether a fire might start. This house would go up in flames in an instant.

Stop.

So much for solving her own craziness. Though, in her own defense, she *had* found a dead body.

The inn's age made moving with any stealth out of the question, but as Hester came off the landing, it was clear that neither Lydia nor Rory cared what anyone saw. Rory held Lydia's head to his chest, tenderly stroking her hair. His eyes were closed, and he rocked her slowly. When floorboards groaned under Hester's weight, Rory's eyes popped open, a flash of guilt coloring his face. He was enjoying this, in a way, at least.

"Can I get you anything, Lydia?" Hester asked.

Lydia squinted as though waking from a dream and pushed away from Rory. "Do you have everything you need in your room?" she asked.

"I don't need anything," Hester said.

Lydia turned toward Rory, steeling herself. "Where is he?" she asked.

"Out by the lighthouse," Rory said. "I pulled his body up the shore to keep him from washing out to sea." Rory caught himself, as though hearing his own words. "Sorry," he said.

"No, I want to know," Lydia said. "Tell me what else you did."

"The state police hadn't left yet, so they've taken over while we wait for the medical examiner."

"Did he drown?" Lydia asked. "Or hit his head?"

Rory caught Hester's eye, and she pictured the knife sticking out of the corpse's back. "We don't know yet," Rory said. "The body hasn't been released. The autopsy will tell us."

"Who drownded?" Oliver asked.

"Jesus Christ," Lydia said, putting an arm out and giving the boy a hug. "We should talk someplace else," she said to Rory. "And there'll be tuna casseroles all over this house within the hour."

"I'll take him," Hester said, crouching to meet Oliver's gaze. "Let's go back upstairs and play."

"*Angry Birds*!" Kate said.

"Or something else," Hester said, leading the two children upstairs, where Kate showed Sebastian to Oliver and told him that the toy was off limits. A moment later, Rory knocked on their open door and looked around for a chair, but Hester patted the mattress beside her. "We have chaperones," she added.

Rory hesitated before perching on the edge of the bed. "Could you tell me what you saw?" he asked. "You'll have to repeat it all to the state cops, but sometimes it's best to talk right away."

The whole scene had pretty much seared itself into Hester's memory, but she went over each detail with Rory, from the visit to the Victorian, to her walk to the lighthouse, to the walk back.

"What about the guy at the house," Rory said.

"Seth," Hester said.

"Seth, right. I looked for him last night but couldn't find him. Seth told you that Frankie had taken Ethan out to the beach. But you never saw her?"

"Nope, not a sign, though I ran into her later. I was hoping Annie might be there, but the lighthouse was empty. The door had been kicked in. And I saw that guy with the black lab. He was sopping wet from collecting buoys."

"Vaughn?" Rory said, sitting up.

"Yeah, that's him. But if he stabbed someone, there was no blood on his clothes."

"But he'd gone in the water. Make sure to tell the state police when you see them. Every detail. Okay?"

"Of course," Hester said. "I have no skin in this game."

"Seems you might have some," Rory said, standing up and heading to the door. "You showed up looking for a friend who disappeared, then a dead body washed up on shore. Doesn't look good for Annie, I'll tell you that much. Got any secrets you should share?"

Hester groaned, at least she did on the inside. She knew it was time to show her cards. "How's this for a secret. Annie . . ." she began.

Rory waited her out.

"That's not her name. Her name is Daphne Maguire. She's been missing for the last year, and she sent me a text in the middle of the night asking me to come here even though I haven't really heard from her the whole time she's been gone. And now I'm really, truly worried. Also"—Hester nodded toward Kate, her voice low—"that's her daughter."

"You didn't think to tell me this earlier?" Rory said. "Like when you got off the ferry?"

"None of this mattered when I got off the ferry. It was just an embarrassing personal situation. And I hadn't found a dead person. But now I have, so now it does. That's why I'm telling you."

"Who's dead?" Kate asked.

"I'll tell you later," Hester said.

"When?"

"Not now."

Hester stood and pulled Rory into the hallway. "Little ears . . ." she mumbled.

"So you don't think it matters that you haven't heard from your friend in a year?" Rory asked. "The friend who abandoned her own child, leaving her with you to raise?"

Hester hated when people vocalized her situation to her. "You'd be surprised how quickly you can adapt to things," she said. "Even caring for someone else's child."

Rory looked her over one more time. "The state cops are at the community center. You need to come in and make a statement to Detective Kelley. Come in an hour or so. Maybe we'll be back from the beach by then."

"Please find Annie. Whatever it takes, and whatever she's done. She can't have just disappeared."

"Her name's Daphne," Rory said.

"Fine," Hester said. "Please find Daphne."

"I'll do what I can." Rory closed his eyes and sighed. "I promise. It's my job."

"Thank you," Hester said.

"Can Oliver stay with you for a bit? Lydia needs to come with me to identify the body."

"Of course," Hester said.

She listened to Rory's footsteps as he made his way down the narrow staircase. She watched as Kate began to let Oliver play with Sebastian, as though the little girl understood the sadness the boy would face in the coming days. It used to be that Hester didn't believe she could care for a child—she hadn't wanted to, and part of her had thought she wasn't capable of doing so. Now, here she was with two of them, neither of them hers. "What are you playing over there?" she asked.

"It's Sebastian's birthday," Kate said.

"How could I have forgotten?" Hester said, joining them on the floor.

Today, Sebastian's birthday was sparser than usual, with mini soaps from the bathroom serving as presents. Kate had never seen a hotel soap and marveled at its tininess, using her imagination to turn them into birthday cake and iPhones, and directing Oliver through the whole game. Oliver took Kate's instruction well, absorbing the bossiness Hester hoped Kate would carry with her into adulthood. They played till the autumn sun began to move toward the horizon. The inn remained quiet, but Hester suspected the doorbell would soon start to ring with the promise of those casseroles and cakes that came with death.

"We should go," she said after an hour had gone by. "It's time to face the music."

"Like the Wiggles?" Kate asked.

"Worse," Hester said. "More like Barney."

"Where did they all come from?" Lydia asked as Rory pulled around the bend on Little Ef.

At least a dozen state troopers stood in a group by the side of the road. A coast guard cutter had dropped the reinforcements off soon after word of Trey's death hit the mainland, because nothing brought out the forces or agency cooperation like a death to one of their own. "Everyone cared about Trey," he said to Lydia. "Will you be okay?"

"Why wouldn't I be?" Lydia said, already back to her stoic Maine self.

"Stay here for a minute," Rory said as he parked the Jeep. "I'll come get you."

Police tape lined the area leading out to the lighthouse, and Trey's body still lay where Rory had dragged it earlier. Barb Kelley was on her radio as he approached her. "Best place to land is by the pier," she said, waving Rory over as she signed off. "Medical examiner is on his way from Portland. But I don't need a doctor to tell me the cause of death on this one. Thanks for handling the notification," she added. "That couldn't have been easy."

Rory wouldn't have let anyone else do it. "Comes with the territory," he said. "She's in the car to do the ID."

"I think we know who it is," Barb said. "But let's make it official." She lifted the tape and ducked under it. "Walk me through what happened again. What you saw and what you found."

Rory gestured toward the water. "The tide was coming in, and he was on the sand, nearly floating out to sea."

"So you did what?"

"I photographed the scene, pulled the body out of the water, and radioed in," Rory said. After a beat, he added, "Following protocol."

"Not exactly protocol," Barb said, letting that smile slip in. "Even a rookie knows not to touch a body till it's released by the medical examiner. But it's what I'd have done too. Send me those photos."

Rory had spent enough time with Barb to know that each of her actions had meaning and that he was both investigator and suspect, both part of the team and miles outside of it. Barb had seen how Trey treated him. She knew what people in town thought of Rory. He hoped she'd see beyond it.

"The body was in the water," Barb said.

"That's not exactly right," Rory said. "The body was on the sand, but the tide was on its way in. Last night was a moon tide, which means the water comes in fast and the final tide will reach to about here." Rory walked to a dark line on the stone. "All this tape will be gone within the next hour."

"Good to know," Barb said, calling Nate over and telling him to move things back. "So much for a secured crime scene, I guess. Let's hope the good ol' doc gets here before then."

She lifted the edge of the blue tarp that covered the body, and Rory caught a glimpse of Trey's hand, the skin rubbery.

"God knows how long he's been dead," Barb said. "My guess is a few hours at the very least, though getting an accurate time of death will be tough. It doesn't help that he's been soaking in seawater. Could the body have floated from somewhere else?"

"My best guess would be maybe."

"Did you see anything around the body?" Barb asked. "Any footprints?"

"Not even footprints from the woman who found it. The tide had washed them away."

"But anything from here up would be fresh," Barb said, pointing to the tide line. "Anything old would have been swept away in last night's rain."

Barb lived on the water in South Portland, and like anyone who lived on the water, she understood tides. But Rory would let her play her game and ask the questions that she already had answers for. He'd play along too, as long as it made sense.

"Two sets of prints," Barb said. "Tiny and tinier."

"That's the woman and the girl."

Barb walked to the water's edge and faced the horizon, hands on her hips, her legs apart, her feet firmly planted. "This is my Superman pose," she said. "Or Superwoman. It's supposed to make you feel invincible. I heard it on a TED Talk, and I do it whenever I don't know what to do next."

"Does it work?" Rory asked.

Barb sighed. "I hate TED Talks," she said. "Why don't we pull together a list of suspects? Good thing is, there are only so many people on this island, right? And who do we start with?"

Rory glanced toward the Jeep as Lydia stepped out of it and headed toward him. "The wife. Always start with the spouse."

Barb followed his gaze. "Will you be okay with that?"

Rory remembered Lydia and Vaughn in the ravine the night before, the way Trey had tried to cut their line. And he remembered sitting outside Lydia's window, watching her. "I'll have to be," he said.

Barb relaxed out of her pose. "What is it with this island, anyway? Missing children. Now a murder. Who else is on that suspect list?"

I am, Rory thought. *Or, I should be.*

"Rory?"

Lydia waited at the police tape. Barb nodded, and he led Lydia to the blue tarp. "Are you ready for this?" he asked, and she nodded sharply.

He lifted the edge of the tarp. Lydia inhaled.

"It's him, right?" Rory asked.

"Have you seen Vaughn?" Lydia asked.

The sound of Vaughn's name hit Rory right in the heart. He had held Lydia as close as he dared when he'd told her about Trey, making sure she didn't collapse from grief. Or so he'd convinced himself. Now, he felt her slipping away again. "Haven't seen him since I tackled him at your place."

"The two of you," Lydia said. "You've been brawling since high school. Fighting over nothing."

You're not nothing, Rory wanted to say, *you're every-thing*. But Barb's radio crackled to life. She ducked under the tape and headed toward shore, then waited to see if Rory would follow.

"Do you want to stay?" he asked Lydia.

"I'm done," she said.

"I'll take you home."

"I'll walk," Lydia said. "I could use the air."

"What about Oliver? He's with that woman, at the inn. With Hester."

"I'll have to go get him, then." She turned back to where a breeze lifted the edges of the blue tarp. "This is gonna be hard," she said.

It took everything he had to turn away from her and get into the Jeep beside Barb. "The woman who found the body showed up at the community center. Let's find out what she saw," she said, watching Lydia out the window. "You and the widow, Pelletier. What's going on there?"

"She's like a sister."

"Not like any sister I've ever known."

Rory put the Jeep in gear and sped toward town, watching in the rearview mirror till Lydia disappeared.

"You really need to get more cars out here," Barb said. "It's like the nineteenth century."

"That's how we like it."

"Yeah, but if you had more cars and tolls on this rock, we'd know where people were. You can track just about anything these days as long as there's some data attached to it."

Rory swerved around a tree that had fallen into the road. "Did you meet Annie?" he asked.

Barb paused, and Rory could almost see her putting a

mental pin in their conversation about Lydia. "Homeless woman from last night? Red hair?" Barb said.

"That's her. We're meeting her friend, Hester. She showed up on the ferry this afternoon looking for Annie, and it turns out that Annie's name isn't Annie, it's Daphne. But now Annie slash Daphne is missing, even though she wrote to Hester last night asking her to come here. Then Hester finds Trey's body. I thought Annie had left the island, but now, I don't know where she went."

Rory pulled in front of the community center, and Barb sat for a moment thinking. "Like I said, murders, missing children. Now missing women who use aliases. Maybe there were two bodies on that beach? Maybe one of them washed out to sea? Come on! Let's find out what we can."

Inside, Hester Thursby waited on a metal folding chair with the little girl and Oliver sitting on the floor beside her.

Barb strode across the room. "I have two, about the same age. Maybe one of the officers can watch them. It'll make it easier to chat."

"As long as I can see them," Hester said.

Barb signaled to one of the troopers, who then led Kate and Oliver to a play area in one corner. Barb waved Hester over to a folding table, where she sat with her foot up. "We went out to the scene," she said. "It was pretty bad. I'm sure it was upsetting."

"I've seen worse," Hester said, which, Rory observed, knocked the smile right off Barb's face. A first.

"Walk us through what happened," Barb said. "Why were you out at the lighthouse?"

"Don't most flatlanders gravitate toward lighthouses?" Hester said. When Barb didn't respond, she added, "I'm pretty sure Rory's already told you why I'm here."

"You're looking for Annie."

"And Annie lives out by the lighthouse. Someone at the house said she might have gone to the point."

"And exactly who is Annie?"

"She's my boyfriend's twin sister. And Kate's mother. And as I'm talking, I'm realizing that none of this sounds that great."

"Annie is that little girl's mother," Barb said.

Hester nodded.

"Can you show me the texts she sent?"

Hester handed her phone to Barb.

"They came in right after midnight," Barb said to Rory, showing him the two texts. "You didn't delete anything, did you? Because we'll find out."

"I'm a librarian," Hester said. "I know you can't delete anything permanently."

"Who is this Morgan?" Barb asked, scrolling through more of Hester's messages. "He seems pretty pissed off at you."

"Daphne's brother. Kate's uncle. My boyfriend. Probably in that order. He's mad because I left in the middle of the night and didn't tell him where I was going."

"Do you live together?"

"Mostly."

"I'd be mad too. And to keep this straight, Daphne and Annie are the same person."

Hester sighed. "Yes," she said.

Barb turned to Rory. "Didn't you say Annie moved here right before the first kidnapping?" When he nodded, she shoved a pad of paper toward Hester. "Write her name down. And her date of birth and Social Security number, if you have them."

"I know them by heart," Hester said, scribbling down the information. "It won't help. I've tried."

"We have a few more resources than you do," Barb said. "Do you have a photo?"

"Give me my phone back and I'll text you one, though everyone says she looks different now."

"This is helpful," Barb said, and Rory noted that her voice softened into good cop. "Is there anything else you need to tell me? Anything you're holding back on?"

"If I think of anything, I'll let you know," Hester said. "It's not like I'm leaving before morning."

"Don't leave at all," Rory said. "Not without telling us first."

Off in the distance, he heard the steady hum of a helicopter.

"That's the medical examiner," Barb said. "In a helicopter. They're pulling out all the stops on this one. We need to deal with him. Afterwards, we'll have more questions."

"I won't be hard to find," Hester said.

"Let's hope," Barb said. "Disappearing seems to be a trend around here."

After Hester left, Barb radioed to shore to put out a bulletin on Daphne Maguire. She opened a laptop. "Do you know anything about this Hester Thursby?" she asked. "She's all over the Internet. There was an Amber Alert out on that kid, Daphne's kid, over the winter."

Rory leaned in and read through some of the results. "What are you thinking?"

"This isn't rocket science," Barb said. "A woman using a fake name moves to town right before a kidnapping and then goes missing the same night that a state police officer is stabbed a few hundred yards from her house. As long as she isn't dead, we have our prime suspect. Now we have to find out where the hell she went."

CHAPTER 16

Hester hadn't expected quite such an interrogation from the police; still, she supposed with Daphne came guilt by association. At the inn, with Kate and Oliver in tow, she found at least two dozen notes addressed to Lydia at the door, and inside, casserole dishes had begun to pile up on a table. Hester called Lydia's name, but no one answered. Upstairs, she found a note from Lydia tacked to her door asking if she could please watch Oliver for a little while longer.

> *I know that we don't know each other, but I am feeling overwhelmed and I need to speak to the police. I should be back later this evening. Have dinner at Cappy's. It's on me.*

Hester crumpled up the note in her fist. Whatever happened, she hoped she didn't wind up with two kids instead of one.

"Help me out," she said, ruffling Oliver's hair.

The three of them moved the casserole dishes into the refrigerator in the bakery and piled the notes up by the door. Then they sat on the floor in the bedroom, and Hester watched as the kids played and drew pictures. When she thought things were calm enough, she stepped onto the landing and called Angela White, level-headed Angela, who picked up on the first ring. Angela was a detective with the Boston Police Department and seemed like the best bet as a consultant right about now. "Have you gone off the deep end?" Angela said. "That husband of yours was on the phone with me all day long."

"Non-husband," Hester said.

"You're impossible," Angela said.

"We're all impossible in our own way," Hester said. "And don't think I've forgiven you for the intervention, but I need your help anyway."

"Fine. Hit me."

Hester walked Angela through what she'd told the cops. When she finished, Angela said, "You handled the interview well. You're being honest and straightforward, which is exactly as I'd have advised you, but none of this sounds too good for Daphne. She'd definitely be one of my prime suspects. Don't let her open her mouth without a lawyer."

"First, I have to find her. Second, I doubt there are any lawyers on this island. Not at this time of year."

"There's always a lawyer around, and even a bad one is better than nothing. I have the next two days off though. Why don't I come up there and give you a hand?"

Hester nearly said yes. It would have been a relief to have a friend to rely on, but she also knew she had to confront Daphne when she found her, and for that she needed to be on her own.

"I may show up anyway," Angela said when Hester declined the offer.

"That's what I'd do," Hester said. "But please don't. Not this time. I'm asking for what I need, and if that changes, you'll be the first one I call."

"Make me second," Angela said. "I should always be second after that husband."

"Non-husband."

"Call him what you want, but we all know the deal," Angela said, hanging up before Hester could respond.

Hester looked at the blank phone and thought about calling Morgan but held off, not because she wanted to avoid another confrontation—though that was part of it—but because she knew a call would only worry him more when she filled him in on his missing sister and the details Hester had uncovered about Daphne's life. It worried her, too, and she hoped that she could find some good news to share before they talked again. "Let's grab dinner," she said to the kids.

At Cappy's they found a warm bar filled with people and a menu with basic pub fare. "We're packed," said a hostess as she led them to a table in the back. Soon enough they'd ordered—fish and chips for Hester and chicken fingers for both Kate and Oliver. They talked through the important things that you talk about with four-year-olds: grasshoppers, Halloween costumes, Kate's imminent return to school. Hester wondered what Kate had surmised from her conversation with the cops. She wondered how many questions it might bring up. But tonight, the girl seemed content to focus on other things.

"Still around?"

The man Hester had seen on the beach, the one with

the black lab, loomed over her. Vaughn Roberts. He'd cleaned up since their last encounter. He'd also clearly had a few already.

"What's another night?" Hester said.

"You've been talking to the police." Vaughn nodded toward the crowd, with their gleaming eyes and excited chatter. "From what I hear, at least."

"That's why everyone's out tonight," Hester said.

Vaughn leaned toward her and nearly fell over. "For the gossip," he said.

Hester pulled up a chair. "Gossip with me."

Vaughn motioned to the waitress and ordered a beer. He cocked an eyebrow at Hester in a way that seemed practiced. In a way that set her on edge.

"Ginger ale and rye," she said.

"How much can you drink?"

"I come from a long line of drunks. I can hold my own."

Vaughn walked a hand across the table and touched Hester's fingertips. She pulled her hand away. "Head back to the bar," she said.

That seemed to sober Vaughn up, but when the waitress brought him his beer, he told her to keep them coming.

"You need to slow down, buddy, before you become gossip yourself," Hester said.

Vaughn shrugged. "It's just one of those nights. I mean, I have a girl. Or, I *had* one. Been divorced six months now. Never thought I'd spend another night on this rock, but here I am, right? Stuck on a woman. Stuck on an island."

"And I'm stuck eating with a maudlin drunk. Find me when you've sobered up."

"Don't you want to find out about your friend? Your friend whose *real name* is Daphne."

Hester saw Kate perk up at the mention of her mother's name.

"News travels fast here," Hester said. "And I know her better than anyone else in the world. Daphne Maguire will be found when she wants to be, and not a moment sooner."

Hester sipped the sweet cocktail. She didn't want to say much more, not with Kate sitting right there, absorbing every word. "What are people saying about . . ." She glanced at Oliver. "About what I found."

"You found it. They're saying that."

"True enough."

"You come to the island to find a woman using a fake name, and a man winds up dead, with a knife in his back." Vaughn leaned forward. "As far as I'm concerned, it was well deserved."

"You were on the beach earlier," Hester said. "Didn't you see anything?"

"Not a thing," Vaughn said. "I didn't go out as far as you did."

But he had, hadn't he? Hester tried to remember where the dog had appeared, and which direction Vaughn had come from.

"You told Rory you saw me," Vaughn said. "He's been looking for an excuse to get me for years, but now more than ever."

"Why?"

"No reason," Vaughn said. "I'll tell you this though. You'll be hard-pressed to find someone on this island who's upset to see Trey gone. He didn't have too many friends."

"Well, his wife's upset."

"Leave her out of it," Vaughn said, smashing his glass to the table. All around, conversation stopped as people stared. Vaughn stood slowly and faced the room, his feet unsteady.

"Get him some coffee," a man shouted from the back, followed by a smattering of applause.

"Sit down," Hester said.

Vaughn felt behind him for his chair, and collapsed.

"You should go home," Hester said. "Whatever's going on . . . it can wait till morning."

"What do you think is going on?" Vaughn asked.

"I don't know and, right now, I don't care."

Vaughn leaned forward and whispered, "I've been sleeping with the Widow Pelletier. Have been for months now. Is that what you wanted to hear? There, do what you want with it!"

While all this had been going on, Kate had finished her chicken fingers and had tried to entice Oliver into eating her carrot sticks for her. Now, the boy cocked his head at the name "Pelletier," while Kate stared at the drunk man in front of her, more fascinated than fearful. Hester tapped her finger on the side of the plate. "You're four years old," she said. "So, how many carrot sticks do you have to eat?"

"Four," Kate said, biting into one of them glumly.

Hester had spent enough time with drunk people to know that this conversation would go nowhere fast. Besides, the last thing she needed was for Oliver to understand even a jot of what Vaughn had confessed. "I've been on Finisterre for less than twelve hours," she said. "And it took me all of five minutes to figure out what was going on between you and you-know-who. I can't imagine anyone on this island doesn't already know. And the police too." She finished her drink in one gulp. "By the way, I can drink you and just about anyone under the table," she added, dropping two twenties on the table. "And about L-Y-D-I-A? Watch yourself. I'm just saying."

"That spells Lydia," Oliver said. "That's my mother's name."

"Excellent job," Hester said.

She held out her hands and waited till each of the kids had taken one. Then she marched out of the restaurant and tried to ignore the feeling of Vaughn staring at her as she retreated.

Back at the inn, Lydia still hadn't come home. Hester told Oliver to go find himself a pair of pajamas and helped both children get ready for bed. She read them a story, and when they'd fallen asleep, she slipped the bottle of Johnnie Walker she'd picked up at the General Store into her coat pocket and searched the first floor for any signs of where Lydia might have gone. The last thing they needed was another missing person, but the only clue she uncovered was a handwritten sign hung on the bakery door that said it was closed until further notice due to "personal reasons."

In was only when Hester had wandered onto the porch and watched as her breath froze in the autumn air that she realized she'd left Kate upstairs. These ten minutes were the longest they'd been apart in weeks, and instead of panic, Hester felt relief. Maybe she could move toward something normal again. Maybe she could heal. She twisted the cap off the bottle and drank down a slug of whisky, feeling the warmth spread through her. She sat on one of the rocking chairs and typed *I'm sorry* into her phone but deleted it before she accidentally sent it to Morgan.

She closed her eyes and had dozed off, when suddenly she sat up, fully alert. "Who's there?" she said, staring into the darkness.

She listened. The island was asleep. She heard the steady rhythms of the sea and the wind. But she'd heard something else. A footstep, the breaking of a twig. She turned on her phone's flashlight and shined it across the garden and into the shadows. Did something move? The weak beam of light didn't reach far enough for her to see. She thought about Vaughn, drunk and angry. Could he have followed her here?

"Coward," she said.

Inside, the small bed-and-breakfast suddenly felt very big and empty, with plenty of places where an intruder could hide. She dug in her pocket for Rory's card, and even considered calling the deputy, but shook it off. Whatever she'd heard could have been anything—an animal, someone walking on the path toward home, a homicidal maniac—or nothing. Upstairs, Kate and Oliver lay sleeping with Sebastian nestled between them. She tucked them in and evaluated the safety of the room. The door to the bedroom didn't have a lock, so she shoved a chair in front of it and slid into bed. She'd had enough nights where paranoia took over, but most nights she wasn't trying to fall asleep on an island far from home where children disappeared and fathers wound up dead. Most nights, Hester didn't have a clue where Daphne was, and the things she worried about were the things doing battle in her own head.

* * *

Hester woke instantly from a deep sleep, every sense heightened. She lay still and listened. Again, she could hear waves pounding on the shore and wind. Endless wind. And the creaks and groans of a two-hundred-year-old house.

She told herself to go back to sleep, to stop imagining, but then the latch on the guestroom door clicked, and the door hit the chair. Gently at first, then with more force. Someone was trying to get into the room. Hester felt beneath the blankets till she found Kate and Oliver sleeping soundly beside her. She imagined the room as it had been before she'd turned out the lights: the television, the braided rug, the bedside table. The lamp.

The floorboards groaned. The chair fell over.

Hester leapt from the bed, hand on the base of the lamp, tearing the cord from the wall. She charged toward the shadow, a cry rising in her throat.

"Stop, stop, stop!"

A cell phone display lit up a familiar chin.

Hester dropped the lamp midswing. It clattered to the floor, the bulb smashing. Behind her, she heard Kate and Oliver sit up in bed.

"You scared the shit out of me," Hester said.

She crossed to her side of the bed and flipped on the other bedside lamp. Morgan stood—cowered—by the door, arms raised to protect himself from her onslaught. He wore a blue fleece and jeans and a wool cap pulled down over his red hair. He opened the door to the room wide and let Waffles lumber in.

"Careful," Hester said. "There's broken glass."

But the basset mix jumped right onto the bed, sniffed Oliver and lapped Kate on the cheek, who squealed with delight. They'd never go back to sleep now, but somehow Hester hardly cared. All the fear and anger had vanished, and she hoped Morgan's anger—at everything—had too. "Come," she said. "We can squeeze onto the bed. All five of us."

Morgan threw an overnight bag onto a chair. He tickled Kate, patted Oliver's cheek, kissed Hester on the lips, lay on the bed, and let Waffles walk all over him. "Who's the little guy?" he mouthed, nodding toward Oliver.

"I'll explain in the morning. How on earth did you get here?"

"Found a fisherman to take me from Rockland," Morgan said. "Cost me a fortune."

"Did you hurl?"

"The whole way."

"Money well spent," Hester said. "Can we fight tomorrow?"

Morgan kicked off his shoes and tossed the wool hat to the floor. Hester curled up alongside his body. "Best idea I've heard all day," he said.

WEDNESDAY,
SEPTEMBER 25

CHAPTER 17

Hester met Morgan for the first time a year and a half after she and Daphne graduated from Wellesley. "She hasn't mentioned me," Morgan said when Hester opened the door of their Allston apartment one February afternoon. A statement. A fact.

"I barely know her," Hester said. Her first sentence to Morgan. A lie.

"She calls when she's in trouble."

"Who are you?"

Morgan walked into the apartment as though he lived there, tossing a ratty peacoat onto an even rattier chair, a cat carrier dangling from one hand. He opened it, and the mangiest cat Hester had ever seen (till then) leapt out, claws digging into the sofa. "I'm her twin brother."

"Daphne's at work," Hester said, though in truth she hadn't seen Daphne in a day or two, which wasn't out of the ordinary, since they worked opposite schedules. Daphne tended bar, while Hester worked at Widener. Still, she peeked into Daphne's bedroom and was relieved to find an unmade bed and piles of clothing.

Anything neater would have set off alarms. "And she hates cats."

"I go to Tufts," Morgan said. "To the vet school out in Grafton. The rest of the family lives in Southie. Good ol' Boston story: father was a cop, mother a kindergarten teacher. There are eight other Maguires running around, most within a stone's throw of this apartment. Ever met any of them?"

All this surprised and didn't surprise Hester. By then, she'd known Daphne for over five years, and it had been five years of the two of them. "We keep to ourselves," she said. "My mother lives on the South Shore."

Those words surprised her all over again, because now Morgan knew more about her childhood than any-one else, including Daphne.

"I ignore most of the Maguires," Morgan said. "But not Daphne. You must know the Daphne Charm."

Daphne had a lot of good qualities, but Hester wouldn't say charm was one of them.

"Yelling," Morgan said, swooping the cat from the ground and cradling it to his shoulder. "She thinks it'll get her what she wants. She'll scream her head off when she sees this cat. But his name is Hamlet, and it would be great if he could stay here for a few days. He has nowhere else to go."

Hester took the cat. It curled onto her shoulder, a gentle purr strumming through its body. She'd dreamed of having a pet her whole life. "What do I do about his fur? It's disgusting."

"That's the thing with cats," Morgan said, "you give them an ounce of love, and they usually fix themselves. And if the fur stays like that, then that'll be Hamlet's Charm. What's yours?"

"I don't have one."

"I bet you do," Morgan said. "But point me to where Daphne works. That's usually the best place to start."

Hester led Morgan the three blocks to the Turin, a German-style beer garden. Inside, they found a dark and warm bar, with a few patrons dotting the floor. Morgan ordered two IPAs, and when the bartender brought the draughts, he asked if Daphne was working.

"She's gone," the bartender said.

"Since when?"

"Since I started."

Morgan took a long quaff, and all these years later, lying in bed in this strange inn on this remote island watching him sleep, Hester could still see him steeling himself for what was to come. "Your manager around?" he asked.

A moment later, a woman with brown hair tied in a sensible ponytail strode onto the floor. "Your friend can go to hell," she said.

"We're not friends," Morgan said. "What did she do this time?"

"She's been gone since I asked her to clean the grease traps," the woman said. "No one likes to, but we all have to sometimes. I found hamburger grease at the bottom of my bag. At least she knew enough not to come back. And if I do see her, she'd better watch out."

Morgan downed the rest of his beer. "The Daphne Charm," he said.

Back at the apartment, he asked Hester what the rent cost and wrote a check for three times the amount.

"Aren't you a student?" Hester asked.

"I'm good for it. And don't tell Daphne I came or about the check, it'll only piss her off. But call me if you need more money. And Daphne'll show up. She always does."

"I can keep a secret," Hester said.

"Maybe that's your charm, then," Morgan said as he put his coat on and gave Hamlet one last pet. "Take care of him, okay?"

Hester shrugged, but after he left, she lay on the sofa and let the cat knead her chest with his paws. Morgan turned out to be right. With a few days of regular food and water, Hamlet's coat grew shiny and healthy, and when Daphne walked in the door a week later, she barely mentioned their new roommate. She didn't talk about where she'd disappeared to at all, and Hester didn't ask. Those were the types of things they didn't discuss.

Two months later, it was Hester who called Morgan for the first time—she always remembered that—and it was Hester who asked to meet him in Davis Square, a world away from Allston, to talk about Hamlet. She wore a dress that day, and makeup, and when they sat in Mike's, an old Italian-American restaurant with picture windows that opened onto the square, a pepperoni pizza between them and a pitcher of Blue Moon to share, Hamlet—who wound up living with Hester till he passed away—hadn't come up once. Neither had Daphne. They talked for hours on a perfect spring evening when cherry blossoms were in bloom and yellow pollen coated the world, and Hester had known that everything had changed. Her last words to Morgan that night had been, "Daphne can't know about this," as he'd pulled her in for a goodnight kiss.

Up until then, it had been Daphne and Hester against the world, united and alone. Meeting Morgan—meeting anyone—felt like a betrayal. Hester knew already that Morgan would understand this better than anyone.

Now, as the sun rose, and light filtered into the tiny room at the inn, she touched Morgan's cheek and brushed red hair from his eyes.

Things had changed again.

When Morgan woke, it took him a moment to remember where he was, or why Kate and another child were asleep beside him in a strange bed. Sun shone through thin drapes, lighting up a small room decorated with antique furniture. In an instant, he remembered the drive to Maine and the late-night boat ride to the island. He remembered spending most of the night feeling the roll of the surf beneath his feet before falling into a deep, dreamless sleep, and he remembered listening to Hester breathe beside him and wondering whether she'd fallen asleep, or whether she was faking it to hold off their inevitable fight. He sat up.

As usual, Hester had taken the opportunity to escape.

He carefully rolled off the bed to avoid waking the children and slipped into the hallway bathroom, where he splashed water on his face and tried to prepare himself. He and Hester would have it out. He'd take his lumps and every insult she hurled at him, and she'd take what he threw at her, and in the end they'd survive this, like they'd survived it all. That much he believed.

He found her sitting on the porch in a rocking chair, staring out to sea, and he suspected she'd heard him coming and dreaded the conversation as much as he did. Part of him wanted her to feel it all, to believe that everything might not work out in the end. He wanted her to feel a fraction of what had coursed through him yesterday when he'd thought that she may have finally left. He wanted her to worry. He gave her a moment, pretending to appreciate the landscape, to breathe in the fresh, salted air, to listen. Then he stretched and let out a long, exaggerated sigh.

"Bakery's closed," she said. "No coffee either. At least they have Charleston Chews at the General Store."

"Where's Waffles?" Morgan asked.

"I don't know," Hester said.

"She wanders," he said. "She's a hound. We'll never find her now."

"We're on an island with no cars," Hester said. "In a place where people watch out for one another. Of all the things to worry about, for once Waffles isn't one of them. Where's Kate?"

"Upstairs. Asleep."

"Did you leave her alone?"

He heard a hint of panic in her voice, and it was all he could do not to snap, to tell her to quit it, that she couldn't protect Kate from everything and everyone, and that if she tried, she'd lose. Then he thought, *Why not?* He'd played nice for long enough, and it hadn't gotten him anywhere. "I left her upstairs asleep in a queen-sized bed," he said. "The same kind of bed she sleeps in at home. And she's fine. What's going to happen to her?"

"Anything could happen. She could fall out of bed and hit her head. She could wake up and wonder where we are. She's in a strange place. She could get kidnapped."

"See that shovel over there, the one leaning against the shed?" Morgan said. "If I hear anyone, anyone at all, I'll bash the motherfucker's brains in."

"Don't swear," Hester said. "It doesn't come naturally. You wouldn't do that. Ever."

"I would, actually, if I thought there was any real danger. I'd protect you, Kate, Waffles, all three of you from anything I could. I'd even protect that other kid."

"Oliver," Hester said.

"Who is he anyway?"

"It's a long story."

"Well, I'd even protect Oliver. I sometimes wonder if you understand that about me. But right now, I don't think there's any danger. Do you?"

Hester leaned forward and rubbed her eyes. "There's danger everywhere."

Morgan didn't know what to say, just as he hadn't known what to say since he'd seen Hester in that hospital bed all those months ago, her jaw wired shut, her eye black, her body nearly broken. He hadn't known what to say when she'd come home from the hospital either, so he'd taken that sledgehammer to the wall behind his closet in a show of brute masculinity while she'd watched, her every movement telling him to stop while her mouth told him it was what she wanted. And he hadn't known what to say when he discovered her first lie, that day a week and a half earlier when he ran into her boss, Kevin, and Kevin mentioned that Hester hadn't been to work in a month and that they missed her.

In their life—their life "before"—things with Hester had been easy. Not perfect, but easy. Now that they weren't, Morgan wondered if he had it in him to fix them. A part of him wanted to take her hand and pretend that the last forty-eight hours had never happened, to let her off the hook, to not only ignore that the intervention had happened but to tell himself it hadn't been necessary all along, that Prachi and Angela, even Jamie, hadn't insisted that he needed to do it, that he needed to take a stand. "Why did you come here?" he finally asked.

Hester took a deep breath and answered in one long exhale. "Because Daphne asked me to."

"Did she ask you to come alone?"

"She didn't say one way or the other. She wrote that she needed me."

"Okay," Morgan said. "Tell me what you know," and he listened as Hester told him about "Annie," and the decrepit house she'd lived in, and about finding Trey Pelletier's body on the beach. She also told him about the two missing boys.

"Missing children," Morgan said.

"Two of them," Hester said. "Oliver. The boy upstairs. He went missing on July Fourth. Another one went missing the day before yesterday."

Morgan could feel the fury he'd managed to keep at a simmer begin to boil over. "Two missing four-year-olds?" he said.

"They turned up safe and sound," Hester said.

The words spilled out on their own. "You do this on purpose," Morgan said. "All this lying to me and creating danger where none exists. And it doesn't even make any sense. The stupid, stupid choices you make. I mean, you won't bring Kate to a daycare center that's five minutes from your work, but now you bring her to an island the size of a postage stamp where two children have already gone missing, and you decide it's a good idea to import a third? Why not put a sign on her back that says *Take Me!*?"

"Oh, no," Hester said, shaking her head. "We're not doing this. Not today."

"Yeah, we are," Morgan said. "You left our house in the middle of the night without bothering to return the thirty or so texts that I sent. I had no idea where you were. And you left to find *my* long-lost sister. As far as you knew, there was still an Amber Alert out when you got on that ferry. Why can't you mind your own fucking business? You nearly got Kate kidnapped once already."

Hester stood, walked into the garden, and turned on Morgan. "You didn't get that one quite right," she said. "I *did* get her kidnapped, and don't ever, ever forget it. And it was all my fault. Do you think that taking a sledgehammer to a wall undoes any of that? Or planning interventions? Do you think any of it will protect Kate from this awful, awful world? And do you want to know how to swear? You do it like this: You are a fucking, fucking fuckface!"

"Excuse me."

Morgan froze at the sound of someone else's voice. He was standing on the porch, leaning forward, jabbing an index finger at Hester, his face bright red as he prepared to unleash a tirade of his own swears. But he glanced toward the source of the voice and saw a deputy who'd let himself in through the garden gate with Waffles in tow.

"Is this dog yours?" the deputy asked.

Hester swept a lock of black hair from her mouth and pushed her glasses up her nose. When she turned to the deputy, she had the decency to look chagrined. "How did you know?"

The deputy thumbed the tag on the dog's collar with Hester's contact info on it. "Aren't too many Hesters around these days," he said. "He was getting into the garbage by the community center. We have leash laws." The deputy laughed. "Believe it or not. But don't worry. Just watch him, okay?"

"Her," Morgan said, putting his hand out so that Waffles trotted to him. He took a treat from his pocket and held it over her nose till she lay down. "She's a female."

Hester glanced from Morgan to the cop. "This is my husband," she said.

A lie.

She lied because it was easier than the truth, or at least that's what Morgan told himself, and it bothered Morgan more than he wanted to admit.

"Morgan," Hester said. "This is Rory. He's the local deputy."

"It looks like you were in the middle of something," Rory said. He caught Hester's eye. "Everything okay?"

"We're fine," Hester said. "Morgan's mad at me, and I deserve it. I was an asshole. But we yell at each other all the time."

"Nothing else? Do you need me to stay?" he asked in a way that made Morgan feel guilty.

"Not at all," Hester said. "It's not that kind of fight." When Rory still wouldn't move, she added, "I know you're doing your job, and you're doing a good job by not leaving, but really, I am fine. This won't escalate. It never has, and it never will."

She took Morgan's hand, which only made him feel worse.

Rory put one foot on the porch and leaned over his knee. "Have you heard from your friend?"

"You'll be the first person I'll call when I do," Hester said. "Are you finally worried about her?"

"You must be Annie's brother," Rory said. "I recognize the hair."

"It's a dead giveaway," Morgan said. "Her name is Daphne."

"I keep forgetting," Rory said. "But call if you need anything," he added as he backed out of the garden.

"Have you seen Lydia?" Hester asked. "I still have her kid. Don't you think it's weird that *she* vanished too?"

"She's around. I'll send her your way," Rory said.

As the deputy left, Hester sat back in the rocking chair and sighed. "I keep thinking about Lydia and everything she has to sort out now. Everything she needs to do." She glanced at Morgan, a trace of a smile starting. "I'm glad I didn't find your body yesterday, even if I do want to kill you right now."

Morgan squeezed her hand. "I want to kill you too," he said. "And I'm pissed off, though I appreciate the third-party acknowledgment of your own assholeness. I'm pissed in a way that means I'll remember this for a long, long time. Like, forgive but never forget pissed off. Like, we *will* get Kate back to school and you back to work. As in, we need to deal with it tonight, not tomorrow. Not next week."

"I do these things to be secretive and manipulative," Hester said. "It's what you love about me."

Morgan leaned across the rocking chair and kissed Hester's cheek. Waffles dashed around the perennial garden. She found a fallen tree limb three times her size and tore at it with a frenzy. "In a month," Morgan said, "winter will probably be here. This whole garden will be unrecognizable."

"Everything will be unrecognizable if Daphne comes home," Hester said.

Morgan knew how much Hester cared for Daphne, and that she also dreaded his sister's return and what it would mean for Kate. Unlike Hester, he couldn't ever weigh one loyalty against another.

"Where else has Daphne been this last year?" Morgan asked.

"Portland, before here. That's as much as I know."

"We could swing through there on the way home," he said, glancing at his phone. It was 8:15, and the morning ferry to the mainland left at 9 a.m. They'd need to hurry or be stuck here till afternoon.

"She may be there," Hester said, and paused before adding, "And she may still be here."

It took a moment for the implication to sink in. "You are not staying," Morgan said. "Not in a million years. Not in a billion."

"Someone has to," Hester said. "Think about it. It's what makes sense. What if she's off hiding out somewhere? What if something happened during the storm and she's hurt? Besides, I did find the body. They want me to stick around."

"Then I'm staying too."

"You need to see if you can find Daphne in Portland. We need to split up and cover as much ground as we possibly can. You should go now. You'll want as much of the day as possible."

"There is no way, no way in hell I'm leaving you here," Morgan said, but he could hear himself losing in his own voice. Still, he scrolled through the contacts on his phone. When Hester asked who he was calling, he shushed her.

"Don't shush me," she said.

"I found her," he said into the phone. "Here, you talk to her."

Hester took the phone, glanced at Angela White's name on the screen, and strolled away through the garden, seeming to mostly listen for the next few moments. When she came back, she handed the phone to Morgan. "Angela has today and tomorrow off," she said. "She's watching *Real Housewives*, but she'll meet you in Portland. Meanwhile, I'll hang out on the porch here. I'll probably die of boredom, but someone has to be here if that redhead decides to show up."

Out in the harbor, the ferry blew its horn.

Morgan narrowed his eyes. "You have to call and tell me if you get any news. Any news at all. Or no news. No secrets."

"Same to you," Hester said. "This'll only work if we talk to each other."

"Agreed. And one more thing. I'm taking Kate with me."

"Nope," Hester said. "She's staying with me."

"You're on an island in the middle of nowhere, with a murderer and at least two if not three missing persons cases. And you have Oliver to deal with too. Don't you think she'll be safer with me?"

Hester had the decency not to answer.

"I'm not debating this," Morgan said. "Dog, kid, with me. You, on the porch, waiting, and I'll meet you in Boothbay Harbor tonight when the last ferry comes in. That's the only way you're getting rid of me."

"I can't," Hester said.

"What's the worst thing that could happen?"

"You lose her at the park. I know you do."

"Angela will be there to keep me in line. She's a police detective! Waffles will be there too."

Hester fought off tears. "What if there's another storm?"

"But there won't be," Morgan said. "And if there is, she'll be with me, and I'll call you, and we'll ride out the storm together. Remember when Kate came to stay with us and all you wanted was a day to yourself? I'm giving you one."

"But I don't want it anymore!"

Morgan took her hands in his and pulled her in. As much as he wanted to, he couldn't help her. When they found Daphne, Kate would be hers again, and Hester would have plenty of time on her own. It was the only way it could be. They stood on the porch for another five minutes till Hester's sobbing subsided. Morgan didn't know how to make this pain end, and as much as he wanted to, he wondered if it ever would. Finally, without a word, Hester put Waffles on a leash, went into the B and B, got Kate and Oliver out of bed and dressed, and walked down to the ferry, where passengers had already begun to disembark. A state trooper watched the few passengers waiting to leave, asking them to leave their names and phone numbers. "In case we need to follow up on anything," the trooper said.

Morgan jotted down his information. Hester handed him Waffles's leash and kissed him on the cheek while Kate and Oliver said their goodbyes and promised to FaceTime each other. "I'll see you in a few hours," Hester said, crouching to let the dog lap at her face. "You need to go."

"Say goodbye to Aunt Hester," Morgan said to Kate.

"Bye, Aunt Hester," Kate said, skipping along a few steps.

"Go," Hester said, shortly. "Now."

Morgan turned and left without another word, holding Kate's hand as they crossed the gangway. He understood Hester better than anyone else in the world, even better than Daphne, and he knew that this decision had broken her in a way that he hoped would help her heal stronger than before. He found a spot on the upper deck, lifting Kate onto his hip and standing at the railing while the crew untied the lines. Down below, Hester's feet were rooted to the ground, her hands balled up in fists, Oliver at her side. Morgan could see her using every bit of resolve to keep herself from leaping across the water as the ferry pulled from the pier. "Wave to Aunt Hester," he said to Kate.

"Bye!" Kate shouted, waving with her whole body.

Waffles sat back and bayed. And Morgan waved too. Hester didn't wave back.

CHAPTER 18

The state police had pulled the plywood covering from most of the windows at the Victorian, but Rory still felt as though he needed a hazmat suit when he arrived and walked into the stench. It smelled like a forest of dead creatures rotting in the walls. Upstairs, he found Barb Kelley in Annie's room. "What a dump!" she said. "You must keep this place hidden from the summer folks, or else they wouldn't come back."

She'd tied her hair back with a teal-colored scrunchie and wore white Keds and a pink sweatshirt with puff paint that read SHOP AHOY! "How often do you come out here?" she asked.

"Not often," Rory said. He tried to squash the defensiveness in his voice, which somehow even made it worse. "I mean, do *you* follow up on every drug call you get? Besides, most of the stuff on the island is legal, prescription. Pills. I haven't seen anything like heroin."

"Listen," Barb said. "I'm asking because I need to know the answer, not because I'm trying to get you fired or reprimanded, though I do need to ask about that little incident between you and Vaughn Roberts yesterday. What was going on between the two of you?"

"Oh, Vaughn and I are just . . . we've known each other too long. We like each other and hate each other at the same time."

"Like brothers, then?" Barb asked.

"Nothing like brothers."

"You're holding something back," Barb said. "Something you're not telling me. Spill." She folded her arms across her chest. "And I'll warn you, it's a little after nine in the morning? We can stand here till nightfall. I can outwait anyone and everyone."

Rory caught himself rolling his eyes. "You make me feel like a teenager," he said.

"It's my super power."

"Fine," Rory said, telling Barb what he'd seen happen between Lydia and Vaughn in the ravine and the way Trey had reacted.

"Sweetie," Barb said. The smile. "That would have been good to know yesterday when that girl found the body. And it would have been good to know when that wifey came in to make her statement. It tells me something that she didn't bring it up herself. Now we'll need to pick up Lydia Pelletier again and get her to spill."

"Maybe it would have come up if I'd sat in on the interview."

When Lydia had come by the community center the night before, Barb had sent Rory home. When he'd tried to argue, she'd said, "We both know having you sit in on this isn't a good idea."

Now she looked Rory right in the eye. "Any other secrets?"

Rory had plenty of secrets. One was that after Lydia had finished talking to Barb, she'd come to him, pounding on his door. He hadn't asked what she'd told Barb, and she hadn't mentioned Pete. He let her into the house, and she collapsed on his bed, fully clothed. He sat in a chair beside her all night, and they grieved in silence. In the morning, he made her coffee and they sat at the kitchen table. When the call came in from Barb asking him to meet her here, he left Lydia at his house, a stream of morning light shining on her sleepy face.

It had been the best night of his life. The best morning too.

"I'll let you know if I think of anything else," he said to Barb.

"If you do," Barb said, "make sure it comes out of your mouth and into my ear."

"Yes, ma'am."

Rory surveyed the room. Annie had done her best to make the space her own. The room was clean, much cleaner than any other part of the house. And the bed, surrounded by furniture, was like a sad island of safety.

Barb lifted one corner of the mattress. Rory took the other side, and they flipped it, but nothing was underneath. A black knapsack leaned against the wall. In it, Rory found a dead burner phone and a wad of money stuffed into an interior pocket. "I'm surprised no one's stolen this," he said. "We should charge this phone up. See what's on it."

Barb nodded toward the bureaus. "Start on that end, and I'll start on this one."

Most of the bureaus were empty, with swollen drawers that groaned when they opened, but a few minutes in, Barb said, "Yuck," and lifted a white towel crusted over with a yellowish substance. "I'm pretty certain that was spew," she said, dropping it into an evidence bag.

Rory pictured Annie, on this mattress, in this house, pawing at another human being while surrounded by strangers and filth and couldn't help but have a little sympathy for the woman. In another drawer, he found a pile of clothing, and in another a small stash of books. When he flipped through a dog-eared copy of *Jane Eyre*, a locket of thin baby hair fell out.

"Probably that girl's," Barb said. "Her daughter."

She placed it in an evidence bag and marked where they'd found it. Rory flipped through another book, and a coffee card from Doughnuts and Pies fell out. It had eight cups checked off. "Two to go," Rory said, "and she'll have a free cup."

"Let's make sure she gets it," Barb said as her phone rang.

She answered and walked into the hallway, only to return a moment later. "That was the medical examiner. There wasn't much trace evidence on the body, but guess the cause of death."

"Wasn't it obvious?" Rory asked. "He had a knife in his back."

"So guess," Barb said, and waited.

When Rory started to say, "Stabbing?" she seemed to snatch the word right out of his throat and finish it for him. "Stabbing!" she said. "You'd think that was right, and if it was, I could have told you that on my own. But there's a reason we paid to bring the good ol' doctor out here by helicopter. I'll give you one more guess."

"Drowning?" Rory said.

"That would be a good one, too! And that would have been my second guess. But it's wrong. I'll give it to you because you won't get it, even if I gave you a hundred guesses. But when I do, you have to tell me on a scale from one to ten how surprised you are. Deal?"

"Deal," Rory said.

"Overdose! Fentanyl."

"The same shit that showed up in Portland," Rory said.

And the same shit that probably killed Pete.

"You got it! And I'll take that as a ten. And it keeps this house right in the middle of things."

Rory took a step into the room. The whole building felt as if it might collapse around them. "Had Trey been using?" he asked.

"Good question!" Barb said. "And the answer is . . . undetermined, at least according to the doc. He says that there aren't any injection sites but that there are lots of ways to take drugs. Smoking. Snorting. You know, the usual, and they'll need to run more tests. Have *you* noticed anything unusual?"

"Just Trey being a jerk," Rory said.

"Trey being a jerk is par for the course," Barb said. "Or was, I should say. You didn't like him, did you?"

"I hated him, but that's between you and me."

"Don't worry, your secret's safe." And she smiled.

Rory should have kept the secret to himself.

Barb paced around the room. "What can you tell me about this house, besides that it stinks?"

"It's been abandoned for as long as I can remember," Rory said. "When I was a kid, we thought the house was haunted and would torture the summer kids by bringing them out here and daring them to go inside on their own. Then we'd find ways to scare them."

"Who's 'we'?"

"Me, Lydia, Vaughn."

"The three of you show up together a lot."

"So?"

"You said it yourself. The prime suspect is the wife."

"I thought the prime suspect was Daphne."

"Maybe she is. But you still need to be objective."

Rory thought about Lydia, asleep, her breathing steady, her arms splayed across the bedspread. He could have touched her. But he'd never have done that, not without permission. He was her protector.

"I'll do my best," he said. This time he knew enough to lie.

"I'll be watching," Barb said as Nate came to the door. "Come downstairs," she added. "We're talking to Frankie Sullivan again, and I need my bad cop."

They descended the backstairs to where Frankie sat on a chair with Ethan perched on her knee. Nate hovered by the back door. Barb produced a candy bar from her pocket. "You mind?" she asked Frankie, who shook her head.

Ethan took the chocolate bar and ripped the wrapper off, eating it like someone might steal it from him.

"Has he had breakfast?" Barb asked.

"Yes," Frankie snapped.

"Good, just checking."

"When can we leave?"

"You can go whenever you want, really," Barb said,

taking a chair and sitting beside her. "As long as you tell me where. But it'd be great if you could stick around another day, maybe two."

"Whatever."

"I'll take that as a yes. Where do you think you'll go?"

"Probably back to Ohio. I don't know where else I'd go. Certainly not to Portland."

"Is Ohio where you started taking drugs?"

Frankie glared at her. "I don't take drugs."

"Sweetie, only the truth, okay?" Barb said. "And let's start with this: Had you ever met Trey Pelletier before you came here?"

"Why would I have?"

"That's not an answer," Barb said. "And he was a state cop, and you, from what I can see and despite what you claim, are a junkie. It's not out of the realm of possibility that you might run across each other."

Ethan tugged on Frankie's sleeve. "Mommy?" he said.

"What is it, sweetie?" she asked.

"Could Thomas take us away?"

"I could use a minute," Frankie said.

"For what?" Barb asked.

"The bathroom."

"Stay put. You can shoot up or snort or whatever you do after we're done." Barb waved Nate over. "Take the boy outside, would you? Find that train and play with him."

"Tank engine!" Ethan said.

Frankie seemed reluctant to give up Ethan and watched as the officer walked out through the back door.

"He seems like a good kid," Barb said. "One who should have a chance, right? Tell me, did you know

Detective Pelletier? Had you ever run into him in Portland or here?"

"I'd seen him around," Frankie said.

"And what about other people in the house here," Barb asked. "What about your brother? Seth, right? Where is he anyway?"

"He'll show up."

"He'd better. And I know he's not your brother, so what is he to you?"

"He takes care of me," Frankie said with a shrug. "He watches us. Me and Ethan."

"Did he take care of Trey for you?"

"No!" Frankie said with as much force as Rory imagined she could muster. "I don't know," she added with a sigh.

"Listen to me," Barb said. "I want to make sure you understand what's going on here. We have a dead cop. That's a big deal. And we have a shipment of drugs that's making its way across Maine. That's a big deal. A woman who lived in this house with you has disappeared, and that's a big deal. And your son disappeared for nearly twenty-four hours and showed up on your back step, which, to me, sounds like someone may have been sending you a warning. That's the biggest deal of all, because somehow I bet all of this is connected to you and this mysterious friend you have wandering around this island." Barb turned to Rory. "Have you seen this guy?"

"He was gone when I came to pick him up. I've only heard his name."

"If you don't start talking," Barb said to Frankie, "I'll start making those connections myself, and it won't be good for you or your son. Bottom line is, we need to find your friend and we need the truth. And that means now, not next week."

Frankie sank into herself right before Rory's eyes. Barb was better at bad cop than she gave herself credit for. "I've only been here a few weeks," Frankie mumbled. "Annie was here much longer."

"Did Annie know Trey?" Rory asked.

"I don't know Annie," Frankie said. "I don't know anyone!"

"You know Seth," Barb said. "And he showed up out of the blue on the day your son went missing. That's what you told me. Walk me through that day again."

"I don't remember it."

"It was two days ago. You got up. What happened then?"

"I looked for Ethan."

"What time was it."

"I don't know. Maybe ten, eleven."

"Eleven o'clock," Barb said. "Was Ethan here?"

"I looked for him," Frankie said.

Barb flipped back through her notebook. She sat up, getting right into Frankie's face. "Do you remember the panic?" she asked. "Last time I talked to you, you told me that you had lunch and put Ethan down for a nap. It says right here that you had peanut butter." Barb jabbed a finger at her notes. "But now, are you saying Ethan wasn't around when you woke up? At eleven in the morning? Because you didn't *panic* till almost four o'clock."

"I thought he wandered off." Frankie looked at Rory. "You said . . ."

"Kids wander off," Rory said. "They do it all the time."

"So," Barb said. "Let me get back to my question. If you thought Ethan wandered off, what made you *panic*? What didn't you know? Or what did you know that made you panic?"

Frankie leaned forward and rubbed her temple. "I'll need a deal," she said.

"We'll talk deals later," Barb said. "Right now, you need to spill."

"I can't."

"Arrest her," Barb said to Rory. "For child endangerment. And call family services. We'll have Ethan in foster care by this afternoon. It's actually a relief to say that."

Rory reached for his handcuffs.

"I've been running drugs," Frankie said quickly. "All over Maine."

"Big surprise," Rory said, but Barb shot him a glare that told him to shut up.

"What else?" she asked.

"Three weeks ago, I got pulled over," Frankie said. "I had balloons in my mouth. I swallowed them, like I'm supposed to, but the cops took me in anyway. And it turned out they weren't cops, they were with the DEA. They kept threatening me, telling me I'd go to jail for an eternity or I could turn state's evidence. So I played along."

"You turned state's evidence?" Barb asked.

"Nope." Frankie stared off. "Believe it or not, I'm not a fucking idiot. They didn't have anything to hold me on. They knew it, and I knew it too. The minute they released me, I got Ethan, took the ferry here, and hid out. I've been here ever since. And I thought it was the end of the world. I thought no one would ever find me here."

Barb leaned forward and spoke slowly and softly. "What. Made. You. Panic?"

Frankie closed her eyes. "Ethan disappeared. And Seth showed up."

"And who is Seth?"

"I said, I need a deal."

"Only the DA can cut a deal. But I can still arrest you and send your kid to foster care."

"Seth is who they wanted me to turn on," Frankie said.

"You should have told us this when Ethan disappeared."

"He had what I needed," Frankie said, her shoulders slumped.

"And you needed what?" Rory said, stepping toward the woman. He despised her. He couldn't wait to slap cuffs on her. "Another hit?"

"Back off," Barb said, her voice barely a whisper. "Frankie," she added. "Did Seth know Annie? Does he have anything to do with where she went?"

"I don't know," Frankie said.

"Where is he now?" Rory asked.

When Frankie didn't answer, Barb called Nate into the kitchen. "Get a description of this guy Seth and start looking for him. I need everyone on this. And don't let her out of your sight."

CHAPTER 19

Hester watched from the pier till the ferry disappeared. If she could have, she'd have leapt into the ocean and swum after it. Instead, she texted Morgan: **Everything okay?**

A moment later, he sent a photo of Kate sitting abovedeck, wearing his sunglasses and posing with Sebastian and Waffles. Hester texted him again.

Don't let her near the rail. And make sure she wears a hat. And sunscreen. The sun is brighter than you think.

She sounded like a harpy, and she knew it.

Will do!

Morgan had the decency to respond, and Hester somehow found the willpower to put the phone in her pocket and start to move. "Ready?" she said to Oliver.

He saluted the state trooper and dashed ahead. At least watching him distracted Hester from looking around, listening, and searching for Kate.

At the inn, she found Lydia sitting in the front room, staring out the window. "You're back," Hester said.

Lydia looked up, and it seemed to take a moment for

her to focus. Then she put out her arms, and Oliver ran to her. She held him tight till he squirmed away.

"We saw seventy-seven ladybugs," he said.

"Seventy-seven!" Lydia said. "See if you can find seventeen more in the garden."

"Where's Daddy?"

Lydia paused. "I'm not sure," she said.

Oliver kissed her on the cheek and dashed out the front door. Lydia watched after him, gripping a mug in both hands. "I thought I saw you on the pier," she said. "I wondered if you'd left without settling up."

"I couldn't really leave if I still had your kid," Hester said. "Where have you been, anyway?"

"I was hiding from the grieving masses. Plus I had to talk to Barb. Detective Kelley."

"What did she ask you?"

"Oh, where I was, what I was doing. If I had a reason to stab my husband in the back. She probably thinks I did this. Isn't the wife always the prime suspect?"

"If you believe what you see on TV," Hester said, wondering how much Lydia had actually told the cops. "I'll be here for the day, but I can check out now if that's easier."

"Take your time," Lydia said, raising the mug in a toast. "I've got nothing much to do. Nothing but planning funerals and writing obituaries."

"I'm sorry for everything," Hester said. "For your loss."

"Don't do that," Lydia said. "I'm sorry I left Oliver with you."

Hester perched on the edge of a chair. "I hate kids,"

she said. "But for some reason I wind up with other people's. I put the casseroles in the fridge."

"Thanks. Did you figure out where Annie went?"

"Not yet, but I'll be on the ferry this afternoon no matter what."

"Rory told me you and your husband were fighting when he came by this morning," Lydia said. "I didn't even know your husband was here."

"There isn't much that you don't tell each other around here, is there? It feels like every time I move, it gets reported back to me. But Morgan and I? We fight and make up. I think it sounded uglier than it was."

"Where'd he go?"

"To the mainland. We're looking for Da . . . for Annie."

A shadow passed over Lydia's face. "Oh, I heard about the fake name too. I knew there was something off about Annie, something not to trust."

"Daphne's complicated," Hester said. "But she's good, at the core."

"I don't know if I saw the good or the bad. But I saw something." Lydia held up the mug. "This isn't coffee, you know. Want some? I hate to drink alone."

It was early, even for Hester. "Is there somewhere I could make actual coffee?"

Lydia waved Hester through the connecting door to the bakery. "Rory told me your husband is good looking," she said as she put the coffee on to brew. "Handsome."

Hester was so used to seeing Morgan that she didn't think of him as anything anymore, but she supposed he was handsome in his own pasty, redheaded way. How could she have taken that attraction for granted?

"Coffee'll be a minute or two," Lydia said. "I'll bake off some scones too."

She turned on one of the ovens to preheat and pulled a half tray of chocolate-chip scones from the freezer. When the coffee finished, she poured two mugs.

"Put in as much sugar as you think possible. Then add one more," Hester said. "Morgan says it'll give me diabetes."

"Annie likes it sweet too," Lydia said. "Daphne, I mean."

The oven beeped, and she slid the half tray in. Hester tried her coffee, added two more sugars, and joined her at a café table.

"I went to the crime scene yesterday," Lydia said. "But can you tell me what happened? What you saw?"

"Are you sure you want to hear it?"

"I do," Lydia said, closing her eyes for a moment. "More than you know."

Hester told her about walking out to the lighthouse and finding the door kicked in.

"It's usually teenagers who do that," Lydia said. "I'm pretty certain Rory and I kicked in that door a few times ourselves."

"There was some graffiti spray painted on rocks."

"There usually is," Lydia said.

Hester told her the rest of the story too, though omitted that she'd seen Vaughn with his dog. Lydia probably already knew that too though. When Hester finally got to the part where she found Trey's body, Lydia inhaled sharply.

"Should I stop?"

"No," Lydia said. "If you don't tell me, I'll sit around imagining something even worse."

Hester understood that, so she tried to remember every detail, to keep Lydia from spiraling after the truth. "He was facedown on the sand," she said. "His feet were over the waterline, so when the surf rolled in, half his body would lift. At first, I thought I'd found someone's lost coat, but I saw his hair. And one of his hands."

"What about the knife? What did it look like?"

Hester would never forget the knife. She pictured it, the blue hilt sticking out of Trey's back. She hadn't wanted to look at it as she'd approached the body and felt for a pulse.

"The hilt, what color was it?"

"Why?"

"There are a lot of knives around here. I'm curious whose it might be."

"Ask the police," Hester said, taking a long sip of her coffee. "Gossip spreads quickly, but you know that already. I heard something about you, about you and Vaughn. And I bet everyone else has heard it too, including the detective. Vaughn was at Cappy's last night, drunk off his ass. Did he find you later?"

Lydia closed her eyes and rubbed her temples. "I used to send Trey away," she said, softly. "Every week, he'd take the ferry to town and be gone for days. You never met him, but we could get a table at the best restaurant in Manhattan without having a reservation. He was that type of good looking. He was used to it too. He grew up in Bar Harbor, a working-class kid surrounded by privilege. He figured out early on that he could use his looks at the country club to get what he wanted. And it's not like I trusted him. I'd search his phone for text messages, look at his browser history, steam open his mail. That kind of thing. But he was careful. He was a cop. He was too good at his job for me to ever catch him in the act. But he had power, and he used it, however he could. It won't take long now for the rest of the secrets to come out. All of them."

"Did he know about you and Vaughn?"

Lydia answered with a shrug. "Not till the night of the storm. The truth is, I didn't really like Trey all that much, and he didn't like me, and we were probably headed toward a divorce, but we hadn't talked about it yet. I'm still sad that he's dead. Strange how that happens. But that night, I was glad he wound up seeing what he saw. He'd messed up one too many times."

"How?" Hester asked.

"It was why we were out in the storm in the first place. Have you met Frankie Sullivan? Did you see *her* on the beach when you found Trey?"

"That's who I was looking for."

"I bet you were," Lydia said. "And you should find out where she was. Have you noticed how much Oliver and Ethan look alike? I did. And that frumpy Detective Kelley's bound to notice too, if she hasn't already. I can't imagine it was a coincidence that both of Trey's sons went missing and returned without incident in the same summer. Can you?"

"Wait. What? Trey is, was, Ethan's father?"

"Yep."

The timer on the stove went off. Lydia yanked open the door and left the tray to cool on the aluminum counter right as Oliver dashed in through the bakery door. He held his palm over a clear plastic cup in which two ladybugs crawled. "That's two," Lydia said. "Fifteen to go."

Hester had assumed that Lydia and Vaughn and Trey had been at a crossroads when Trey had died, that something was ending so that something else could begin. Out with the old, in with the new, because if Hester were to cheat on Morgan, that's the only way it could work. But some people, she reminded herself, had more tolerance for the in-between.

"How long have you known?" Hester asked.

"Since the moment I saw Ethan's photo on that poster. I hadn't seen him in town, or if I had, I hadn't noticed him. It was why I gave in and let Trey see Vaughn touch me while we were in the ravine."

"Did Trey know you'd figured it out?"

"Maybe? Maybe not. We never talked again."

"You told all this to the detective, right?" Hester asked, and when Lydia shook her head, she added, "Well, you should. All of it. She should hear it from you."

"Yeah, maybe. Or you tell her. I don't care anymore." Lydia took Oliver's hand and headed toward the back door. "Come on," she said to him. "Let's let these girls fly free."

After Lydia and Oliver left, Hester poured another cup of coffee and ate two scones. She checked her phone. The ferry would be getting into Boothbay Harbor right about now, and she thought about texting Morgan, if only to be reminded of everything she took for granted every day and to update him on what she'd just learned. If Hester knew one thing, it was that Morgan, like her, would have the decency to leave before betraying her. It wasn't a romantic quality to have in a partner, but it was one she cherished.

She found a paperback and set up camp on the front porch, but after an hour of rereading the same page while thinking through everything Lydia had confessed and eating three more scones, she put the book aside and stared out over the water. She couldn't sit here doing nothing, no matter what she'd promised. She thought about heading to the Victorian to see what else she could learn from Frankie. But then, in the harbor, a boat rounded Bowman Island, and Hester recognized the black lab running across the deck. A few moments later, down on the pier, she found Vaughn in his slip hosing down the boat. Mindy ran with the stream, jumping from the deck to the dock and back again.

"Can your stomach handle a scone?" Hester asked, offering up a white paper bag. "Or are you still hung over from last night?"

Vaughn groaned and covered his face.

"Permission to come aboard?" Hester asked.

"Permission granted," Vaughn said, giving her a mock salute. "Apologies for anything and everything I said last night. I guess yesterday's bad news hit home more than I realized."

Or maybe he hadn't gotten what he wanted out of that bad news. "Good day on the water?" Hester asked.

"Made my quota, and that's as good as it gets."

Hester called the lab over. She scratched her ears, and the dog pressed into her thigh with her whole body.

"Heard your husband showed up last night," Vaughn said. "He hurled all over Chris Abbott's boat."

"I can't take a shit on this island without everyone hearing about it," Hester said.

Vaughn raised an eyebrow but didn't reply. Hester crossed the deck and peered into the gray water. The swells from the storm had gone, replaced with water as still as a lake. "Morgan went to Portland. You lived there, right? Did you know Daphne? Annie?"

"The first time I met her was two days ago," Vaughn said.

"How was she on the boat?"

"Followed directions," Vaughn said. "There isn't much more you can ask for from a sternman. Now that I get how much she was hiding, I can see how adept she was at keeping things to herself. She told me she grew up in Boston. I take it that was true?"

Mindy licked Hester's hand. "It's true," she said. "I'm worried about her. Really worried."

"I would be too," Vaughn said, the first person on the island to affirm Hester's concern.

"Your wife lives in Portland, right?" she asked. "Did Daphne know her?"

"Sophie and your friend have definitely not crossed paths," Vaughn said. "Sophie doesn't know people like Annie even exist. But for what it's worth, here's my story. I got married right out of college. My wife has a ton of money, and she got bored being married to a lobsterman, and I got bored talking stocks at the yacht club. Pretty simple. In the end, she wanted me to honor every clause of the prenup her daddy insisted on when we were madly in love, and I was only too happy to oblige. By then I didn't have the money I'd need for a lawyer, which is how they get you anyway. Now she's kind enough to rent me this boat. But if your boyfriend starts asking questions, it'll cause me trouble." He paused. "Have you talked to Lydia today?"

"Just now," Hester said. "She finally showed up."

"Any idea where she went?"

Apparently, she hadn't been with Vaughn. "I didn't ask," Hester said.

Vaughn stripped off his yellow gloves, one at a time. He tossed them onto the deck and took one step toward Hester. "I did my own research," he said. "You're nosy. And it gets you in trouble. Watch yourself. Don't get in trouble again."

"I don't like being threatened," Hester said.

"I'm not threatening you," Vaughn said. "I'm telling you to be careful, especially if you're wandering around the island asking questions. You might talk to the wrong person."

"Thanks for the warning," Hester said.

She leapt from the boat to the dock. As she retreated up the ramp, she felt Vaughn's glare following her. She checked the reception on her phone and texted Angela White with Sophie Roberts's name. The text failed to send the first two times she tried, but when she moved closer to the General Store, it went though.

A few moments later, Vaughn left the boat and headed into the trees. Hester couldn't help herself. She followed him.

When it came to finding missing people, Morgan was hopeless. Unlike Hester, his more fearless partner, he either didn't ask the right questions or didn't ask the questions at all, withering under the threat of speaking to a stranger. Where Hester would have rushed right in, probing and peeling away layers from a secret, Morgan believed it was best to leave well enough alone. In the time since he and Kate had arrived in Portland, they'd managed to have French fries cooked in duck fat, followed by ice cream. They'd shopped for olive oil. They'd debated whether they'd like living on an island (Kate: yes; Morgan: no). Now they stood in line at a doughnut shop, but they hadn't asked a single person a single question about Daphne.

"Don't tell your aunt Hester," Morgan said to Kate.

"Don't tell Aunt Hester," Kate said to Waffles. "Don't tell Uncle Morgan."

"You're too smart for your own good," Morgan said.

"Did Mommy take Oxy?" Kate asked, her words skipping along like a stone on water. "Ethan's mommy snorts Oxy."

"Where did you hear that?" Morgan asked.

"Oliver told me," Kate said. "What's snorts?"

"It's like when you blow your nose," Morgan said, and he could see Kate reasoning her way through it.

"What's Oxy?" Kate asked a moment later.

"A pill."

"Ethan's mommy blows pills out of her nose?"

Kate laughed at the image, and Morgan wrestled with what to say, whether to take the easy route and let her believe the image or to correct her and suffer the consequences. No matter what he said, Kate would go to daycare tomorrow for the first time in weeks and tell the other kids all she knew about snorting. He was saved from the predicament, though, when Angela White pulled up along the curb in her tan-colored minivan

"Get in," she said. "Car seat's in the back."

Once they'd pulled away, Morgan admitted he hadn't gotten very far with the search.

"Who cares," Angela said. "Spill what you know. And I mean all of it."

There was something about Angela—maybe it was because she was a cop, or maybe it was because she was kind and stuck with Morgan during the darkest of times, when she'd barely known him—but she made him want to bare his soul. He told her how angry he'd been yesterday as he'd driven up the coast and night fell. He told her that he'd truly believed that he'd see his sister again when he arrived on the island, that she'd scowl at him and he'd ask her where she'd been, and she'd tell him to mind his own goddamn business, and it would be like when they were kids, when they fought over anything and everything, but still defended each other at home, at school, against the world.

"How are *you* doing?" Angela asked. "We know our girl Hester is all types of screwed up, but how are you?"

No one had asked Morgan that question, not since Daphne had left, not since Hester's kidnapping over the winter. "Nothing's quite working out right now," he said.

"That's an understatement," Angela said. "I would say more that everything's wrong. It's all Prachi and I talk about, and we're not really even friends, but we both love Hester and worry about her and see how much she's hurting."

"Hester would do anything for my sister," Morgan said.

"Even lie?"

"Especially lie. It's what they do best."

"Is she lying now?"

"I don't know," he said.

They rode in silence for a few moments, till Angela glanced in the rearview mirror at Kate and whispered.

"What will you do if you-know-who comes to Somerville?"

"We'll go back to the way things were," Morgan said. "What other choice is there?"

"There are always choices," Angela said as she eased her car onto the bridge to South Portland, a beachy enclave to the city. "Even if they aren't always easy. Like the intervention the other night. That wasn't an easy choice, but it was the right one, even if it was a disaster. Now we can all talk about what's happening. It's in the open, and it's our shared truth."

Morgan knew that Angela was right. In his heart he did, at least.

"Let me tell you what I found out," Angela said. "We're about to talk to Sophie Roberts, nee Johnson. The Johnsons are a prominent family here in town. Her mother was mayor for two terms, and her father runs a major fishing conglomerate. Until last year, Sophie was married to Vaughn Roberts, a lobsterman living on the island. According to Hester, Vaughn's been having an affair with Lydia Pelletier. We're not sure whether the end of Vaughn and Sophie's marriage had anything to do with the Pelletiers, but we'll find out."

Angela pulled up a stately driveway lined with hydrangeas that had begun to lose their blue color and drop their leaves with the season. At the end of the driveway, an enormous white house perched on the edge of a cliff. Angela parked and told Morgan to sit tight for a moment. He watched from the van as she took out her badge and flashed it to the woman who answered the front door. They exchanged what seemed like pleasantries till Angela waved Morgan toward her. The woman moved her knee, and two golden retrievers dashed out the front door and wrestled across the seashell driveway. Morgan opened the rear door, and Waffles leapt into the fray, the three dogs running in tandem across the perfectly manicured lawn. He lifted Kate from the car seat and approached the elegant front door.

Sophie Johnson looked to be in her early thirties. While she wore expensive yoga pants and had clearly spent money on her hair, she also had the look of a woman who could haul in a tuna. Her skin was freckled from plenty of sun, and a tiny tattoo poked from beneath her t-shirt sleeve.

"Vaughn's not a horrible person," she said to Angela, clearly mid-conversation. "But I really don't want to hear from him either."

"Are you two in touch?" Angela asked.

"Not really," Sophie said. "Only when something happens with the boat. I rent it to him for a dollar a year, which gets my dad going. But what else can I do?"

"I've been there," Angela said. "Divorce sucks."

"I try to be Zen about it, but don't always succeed." Sophie brushed her hair behind her ears and called to her dogs, who trotted over with Waffles at their heels.

"What happened?" Angela asked.

"Nothing anyone hasn't heard a thousand times before," Sophie said. "There was a third party in our marriage, a flame of Vaughn's. Vaughn would say my dad was a fourth, but I won't go there now. It was okay at first, though I always felt her there. When Vaughn reconnected with her last year, our marriage never recovered."

"So you knew about Lydia Pelletier?" Angela asked. "I thought they'd kept that to themselves."

"Vaughn . . . he never understood what it meant to be married—I mean, married to *me*. You don't know this because you're not from around here, but in Portland I'm a big deal. Whether I like it or not, people talk about what I do. And they talk about what my husband does. Gossip gets around, and it gets around quickly. Plus, people at the club . . . they can be cruel . . . some people thought I'd stooped low when I married him."

"What did you think?" Angela asked.

"I didn't think that. Not at all," Sophie said. "If Vaughn asked, I'd probably take him back today." She rolled her eyes. "Pathetic, right?"

"Do you know Trey Pelletier?"

"A bit. The four of us went to college together," Sophie said. "That's where I met Vaughn, and I knew Lydia, too, because the two of them hung out. *All. The. Time.* Once she started dating Trey, she and Vaughn seemed to drift apart, or at least I thought they had. Vaughn and I even broke up once because of her! I should have listened to my instincts there. Anyway, Trey comes to town when he's working a case, so I see him every now and then. Mostly I stay away from him."

"Why?"

"Because I didn't like him in college, and I don't like him now. But if I have to, I'll say hello."

"Well, you won't have to anymore," Angela said. "He's dead."

Sophie looked stunned. "Jesus. You buried the lede there," she said. "Now I feel like a jerk. I didn't like the guy, but he doesn't deserve to be dead."

Angela flashed the photo of Daphne. "Have you seen this woman?"

Sophie took the phone and examined the picture. "She may have worked at the club for a while, but I wouldn't swear to it."

"Would she have known Vaughn?" Morgan asked.

"He only went to the club when I made him go," Sophie said. "I'll give him that. And I didn't make him go much toward the end. What's the connection anyway?"

"She lives on the island, or at least she did till yesterday. She went out on Vaughn's boat to help pull traps right before the storm."

"Is he still pulling traps?" Sophie asked.

"What else would he be doing?" Angela asked.

Sophie crouched down and said hello to Kate.

"Please, Ms. Johnson," Angela said. "Anything you can tell us would help. We have two missing kids, a missing woman, a rogue shipment of fentanyl, and a dead body. This is pretty serious."

"I don't want to get Vaughn in trouble," Sophie said.

"And I don't want anyone else to get killed."

"Please," Morgan said. He never should have left Hester on that island.

"Start with the fentanyl," Sophie said. "Ask Vaughn about it."

CHAPTER 20

Hester's phone beeped. She fumbled with it, turned it to silent, and shoved it deep into her pocket as she followed Vaughn up a hillside and along a path lined with small cottages. Ahead, one of the rare trucks on the island rolled out of the trees with a state trooper at the wheel, and Vaughn stepped to the side of the road to let it pass, forcing Hester to dive behind a clump of beach roses. When she peered out, dust still settling, he'd disappeared onto a narrow path that led into heavy forest, and she scrambled after him. Here, the leaves had already turned brilliant shades of yellow, orange, and red. The path hugged cliffs that dropped off to the left, and houses were sparser, most labeled with simple signs pointing into the trees. At one, a woman stood at an easel painting the rocky cliffs, and Hester wondered how many times she'd stood in that same spot, painting that same scene.

Up ahead, the path forked, and Hester caught a glimpse of Mindy's wagging tail. She gave them a moment before hurrying to where the coastline opened, and a small house clung to a cliff. Vaughn stood on the front stoop of the cottage, holding the screen door open with one foot. "You should come in," he called to her. "And stop lurking. You'll get a reputation."

He released Mindy, who bounded toward Hester, nearly knocking her to the ground.

"You're terrible at surveillance," he added.

"So I've been told," Hester said.

"I'd have followed me too," Vaughn said. "I was acting suspicious back there. But come in. We'll have a drink. I'll tell you what I can. Snack?" he added, this time directed at Mindy, in the uninhibited voice of a dog lover, in the same voice Morgan used when he spoke to Waffles. No one who spoke to another creature like that could be a bad person. As much as she wanted to listen to her instincts and run, very little about Vaughn felt dangerous. Hester followed him into the bungalow, a tiny one-room house with a stone fireplace that took up an entire wall. She ran her hands along shelves filled to overflowing with books, CDs, and DVDs. A stairwell led down to what must have been a basement, and a set of French doors led out to a deck that overlooked the sea. "It's tiny," Vaughn said.

"Perfectly tiny," Hester said.

The tininess of it reminded her of her Somerville apartment, before she'd stripped it of all personality. She could have stayed in a place like this for months.

Vaughn lifted the kettle. "Or something stronger?" he asked.

"This house is built for long winters and brown liquors," Hester said.

Vaughn poured two shots of Wild Turkey. He offered her one, but she took his instead. "To be safe," she said.

"To safety," Vaughn said. "And new friends."

Hester drank the shot down, feeling the alcohol warming her body.

"Those troopers we passed told me there's a manhunt going on," Vaughn said. "For some guy named Seth who was staying at the Victorian."

"I met him yesterday," Hester said. "Do they think he killed Trey?"

"Would you be surprised?"

"Not in the slightest," Hester said, walking through the room. "Is this the house you grew up in?"

"Here?" Vaughn said. "I have three brothers and sisters. Imagine us here all winter long? The house we grew up in is back in town, but my parents gave up and moved to Florida a few years back. This is a rental we hung on to. I come out here only when we don't have renters and I want to get away."

"Where do you live?"

"In a dumpy apartment by the marina. But the summer's over. No more renters—the last ones left with the storm. Now I'll be able to come out here whenever I like."

He poured himself another shot and held up the bottle as a question mark.

"Like I told you last night," Hester said. "I can drink anyone under the table."

He filled her glass. "I'll leave it here, then," he said. "Help yourself, but be careful. The island is too small to get lost on. What gets people are the cliffs. Don't drink so much that you fall off one of them."

He opened the French doors and waved Hester outside onto the deck, where the air smelled of salt and granite spilled to the sea below. "You need a coat or something?" Vaughn asked.

"I'm good for now." The bourbon was doing its trick.

Mindy joined them, her tail wagging as she nuzzled Vaughn's legs.

"How do you ever leave?" Hester asked.

Vaughn turned his back to the sea and scrutinized her. "You'd be a One and Done," he said. "Every summer, some guy from away, usually a prick, always rich, makes his whole family move out here to *escape*. Most of the time, he's working on a novel or he recently took up black-and-white photography. Don't they know that whatever they're running from, it's here too? But they see the post office and the one-room schoolhouse, and the lobster boats, and they forget about the crap Internet service or that building a McMansion requires board approval, which never happens, or that it's hard to get your douchebag friends to an island where there's no helicopter pad and nothing to do. And the bets start the moment these guys close on their houses, because what they really don't know about is the winter. You can't know about the winter till you live it, but come November, when the wind is high and the darkness descends and the only thing left to buy at the General Store is canned lima beans, these guys want *out*. Sure, this place is fun for a summer, but it's hard for life, and you have to be special to live it. If they're lucky, they wise up before they commit. If they aren't . . ." Vaughn paused and drank down the rest of his shot. "At least we have AA. Alcohol's the best of the worst."

"Why'd you come back, then?" Hester asked. "You had the whole world to run to."

"The whole world doesn't have Lydia." Vaughn tossed the dregs of his shot into the sea.

"Have you talked to her since they found Trey's body?"

"Another drink?"

"I'm good." Hester set her glass down.

"I still have the whole world to run to if I need it," Vaughn said. "But this is the only world I can see right now." He forced a smile. "But enough. It makes me feel pathetic, and I don't like being pathetic. Tell me about Annie. She must be special for you to come all the way here."

"I'd do anything for her," Hester said. "She would for me too."

"Would she take in your kid?"

"Word spread about that, did it?" Hester said.

"Word spreads about everything."

"We've known each other for years."

"I've known a lot of people for a long time, but I wouldn't take their kids for a year."

Hester watched as the waves rose and crashed. She remembered a day, years earlier, when Daphne had rented a red convertible and they'd sped along the narrowing roads to the Cape, all the way to Provincetown. It was their first year out of college, when they lived in that Allston apartment. Hester couldn't remember if it was before or after she'd met Morgan. Daphne parked the car in a hot, crowded lot and grabbed a cloth bag overflowing with towels and snacks from the back seat. "Come or stay," she said to Hester. "Your choice."

She disappeared into the throngs of people shuffling along in flip-flops. The very idea of following, of sitting on sand, of sweating, of the smell of sunblock, made Hester fume, but she eventually gave in when the air in the car grew too hot to breathe.

"You don't leave dogs in hot cars, let alone people," she said.

A trickle of sweat had started in the middle of her back and ran right down to the waist of her skirt. Even in the summer, Hester wore black from head to toe, covering herself to keep from standing out.

"Come," Daphne said, taking Hester's hand and leading her down the beach.

It seemed like all of Massachusetts had descended on this tiny strip of land. People lined the beach, men and women, all shapes and sizes, but Daphne kept walking till the crowds thinned and finally disappeared, and Hester's black Doc Martens had filled with sand. At last they followed the path to where it skirted two dunes. Here, there were plenty of people, but, Hester realized, they were all men. Only men. Fat men, thin men. Buff men playing paddleball in bulging Speedos.

"Where are we?" she asked.

Daphne knelt and unpacked her bag. A blanket to lie on. Lunch. A pink bikini for Hester. A set of cards. She stripped off her own shirt and shorts and stretched out on the blanket.

"We're invisible here," she said, undoing her polka-dotted bikini top and setting her breasts free. "See, none of them even notice!"

"We notice," one of the men playing paddleball shouted. "We just don't care."

Hester stood on the sand surrounded by people who couldn't be bothered to see her and tethered by her faith in Daphne. A bond she never imagined would break. And she'd let her woolen coat fall to the sand

and slipped out of her clothes and into the bikini. She felt the sun on her skin and the breeze in her hair for what seemed like the first time in her life. She'd felt like Daphne had woken her from a dream. Again.

"The thing about Daphne," Hester said to Vaughn, "is that she sees me. She sees who I really am."

"But you're hard to miss," he said. "You are seen."

"She helps me remember that."

"Then she's a good friend."

Mindy had fallen asleep in the sun, stretched out on the warm pine boards of the deck. Now she lifted her head and woofed. Then she leapt to her feet. The woof turned to a snarl.

"Hold on, girl," Vaughn said, putting a hand to her collar. "You're all right."

Hester reached for her phone.

"No reception out here," Vaughn said. "Who's there?" he shouted, edging toward the French doors.

Hester followed. "Is it Seth?" she asked.

"Stay here," he said.

"I don't think so," Hester said.

"Then hold the dog."

Hester gripped Mindy's collar. Vaughn slid the screen door open with one finger. "Hello?" he said, stepping over the threshold.

The darkness swallowed him.

"What the hell?"

Hester heard a thump and what sounded like a bag of wet cement falling to the floor. She let Mindy go. The dog hurtled through the open door, with Hester at her heels. It took a second for her eyes to adjust from the bright sun. Vaughn lay slumped on a rug, blood gushing from a gash on his forehead. Over him, Daphne clutched a log from the fireplace, using it to fend off the dog. Dried blood caked her hair, and she had a black eye. Lydia was right—she didn't resemble the woman Hester had known for all those years. She looked sick and broken.

Vaughn groaned and tried to stand. Daphne raised the log to hit him again, but Hester shouted, "Stop!"

Daphne froze.

Mindy growled.

"You came," Daphne said.

"I did," Hester said.

CHAPTER 21

Daphne.

The name felt strange, like an old sweater that didn't quite fit—one that had stretched out and hung to her knees and made her look like a rectangle—but that she still loved. Was she *Daphne* or *Annie*?

Daphne.

It was another lifetime, one she didn't want to slip back into, but *Annie* was gone, probably for good. For now, she'd need to make that sweater fit.

She—*Daphne*—gripped the log, looming over Vaughn, ready to strike again. Someone had locked her in the cellar, and as far as she was concerned it had to have been him. When would he come at her? When would she have an excuse to bash in his brains?

The world around her revealed itself bit by bit. She took in the sun first. It shone through panes of glass, blinding her after hours or days in the darkness, after all that time lying on a cot, wondering, hoping, dreading. The details in the little house came next, with its walls of books and its secondhand furniture. She heard the barking dog. And she saw her.

Hester.

In her pink sweater and green-checked shorts, and those orange sneakers they'd bought together at Marshalls a decade ago, the orange shoes she still wore every fall. After all these years, Hester hadn't learned to dress herself.

Hester.

She tried to say the name, but she couldn't form the sounds.

Her friend. Daphne's friend. Her best friend. She'd come. After everything. She'd come when Daphne had needed her and maybe, she hoped, Hester didn't hate her for leaving.

Vaughn groaned again and put his hands to his head. Daphne lunged forward, and Hester's lips moved, and even though Daphne couldn't quite put the words together, she stopped. Hester held the dog back, both hands on its collar, her thigh muscles bulging under those shorts. Memories of the dog, of that day on the boat, of the way Mindy had nestled against her as she'd pulled traps from the water, flooded through her.

"Daphne," Hester said. "Are you okay?"

"I don't know," she managed to say, her lips dry, her throat parched.

The thoughts ticked off. Time and space expanded. How long had she been here? And where was here? How long had she been locked in that cellar? A windowless dirt room, really, where no one had come. She remembered the beach. She remembered someone attacking her. And screaming to Ethan, telling him to run. And she remembered waking later, barely being able to open her eyes. They were swollen and heavy. Darkness surrounded her, and she took in what she could with her other senses, the scent of mildew, the dig of a mattress spring in her back, the dampness of the narrow cot.

And silence.

Pure silence.

She'd listened. For wind. For rain. For crashing waves. For the cry of seagulls. The sounds of the island that followed you wherever you went.

Nothing.

She'd tried to remember how she'd gotten there, and when she did, she'd called out in desperation. For the boy. "Ethan!" she whispered as loudly as she dared. She listened again, this time for a voice, for crying. For a breath.

Again, nothing.

She'd touched her head. It throbbed. She'd rolled to the side, and a sharp pain hit her. It spread through her body from so many points, she couldn't tell what to tend to first. She'd managed to roll off the mattress and onto a cold, dirt floor. Her clothes were damp. She shook. All over. She willed the tremors to stop, for all of this to end, to be safe. And then she could see. Barely. A tiny shaft of light emanated from the base of a door. She'd crawled toward it. One knee and then the next. The five feet seemed endless, but when she got there, she felt her way up to the knob. It turned, but the door wouldn't budge. She struggled to her feet, yanking at the unforgiving handle, ignoring the pain surging through her body. No way out. She had felt herself losing control. Panicking. Hyperventilating.

Stop.

Think.

She'd used the little light she had to scan the room.

A black rectangle had to be the mattress. Another shadow outlined a chair. She followed the edges of the room, the pain of moving trumped by panic. She ran her hand along a stone wall, damp with trickling water.

And the silence ended. Outside, beyond the door, footsteps crossed solid dirt and a shadow fell across the line of light. "Help!" she shouted. "Please. Let me out!"

The footsteps retreated.

"Come back!" Daphne shouted, pounding at the door.

But when she stopped to listen again, all she heard was silence. She put her back to the wall and slid to the ground. When she crawled toward the cot, her hand hit a cellophane bag, and her stomach grumbled. She'd torn the package open, her hands shoveling something salty and cheesy into her mouth. Combos. Pizza flavored.

They'd never tasted so good. It didn't even occur to her to save any.

She'd felt along the floor and found a plastic bottle. Carbonation burst as she twisted the lid and sucked down sweet, spicy ginger ale, drinking half the bottle in one long gulp. When her hand found a small vial that shook with pills, she twisted the lid off and sniffed. What did Tylenol smell like? She ached, and she yearned to take some of the hurt away, and someone had been kind enough to leave her food, even if he'd locked her away in the dark, so she'd taken a chance and swallowed the pills, two, not three, with a gulp of ginger ale.

On the cot, she'd fallen into a deep, fitful sleep, drugged, she was sure. She'd awoken, cheek wet from a pool of her own drool. She had no idea how long she'd been asleep. No idea how long she'd been in the room at all, but the door that had been locked was ajar. Gray light had filtered in, and she'd heard murmurs above her. Voices. Outside the room, she'd found another dirt room, this one lined with firewood, a long table covered in vials, pills spilling to the floor. Pills like the ones she'd seen Frankie snorting. And a staircase leading toward the light. This was her chance. Her one chance to survive. She'd taken a log and headed upstairs, where she'd waited. To attack.

Vaughn moaned and sheltered his head with his arms. The dog lunged again. Daphne held the log between her and the snarling teeth, but Hester dug a random treat from her pocket and coaxed the dog outdoors, slamming the French doors shut. The dog pawed at the glass and then sat and panted.

"She's a lab," Hester said. "How vicious can she be?"

"Not very," Vaughn managed to say from the floor.

"Shut up," Hester said.

She crossed the room, throwing open drawers till she found a pile of dishtowels.

"What day is it?" Daphne asked.

"Thursday. You've been missing since yesterday," Hester said, tearing the towels into strips. "Don't move," she said to Vaughn, "or we'll bash your brains in."

"Yes, ma'am," Vaughn said.

Hester bound Vaughn's hands behind his back with the strips of cloth and folded another towel and held it to the gash on his forehead. "Press here," she said to Daphne, giving her a kiss. "There's no phone. But don't go anywhere. Please. We'll talk when I get back."

Hester ran from the house, slamming the front door

behind her. Daphne crouched beside the barely conscious man—her kidnapper—and pressed the cloth to his wound till blood seeped through the fabric. Outside the French doors, the dog stopped barking and took off, and Daphne imagined Hester running through trees, a blanket catching on a limb, the dog in close pursuit, like in a postmodern fairy tale.

"Hey, Red," Vaughn croaked, struggling to sit up.

Daphne let the cloth drop and scrambled away.

"Where'd Hester go?"

"She went for help."

"She'll bring Rory, I bet. This'll make his day. He's had it in for me since, well, since as long as I can remember. I'm feeling a bit like that thirty-pound lobster right now. Like I could use a little pity. Could you show me some mercy?"

Vaughn's voice was as soft as Daphne remembered. She'd thought about him in that cellar, in the dark, about his kindness. No one had been truly kind to her in so long, she'd forgotten what it felt like. She'd believed that they were friends.

She moved in closer and pressed the cloth to his head again. "That lobster didn't weigh thirty pounds," she said. "Twenty, maybe."

"You're probably right," Vaughn said. "And your friend must have been a Girl Scout. She ties a good knot. I'm not going anywhere. But listen to yourself on this one. Listen to your own judgment."

"The boy," Daphne said. "Ethan. What happened to him?"

"He's fine. Wandered home after the storm. He got stuck by the lighthouse when the tide came in."

And she remembered. She *could* run toward danger.

She could protect. Hadn't she done something good, something that mattered? "He was on the beach," she said.

"Were you on the beach?" Vaughn asked.

"By the lighthouse. As the sun came up."

"Who else was there?" Vaughn asked. "Who did you see?"

Trey. She'd seen Trey. He'd come at her. He'd attacked her, and she'd woken in that cellar. But she didn't want to believe Trey would do that. She didn't want to believe he'd hurt her. "Why do you have all those pills?" she asked.

"Pills?" he said.

Daphne lifted the cloth. The bleeding had stopped. "There are pills downstairs. Vials and vials of pills."

Outside, a Jeep roared up the narrow path. She had to decide who to trust. Now.

"Trey was on the beach," she said, quickly. "And he knows. About you and Lydia. He knows you're having an affair. Be careful. Don't say anything. He wants to take you down."

Saying Trey's name still made her heart beat faster, even as she remembered his face as he screamed at her. She remembered the sand rushing toward her and telling Ethan to run. She'd kicked at him, hadn't she? She'd swung that rock. In her heart, she knew that Trey had never loved her, but she still wanted him. How could she have been so pathetic? How could she be so pathetic?

"Oh, Annie," Vaughn said, and the look in his face gave something away. It woke up a little voice, a whisper that told her not to listen. Not to trust, no matter what.

"My name is Daphne," she said. "Annie wasn't real. She wasn't anyone."

"She was someone to me," Vaughn said. "We were friends. I liked her."

The door flew open. Rory crouched, gun gripped in both fists. He shouted, telling Daphne to put her hands up, to roll on her stomach.

"Really?" she said.

"Now!"

Even though it made her feel like a criminal, she faced the braided rug, with its grains of sand and dog hair. She wasn't sure how much fight she had left in her anyway. Rory moved forward. He passed her, and in a few deft moves he'd snapped a set of handcuffs onto Vaughn.

"I'm not going anywhere, buddy," Vaughn said.

"Shut up," Rory said. "Try anything. One thing, and I'll hurt you worse than she already has."

"We'll get this sorted out," Vaughn said.

"Don't talk," Rory said. "I don't want to hear it. You're under arrest."

He read Vaughn his rights and hauled him to his feet. As soon as the door clicked shut, Daphne leapt up and ran after them, into the sun. The sun. The bright warmth on her face. She breathed deeply, letting oxygen flow into her lungs, letting the world swirl around her in a sea of shapes and colors. At the Jeep, Rory guided Vaughn's head as he eased him into the back of the car. By the trees, Hester held the dog by a burgundy-colored leash. Once Vaughn was safely locked away, Rory ambled toward Daphne. "I was worried about you," he said, his voice kinder than she'd expected.

"I'm glad you turned up. I'll need to get you to a doctor."

"I'm fine," she said, ignoring the aches and pains.

"You don't look fine. You got a beating. Come in the car."

"Nothing's broken, and I want to be outside. I'll walk."

Rory looked as if he might argue, but he gave in. "Go right to the inn and wait there," he said, glancing at Hester. "You too. I'll send the doctor around. And you'll need to talk to the state police about what happened here. There were pills all over the place in there. And a lock on the door." He glanced toward the Jeep. "Sick."

He slid into the driver's seat, revved the engine, and drove too aggressively into the trees. The dog, which had seemed so menacing at the house, wagged her whole body as Daphne approached. "Strays always manage to find you," she said to Hester.

"We'll take her with us," Hester said. "Figure out what to do. Vaughn has plenty of friends who'll look out for her."

Daphne surveyed the coast, holding a hand up to block out the sun. She was safe. Ethan was safe, for now at least, and it was because of her. She was a hero, even if no one knew it yet, a hero like Hester had been with Kate last winter. Daphne had read everything about the kidnapping. More than once over these months, she'd wondered if she'd have done the same, whether she could have found the strength to save her own child.

Kate.

If she was a good mother, Kate would have been her first thought when she saw Hester, her sole thought, but she'd remembered the girl only now. "Is she here?" Daphne asked.

A subtle shift in Hester's expression revealed that need to protect at any cost. Daphne remembered wanting to feel that way, watching mothers bonding with their children and asking what she'd done wrong to never have that. Hester's every waking thought probably involved a child now. The way Daphne's should have.

"Kate's with Morgan," Hester said. "In Portland. He's looking for you. We both are."

Daphne imagined her little brother—they were twins, really, but Morgan was twelve minutes younger, something she'd never let him forget—she imagined him trying to interrogate the people he'd need to talk to, the ones she'd known, the desperate and the destitute. He'd never understand that world, because he wouldn't be able to comprehend how far she'd fallen.

"The last ferry is at four," Hester said. "And we need to get you to the doctor and talk to the police before it leaves. If I'm not on it, I think Morgan may actually give up on me. He's meeting us in Boothbay Harbor."

"Will Kate be there?"

"Unless he manages to lose her," Hester said, glancing at her phone. "No service here."

"Not till we get closer to town."

Daphne kept smiling, a mask to hide behind. She protected herself, even with Hester. It would take ten minutes to get to town, where phone service was reliable, ten minutes before Hester texted Morgan something like, *Mission accomplished!* Ten minutes before she asked Daphne to pose for a selfie, to smile into the phone, to grin for her brother and daughter. What did Daphne want? She had to decide and get Hester to trust her again. First step, a hug. Tentative. Let Hester believe Daphne didn't know whether she'd earned it. Hester held her tight, though, without inhibitions, like she always did, and released her long after Daphne was ready to stop.

"Let's go," Hester said, already hurrying.

The dog trotted along beside them as they headed into the trees.

"Tell me what happened," Hester said.

And Daphne told her what she could, about the storm and the lighthouse and releasing Ethan and waking up on the cot and taking the pills that she hoped were Tylenol. She told her about finding the door ajar. She didn't tell Hester about Trey. Not yet. When she saw Trey, she'd know. She'd know whether he'd meant to hurt her. "Are the state police still here?" she asked. "Have they been looking for me? Did Trey raise the alarm?"

Hester took a deep breath.

"What's wrong?" Daphne asked.

"Trey Pelletier," Hester said.

There had to be a reason why he'd been on the beach.

"Did you know him?" Hester asked.

Of course, she knew him. She loved him. "A bit," Daphne said. "He's married to my best friend."

"Lydia Pelletier is your *best* friend?" Hester said.

"She's *Annie's* best friend," Daphne said.

"Well, I'm glad. Lydia needs friends. Trey is dead."

The words didn't make sense. Nothing did. Daphne saw herself, her legs moving, her arms swaying, as she floated across the mossy forest floor. She tried to latch on to what Hester had said, to string words together into a whole. Hester glanced at her phone again, and she remembered that Hester had hated technology, hated being bothered by the world. But a year could change anyone. It had certainly changed her. It had made her into Annie.

"What did you say about . . . Trey?"

"I found him on the beach by the lighthouse with a knife in his back. I suppose they'll try to pin that on Vaughn now too," Hester said.

This time Daphne heard all the words. And they brought her crashing to earth. "I saw Trey on the beach," she said. "After I found Ethan. He attacked me. I swear he had a knife."

"Why would he attack you?"

"I don't know!"

Hester turned to her. "He had a knife? What happened to it? Are your fingerprints on it?"

"I don't even know if he had one."

"You just said he did."

"It was dark. I saw something flash. I thought he put me in that cellar."

"Maybe he did put you there," Hester said. "But he couldn't have unlocked that door to let you out, because he's been dead since yesterday. Besides, I thought Vaughn attacked you. You hit him with a log. You were in his basement."

"It *was* Vaughn," Daphne said, trying to convince herself. But she hadn't seen Vaughn on the beach. It had been Trey.

Hester stopped. She held out a hand so that Mindy sat. "Where have you been for the last year?" she asked. "You look terrible. And who is *Annie* anyway?"

Daphne could see her friend had moved beyond relief—or whatever emotions flooded through you when you found a long-lost and imprisoned friend—beyond that hug and to anger.

"Annie's someone nicer than I am," Daphne said. "Or, I thought she would be. She's someone with friends."

"What do you call me?"

"My friend. I've always had you. But Annie sipped chardonnay and joined book clubs, or at least that's who I wanted her to be. It didn't work though."

Hester started to say something and stopped.

"What?" Daphne said.

"I told myself you'd left to become something, to become someone you've always wanted to be," Hester said. "I thought you'd be—I don't know—I thought you'd be starting a new career or saving the world. Or even just dating someone fantastic. I thought you'd fix yourself. I'd never have let you go if I'd known it was for . . . for this." Hester waved at Daphne's clothes, at her hair, at her pockmarked skin and yellowing teeth, at everything that had shamed her. "Kate needs someone she can trust!"

"I can't wait to see Kate," Daphne said quickly, the words spilling out. In part, she said them because she thought they might be what Hester wanted to hear, and in part she said them to convince herself. "I can't wait to hold Kate in my arms. I have missed her more than you can possibly imagine. A mother loves her child more than life itself. More than oxygen. I made the choice to leave, and now . . ." She let her voice trail off.

Hester turned toward town. "She misses you too. She has a photo of you by her bed. Sometimes when I'm reading her a story, we switch out your name for whoever the story is about."

"Princesses?"

"Mostly."

Daphne hated princesses. She hated that they were weak and girly and needed men to complete their stories. Mostly, though, she hated that they'd infiltrated her life with Kate, and that Kate had made them hers, that she'd accepted them and welcomed them without asking permission. And that Daphne had somehow lost control. What else had Kate embraced in this last year? Did she love broccoli or the Greek myths or making bubbles in the tub? Did she have friends at school, ones Daphne wouldn't like, ones that could turn her mean or sad or lonely? Had she become so much her own person that Daphne wouldn't even recognize her anymore?

They stepped out of the tree line, and Hester's phone beeped to life. And she was typing a text. Daphne put a hand to Hester's, holding it tighter than she'd expected.

"What is it that you want?" Hester asked, her index finger hovering over Send.

"I don't know," Daphne said. "I haven't known."

"I can't help you if you don't tell me."

On the path, the sun caught the shiny face of a quarter. Daphne imagined a world where a quarter no longer mattered.

"I want a beer," Daphne said. "And something to eat. I want a burger, and an enormous slab of blueberry pie."

Hester glanced at the time on her phone and deleted the text message. "First a doctor. If it's okay, we'll have a beer. You have till four o'clock. Not a minute longer."

Rory drove too fast down the narrow lanes. He'd done it!

He'd secured the scene and apprehended the suspect. He'd cuffed him and read him his rights, and in a few moments he'd deliver him to the state police.

He checked the rearview mirror. Vaughn stared out the window, watching the people in town trying to look in, trying to get a glimpse of the kidnapper, the murderer, the drug dealer. "You took those kids, too, didn't you?" Rory said. "You used them."

"You know I didn't," Vaughn said, his voice too cool.

Vaughn should be afraid, but he hardly seemed to care. He grinned in a way that made Rory want to haul him out of the Jeep, make him kneel, and then kick him in the face. Always, since the very first day Rory had known him, since before time, Vaughn had had that easy charm. He had it now, even as he faced a life in prison.

"Motive and opportunity," Rory said. "You have them both."

"You done good today, Rory-boy," Vaughn said.

"Don't. Don't call me that."

"Annie said there were pills in my basement," Vaughn said. "Bet you saw 'em too. I wouldn't be much of a drug dealer if I left evidence like that out for the world to see."

"I saw what I saw."

"And Annie. She's been locked up since yesterday, but the door was suddenly open. It was like someone wanted her to be found or wanted her to escape."

"Stop talking," Rory said.

At the community center, a small crowd had gathered.

"I've always watched out for you," Vaughn said.

"I don't need you."

"I hope to hell not," Vaughn said.

Rory hauled him out of the Jeep and led him through the crowd.

"Hey, Vaughn," someone shouted. "Do you need me to clear your traps?"

"Check with me in the morning," Vaughn said. "I should know by then."

"You should take him up on the offer," Rory whispered. "You won't be here in the morning. You'll be on the mainland at the county jail."

He opened the door to see Barb Kelley hunched over a laptop computer. She smiled. *That's right, Vaughn, you're done*, Rory thought. Barb took Vaughn's arm from Rory. "Keys?" she said.

Rory handed her the key to the cuffs, and in one swift move Detective Kelley had slipped them off Vaughn's wrists.

"Coffee?" she asked.

Rory started to answer, but Vaughn said, "Got anything stronger?"

"Not right now," she said.

"Then I take it black."

"Hah! Get it yourself, Roberts," Barb said, like she

was talking to her annoying little brother. "And do you recognize this?"

She laid a photo of a bloody knife with a blue hilt on the table.

"Looks like my knife," Vaughn said. "The one I keep on my boat. Maybe *I* killed Trey."

"Hilarious," Barb said.

"What the hell is going on?" Rory asked.

But no one answered.

CHAPTER 22

There was no news from Hester. Morgan could tell himself it was because parts of the island didn't have service, but why give her the benefit of the doubt? She'd been lying to him for days now.

He looked out the window as Angela drove over the bridge toward the marina, and he thought about what they'd learned from Sophie Johnson, if only to keep his mind off what Hester might be doing. Back at the house, when Angela pressed her for more details, Sophie had insisted that she'd already said too much. "There are drugs all over Maine," she added. "The rest you'll have to get from Vaughn."

Now Angela pulled the minivan into the parking lot of an unassuming building on the edge of a marina. This was the club where Sophie said Daphne may have worked.

"You holding up?" Angela asked Morgan.

"Sure," he said, shaking the thoughts about Hester away. "What do we know so far? Vaughn Roberts is having an affair with Lydia Pelletier."

"And fentanyl is making its way through Maine.

And it's killed at least one person on the island that we know of."

"How could Daphne have anything to do with any of this?" Morgan asked.

"I've never met Daphne," Angela said, catching his eye and glancing in the rearview mirror to see what Kate was up to. Morgan turned to his niece, who'd been quiet for far too long. Kate was pretending to play with Sebastian, but he could tell she was hanging on every word they said. He forgot how much the girl heard and how much she understood, or that finding Daphne was important to her, too.

But to Angela, he realized, Daphne was a blank slate, waiting to be filled. And from what Angela had learned in the months since she'd come into their lives, Morgan suspected she didn't have many charitable thoughts toward his sister. Why would she? Daphne was the woman who'd abandoned her own child. She didn't know his sister, the girl who'd crawled into bed beside him and cried with him when their father died, or the high school senior who'd led Liechtenstein through the Model UN. And she certainly didn't know the young woman who'd taken three busses to get from Wellesley to Amherst on the day Morgan's high school girlfriend, BranDee, dumped him via e-mail. Daphne had shown up at the UMass campus with a bag of weed and six boxes of Oreos and had refused to leave till he'd written out a list of reasons why it was good to be free.

"I'll leave number one to you," Daphne said. "But spelling your name with a capital D? That has to be number two."

Morgan was stoned enough to laugh.

"It's a terrible joke!" Daphne said. "I was being mean! She can't help what her parents named her!"

"But she can," Morgan said, Oreo crumbs spewing from his mouth. "Her real name is Jennifer."

"Then maybe it should be number one," Daphne had said.

"My sister's more than what you know," Morgan said to Angela. "More than what you've heard about."

"I don't know anything about your sister or her choices," Angela said. "I do know that you and Hester have done pretty well in an extraordinary situation, and sometimes I don't know if you realize how extraordinary it is. You both plod through this as if it's normal. It isn't, but you make it as normal as you can, and that's good. I'm a cop. I see ugly things, every day. This situation"—Angela jerked a thumb toward Kate—"doesn't compare. You have a good thing here. You watch out for each other. You care about each other. It could be so, so much worse, and I hope you know that."

Morgan knew more than he got credit for. But he still wanted to find his sister, to see that she was safe and healthy. He wanted her to be the person _he_ wanted her to be, instead of the person she was, which could only lead to disappointment. And he knew that too.

Inside the club, with Kate at his side and Waffles on her leash, Morgan watched as Angela showed a photo of Daphne to anyone they could find, till finally, in the kitchen, the chef nodded. "Sure, she worked here, but not for long. Maybe a week."

"What happened?" Angela asked.

The chef shook his head and went back to chopping carrots.

"This isn't official," Angela said.

"Then what am I doing, talking to you?"

"We're hoping nothing happened to her."

"She had a run-in with the manager and didn't show up the next day. She'd have been fired anyway."

"Why?"

"We always lose stuff to staff. Saltshakers. Silverware. That kind of thing. It was a bit much with that one."

"She was stealing?"

"You'll have to ask the manager."

"Do you know where she went?"

"Someone like her?" the chef said. "She was pretty down-and-out. I'd start out by Northfield. There's a homeless contingent there. See if anyone recognizes her."

Out in the parking lot, Angela put a hand on Morgan's arm. "We don't know if anything he said was true."

"Let's find out, then," Morgan said.

Northfield Street turned out to be a run-down section of town where desperate-looking people hung out in doorways and alleys. A woman who looked as if she hadn't eaten or slept in a month wandered from one empty doorway to the next. A man in a dirty army jacket waved a cup and grinned through missing teeth. Angela parked the minivan but kept the engine running. "This is where you and the rest of your team stay on the ark," she said. "Doors locked. Phone on. Nine-one-one primed to go. I'll see what I can find out."

"You shouldn't go in without backup," Morgan said.

"I'm not *going in* anywhere," Angela said. "I'm

talking to those guys there and coming back here. But remember, you ain't the backup. Call the cops if you see anything. Otherwise, I'll be back in two minutes. Got it?"

Morgan nearly protested.

"There's no argument," Angela said. "Either you stay here, or we leave. Those are the choices."

"Fine," Morgan said, and watched as Angela approached two men playing chess. She flashed her badge, and one of the men held up his hands as if to say he had nothing to offer, and Morgan could imagine Angela's reassuring voice, a voice that told the man she was looking for a friend, nothing more. Angela was one part Earth mother, one part counselor, and one part warrior. He often wondered how they'd gotten along before knowing her. He also wondered how any perp could avoid spilling his whole story once Angela started in on an interrogation. She made you want to bare your soul. Or at least she made him want to.

"Uncle Morgan?"

Morgan glanced into the back seat. "Hmm," he said.

"Does Mommy live here?"

"I don't think so. Not now, at least."

"What's down and out?"

"It's when . . . I guess it's when you don't have a lot of luck."

"Are you down and out?" Kate asked, and Morgan thought that, no, he's wasn't. Not now, at least. He hadn't been down and out since his first date with Hester.

"Waffles wants to get out," Kate said.

"We'll sit here for a bit longer," he said.

"How much longer?"

"A minute, maybe two."

"I can count to sixty."

"You might need to do it a few times."

As Kate began to count, he watched as Angela moved on to a man with greasy, dark hair that hung to his shoulders. They spoke intently, the man's wiry limbs waving with kinetic energy.

"Uncle Morgan?"

"Hmm?" He turned in his seat.

"What comes after thirty-nine?"

"You know."

"Forty."

"That's right."

"Uncle Morgan?"

"What is it, sweetie?"

"Look."

Kate pointed to where Angela was on the ground. And the man was running. Morgan didn't think. He moved, stepping out of the car and into the man's path. It had been a long time since anyone had run full force into him, and it hurt more than he could have imagined to be flung to the ground. The man fell too, head over heels into a pile of arms and legs, and before he could flee again, Angela had tackled him to the ground.

"Don't move," she said. "Not even your little toe."

The man rolled onto his stomach and held his hands at his sides. He'd done this before. Angela frisked him and told him to sit with his back to the car. A gash across his forehead dripped blood. "Police brutality," he said.

"Shut up," Angela said.

With adrenaline coursing through him, Morgan understood now how Angela did this every day.

The man started to cry, begging not to be arrested.

"Oh, for Christ's sake," Angela said. "Stop blubbering and sit on your hands. Answer my questions and you can go. Give me lip, and I'll haul you in for dealing."

"I ain't dealing."

"Then why'd you run?" Angela said, and when he didn't answer, she showed him a photo of Daphne. "Tell me what you know about her."

"Don' know her."

"Let's go."

"I seen her around."

"When?"

"Few months ago."

"And how did you know her?"

"She was around, you know. Like everyone else. We get to know each other. Or at least the look of each other. She smart, angry, ready to blow. Goes to the Walmart."

"Where's that?"

"Outside of town. About a mile. You can walk there."

"She'd walk there to work?"

"Nah, to return things," the man said.

"Got it," Angela said. "Who else did she hang out with? Who were her friends?"

"I don't know nothing," the man said.

"I'll get the cuffs," Angela said.

"Okay, okay. Some girl named Emily. Haven't seen her, not since the spring. She used to come here to score."

"Emily what?"

"Don't know. But I think she live over in Gorham. She blonde. Young. Maybe twenty. That's all I got."

"Get out of here," Angela said.

After the man scurried away, Angela turned on Morgan. "I told you to stay in the car."

"I wanted to see better."

"No, you didn't. You wanted to be a hero, and you could have gotten yourself killed. I need a lot of things. Like a new dishwasher. One thing I don't need is a dead friend."

Morgan had spent the last year sitting on the sidelines. Blocking that guy and slamming into the pavement had woken something in him. Maybe he'd needed an intervention as much as Hester had. As much as he wanted to find Daphne, even more he wanted answers. He wanted the truth, whatever it might be. And he wanted to find a path to where he and Hester should be, away from where they were right now. "What was that about Walmart?" he asked.

Angela glared at him. "It's a junkie trick," she finally said. "Steal things and return them. It's how you make cash out of nothing."

"Daphne's a junkie?" he asked.

"We'll have to find her to ask," Angela said.

Dr. Feldman was probably in his early fifties, with the easy charm of someone who had it good. "I'm a shrink," he said as he cleaned the cut on Daphne's head in the room at the inn. "But I'm also usually the only doctor around on this island, so I'm up on my skills. Head wounds bleed," he added. "This one's not as bad as you might think. You won't even need a stitch."

He applied a butterfly strip and checked Daphne's other cuts and bruises. "Nothing seems broken besides that tooth," he said after a few minutes. "You'll have to see a dentist about that. Advil's the best cure for the pain right now."

"No concussion?" Hester asked as she watched from the corner of the room, Mindy sitting at attention beside her.

"Nope, nothing much on the physical side," he said. "But, like I said, I'm a shrink. Come talk to me if you want. This couldn't have been easy, and sometimes it's good to talk things through."

"Sure," Daphne said, in a way that meant she wouldn't. "Thanks."

"For real," the doctor said. "Session's on me."

"Maybe tomorrow," Daphne said. "Right now, what I really need is something to eat."

"Is she okay to eat?" Hester asked.

"Absolutely. Though you'll need to watch that tooth."

"How about a drink?" Daphne asked.

"One drink. No more."

Hester watched him pack his bag up and leave, listening as his footsteps descended the narrow staircase. "Maybe you should go talk to him," she said.

"Not a chance," Daphne said. "Come on. I'm ravenous."

A few moment later, they'd hiked with Mindy to the Finisterre Brewery, where a few remaining summer people lounged on picnic benches in the cooling autumn air. The brewery was in a one-room log cabin. A chalkboard hanging on the wall listed the available brews, and growlers were lined up on an A-beam ready to be filled. Outside, a food truck sold burgers, pot stickers, and blueberry pie. "Watch the dog," Hester said to Daphne and then grabbed two lagers from a girl with a nose ring and purple streaks in her hair.

"It's like a slice of Brooklyn here in Maine," Hester said, bringing the beers to Daphne. Mindy had already fallen asleep under the picnic bench.

"I wanted to come here all summer," Daphne said.

Hester glanced around. Long strings of white bulbs hung over the seating area, and she imagined them lit up, music playing, crowds spilling across the grass on a perfect summer night. She also imagined Daphne outside, looking in, hoping to be asked. "When was the last time you ate?" she asked.

"I don't know."

"Don't drink too fast, then. Let's get some food in your belly."

At the food truck, Hester ordered burgers and pie; waited till they called her number; and, at the table, watched as Daphne gave herself over to hunger. When she finished, Hester slid her own burger to her. "How's that tooth?" she asked.

"Barely feel it," Daphne said.

Hester split the pie in half but took only one bite. When Daphne finished devouring it, a smear of blue across her lower lip, Hester laid her phone on the table, and like cell phones always did, it tugged at them and made its presence understood. The phone connected them to the rest of their lives, to their future. Daphne's eyes drifted toward it, and as if on command, it rang. Morgan's photo flashed onto the screen. "He's worried about you," Hester said. "And Kate's with him."

"I need more time," Daphne said.

Hester clicked into the call. "The service is spotty

around here," she said, attempting to add a note of cheer in her voice.

"Any luck?" Morgan asked.

Hester glanced to Daphne, who shook her head slightly.

"I may have a lead," Hester said, the lie coming too easily. "But it hasn't panned out yet. How about you?"

"We talked to Vaughn Roberts's wife," Morgan said. "Rich as can be. She told us to ask Vaughn about the drugs."

Hester stood, stepping out from the picnic bench. Daphne sat up, alert, and Hester moved away from her toward a line of trees. Morgan walked her through what he'd learned, and it took all Hester had not to tell him that Vaughn had been arrested.

"I could make a living doing this," Morgan said, and Hester could hear that the distraction had done him good. It made her feel the tiniest bit less terrible about lying to him. "Finding people," he continued. "I get why you do it. We're at the Walmart now, following up on another lead. Finding the mysterious Emily. But there are a lot of Emilys in this world. I don't know if we'll have much luck."

"You'll be surprised," Hester said. "You'll ask the right questions, and there will be your Emily." She paused. "It sounds like you may need more time in the city."

"I take it you want another night on the island. Didn't we get in a huge fight about this?"

"I'm at a brewery," Hester said, relieved to tell the truth. "Once you get used to having nothing to do, this place is pretty relaxing."

"I want to find this woman, and Angela has one more day off before she heads back. . . ."

"And I talked to someone who said he saw Daphne earlier today. I wonder if she's lying low, waiting for the right time to appear."

"You'd let me know if she did, right?"

"Of course," Hester said.

"Okay, I'll see you tomorrow on the morning ferry, Daphne or not. And Kate wants to talk to you."

At the first sound of the girl's voice, Hester felt her heart travel right through the phone to that Walmart parking lot. They talked for a few minutes about the boat ride and Waffles and seeing Uncle Morgan tackle a man outside the car, and the whole time Hester wanted Kate here, with her, just being herself. She didn't want to miss a single moment of seeing Kate become who she'd be. "Is Mommy with you?" Kate finally asked.

"Not yet," Hester said, and this time, the lie felt absolutely right. The first and only thing she cared about was protecting Kate.

"When will she be with you?" Kate asked.

Hester glanced toward the picnic table, where Daphne sat at attention. It should be Daphne, here, on the phone. It should be Daphne's heart zooming across the Gulf of Maine. And it should be Daphne clinging to every moment of this precious childhood, hoping to make it last forever. But it was Hester. It had been Hester all along. And she wasn't willing to give any of it up or to let Kate love someone else instead of her. Not yet, at least.

"Soon," she said, "I promise," and regretted it almost at once.

When she hung up, Hester kept the phone to her ear for a few moments, pretending that the conversation hadn't ended.

"I bought you another day," she said, back at the table.

"I don't know what to do," Daphne said.

"Kate isn't three years old anymore," Hester said. "She isn't a toddler, she's a girl, and she knows why I came here."

Hester scrolled through her phone till she'd found the right photo of Kate, the one she'd have used on a missing child poster. In it, Kate sat on a swing at the park, her curls flying behind her, a grin plastered across her face. She looked smart and curious and kind, like the girl Hester had dreamed of being herself. She'd learned to count on that swing, moving through the numbers with every push, a first that Daphne had missed. And when Daphne took the phone, Hester expected tears, but Daphne's eyes stayed dry.

"I get it," Daphne said. "I screwed up."

"It's not that easy," Hester said. "You messing up is about you, but this isn't about you or me, and it took me a long time to figure that out. I hate it when people say things like they were never a real adult till they had kids, but whether you're an adult or not, it changes your responsibilities. It changes your perspective. It changed mine."

"Kate was mine first," Daphne said.

The words burned. And a part of Hester wanted to let Daphne know what it meant to be a parent, what it meant to take responsibility. But, she reminded herself, Daphne had the power. Kate had been hers, and she could be hers again. One wrong move and they'd be on that four o'clock ferry heading toward a future Hester never wanted to face, toward years without Kate. For so long, Daphne had been Hester's confidante, her sole friend, the one person she could go to when the world hurt. She had other friends now, more than she'd ever had in her whole life, and Daphne's departure had made that life possible. What could she do now that Daphne was the source of her pain?

By the brewhouse, a young man with a beard set up a microphone and strummed a guitar, and Hester was glad for the distraction. She wrapped an arm around Daphne, and they listened as he played. Daphne drank in the small kindness, melting against Hester, her eyes closed. Mindy woke and laid her head on Hester's thigh. The singer played a Bob Dylan song, and moved through his set. An hour later, off in the distance, the ferry blew its horn as it docked at the pier. It would leave soon, and Hester would have seventeen hours. Seventeen hours to figure out what to do.

"I could use a bath," Daphne said as the singer finished.

"You really could," Hester said, playing her part. Being a friend.

"You're awful."

"I know."

CHAPTER 23

Barb's head tilted toward Vaughn as they talked like old friends. This, whatever it was, wasn't an interrogation, and it certainly wasn't the reception Rory had expected when he'd hauled Vaughn in. "What the hell . . ." he said. "I found Annie in this guy's cellar. Daphne, I mean. Someone beat her up. And there are pills all over the place. I bet it's the same drugs . . ." Rory's words caught in his throat.

"What did you see?" Barb said to him. "Tell me. Quickly. Before you forget anything. What did you see in the house?"

Rory's eyes darted from Vaughn to Barb. "Where's Frankie?" he asked.

"At the Victorian," Barb said.

"Why isn't she here?"

"We don't have anything to arrest her on. Nate's keeping an eye on her."

"Did you find Seth?"

"Still looking," Barb said. "Tell me what happened."

"I apprehended the suspect and brought him in,"

Rory said. "By the book. The victim was locked in his basement for at least twenty-four hours. She'd been assaulted and needed medical attention. I called Dr. Feldman on the way here and sent him over to check her out."

"Anything else?" Barb asked.

Rory broke. He'd won. For once, Rory had won. Trey was gone, and now Vaughn was out of the picture. Lydia would have to see him now. "He's a kidnapper and a drug dealer and God knows what else. You need to ask him about those missing kids. The ones everyone said *I* took. Ask him about Oliver!"

"How did you know to go to the house?" Barb asked.

She wasn't listening to him. Calm, he reminded himself. Treat this like any statement. The pieces were in place, and all they had to do was follow the evidence. Walk through the facts, because in the end, that's all he had. "I was participating in the search when the woman from the ferry, Hester, she ran out of the woods. She was shouting. About Annie and Vaughn. And the dog came running after her."

"Where's Mindy?" Vaughn asked.

"I think you have bigger things to worry about," Rory said. Damn it! Why did he answer? Stay in control. Don't engage.

Barb glanced at Vaughn, and he made a zipping movement over his lips. "What did Hester say?" she asked.

"Only that she'd found her friend and that they'd managed to incapacitate the suspect."

"Taken down by a woman?" Barb said to Vaughn. Was that a glint in her eye?

"What can I say?"

"Don't say anything," Barb said.

"Got it," Vaughn said.

"Once you were at the house," Barb said, "what did you do then?"

"I secured the scene," Rory said. "The suspect was bound with what looked like strips of cloth. He was lucid and alert."

"Just barely," Vaughn said, rubbing the back of his head. "She packed a wallop. And I didn't see it coming."

"Roberts!" Barb said, with enough irritation that even Vaughn shrank away.

"I cuffed the suspect."

"Did you touch anything?"

"I don't know," Rory said.

"You should know."

"Okay, I did."

"What next?"

"I escorted the suspect to the car, made sure the victim could make her way to town, and brought him here."

"Where's Daphne now?" Barb asked.

"At the inn!" Rory said, frustration exploding in his answer. "Do you know what I deal with out here? Frat boys getting drunk. Noise complaints. Lost dogs. Domestic disturbances. And drug overdoses. I know how to deal with all those things. I haven't a clue what to do with kidnapping and murder, and certainly not when they all happen at the same time. And why isn't he in cuffs?"

Barb pulled up a chair. "Sit," she said.

"Not till I get some answers."

"Sit and you'll get some."

Like usual, Barb made Rory feel like a teenager. And he did what he was told.

"Earlier this year we started noticing an influx of a new drug in Portland," Barb said. "Potent. Deadly. We've had our challenges, but this was different. We followed a few leads, got in touch with the feds, but these drugs were new, and not the kind they'd seen coming in from Mexico or out of pill mills."

"Yeah, the kind I found in his basement," Rory said, jabbing his thumb toward Vaughn. "The same kind that killed my brother. He's at the morgue, you know, waiting to be cut open."

"I know," Barb said. "The problem is that when word gets out about these new drugs, people want them, whatever the cost. They want the high. People chase the highest high they can find, even if it kills them in the end. That's what happened to your brother. To Pete. We couldn't figure out where the drugs came from, though."

"I think you have your guy," Rory said.

"But Vaughn's one of the good guys," Barb said. "He's been working with us. We needed someone who knew fishermen, who knew the island. And we needed him to be undercover. The drugs are coming from many places, but this island is one of them. And that house where Frankie and Daphne live seems to be at the center of it. So we need to talk to Daphne. And we need to talk to her now. And, you," she said to Vaughn. "You're out of commission. We need people to think you did this."

"Do I have to wear cuffs?" Vaughn asked.

"No, but you do need to keep your trap shut," Barb said.

"Why is Vaughn working for the cops?" Rory asked.

"I am a cop," Vaughn said. "Sorry to keep it from you, Rory-boy, but I work for the DEA."

"Did Trey know about this?"

"I hope not," Barb said. "Trey Pelletier was our main suspect."

For the first time in over a year, Daphne felt full, really full, like she'd throw up if she ate another bite full, and now, in a way, following Hester and Mindy up the narrow staircase and into the little hotel room made her feel like Charlie walking into the chocolate factory. Anything she could dream of was at her fingertips, though her dreams weren't that big. Here, the air smelled fresh, and when the door closed she didn't have to worry that a strange man might walk in, that someone might steal her meager belongings.

Or worse.

The bedsheets were clean, the pillows soft. A TV waited. She touched the duvet, her fingers running along the smooth, white cloth, and remembered TV reports about hotel duvets, how unclean they could be, how they stored up germs from one hotel guest to the next. *Take it off the bed!* the TV reporter had exclaimed. *Use gloves! Worry! Feel terrible. Know this: The end is coming, and it will come because you touched your hotel duvet!*

These people had never wrapped themselves in a

stained beach towel, grateful for any protection from the wind it could provide. They'd never found a half-eaten steak bomb in the trash and wondered where it had gone, unable to remember eating all of it, even the bit of bread with a lipstick stain on it.

The sheets were clean and dry, fitted to the mattress. She lay down, and the bed shaped to her body. When was the last time she'd lain down on a mattress this soft? She shifted the pillows till they conformed to her head, and she told herself, somehow, some way, she'd remember this moment, in all its perfections. In all its simplicity.

"Do you need anything?" Hester asked.

Daphne didn't need a thing.

"Do you want to sleep?"

"Maybe."

"I'll be back," Hester said. "Lydia was worried about you. She'll want to know you're safe."

"You can leave the dog here," Daphne said.

"I'll take her with me," Hester said.

No, Hester wouldn't even trust her with a dog, but Daphne deserved that. She listened as the door clicked shut and Hester's footsteps tapped softly down the stairs.

Lydia.

Would it matter now, about Trey? Would Daphne need to confess to the affair?

She rolled onto her side. She thought about Kate, about the Post-it. A year ago, when she'd left, when she'd written that message—*Back in an hour. Tops!*—she'd truly believed that she'd return. She'd wanted a moment of peace, that's it, so she'd surrounded Kate with a moat of cushions and left the house without a plan. She walked to the corner store on Highland Avenue, bought a pint of Chubby Hubby, and sat on the lawn in front of the Somerville Library and ate all of it. The night was dark and cool but not cold. And when she finished, she saw the 90 Bus idling as though it were waiting for her, the interior lit up and welcoming.

It was so easy to get on.

She was the only passenger, and she rode it to Sullivan Square and transferred to the Orange Line. She walked the few blocks to South Station as though in a dream, and when she got there, fate took her to Portland and to this life, because it had been the only bus still scheduled to leave that night. What if she'd gone to Worcester instead?

Annie had allowed Daphne to wipe the slate clean. Annie had a different past, a different story.

But she was Daphne now. Again. And Daphne's story involved Hester and Morgan.

And Kate.

The bed no longer felt soft. The feathers in the pillows had compacted. A breeze blew the scent of low tide through the window. She went into the hallway and crossed to the bathroom, where she filled the tub with the hottest water she could stand. While steam filled the air, she loaded Hester's toothbrush with toothpaste and brushed for five minutes. Daphne could have brushed for an hour and her mouth still wouldn't have felt clean. She undressed, leaving her clothes in a pile. How long had it been since she'd changed? She examined her body. The cuts and the bruises first. Then her emaciated arms and legs, and the wounds that didn't yet show. She lowered herself into the scalding water, feeling her skin redden from the heat. The stench from days without bathing rose up, hovering in the steamy air. She scrubbed till the dirt and dried blood lifted from her skin. She ran shampoo through her hair and sank down into the water, beneath the surface, letting the water shut out the world. But this was when the thoughts took over.

She could escape. Still.

But what about Kate? What about her little girl? She didn't deserve Kate, she knew that much. She hadn't been young when she'd gotten pregnant—thirty-two isn't young, is it?—but she'd still lived in denial. She lived in the Allston apartment then, by herself, since Hester had abandoned her for Somerville and Morgan. She worked as a home health aide at twelve dollars an hour—no benefits, no fixed schedule—so when the pain began, she went to the emergency room, complaining of heartburn. The doctor had prescribed an antacid. "Unless you're pregnant?" she said. "Is there any chance?"

"None," Daphne said, with what she hoped sounded like confidence, because there had been many chances.

As the months went on, she wore big sweatshirts and ate brownies like a sorority girl from a bad TV movie. When she visited Hester, Morgan would whisper that he worried about her weight when he thought she couldn't hear. She left the job as a home health aide and started another at a pharmacy, also without benefits, where, she supposed, they knew her as the fat girl. And then one afternoon her contractions started. She was alone. Her landlord had come by, asking about the rent earlier that day, but besides him, she couldn't remember having spoken to anyone in days. She'd been fired from the pharmacy by then.

She gave birth on the bathroom floor, blood spilling across the white tiles, scrolling through her phone frantically for instructions on what to do with the umbilical cord. The baby—Kate, though she didn't have a name yet—cried and gurgled, a fist clenched in her mouth. Daphne wrapped her in an old sweatshirt and left her outside behind the trash.

Not in it, behind it.

It was August, so it hadn't been cold out. Or raining. And she could claim now, here, soaking in the tub, alone with her thoughts, that she'd done it without thinking, that she'd been a victim of her own confusion. Hell, she should blame hormones. But when she was completely honest with herself, she remembered that sense of relief at solving the problem. At making it disappear. And she remembered turning on the TV and watching a rerun of *Bewitched*, and the helplessness that had replaced that relief when she went outside and found the baby still wrapped in the sweatshirt, still hidden behind the trash, and brought her inside.

Hester came over as soon as she called.

She swaddled the baby in a towel from the closet and held her to her shoulder. "How about Katherine?" Hester said, kissing the baby's cheek, and bouncing her as she cried. "Like Katharine Hepburn, but not spelled in a way that she'll have to spell her name for the rest of her life. That's annoying. We'll call her Kate. And she's hungry."

"I like Caitlin better," Daphne said.

"Okay, Caitlin it is."

"But we'll still call her Kate. With a K. You're right. She shouldn't have to spend her life spelling her own name."

Hester had never had a child. She didn't even have brothers or sisters, at least not any that Daphne knew of. She didn't know how to do any of this, either, but it didn't stop her from trying. And the moment Kate had a name, Daphne understood what she'd done, the secret that she'd carry with her till the day she died, and she wondered how much of it Hester might have managed to guess. She held out her arms, and after a moment Hester let her hold Kate while Daphne promised herself to always, always put the girl first.

Later, Morgan came to the apartment and examined Kate like a puppy, but Hester insisted that Daphne and Kate go to the hospital. When they were released the next day, everything in the Allston apartment had already been moved to Somerville. "It's easier this way," Hester had said.

The water in the tub had cooled. Daphne lifted the plug with her toe and listened as the quiet drained away, taking some of her torment with it. With the stink washed from her skin and hair, her clothes smelled even worse. But then she heard the voices. They drifted through the window on the breeze. She stood in the last of the draining water and craned her neck to look out the tiny bathroom window, where she saw Rory and that detective, the one who dressed like a housewife, coming up the path, unlatching the gate, walking with purpose. Rory paused to take his cap off.

Daphne toweled off and dressed quickly. She slipped into the hallway, down the back staircase, and outside.

They knew.

They knew that she was terrible and dangerous and

could never be forgiven for the things she'd done. They knew that she could never be trusted, certainly not with Kate. But no one knew better than Daphne how easy it was to make mistakes. She'd seen how dangerous she could be. And she wondered whether she still was. She also believed that she could be a hero.

She could be Kate's hero, because she already had been.

She *had* known what she was doing that night she'd left the Post-it. She'd known more than she ever gave herself credit. She'd written the note with tears streaming down her face, and a bathtub, like the one she'd just soaked in, filled, waiting for both of them, one where they could sink down into oblivion, into that quiet world, and never return.

And she hadn't felt more alone in her whole life.

She'd written that note to save Kate and to save herself, because if she knew one thing to be true, she knew this: If she'd stayed in Somerville, if she hadn't fled that life, if she hadn't trusted Hester with every single thing that she held dear, neither she nor Kate would have survived the night.

Daphne had saved her daughter twice now. From herself.

She slipped out of the garden and ran down the road, stepping out of sight behind a house, her back pressed to the weathered shingles. She took in a deep breath and closed her eyes. And she sensed his presence even before he spoke. "Don't move, Red."

It was Seth. He had the barrel of a gun pressed to her temple.

CHAPTER 24

Hester followed the smell of floor cleaner through the inn and into the bakery's kitchen as Mindy tugged at her leash. Lydia knelt down, scrubbing, her hair tied in a red kerchief. Mindy woofed.

"You have her," Lydia said, sitting back and letting the sponge fall to the floor. "I'd wondered if I'd have to go out and find her." She took a deep breath. "I heard they arrested Vaughn. And that you had something to do with it."

"More Daphne than me. I found her, but I bet you've already heard that too."

"Most of it," Lydia said. "I heard there were drugs. Lots of them. The ones that killed Rory's brother. And that Vaughn installed a padlock on the cellar door, and that your friend there survived on pretzels. How could any of this be true? Vaughn wouldn't do these things."

"Rory told you a lot," Hester said.

"Not me," Lydia said. "The two of us are back to not talking."

Right then, the front door to the bakery slammed open and shut. Oliver ran through to the kitchen, stopping to show his mother a fistful of worms. "I think they're rattlers!" he said, running through the inn and back into the garden.

"He just learned about rattlesnakes," Lydia said.

"You haven't told him about Trey, have you?"

Lydia shook her head. "I need to before someone else does." She stood, wiping her hands on her apron, lifting the bucket, and setting it next to the sink. "I have to stay busy," she said. "Otherwise I might lose it. I scrubbed this floor. And I'll scrub the rest of this place till it sparkles. That's about as much as I can focus on right now."

The bells over the bakery door rang as someone let themselves in. "Can't people read?" Lydia mumbled, and then added in a shout, "We're closed. I'm in mourning."

Mindy's ears perked up at the sound of boots crossing the store. Rory stepped into the tiny kitchen, followed by Detective Kelley, and as soon as Lydia saw him, she tossed the sponge into the bucket and faced him. Everything on this island had changed in the past twenty-four hours, especially in Lydia's world, and no matter what happened in the end, Hester could see that Lydia's life would never be the same again. "I defended you all summer long, and now I wish I hadn't. You arrested Vaughn? I bet those rumors about you taking Oliver are true."

"I didn't touch Oliver," Rory said.

"Take it down a notch," Barb said. "Both of you. Mrs. Pelletier, we need to talk to you."

"Why?"

"I bet you can guess," Barb said.

"Everyone in town knows about the affair," Lydia

said, untying her apron and tossing it onto the counter. "All of you can go to hell for all I care."

She left the kitchen and slammed the bakery door behind her. Mindy woofed and wagged her tail, and Rory let the dog lick his hand.

"Where's Vaughn?" Hester asked.

"He's locked up," Rory said. "At the community center."

"Someone told me to ask him about the drugs."

"Why don't you let us ask the questions," Barb said.

"Well, before you start, let me tell you something, then," Hester said. "Lydia thinks that Oliver and Ethan are brothers. She told me earlier today. Her husband got around."

"Did you know this?" Barb asked Rory.

From the look on his face, Hester could tell he meant it when he said, "I had no clue."

"You could have told us earlier," Barb said.

"I've been a little distracted," Hester said.

Barb paced across the floor. "First things first," she said. "Daphne. We need to talk to her. Now. We need to know her connections to Seth and Frankie, and why someone would lock her in Vaughn's cellar."

"She's upstairs," Hester said, leading them to the room. She knocked on the door and peeked in, only to find an empty bed where she'd last seen Daphne. She crossed the hallway and tried the bathroom door. Inside, the air was steamy, with the gray dregs of a full tub drained.

"She must have gone down the back way," Rory said.

Out in the harbor, the ferry blew its horn as it backed away from the pier.

"Shit," Rory said, running down the stairs, his boots pounding the floorboards.

"We need her," Barb said. "We need both of you. Stay put. Do *not* move."

She followed Rory. Hester watched out the window as Rory ran down the path, waving his hands over his head. He pulled a radio from his waist and shouted into it while Hester scanned the upper deck of the boat for a flash of Daphne's red hair. The ferry's engine stopped, and the boat reversed course. Hester retreated to the room, where she sat on the bed, her knees tucked in. Mindy leapt up, and she let the dog snuggle in beside her. She checked her wallet, which she'd left by the TV. Nothing was missing. Daphne wouldn't have gone anywhere, not without money. If Daphne hadn't taken the boat, she must have gone to Little Ef, to the Victorian. Hester could probably make it there and back before Barb and Rory had finished searching the ferry.

Outside, the air had grown cold. Leaves swirled from trees as Hester set off, letting Mindy run off the leash. Little Ef seemed abandoned. The houses she passed were empty, boarded up for the season. She rounded the last bend in the path and stepped into the darkness of the forest. The house still rose from the rhododendrons, but now, with most of the plywood removed from its windows, it looked naked and sad, and certainly uninhabitable, once the cold of winter set in. At least Hester didn't have a four-year-old with her this time. She called to Mindy, who dashed toward her from out of the trees and sat expectantly. Hester's pockets almost always had spare treats from her morning walks with Waffles, and today was no different. The dog accepted the biscuit and waited patiently for another.

"Daphne!" Hester shouted toward the house. "Are you here?"

A movement caught her eye. She glanced up, toward the second floor, where Frankie stood in one of the open windows staring out, her face blank. She held Ethan against her shoulder, rocking him back and forth. "Frankie!" Hester shouted. "We met yesterday. Come outside. I want to talk to you."

She heard a groan from the forest. "Who's there?" she said, stepping toward the brush. Beside her, Mindy whined. She heard another groan and followed it to where she found a state trooper lying on the ground, unconscious. His name tag read NATE GARDNER. She shook him, but he didn't wake. "Frankie, come help me," Hester shouted. "Someone's hurt."

As she took a step toward the house, a blast threw her to the ground. Flames erupted from the kitchen, black smoke pouring into the air. Mindy spun around, barking at the fire. Hester shouted Frankie's name again and shoved the dog toward the road. "Run," she said. "Get out of here. Scat!"

She hurled a stick into the trees, watching as Mindy ran to retrieve it. The flames had spread up the back of the house, engulfing the century-old wood. Hester held her hand in front of her face and squinted into the heat. Frankie was at the window, still holding Ethan to her chest. "Go toward the front!" Hester shouted, waving her arms. "Down the front stairs! The fire is in the back of the house."

Frankie screamed as smoke engulfed her.

And Hester ran. Forward. Toward the burning building. She ran without thinking, shoving the oak door open with her shoulder and nearly falling back as a wave of

scorching heat swept over her. She took her phone out
and dialed 911, praying the call would go through. She
covered her face with her fleece and pressed forward.

The fire had swept from the kitchen and through the
front room. Hester found a path up the front stairs.
Smoke burned her lungs as she shoved open the door
to Daphne's room and shouted her name. The room
was empty. Back in the hall, she nearly fled. But she
forced herself to keep moving, into smoke as thick as
night. She fumbled with her phone. It slipped from her
fingers and clattered to the floor. *Leave it!* she thought.
There isn't time. "Come toward me!" she shouted.
"Anyone!"

She gasped for oxygen. The heat had grown unbear-
able. Safety beckoned. How long could those front
stairs last? She turned, crawling away. Retreating. And
then she heard it. The boy. Crying. "Ethan!" she screamed.

She lay flat on her stomach, as close to the floor as
possible, and moved, toward the noise, till she came to
a wall. She felt along it till her hand landed on the
seam of a closet door. Inside, she found Ethan, pressed
into a corner. "Come," she said, but he pushed away
and refused to move.

"Where's your mother?" Even those words hurt to
say.

She crawled into the closet, where the air was
clearer for the moment. She took a deep breath. Oxygen filled her lungs, and a part of her wanted to stay
here. To breathe. But she lifted the squirming boy
under her arm. He struggled, clawing at her as smoke
seeped under the door.

What would she do if Kate were here? What world
would she create to get them out of this? What would

she ask Kate to count? "I need your help," she whispered in Ethan's ear. "I need you to be brave and to run as fast as you can when I tell you to. Like Superman. Do you like Superman?"

He pushed away from her.

"Thomas!" Hester said, remembering the conversation outside the General Store. "Thomas the Train."

"The tank engine!" Ethan said.

"The tank engine," Hester said. "What would Thomas do?"

Ethan stopped squirming. "Bash his way out," he said.

"Then that's what we'll do too," Hester said.

He rested his head against her shoulder and wrapped his legs around her waist and mumbled, "Okay."

"Don't let go of me," Hester said.

She opened the closet door and smoke poured in. The air was hot enough to melt skin. Flames had spread into the room, licking at the ceiling, and as she tried to retrace her path to the front stairs, the ceiling collapsed. "There's another way," she whispered.

There had to be.

She felt along the walls to where the windows should have been. They were still boarded up. "We'll bash our way out, right?" she said to Ethan.

"Like Thomas," Ethan said.

Hester balanced Ethan on her hip and shoved her shoulder into plywood. It barely moved. She kicked at it and kicked again and again till the wood buckled. Her head had grown light. She kicked one more time. The plywood cracked, a shaft of light shining through. She kicked again, and a chunk broke off. She lifted Ethan through the hole and lowered him to the top of a bow window on the first floor, and then followed. Black tears filled her eyes. There had to be at least fifteen feet to the ground. Flames burst from the windows around them, and she felt the burn as the flames caught her fleece. This was their chance. "Me first, then you."

She leapt, hovering in midair for what seemed like forever before plummeting. After hitting the ground with a jolt, she rolled to the side. But she was on her feet again, reaching up. "Now!" she shouted to Ethan, her arms held wide.

He stared down at her.

"Thomas can fly," Hester said.

"Thomas can't fly."

"Who can?"

"Harold," Ethan said. "He's a helicopter."

"Then be Harold!" Hester said.

He leapt as flames shot from the wall behind him. And he came at her, slamming into her chest and knocking them both to the ground. Hester rolled across leaves and pine needles. Ethan's sweatshirt was on fire. She pounded at it with her bare hands, ignoring the burns. She took the boy's hand and fled into the trees, toward the water. Off in the distance, a bell rang, a chime from another time alerting the town to danger. When they reached the water, Hester plunged into it, despite the cold, to stop the burning, to save her flesh. Water enveloped her, a world away from this one, a world of peace where mothers didn't die horrible deaths while wondering if they'd saved their children, where friends didn't go missing, where children stayed at home. She crawled to the beach. Ethan sat on the sand, and she examined him from head to foot. His hair had singed on one side, but otherwise he seemed fine, at least on the outside.

"What happened?"

Hester spun around. Daphne stood a few feet away. Behind her, flames burst over the tree line. The ends of her red hair had burned. Hester lifted Ethan from the ground. He was lighter than Kate, skin and bones enrobed in a University of Maine sweatshirt. Still, he smelled of innocence and everything good. And of urine. And smoke. She'd need to bathe him at the hotel. She'd need to figure out what to do, where he should go. What the next step was when a kid had no parents. She'd have to do all of this. And she'd make Daphne watch. Make her see what it meant to take responsibility.

"What did you do?" Hester asked. No, she shouted. She was tired of being nice and trying to understand. She was tired of waiting and wondering. She was tired of putting Daphne's presence and absence and her every decision at the center of her world. And she was tired of pretending that any of this was normal. "You did this," she said.

Pop.

A bullet ricocheted off granite. The rifle went off again, and everything slowed. Hester's first instinct was to dive to the ground, to cover Ethan's body with her own, to crawl and to hide. Her second impulse was to be grateful, grateful that she'd sent Kate off with Morgan, to know whatever happened here, whatever happened with this other person's child, that for once, Hester had made the right decision and Kate would be safe. She'd choose Kate any day. Her third impulse was the one she followed. She slammed her shoulder into Daphne and tackled her to the ground right as another bullet ricocheted off a boulder. A wail began in the base of Ethan's throat, and she pulled him close, putting her lips to his ear, kissing him, tickling him, hoping the tricks she used to keep Kate on the right side of a tantrum might work here.

"How many friends does Thomas have?" she mumbled, right over his ear, barely a murmur. "List them off, but as quiet as you can, and I'll try to remember. It's a game."

"He has a lot of friends."

"That's why you have to list them all."

"There's Toby," Ethan said.

"Even quieter," Hester whispered. "Right in my ear."

Reasoning almost never worked with Kate, and maybe, if Ethan had known Hester, it wouldn't have worked with him, but he relaxed into her arms as he went through the list of names, Gordon and James and Percy.

"You're bleeding," Daphne said.

"Shut up before you get us killed," Hester said.

Daphne lay flat on the sand. She took Hester's hand in hers and squeezed.

"It's just a scratch," Hester whispered, scanning their surroundings. "Come," she said, crawling to a thicket of roses. "And watch the thorns," she whispered to Ethan as he continued to list off names, as if a thorn could matter now, but even as she said it another shot rang out. "It's coming from over there," she whispered, nodding her head toward an outcropping of rock two hundred yards down the beach. The shooter was positioned to block them from returning to the Victorian, to the fire, to the safety of a crowd.

"Where should we go?" Daphne asked.

"Down there, around the bend?" Hester said. "If we can get there, we should be out of the line of sight."

"Then that's what you should do."

Daphne was on her feet, running and weaving, dashing toward the trees, shouting at the top of her lungs. At the tree line, bark exploded around her. Hester lifted Ethan onto her hip and ran, stumbling over rocks, her feet splashing through tidal pools. The rifle went off again. And Hester was around the bend, and the spit leading to the lighthouse was in front of her. And she didn't dare turn.

They could hide in the lighthouse, barricade themselves in. They could wait. If they waited long enough, the tide would come in and the spit would disappear. Six hours of safety. Six hours for anyone but them to find the gunman.

Hester's arm ached. She could put Ethan down, hold his hand, tell him to run beside her. She could put him down and leave, save herself. For Kate. Or at least that's what she could tell herself for all the years going forward, for all the years of guilt and regret. But she pushed that thought away and held Ethan to her chest, even as she dared to ask what Kate would face without her. "We're all right," she whispered in Ethan's ear, her breathing labored. "Everything will be all right."

"There's Donald and Bill and Whiff," Ethan whispered.

Sand fell away. She hurtled forward, crashing across the beach. Ethan rolled away from her. And she crawled even as he fell, scrambling toward him, hand to his mouth. "The game," she said. "Who's next? Who else is friends with Thomas?"

"Rosie?" Ethan said.

And they somehow moved as one, crawling and crab walking till they sat, backs against a rock, out of sight. She held Ethan between her legs. He'd skinned his cheek. She resisted touching it or asking him about it, because it was the kind of hurt you felt only when you knew it was there.

"I don't like this game," he said.

"You're good at it, though," she whispered. "Much better than me. And I think you're winning." She closed her eyes and listened to the quiet of waves lapping at the shore. She rested her burned, blistered palms on the cool, damp sand.

"I'm scared," Ethan said.

"What color is Thomas? Is he pink?"

"Thomas is a boy."

Hester resisted arguing. Arguing made noise. "Tell me about all of Thomas's friends. Start again. From the beginning. But this time tell me what color they are. As quiet as you can."

CHAPTER 25

Emily Broward lived in a ranch-style house that had seen better days, as had most of the houses in the cul-de-sac outside of Portland. The vinyl siding had cracked, windows sagged, and the little grass on the front lawn was covered with brown patches Morgan recognized as pee stains from a dog. As Angela parked along a dusty sidewalk, Waffles, in the back of the van, sat up. A woof at the back of her throat turned into a growl. Inside, the lacy curtains swept aside as another dog snarled and pawed at a window.

Hester had been right when she'd told Morgan he'd ask the right question. At the Walmart, he'd shown a photo of Daphne to any employee who would look at it, till finally a greeter had simply said Daphne was friends with her niece, Emily, and had given him directions to the house.

"How do you want to do this?" Morgan asked Angela.

"I shouldn't, but I guess I can let you go this time," Angela said. "I don't like dogs," she added. "Except for yours, of course, but definitely not the vicious kind.

Put my number in your phone and hit Send if anything happens. And don't go inside the house."

Morgan told Kate to listen to Angela while he was gone. He walked up the flagstone path toward the front door. In his place, Hester would have told a story, one that would help her maneuver her way into the lives of the people who lived there, and she wouldn't stop at a few questions. She'd learn who these people were, what made them keep going. He'd be lucky to say hello. As he got closer, the dog—what he'd have called an "American Mix" at work but was probably part German Shepherd, part pit bull, and part many other breeds—seemed as if it wanted to force its way through the glass, right to his throat. Morgan handled much worse than this at work. He knocked and waited. He knocked again. "Anyone home?" he called, till finally a woman answered, blocking the space in the door with her body. She was more of a girl, really, twenty at most, with thin, light brown hair that fell on a round, gentle face.

"I don't have any money," she said.

Morgan made a clicking sound in his throat that got the dog's attention. "I'm a vet," he said. It seemed like a good-enough place to start.

"Did the neighbors call?" the woman asked. "They're always calling, and they want me to do something."

"You're Emily, right? Who's this?"

Emily eyed him warily. "Trouble," she said.

"Can she have treats?" Morgan asked.

"It's a he. And only if you want to lose a hand."

"People call my dog a boy all the time," Morgan said. "It drives me nuts, so I overcorrect. And I'll be fine. The only dog that ever bit me was a Shih Tzu named Maddie. She was the most vicious creature I've ever met. Trouble will be a piece of cake. How old is he?"

"They said he was two years old when I brought him home, but then he got bigger and bigger."

Morgan took a treat from his pocket. He glanced over his shoulder to where Angela waited. "Can I come in?"

"Don't let him out," Emily said. "He won't come back, though that might be a good thing."

To Morgan, the dog seemed more bored than dangerous. He dropped a treat on the floor to distract it and got on all fours to meet the dog on his level. When Trouble stopped barking, Morgan coaxed him to his side and, not being able to help himself, gave the dog a cursory exam. "He has some mange," he said. "And his teeth need cleaning. How are you exercising him?"

"Walking," Emily said.

"Every day?"

"Mostly. And I put him in the backyard, but he barks. All day. That's when the neighbors call."

"He's a big dog and still young. He needs at least an hour of exercise a day. He's a good boy but protective and bored. You have a kid, right?" Morgan asked.

"What do you want?" Emily asked, recoiling from him. "And who are you?"

"Sorry," Morgan said, nodding toward a photo of a girl in overalls sitting by the door. "I assumed."

"I forgot that was there. I get jumpy. Still, why are you here anyway? Are you some, like, social worker for dogs?"

Morgan moved away from Emily. Trouble followed him. A message from Angela popped up on his phone.

I told you not to go inside!

"Dogs are pleasers, and every one of them has it in them. Sometimes you have to look." He closed the message from Angela and pulled up the photo of Daphne on his phone. "I'm looking for someone I think you might know."

Emily took the phone from him and smiled. "Susan!" she said. "Is she okay?"

"Why do you ask?" Morgan said.

"Because I don't know where she went. We were friends—at least I thought we were—but now that I think about it, I haven't seen her in months. Not since the spring."

Morgan nodded toward the living room. As he sat on an old La-Z-Boy, Trouble leapt onto his lap. The dog was too big to sit on anyone, but Morgan let him stay anyway, scratching at his belly. "Susan's my sister," he said.

"You don't know where she is either?"

"I haven't for a while. But I found out she was here. And someone told me that she knew you. Now I guess she's gone someplace else. Any idea where?"

"I thought she . . . really, I lost track of her. I thought she might pop up one of these days. You know, ask me to go get a manicure."

"She's not really the manicure type," Morgan said. "Or at least not the side of her that I know. She's more of a jock."

"I guess you're right," Emily said. "But you know what I mean. I thought she'd come by."

"Tell me how you met," Morgan said.

"Oh, you know. Around."

"Don't like to share much, do you?" Morgan said. "Here, I'll share something with you: A dealer down by Northfield told me about you. He knew my sister, and he knew you. Seems like those were the circles you lived in."

Emily's face turned to stone.

"Did she deal?" he asked, not wanting to hear the answer.

"Not Susan. That wasn't her thing. Her thing was being kind. To me. To Jordan. That's my daughter."

"And what happened? Why aren't you friends any-more?"

"We *are* still friends, but you know how things go. You talk to someone every day, and it's intense and real and special, but it can't stay that way. Then it turns to every other day. And then once a week, and then a few months have gone by and you haven't really even noticed. That's where we're at. People come and go. I don't think I realized that I hadn't heard from her till you showed up."

Emily stood and glanced out the window to where Angela sat in the minivan, looking in. Trouble leapt off Morgan's lap and joined her, barking again. "You're not a vet," Emily said. "You're a cop. I can spot a stakeout a mile away."

"I guarantee you I am not a cop," Morgan said, taking his vet license from his wallet to show her. "I'd be the worst cop in the world. My friend out there, she is a cop, but she's off duty and watching my niece, so you don't have to worry about her. I just want to know what happened to my sister."

Emily suddenly seemed so small and young to Morgan, too young to have dealt with everything life had thrown at her, too young for a troublesome dog, let alone a child.

"You met at the Walmart, right? Returning things," he said.

She sat in a chair, one leg dangling over the arm. "Susan used to come with me to the Walmart and help me find receipts in the parking lot. You take them into the store, find the item on the shelf, then return it. Most people at Walmart are lucky if they make more than minimum wage. They don't care if 'the man' loses some cash."

"What was the money for?"

"What do you think?" Emily said. "First it was Oxy, then heroin." She rolled her eyes. "I got hooked in high school, got pregnant, dropped out, lived on the streets for a while. OD'd a few times. It's not a very original story."

"Did you deal?" Morgan asked.

"I did anything I could to score," Emily said. "And when I say anything, use your imagination. But I wanted out. I just couldn't stop no matter how much I tried. I'm clean now, and I'm not ashamed, not of anything I did. I'm safe. Jordan's safe, and I got those people out of my life."

"Like Daph . . . like Susan?" Morgan asked. "Is she one of the people you cut out of your life?"

"No!" Emily said, sitting up. "Not at all. Susan saved me. She saved Jordan too. Neither of us would be here if it hadn't been for her."

"Tell me what happened," Morgan said.

"I can't," Emily said. "I can't tell you. I can't tell anyone."

"Please," Morgan said. "My sister is missing. She might be in danger. Her name isn't Susan, it's Daphne. Daphne Maguire. She moved to Finisterre Island this summer and sent a note two days ago asking for help." Morgan scrolled through his phone to a photo of Vaughn Roberts. "Do you know this guy?"

Emily shook her head.

Morgan found a photo of Trey Pelletier. "How about him?"

Emily took the phone. "Yeah," she said. "I knew him, but not that well. He's a cop, but not a good one."

"Well, now he's dead. Someone I care about found his body." Morgan pulled up the Amber Alert for Ethan Sullivan. "Did you know this boy? His mother's name is Frankie, and she used to live here in Portland too. Probably did some of the same things you used to do. There was an Amber Alert out for Ethan two nights ago. I have a kid about his age." Even as the words came out of Morgan's mouth, they sounded right. He'd claimed Kate as his own. "If anything ever happened to Kate, I don't know what I'd do," he added, realizing how much truth there was in that simple sentence. "Tell me what you know."

Emily looked at Ethan's photo. "Poor boy," she said.

"He's fine," Morgan said. "He wandered home on his own. They found him sitting on the back stoop in the morning."

Trouble whimpered and rested his head on Morgan's thigh. Morgan ran his hand through the dog's mangy coat. "Please," he said. "Tell me."

* * *

A few moments later, outside, Morgan took a moment to collect himself. He faked a smile as he strode toward the minivan, Kate waving, Waffles's nose pressed to the rear window. In those steps, he gave himself over to this life, to Kate, finally and completely. He gave himself over in a way that Hester already had done months ago. She'd been waiting for him, all this time, unwilling to turn back to what had been. The whole time he'd seen problems with her, where the only problem had been him. This was their family now. It was time for him to step up and protect them.

"We need a hotel that takes dogs," Morgan said as he climbed into the passenger seat. "You and Kate can have one room. I'll take the other. And we can go to Fore Street for dinner. You can handle dinner in a restaurant, right, Kate?"

"Yes!" Kate said.

"Tomorrow we'll drive to Boothbay Harbor, pick up Hester, and we'll head home."

"What happened in there?" Angela asked.

Morgan turned toward the house, and Trouble came to the window, barking, pawing at the glass again. Desperate. Morgan counted out $120 from his wallet. "Do you have cash?" he asked.

Angela handed him four twenties. "That's all I have."

"I'm good for it," Morgan said. "I'll be back in a sec."

At Emily's front door, he handed her the cash and put Trouble on a leash, and the girl seemed more relieved than anything else. "Dogs take a lot of work, so don't feel bad," he said. "You focus on making for Jordan the best life you possibly can, and if you ever want another dog, give me a call. I'll get you set up with the right one. In the meantime, Trouble will be in good hands."

Morgan ran with the dog around the cul-de-sac four times, till sweat poured down his forehead and he gasped for breath. When he'd finished with the run, he tied the dog to a tree and let Waffles jump down to meet on neutral ground. A few moments later, they were in the back of the minivan, wrestling.

"Another dog?" Angela said.

"Trouble," Morgan said. "But a dog like this one needs a lovable name." He'd learned years ago to leave names like Butch or Rambo to pugs or French bulldogs. Mixes, especially pit bull mixes, needed sweet names, like Honey or Baby. "Any ideas?" he asked, turning to Kate.

"Daphne!" Kate said.

The name hit Morgan in the heart, but he absorbed the hurt the way Hester would. "I don't know how your mother would feel about that," he said. "Besides, he's a boy."

"Pancakes," Kate said.

Pancakes and Waffles. It was too much, even for Morgan. "How about George?" he said. "That's easy enough to remember."

"George, meet Waffles!" Kate said.

"George, it is," Morgan said, turning to face forward.

Angela sat quietly beside him, waiting. Finally, Morgan said, "If she wanted us to find her, we'd have found her by now. Let's eat. Let's have some fun. Let's find a way to relax for once. Hester's been crazy ever since the winter, but so have I. Let's forget that today ever happened."

Angela went to say something but stopped.

"I'm done making excuses," Morgan said.

"What did you learn in there? I'm not on duty."

"You are for this."

"Then you should say something."

"I can't," Morgan said.

A moment later, Angela put the car in gear and headed toward town.

As the alarm bell rang out, Rory ran to the upper deck of the ferry. From there, he could smell the acrid smoke of a house fire, and he scanned the horizon for the source.

"Daphne's not here," Barb said, joining him.

Behind them, the sun hovered near the horizon beyond Bowman Island. Opposite, on Little Ef, thick black smoke and another orange glow rose over the tree line.

"It's near the Victorian," Rory said.

Barb tried to radio Nate, but he didn't answer. "Something's wrong," she said.

Three men and a woman in fire gear unlocked the doors on a shed by the pier, backed the island's only fire truck out, and sped off, the lights flashing and the siren blaring. Like most coastal Maine communities, Finisterre Island had a volunteer fire brigade. A single fire could easily spread and wipe out all of the structures in an area, especially after a dry summer. The few passengers on the boat were all from town. They joined Rory and Barb as they ran up the gangway toward the community center. All around, Rory could feel the town arising. "Get in the Jeep," Rory said, taking charge. Vaughn appeared out of nowhere and got in on the passenger's side. "You need all the help you can get," he said.

"Fine," Barb said, as she climbed into the back seat. "But the two of you need to play nice. I don't want to have to pull you apart again."

"I'm game if he is," Rory said, starting the Jeep and speeding off. A crowd of people ran along the path, fire gear in their hands. They cleared the way to let Rory drive by.

"How long?" he said to Vaughn.

"How long what?" Vaughn asked.

"Everything."

"How long have I been working with the cops? Since I passed the test. You should try it one of these days."

"Fuck you," Rory said.

"What did I say?" Barb said from the back seat. "Get along, or I'll toss one of you out onto the side of the road."

"Right, boss," Vaughn said, and Rory hated him all over again for the twinkle in his eye. But he told his story. "I joined the DEA right after college. And I've been deep undercover almost ever since, working for my father-in-law on the docks. We've seen drugs coming in from all different sources, but one of those was the sea. About six months ago, we picked up a woman who'd been running heroin from Portland up through Augusta. One of the balloons she had in her mouth burst when she swallowed it."

"Sounds like Frankie," Barb said.

"Sounds like a lot of people, unfortunately," Vaughn said. "We had to deal with an OD, but once she came around she implicated the state police. That's when the focus turned to Trey, and I came to the island. He was smart, though. He didn't leave any kind of electronic trail, and he changed up his sources. For a while, they were leaving the shipments in his lobster traps, or at least that's the theory, but I've checked them a few times and they've been empty. I think Trey got wind of the investigation, because whatever was happening here seemed to stop, at least till this last shipment came through."

"The one that killed Pete," Rory said.

"Yeah," Vaughn said. "Again, I am truly sorry about that."

"I've known you forever!" Rory said. "And I'm a cop. Maybe if you'd let me know what was going on, I could have helped. Maybe Pete wouldn't have died! I thought you were my friend. And you knew Pete was an addict. Why the hell didn't you tell me?"

"It's not how it works," Vaughn said. "I was already investigating the police, and I was on my own. I can tell you that I didn't know the fentanyl had made it to the island till Pete died."

Rory punched at the steering wheel and glared at the road. He couldn't cry. Not here. Not in front of Vaughn, of all people.

"Working undercover does something to you," Vaughn said. "You lie to everyone, all day, and it makes you dishonest. But you know I'd do anything for you that I could, right?"

"And Lydia?" Rory asked. "Were you using her?"

"No," Vaughn said. "But I doubt she'll see it that way. Not in the end. Not when she finds out everything I've done, everything I've lied about. Be a friend and let me be the one to tell her. And then be a friend to her and listen to what she has to say. It's all I can ask."

"I can try," Rory said as he rounded the bend.

Down the road, a crowd had gathered by the Victorian. The fire truck had pulled as close to the house as possible, and a team had attached a hose to the nearest hydrant a few hundred yards away. Rory jumped out of the Jeep to join the group. "Do we know if anyone's inside?" he asked the head of the fire brigade.

"If anyone was still in there, God help them," she said.

"Have you seen a woman with blond hair, or the kid who went missing the other night?" Rory asked. "They live here."

"There was an officer here too," Barb said. "Nate Turner. He was watching her."

"We haven't seen anyone," the chief said. "And we can't send anyone in, not now. It's too dangerous."

"Damn it!" Rory said. They'd spent too much time and energy trying to save Ethan to have it come to this, but the house was an inferno, and no one had the equipment or training to do more than contain a fire like this one. Rory watched the house burn, the turrets collapsing in on themselves. Whatever had gone on here, whatever this house brought to the island, would still be there in the morning. The rot would be impossible to cut away, but maybe with the house gone, a part of that evil would go too. Rory took a turn at the hose, and when he finished, a group had tapped a keg and started handing out cups of beer. "There may be a dead woman in that house," Rory said to them. "A kid too. And a cop. Let's show respect."

He joined Vaughn and Barb, who stopped talking as he approached. Barb took a few steps toward the fire. "See that line there, toward the back," she said. "I don't know much about arson—and just like with the murder, we'll need an expert to come out here and confirm it—but to me, that looks like someone poured accelerant along the foundation of the house."

"And the arsonist knew that the house would go up like a tinderbox," Vaughn said.

"What else were you talking about?" Rory asked.

"We're wondering where Daphne or Annie or whatever she wants to call herself might have gone," Barb said. "Anytime something happens on this island, she seems to be right in the middle of it."

Rory heard a rustling in the tall hedges beside him. Nate crawled out of the trees, and Barb rushed to his side. "What happened?" she asked.

"Someone hit me," Nate groaned. "From behind. I didn't see it coming."

Right then, Mindy ran through the trees toward them. Vaughn called to the dog and knelt to let her lap at his face. He glared at Rory. "Tell me you didn't just leave her at my house when you arrested me?"

"I just saw her at the inn." Rory scanned the burning house. "She was with Hester. The question is, what's happened to her?"

CHAPTER 26

The light had begun to fade. The ocean consumed the sand on each side of the spit as, little by little, it narrowed with the incoming tide. Hester and Ethan had managed to make it through the list of Thomas's friends twice during the time that had passed. An hour, maybe? An eternity? Hester still didn't dare move them from their hiding place. Her damp clothing clung to her skin, and as the autumn chill set in, she could feel the cold, right to her numb left pinky, and it brought her back to last winter. To feeling helpless and afraid. She checked her pockets one more time for her phone, if only to distract herself, though she could still hear it clattering to the floor in the fire. She piled up rocks, each the size of her palm, and tried not to worry about Daphne or wonder why her friend had been at the house. And she held Ethan.

By now, the fire at the Victorian was dying down. Only plumes of dark smoke against the darkening sky remained. Hester could hear a celebration beginning by the burned house, and she imagined people gathering, a keg being tapped, children running, music playing. They couldn't be more than a few hundred yards from the crowd, from safety, but she couldn't risk the exposure of crossing the sandy spit in the open.

"I'm hungry," Ethan said.

Hester had learned not to travel without a ready supply of snacks—cellophane packages of raisins and Goldfish—but a day without Kate had freed her from all sorts of restrictions. She felt in her pockets and came up only with dog treats. They could resort to eating those if they had to, but not yet. "We'll find something soon," she said.

"Okay," Ethan said, and Hester heard in his voice that he'd grown used to hunger.

"For real," she said. "Anything you want."

A wave crashed on the shore, the water coming in far enough to meet her toes. The spit would disappear soon.

"We have to go out to the lighthouse," she whispered.

It was almost dark. The sun had disappeared, and only the grayest of light still filtered over the horizon. It had to be safe to move.

Hester lifted Ethan onto her hip. Kate would have demanded to walk on her own, but Ethan seemed content to cling to her, his arms encircling her shoulders. Her joints had grown stiff with the cold, so she was glad to move slowly, glad to hold Ethan, his legs wrapped around her waist and his head pressed to her chest. She stumbled across the sand. Behind her, she imagined the waters surging in, swallowing their escape route. Allowing plenty of time for the police to find the shooter, for Daphne to raise the alarm. But where was Daphne? The alarm should have been raised by now, and the troops should have come. Maybe, at the lighthouse, she could entice Ethan to sleep. Maybe they both could sleep and later, they could slip into town under the cover of darkness. Maybe, when they got to the inn, Daphne would be in bed, asleep. Or maybe she'd be reading with Mindy curled up beside her on the bed. She'd put a bookmark between the pages and say, "I've been waiting for you!"

But that wouldn't make sense either. That would only piss Hester off.

They reached the island, and Hester collapsed to the ground. It was drier here, above the water, and the stone still held warmth from the day's sun.

"Where's my mommy?" Ethan asked, and Hester didn't have the resolve to lie.

"Your mom saved you," she said. "She did everything she could for you."

They sat in silence, Hester letting her mind wander. Ethan grew restless, kicking his feet against stone.

"Are there songs you like?" she asked.

"Def Leppard," Ethan said.

"What are you, like fourteen years old or something?"

Ethan giggled. "I'm four," he said, grinning into her chest.

"Well, I like Def Leppard too," Hester said. "'Pour Some Sugar on Me'? Do you know that one?"

Ethan sang a few lines, and Hester joined in. At first, she thought about changing the lyrics, skipping over the dirty parts, but what did Ethan know? Peaches were peaches to a four-year-old.

"Do you know the Wiggles?" she asked when they'd finished singing, and Ethan shook his head. "I wish I didn't know them either," Hester added. "How about 'Like a Virgin' by Madonna?"

Ethan shook his head again.

"I'll teach you. And when it's darker, we can dance."

Hester sang a few of the lyrics, listening as Ethan sang them back at her, his voice soft and high-pitched. She wondered what he'd sound like as a man, whether he'd be a bass or a tenor, or whether he'd be one of those people who mouthed the lyrics when forced to participate. She remembered, however fleeting the thought, when she'd considered abandoning him, and she committed right then, no matter what, to see him through to what came next, and beyond. And she sang a little louder. Her own voice was a low and croaky contralto that hit the right note only by luck.

"Your turn," she said when they finished. "What's another song?"

"'Baby Got Back'?" Ethan said, and this time he laughed in a way that told Hester he knew this one was dirty.

"I like big butts . . ." she sang, pointing to him.

Ethan picked up the lyric and finished it. "And I can-not lie."

A light blinded her. A voice from behind it said, "How sweet."

Hester stepped in front of Ethan. She'd been so focused on entertaining the boy that she'd stopped listening. A sharp cry followed, and Daphne stumbled forward, shoved from behind. Then the light went out.

"I thought we might find you here."

As her eyes adjusted to the dark, Hester could see Seth's silhouette outlined against the water. He held a rifle and pointed it at them.

"Fire's out," he said.

"What happened to Frankie?" Hester asked.

"I bet you can guess. Though she managed to save the little one, for now. And it's the same thing that'll happen to you," Seth said, rubbing the barrel of the rifle against Hester's cheek. She gripped it and shoved it aside.

"Don't make this into a porn movie," she said.

"Then how about a snuff film?" Seth said. "Better than porn."

"You'll be lucky to make it off the island."

"I have people," Seth said. "They're coming to pick me up. Frankie should have remembered that. We both had people to count on, if we played the game right. But she wanted out."

"Did he hurt you?" Hester asked Daphne.

"No," Daphne said. "I tried to stop him. That's when I got burned."

Seth aimed the rifle at Daphne. "Did you know that even Frankie thought you're a nasty whore? She told me all about you."

Hester ignored him, turning to Daphne. "Look at me," Hester said. "You saved me last winter. I didn't get a chance to tell you. You were with me the whole time, in the snow, in the cold. With Kate. I kept thinking about that class, the one where we first met, the one you were teaching. Do you remember it?"

The self-defense course. Please remember.

"I remember," Daphne said.

"You," Seth said to Hester. "You also need to shut up."

He shoved her, and she purposefully fell to the ground and palmed a stone.

"Get up," Seth said.

He wrenched her arm, and she shoved him off her. He took a step back and fell off balance. And she swung. Hard. Smashing the side of his face.

Seth staggered. When the rifle went off, Hester tried in vain to grab it as it clattered across the stones. Daphne crouched and sprung at Seth, driving her bony shoulder into his gut. He doubled over and fell. Hester lifted Ethan, clutched at Daphne's hand, and they fled into the darkness.

"Run," Hester said, shoving Ethan into Daphne's arms. "Get back to shore, even if you have to swim."

Hester turned and bolted across the granite, making as much noise as she could. Behind her came footsteps, pounding, the sound of heavy breathing. But she turned to face off. And when Seth came at her, she slammed another rock into the side of his head. A hand hooked around her ankle. She fell forward, her hands slipping. Blood flooded her mouth as she bit her tongue. She swung again. The rock connected with something hard and fleshy, and Seth let go enough so that she could scramble forward into rosebushes, her hands waving wildly in front of her, shoving branches away. Her shin snapped as she hit a boulder. She tumbled over it headfirst. She was on her feet again, rounding the lighthouse. She imagined Daphne, on the beach, lit by the moon, with Ethan clinging to her. She imagined them safe. Hester stopped, back to a boulder, facing the sea. She willed herself not to breathe. Daphne would bring help. Soon. In front of her, the inky water rose and fell. A sleek motorboat sped toward where she hid, a bright light glaring from the bow.

"Here they are." A voice in her ear once more. "My friends. Just in time."

Seth jabbed the barrel of the rifle, hard, into Hester's temple.

"I shouldn't say friends," he said. "They'd get rid of me, just like I got rid of Frankie. They're business acquaintances. With a boat that will get my ass out of here."

"Go," Hester said. "I'm good at keeping secrets. I'm even better at lying."

"What's my secret?" Seth asked.

"You burned the house."

"That's hardly a secret. Your friend saw me do it."

"And you aren't Frankie's brother."

"Look, Frankie was an idiot. She was about to go to the state cops and cut a deal. So she had to go. Pretty straightforward."

"And you killed Trey Pelletier."

"Did I?"

"Did Frankie?"

"Give me a break. She wouldn't have killed Trey. She was banging him. Frankie thought she could move here and make Trey pay for everything he'd done. She threatened to reveal their affair to Trey's wife, where that kid came from. She thought she could make him do what she wanted. Then Trey turned up dead, and she had no cards left to play. And why would I kill him? He protected the coastline and made my job easier."

"But you took his kids," Hester said. "You kidnapped Ethan and Oliver."

"I wasn't even here when those kids disappeared. That was the cop, the one who has a thing for Lydia." He paused, adjusting his hold on the rifle. "But what do you care? You're dead anyway."

"Is she?"

Daphne stepped into the moonlight. She swung a piece of driftwood into Seth's temple. He fell back. Then Daphne lifted the wood over her head and smashed his skull. Out on the water, the engine revved and the boat sped away, its headlamp fading into the dark.

"Where's Ethan?" Hester asked.

"In the lighthouse."

Hester ran, throwing the door open, lifting the boy from the ground, checking him all over. He seemed fine. Safe. Or as safe as he could ever be. "Do you still like big butts?" she asked.

Ethan smiled. "Yes," he said.

"Better than Thomas?"

"No."

"Keep it that way."

Back on the beach, Seth was unconscious but still breathing. They rolled him to his side and tied his hands behind his back using rope from a buoy that had washed up. Then they sat with the lighthouse to their backs, Ethan sandwiched between them, and the boy talked in excited whispers about running, about the fight. Finally, his eyes grew heavy, and he fell asleep. By then, the tide had swallowed the spit and marooned them. They could hear the party by the extinguished fire, the music growing in intensity, the laughter and conversation filling the night.

"Did you ever . . ." Hester began. "Were you sleeping with Trey?"

"Annie was," Daphne said, after a moment. "Annie did that kind of thing."

"What else did Annie do?" Hester asked.

"She survived. Any way she could, but she didn't

kill anyone, and she didn't burn down a house, if that's what you're asking."

"It is, actually. I'm asking you if you killed Trey. Or, if you want, did Annie?"

Hester focused on the horizon, where the dark night sky met the nighttime ocean, illuminated by a waning gibbous moon. A thought emerged, a connection, something she'd heard earlier that hadn't fit. Hester turned to Daphne.

"When I left you with Vaughn, after we'd tied him up, did he say anything?"

"He tried to charm his way out of it."

"What did he do when Rory arrested him?"

"More of the same. More negotiating. He treats Rory like a little brother. It gets under his skin."

"What did Rory do?" Hester asked.

"He had his gun drawn," Daphne said. "And he told me to roll on my stomach and put my hands over my head. It pissed me off. Made me feel like a criminal. Then he cuffed Vaughn and brought him outside. I followed a few seconds later."

The noise from the party on the mainland stopped abruptly, and Barb Kelley's voice rang out through the trees. "Everyone, go home," she said into what must have been a bullhorn. "We need to clear the area."

"Oh, Jesus," Hester said, thinking again of the fire, of Frankie standing in that window, of what they'd probably found. She ran her fingers through Ethan's thick hair, and he woke from his sleep.

On the beach, people began to pass by, flashlights and headlamps bobbing along. Hester, Daphne, and Ethan waved their arms and shouted till someone finally heard them. A dinghy launched from the shore, and as it approached, Hester saw Vaughn Roberts standing at the bow with Mindy beside him while Rory rowed. "We were worried about you!" Vaughn shouted.

"We were too!" Hester shouted back. "And we'll need a medevac here. Someone's pretty badly hurt."

"I hope it's one of the bad guys," Vaughn shouted.

Rory pulled at the oars again, his back strong. Hester touched Daphne's hand. "Before Rory arrested Vaughn," she said, "did he search the house? Did he go downstairs to the cellar?"

The boat glided to the shore, and Mindy leapt to the sand, dashing toward them. As Daphne stepped into the surf to grab the bow, she said, "Not that I remember."

It wasn't the answer Hester had hoped for.

CHAPTER 27

For what seemed like hours, Hester answered Detective Kelley's questions about Seth and Frankie and Trey, about why she'd come to the island in the first place, why she'd gone to the house, and why she had the child of a dead woman with her.

"If it helps," Barb said, "it looks like Frankie died of a gunshot wound before the smoke or fire got to her."

"I tried," Hester said. "I ran into the fire but couldn't find her."

"You did your best."

Barb jotted something in her notebook anyway.

Hester balanced Ethan on her knee, rocking him gently and letting him fall asleep against her chest. She refused offers to take him away. Where would he go, anyway? She was all he had, at least for the night.

Vaughn had taken Daphne to another room to question her, and Hester hoped that Daphne would stick to the facts. The truth would be the only way through this.

"You had never met Seth, not before coming to the

island?" Barb asked for what must have been the fourth time.

Hester was tired, but she kept her cool. "Besides Daphne, I'd never met any of these people, including Seth. Not till yesterday when I gave him twenty bucks," she said.

Had she mentioned the twenty dollars before? She wanted to keep her answers straight, to stick to the story. But Barb was better at this than she was. Besides, it was late, well after midnight.

"Why the twenty?" Barb asked.

"Because he answered my questions. And he seemed like he needed it."

"What were your questions about?"

Hester *had* answered that one already. She sighed to let Barb know that she knew they were playing the same game. "Daphne. I was looking for Daphne."

"And this Seth. Do you know if that was his real name?"

"How could I? I'd never met him. Who was he anyway?"

Barb contemplated the question for a moment, clearly deciding what to share. Finally, she relented. "He was a midlevel drug dealer in a much bigger network," she said. "As least that's what we know so far. It looks like Frankie worked for him, till recently."

"Daphne saw them together though," Hester said. "She told me they seemed close."

"Maybe Frankie didn't want to get away as much as she thought she did. Seth probably helped her get high again." Barb's phone rang. "Kelley here," she said, listening for a moment. "That was the hospital," she said when she hung up. "Seth is out of surgery but still unconscious. If he wakes up, we'll be able to ask him some of these questions."

Hester was more relieved by the news than she'd expected to be. "I thought I'd killed him," she said, and immediately regretted it when the detective jotted a note on her pad.

"He's not out of the woods," Barb said. "But we'll see. What do you think he'll say if he wakes up?"

"It'll depend on what kind of deal you cut."

"He's smart enough for that?"

"Probably not. He'll tell you that he's one piece of a big puzzle—and maybe he'll lead you to a few more pieces—but that you'll never put the whole thing together."

"You got that one right." Barb put her feet up on the table. "Next time something like this happens, call in the cops. We're here to help."

"There won't be a next time," Hester said.

"Let's hope."

Hester stood, lifting Ethan onto her shoulder. "He'll stay with me tonight," she said. It wasn't a question.

"Someone from family services will be on the ferry tomorrow," Barb said. That wasn't a question either.

"Where's Daphne?"

"She'll be done soon too, and we'll bring her to the inn. Go get some rest. That kid is tuckered out."

Hester rocked Ethan gently, but when he refused to wake up, she decided her biceps could handle a few more minutes of holding him. Outside, the night air was crisp and clear, though the smell of the fire still hung over the town. The sky was filled to overflowing with stars. When Hester reached the inn, she wasn't quite ready to go inside for the night and headed toward the pier instead, where she saw someone standing by the gangway. It was Rory, who stared out over the water even as she joined him. "This child feels like a bag of cement," she said.

Rory took Ethan from her, resting the boy's head of dark hair on his shoulder. "How is he?"

"He seems fine on the outside," Hester said. "That psychiatrist, Dr. Feldman, gave him a once-over, for whatever that's worth, but we all have bruises, right? Ones that never quite heal. Sometimes it's best to tell someone the truth. Sometimes it's the only way to survive."

"You mean Lydia and me? Everyone knows that already." Rory laughed, as though realizing the gravity of the situation for the first time. "The whole town. Everyone I grew up with, everyone I've ever known, they think I kidnapped Oliver to steal his mother away from his father. They actually think I could do that."

"Well, didn't you?" Hester asked. "Take Oliver?"

"I've done a lot of things," Rory said. "But that's not one of them."

Hester glanced around the pier. They were the only ones out at this hour, the only ones who could hear what was said. This was a place meant for secrets.

"Like what?" she whispered.

Rory glanced up. Would he deny what she knew must be true? But Rory laid Ethan on a bench and placed his coat over the boy. "You don't know anything," he said.

"I do, though," Hester said. "I know that things you said didn't add up. Things you claimed that you saw.

At Vaughn's house, you never went downstairs. You couldn't have seen the lock on the cellar door or the drugs. But you told people about them as if you had. You told me about them."

"How do you know I didn't search the house?" Rory asked, his voice tipping toward anger.

"Daphne was there."

"And she'd been held in a cellar for almost two days. Beaten, confused. What she says won't matter."

"None of this does, even if you tell me," Hester said. "It'll all be hearsay. Right now, it's us. You and me. And you can tell me. You can let all of this go. It's better to share."

Rory put both hands on the iron railing and bounced on his toes like a gymnast getting ready to launch himself high in the air. "Barb will be disappointed," he said. "That's what really hurts. She likes me and believes in me like no one else ever has."

Hester felt the winter again. She felt the cold. She thought about Sam, about Gabe as he sat in that cell in Devens. Those unread letters in plain white envelopes in her closet at home. "I've seen awful things," she said. "And I've known terrible people. Dangerous people. You aren't one of them."

She heard him catch his breath and exhale slowly, steeling himself for a future he didn't need to choose, and Hester wanted to tell him to push this down, to forget it ever happened. Good people do bad things. She'd done plenty herself. He could live his life, one with value, but he'd have to give himself a chance. He'd have to forgive himself. He could let Seth take the fall. Seth had killed Frankie. He'd burned that house, and what was the difference between one and two murders anyway? "Don't say anything," she whispered. "Not even to me."

But he did. He told her everything.

The town was asleep. Quiet. Rory passed by Cappy's and The Dock. At the inn, he stopped outside the picket fence. A light burned in the first-floor sitting room, where he imagined Lydia on the sofa with Oliver beside her, like the night of the storm. He could have let himself in through the gate and stood outside the window looking in as he had on so many other nights. Did Lydia know? Did she know that he'd watched over her all these years? He wondered a lot of things about Lydia, like how much she'd learned about Trey, what she'd participated in and what she'd chosen to ignore. But there was enough blame already, enough for him to take on. And even though a part of him wanted to walk through the garden and tap on the glass to ask her to come outside, to have one more conversation before the end, he knew he wouldn't know what to say. And no matter what he asked, he didn't want the answers.

On the night of the storm, as the rain had begun to slow and the sky had turned gray with the coming sun, he'd been right here, thinking about Pete.

When a truck rumbled down the path, Rory stepped behind a tree, if only because he didn't have the strength to face anyone, not yet. But when the truck passed by, its headlights extinguished, he recognized Trey behind the wheel. Why drive without headlights? Why pass by his own home? It was easy enough for Rory to follow him, into the woods, along the paths till

Trey parked outside Vaughn's house and lugged something inside that looked like a body.

Trey had killed Vaughn. Or at least that's what Rory believed. And for a moment, he also believed that all his problems had been solved for him. And that he could be a hero. Lydia's hero. He drew his firearm and edged into the house. Downstairs, Trey breathed heavily. Rory slipped down the stairs, where he saw Daphne slumped on the floor while Trey dumped prescription vials onto a table from a duffel bag. He spun around at the sound of Rory's footsteps.

"Jesus, Rory," he said.

Rory pointed the gun at him and descended the final few steps.

"Put that away," Trey said, in a voice of someone used to getting everything he wanted. It was a voice that incensed Rory. "I found this crazy bitch," Trey said. "She had that kid locked up in the lighthouse the whole time. She took Oliver too. For *them*. I'm trying to get out, you know. I've been trying to get out all summer. And they keep threatening me. They sent her. And she attacked me."

"Where's Ethan?" Rory asked.

"I brought him home," Trey said. "I left him outside the back door. They'll find him soon enough."

"Then why is she here?" Rory asked.

"To help me," Trey said.

"Do what?"

"Put her in that room. We'll lock her in."

"If she kidnapped Ethan, then I'll arrest her," Rory said, still pointing the gun.

Trey pulled a wad of twenty-dollar bills from the

duffel bag and tossed it on the floor. "There," he said. "How's that for motivation? There's more, you know. Plenty more. Don't be an idiot. We can both win."

Rory was across the room in two steps. He was bigger than Trey. Stronger too. And when Trey tried to tackle him, Rory got him into a headlock, one that reminded him of being on a playground, of knuckles digging into skulls. They slammed into the table, and amber-orange prescription bottles scattered across the floor. One of them opened, and pills spilled out, and for Rory, all the pieces fell into place.

"What are those?" he said.

"They're nothing," Trey said.

"Then you take one."

"Are you serious?"

Rory dug the barrel of the gun into Trey's head. He pulled the man across the small room to a sink, where he filled a dirty glass with water. He shoved the pill into Trey's mouth and forced him to drink.

"Come on, man," Trey said. "Enough, okay?"

"Enough?" Rory shouted. "Pete is dead. My brother is dead. My whole family is dead. And you've been in the middle of it this whole time. Take another one!"

"No!"

Rory hit him in the head with the gun. "Take another, or I'll blow your brains out."

Afterward, Rory sat outside the locked room and listened. Soon, a voice crackled over the radio. They'd found Ethan, sitting on the stoop outside his house, like Trey had said they would. Rory could still have done the right thing then, and he'd have forgiven himself for everything that came before. He could have taken the padlock off and left all this behind. But he wanted Lydia, and for that, he needed Vaughn out of the way. So he left what food he could find in a pile on the floor while Daphne lay unconscious on a cot. He waited till he heard Daphne move. She crawled to the door and shook it. He heard her cry out, though the panic hadn't hit her voice yet. And then he left her there, lifting Trey's body into the car, taking Vaughn's knife from his boat in drydock, and bringing the body to the shore, where he plunged the knife into the man's back to be sure he was dead. And to frame Vaughn. He hoped the seagulls would peck out Trey's eyes before the tide carried him out to sea. Neither wish had worked out.

Vaughn was leaving the community center as Rory approached. "We're finished up for the evening," Vaughn said.

"You off to see Lydia?" Rory asked, and Vaughn had the decency to look at the ground. "Be honest with her," Rory said. "It's all you can do."

"Thanks, man," Vaughn said, shaking his hand. "See you around."

Inside, Barb was on the phone. She rolled her eyes when she saw him and made a talking gesture with her hand.

"I need to tell you something," Rory whispered to her. "But I can wait."

This would be his last night here on the island. His last night at home. She could take as much time as she needed.

CHAPTER 28

Hester watched where Rory had disappeared into the dark long after he left. She wished she could have convinced him to keep his secrets—their secrets now—but he was a better person than she was.

She reached for her phone, forgetting for a moment that she'd dropped it in the fire. She imagined the unanswered messages from Morgan, piled on top of one another. How much longer would he put up with her? When would they be whole again? When would they put the arguments and lies behind them? How she yearned to be able to send him a text right now, one that simply said *I need you*, though she imagined typing it, her finger hovering over the Send button before hitting Delete instead. Why was it so difficult to admit? What did it mean to confess to her heart?

She lifted Ethan onto her shoulder and headed to the inn, which was quiet and empty. She found a phone in the kitchen and managed to dig Morgan's phone number from the recesses of her memory. His phone rang until it went to voice mail, and she suspected he'd ignored it because he didn't recognize the number. When she called back, he answered.

"Where are you?" she asked.

"In bed," he said. "It's after midnight."

"Is Kate there?"

"She's in the other room. With Angela. We celebrated tonight."

"What's the celebration?"

"Nothing, really. We made fun out of nothing."

I need you.

"I found Daphne," Hester said. That was easier to say. "She's safe."

There was a silence on the other end of the phone. "Good, I'll talk to her tomorrow."

"Does Kate want to talk to her?"

"I don't want to wake her. And you never know."

"You don't," Hester said. "And you'll need to come to the island in the morning. We're still in the middle of something here."

"We'll be on the morning ferry."

Hester's mouth felt dry. She swallowed. "I need you," she said, wishing instantly that she could reach into the air and pull the words back.

"I love you too," Morgan said.

It was just what Hester needed to hear.

Upstairs, Daphne sat on the bed as Hester let herself into the room. She carefully laid Ethan down and ruffled the boy's hair. "How long have you been here?" she asked.

"Just a few minutes," Daphne said. "They had a lot of questions."

"Did you tell the truth?"

"As much as I could."

"Then I guess we'll be fine."

Daphne nodded at the sleeping boy. "You still have him."

"I need to be sure he's safe," Hester said. "Now. In the morning. Always."

"He's not yours," Daphne said.

"But he's not anyone's," Hester said, pushing her hair behind her ear and kissing the boy's cheek. "Everyone should belong somewhere."

She took out her wallet, where she kept $200 in cash hidden behind her credit cards for emergencies. Now she fished the bills out, folded them in half, and left the wad tucked under a lamp by the TV.

"Come to bed," Daphne said. "It'll be like the old days in Allston. Just the two of us."

"There are three of us tonight," Hester said.

"You know what I mean."

"Can you watch him for a minute?" Hester asked, and in the bathroom she stood under a hot stream of water hoping to feel clean, hoping to wash away the day, even if she had to change back into the same smoky clothes she'd been wearing for days. When she returned to the room, the money still sat where she'd left it.

Ethan had woken, and Daphne crawled on the bed beside him pretending to be an elephant and then a chimpanzee. Hester remembered that, the way Daphne could transform into any animal. She remembered watching as a three-year-old Kate sat transfixed by her mother the lion. Now, Hester watched till Ethan fell back to sleep, and then she crawled into bed. The mattress was soft, and Daphne was warm, and when they turned out the lights, it could have been any time or any place. "Should I be a hyena?" Daphne asked. "Or how about a gorilla?"

"Shh, you'll wake him."

They lay for what seemed like hours, silent and together, listening to each other breathe. When Daphne said, "Tell me about Kate," Hester let the words flow. She told her about Sebastian the rabbit and making homemade Play-Doh. She told her about trying to drop Kate off at daycare and failing day after day. She told her about pushing Kate on that swing as they practiced their numbers. What Hester didn't tell Daphne about was her heart, that her heart traveled with Kate, that it beat with Kate's, or that she couldn't imagine having her own child, because if she'd ever love anyone or anything more than Kate, it would consume her.

"I probably messed Kate up for the rest of her life," Daphne said.

"Children have short memories," Hester said. "And Kate loves you. She loves all of you, every part."

"And I love her," Daphne said, a hitch in her voice. A hitch that gave Hester hope.

"She'll be here in the morning. They're coming on the ferry, and she'll be ready to let me go and to be yours." Hester paused and added, "Completely yours, all over again."

"Will she want that?"

"She wouldn't want anything else."

Hester could play this game. She could play it better than Daphne. She could play it better than anyone.

* * *

In the morning, Hester lay still as the dawn light filtered in through the window. And she listened.

Daphne's breath was soft, even, gentle. Her face was peaceful and at rest, like those times when they'd slept side by side in their dorm room, or in the apartment, or those long nights when Kate first came home.

Daphne shifted, and Hester closed her eyes. When Daphne sat up, Hester lay as still as she could. She sensed a hand hovering at her shoulder, as Daphne decided whether to wake her. This was one of those times when paths were chosen. Hester could say good morning. She could take those choices away. Or she could lie here for a while longer and let Daphne decide.

The early-morning ferry to Bar Harbor blew its horn as it chugged into port.

Daphne swung her legs around. She sat for a moment. And then she stood. The alarm clock on the bedside table clattered to the floor, and Hester wondered if Daphne had knocked it over on purpose to see what Hester would do, whether Daphne knew that when Hester's eyes didn't flutter open, she had permission to leave. She gathered her things and stood in the doorway for a moment. Then she left.

But Hester still didn't dare move. Not till the ferry sailed away.

When she did get up, she found a note in Daphne's handwriting folded under the lamp where the two hundred dollars had been.

The truth is, I'm tough to love, and almost impossible to like. Somehow, you've managed both.

You're a good friend. I love you. More than you know. Don't try to find me.

Hester read the note through again, then folded it and put it in her wallet where the two hundred dollars had been. It would help her remember.

Later, a breeze blew through Hester's hair. All around her, boats came and went as lobstermen brought in their hauls. She stood by the pier, holding Ethan's hand. "Is Mommy coming?" he asked.

"Not today."

Hester prepared for an onslaught of questions, but Ethan seemed to understand that the truth was still too hard to face.

"I miss her," he said.

"I know," she said.

Off in the distance, the ferry chugged into the harbor. Hester couldn't wait to see Morgan and Kate, despite what lay ahead. She'd find the right words to explain what had happened and what she'd done. She'd tell Kate a story that would help her understand where her mother had gone. And she'd tell Morgan the truth. And she'd hope, somehow, that he'd forgive her.

Someone joined Hester at the railing.

"Big night," Barb Kelley said. "Rory came by after you left. Told me some things, but I think you know some of them, don't you?"

"I don't know anything," Hester said.

"Do you know where Daphne is? I need to talk to her."

"She left," Hester said. "She took the morning ferry. She could be anywhere by now."

"I wish she'd stayed," Barb said. "Now we'll have to find her."

They wouldn't be able to, no matter how hard they tried. Daphne was too good at disappearing.

"Before the fire," Barb said. "We searched her room at the house and found a few things. Had them tested. Normally these tests take a few weeks, but not when you have a dead cop."

The ferry was getting closer.

"There was a 'sample,'" Barb continued. "It was from Trey. Did Daphne say anything to you about him?"

"No," Hester said. "Nothing. I don't even know if they knew each other."

"There was something else," Barb said. "Last spring, there was an Amber Alert in Portland for a girl named Jordan."

Someone on the deck waved. Hester raised a hand and waved back.

"The girl showed up in her own backyard," Barb said. "Her mother walked out and found her sitting there."

"Sounds like she wandered off and made her way home again." Hester ruffled Ethan's hair. "Like this one."

"Exactly. Any idea why Daphne might have had a lock of Jordan's hair tucked into a book?"

Hester turned to face Barb. "I don't," she said.

"You sure?" Barb asked.

"More than I've ever been in my life," Hester said. "I don't know anything, and I don't need to know anything else." She glanced across the water to where Morgan stood on the deck of the ferry. "Morgan doesn't want to know anything either."

"But I bet he does," Barb said. "I bet you both do."

"He doesn't."

"I may have questions."

On the deck, Morgan lifted Kate in the air, and the girl waved both arms over her head. When Hester shook her head, he shrugged. Daphne was gone. Again.

"Then come to me," Hester said. "I'll have the answers."

Hester would do anything to protect Morgan, like she protected Kate. Like she protected Daphne.

But tomorrow was Friday. Tomorrow, Hester and Morgan would bring Kate to daycare together. Not just Morgan, but Angela and Cary and Prachi and Jane and Jamie and Ms. Michaela and even Daphne, in her own way, all of them, everyone who Hester loved, lined up along Mass Avenue to cheer her on, to guide her forward, to help her push away the pain and terror that came with life. She didn't live in that apartment in Allston anymore. She wasn't alone. She had more people than Daphne to rely on as she forged her way through this world.

She waved again. Beside Morgan, Angela held Waffles by a leash. Hester lifted Ethan up into her arms. Children didn't disappear, not in this world. Neither did problems.

"Who is that?" Morgan shouted.

"This is Ethan," Hester shouted back. "He likes Thomas the Train!"

"The tank engine!" Ethan said.

"The tank engine!" Hester shouted. "He likes Thomas the Tank Engine. And I don't know what to do with him!"

"We'll figure it out!" Morgan said.

"You know you can't leave with him," Barb said. "Someone from family services is on that boat. They're here to take him."

Maybe, in the end, Ethan would stay on the island with Lydia, with his half-brother Oliver. Maybe he'd go with that social worker. And maybe he'd wind up coming to Somerville with Hester. Whatever happened, she'd be sure he was safe, always and forever.

Another dog ran around Morgan and lifted its two front paws onto the ferry's railing.

"George!" Morgan shouted, pointing at the dog and grinning. "This is George!"

"George!" Hester shouted.

George was huge, with a mangy coat and giant teeth and the kind of face that made people cross the street when they saw him coming. He was the kind of creature only a lunatic could love.

Hester couldn't wait to love him.

December

Hope wakes to the smell of warm croissants wafting through the cold inn. She burrows into the quilts and blankets that cover her bed. They're soft. And safe. When she finally wakes fully, she tests the frigid morning air with a finger, then her whole arm. Like diving into the ocean, she shoves the bedding aside and leaps into her day.

After showering under hot water that pulses from the showerhead and changing into jeans and a red sweater, she heads down the narrow back staircase. Christmas decorations hang along the bannister, into the living and dining rooms, through to the kitchen where the croissants cool on racks. There are four dozen—plain, chocolate, and her favorite, almond. They come frozen, shipped here from a factory, ready to bake, hardly homemade the way the guests at the inn expect them to be.

The tiniest of lies.

Hope tears into an almond croissant, shoving the pieces into her mouth before Sandrine catches her.

Sandrine believes that she sees everything.

Hope fills two baskets with the croissants and strides into the dining room with confidence. Because Hope is confident. Happy.

She's hopeful.

"Let's invite Hope!" Sandrine had said only the other night as she'd made plans with friends. She'd said it into the phone while Hope listened from outside the room.

"*Bonjour*, hello," Hope says, delivering the baskets.

The French sounds like a song, and it still feels like everyone who speaks it is pretending, that they're all in one long high school *exercise* and that the bell will ring and they'll all return to speaking English.

In the kitchen, Sandrine has appeared, her springy hair tied in a ponytail, that apron screaming *Tres Bien!* tied around her ample waist. Despite their location in southern Québec, despite her name, Sandrine doesn't speak a word of French. Oh, she tries, but she only manages to sound like a three-year-old. She moved here from Vermont, two generations removed from her Québécois heritage. She told Hope that she dreamed of owning an inn, of making happy people feel "at home." But Hope can tell, and Sandrine doesn't try to hide it, that the woman has stepped into her own hell. She hates standing all day, and the varicose veins that have spread down her legs, and the way those uneaten muffins and croissants and poutine—endless, endless poutine, the only thing that Americans think they eat in Québec—somehow make it into her mouth and onto her hips. "Before I had Jean-Marc . . ." Sandrine had said only the other day, looking at herself from the side in the mirror and leaving the sentence unfinished. Practically begging Hope to finish it. To give it a hopeful flourish. Hope had split a muffin in two and watched while Sandrine succumbed in two quick bites.

This morning, Sandrine looks as if she hasn't slept. Her husband, Henri—he speaks French—came home last night drunk, and the screaming had started with a whisper, seeping through the vents and into the cold air like frozen breath. Henri moved with ease between French and English. Soon the whisper turned to a roar, and Henri shouted words like *salope* and *ta gueule*, the words that Hope had loved tossing off in high school French, the words that had stuck. She caught those that she could, piecing together bits of the conversation in the Québécois she was only beginning to learn. So it took a moment for Henri's words to take hold. *Je vais te tuer*.

Hope sat up, the cold flooding her blankets.

I'll kill you.

The yelling stopped. Even Sandrine, in her ignorance of French, had understood what Henri meant.

"Two eggs benedict, Table 5," Hope says.

Sandrine pulls a skillet down from over the stove. She seems to be moving in slow motion, cracking eggs into a pot of simmering water and mindless of the shells that follow. "All those years of high school Spanish," she says. "And I could have ridden my bike over here to practice French." She clucks her tongue and watches the eggs simmering. She tilts her head. "I saw you," she says.

Hope's stomach drops.

"I saw you eat that croissant," Sandrine adds. "You don't have to sneak food. We're family."

The panic subsides almost at once. Hope mumbles thank you and grabs two more baskets and retreats to the dining room, only to see Henri at reception. He's different this morning, removed from last night's disembodied voice. He has thick, unruly black hair and piercing blue eyes. He makes customers want to return year after year. But most of the people who come to the inn are American and blissfully monolingual. Henri could threaten to gouge Sandrine's eyes out, and all that these people would notice would be his smile.

But not Hope.

Last night, she snuck out of bed, her feet going numb when they hit the cold floor. Down the hallway, and to their bedroom door, where she put an ear to the keyhole and listened as a fist hit soft flesh, the parts of the body easily covered with a *Tres Bien!* apron.

Now Hope passes by Henri, waiting till he meets her gaze before letting her eyes fall. A coquette. That's her part to play. He wants his women to be thin and pretty. Submissive. She heads upstairs and into an empty bedroom. She remembers hearing him last night, his voice barely a whisper. "*Ton fils*," he said to Sandrine, "*il sera la prochaine.*"

Had Sandrine understood? Had she been relieved this morning to find Jean-Marc safe, asleep, his thumb in his mouth. Unbruised. What will she think later, when he goes missing? What will Sandrine imagine? What will she convince herself she should have done? When the police do show up, Hope will tell them that she spent the morning serving breakfast and going from room to room, cleaning bathrooms, changing sheets. She'll say it in broken French, more broken than necessary. It'll make her seem simple. Easy to ignore. And if they get too close—if they point the finger at the stranger, the outsider, the one from away—it'll be easy enough to start a whispering campaign to fend them off. To discredit them. To deflect the blame right back at them.

She's done it before.

The door to the bedroom opens and closes. Henri holds the knob behind him, his hips thrust forward, a grin forming at the edges of his mouth. He likes to stand, to watch in the mirror. Hope looks at herself, at her black hair. It felt best to make a change. To be someone new. Is coloring your hair a lie, however tiny, when it's out there for all the world to see, when the roots, still orange like a carrot, sprout from her scalp? But she'll need to take care of that soon. To let Daphne remain Hope.

He kisses her, a hand groping at her breast. He squeezes a nipple. And she remembers, another time, another place, a Fourth of July celebration, another child in danger. She remembers covering her hair with a cap. "Oliver," she'd said, crouching and holding out a hand.

"Who are you?" he asked.

"A gorilla." She puffed out her cheeks and scratched her armpit. "Or a spider." She walked her hand up his neck. "I can be whatever you want."

And he took that hand in his, as they walked away from the crowds, toward another life.

ACKNOWLEDGMENTS

I originally set this story on the very real Monhegan Island off the coast of Maine, but as I drafted, I realized I needed to change some details about the landscape of the actual island, and I needed to borrow the police force from Peaks Island in Casco Bay. So I created the fictional Finisterre. Still, anyone who has lived on or visited Monhegan will recognize many of the details from this beautiful and special place.

In researching this story, I relied on several resources, including *The Lobster Chronicles: Life on a Very Small Island*, by Linda Greenlaw and *Dreamland: The True Tale of America's Opiate Epidemic*, by Sam Quinones. I am also forever indebted to Bruce Robert Coffin, former Portland detective and current author, for helping me refine the details in the novel around police investigations. If you like expertly plotted procedurals, check out his fantastic Detective Byron series (brucerobertcoffin.com). Also, thank you to the many, many people who answered a desperate Facebook plea about the differences between three- and four-year-old children, including Mara, Traci, Jennifer, Beth, Dave, and Matt. You'll see some of your stories in Kate, Oliver, and Ethan. As always, any and all errors are my own.

To my fantastic agent, Robert Guinsler, thank you for your friendship and for making so many things possible. I am eternally grateful to Ellen Thibault for burning the midnight oil as deadlines approached. I couldn't have finished this novel without your kind guidance and support. And to the incredible team at Kensington, starting with editor extraordinaire John Scognamiglio; the publicity team of Vida Engstrand, Lulu Martinez, and Lauren Jerningan; and Steve Zacharius, Lynn Cully, Lou Malcangi, Tracy Marx, Robin Cook, and everyone else behind the scenes, I couldn't ask for a better publishing team.

I've had the privilege of getting to know so many generous people in the writing community. Thank you to Maggie Barbieri, Mario Giordano, John Keyse-Walker, Bracken MacLeod, Carla Neggers, Hank Phillippi Ryan, Joanna Schaffhausen, and Jessica Treadway for taking the time to read and comment on a manuscript by a very unproven writer. And thank you to Shawn Reilly Simmons for being kind enough to say hello.

To Betty and Jack and the rest of my family, thank you for your continued love and support. And to Michael and Edith Ann, thank you for sticking with me though this journey. It wouldn't happen without you. For real.

To anyone who took a chance on this book, thank you a million times over. Please be in touch: edwin-hill.com.

This book, the whole series, really, is about the power of friendship. I am forever thankful for the many people I've called friends over the years. I dedicate this book to Jennifer Gormley. What a gift it was to call each other friends for over thirty years. I miss you.

Please turn the page for an exciting sneak peek of
Edwin Hill's next Hester Thursby mystery
WATCH HER
coming soon wherever print and e-books are sold!

Freezing rain splattered the windshield as Hester Thursby's non-husband Morgan tried to parallel park their truck for the third time. Heat poured from the vents. A week into spring, and winter had a hold on Boston.

When Morgan finally succeeded in parking, he cut the engine, leaned across the cab, and kissed Hester on the cheek. Tonight, he'd tamed his red hair and changed out of the scrubs he wore at the veterinary hospital and into a navy blue suit that fit perfectly, a suit that made its way out of his closet about once a year. The two of them didn't get out much these days.

"Hello, Mrs.," he said, kissing her again.

"Yuck! Quit kissing."

Hester's five-year-old niece Kate glared at them from the rear cab. These days, the girl seemed to drink in everything and anything that happened around her and didn't think twice about voicing her opinions. Kate would finish kindergarten in a few months, and Hester knew she'd blink and soon enough the girl would be heading off to college. She tried to cherish every moment with her niece, even these ones, the ones that gave her a glimpse of the teenage years.

"How's this?" Morgan asked, kissing Hester with exaggerated smacks. He rolled over the seat and into the back, and kissed Kate, too, who shrieked and shoved him away. "Uncle Morgan, you are disgusting."

"Guilty as charged," Morgan said.

"And saying no is your prerogative," Hester said.

"It is!" Morgan said, letting Kate shove him away and having the good sense not to go in for a final smooch.

"What's prerogative?" Kate asked.

"Your choice," Hester said, quickly adding, "But not when it comes to eating vegetables."

"None of us has a choice when it comes to vegetables," Morgan said.

Kate was Morgan's niece, his twin sister Daphne's daughter, though the girl had lived with Hester and Morgan for more than two years now, ever since Daphne had skipped town. For most of Hester's adult life, she'd thought of Daphne as her best friend. Now, she wasn't sure. She had more friends than she'd ever had in her life, more people who loved and cared for her, and the years she'd spent with Daphne, first as undergrads at Wellesley College, and later as roommates in Allston, was beginning to feel like a different life.

Since her friend had left town, Hester had seen Daphne once, briefly, a year and a half ago, a meeting that had nearly ended Hester's relationship with Morgan, but one that had helped them heal stronger than they were before. Now, Hester and Morgan did their best to keep Daphne real and present in Kate's life, talking about her in big and small ways when it made sense. For a long time, Kate had spoken about her mother with reverence and what Hester had seen as a deep longing. Recently, though, she'd noticed that Daphne came up in conversation less frequently, and when she did, it was Kate who often steered the conversation away to another topic.

"It's pouring out," Hester said. "We'll have to run between the raindrops."

"You can't run between raindrops," Kate said.

"And I can't fool you with anything these days," Hester said.

She opened the door and leapt to the asphalt below, yanking up the hood on her blue raincoat. When she stepped on the running board to help Kate out, Kate had already undone her seatbelt. "I can do it myself," the girl said, slipping right past Hester's outstretched arms and leaping to the ground.

Yes, you can.

Morgan dashed to their side. The three of them hurried through the rain, down Amory Street in Jamaica Plain, a neighborhood on the outskirts of Boston, and toward a brick building that took up most of the block. Banners for Prescott University, a local art school, spanned the building's street face, and lights blared from plate-glass windows.

"This is a change," Hester said. "I haven't been over here for a while."

Until recently, this neighborhood had been industrial, filled with mostly abandoned factories.

"I went to high school a few blocks from here," Morgan said, which took Hester by surprise.

She and Morgan had an unspoken rule: they didn't talk about their pasts. They didn't mention dating history or their families. It was like they'd both appeared on the earth fully formed on the day they met. In the nine years they'd been together, Hester had learned that Morgan grew up in South Boston, the youngest of ten children, and that his father, a cop, had been shot in the line of duty. Hester knew Daphne, of course, but she hadn't met any other members of the Maguire clan. Now, she also knew that he'd gone to high school in Jamaica Plain. For his part, Morgan had managed to ferret out that Hester had grown up in a small town on the South Shore—though she couldn't confirm that he knew which one—and that she didn't speak to her mother anymore. She had no plans of letting him find out anything else.

Hester liked their arrangement, even if it might appear unhealthy to anyone on the outside. She focused on the present and the future and let the past go. So, now, even though she could have asked a follow up question—what school? Were you in the marching band? Did you date the head cheerleader?—she let the statement hang between them.

Kate, however, did not.

"Can we see your school?" she asked.

"I don't think it's there anymore," Morgan said. "They tore it down."

"When?"

"Maybe ten years ago."

Kate thought about that for a moment. "Before I was born," she said, her latest obsession as she'd figured out there was a time before her own existence.

"Long before," Morgan said.

They reached an awning stenciled with blue dolphins, where, behind a set of glass doors, a crowd had already gathered in an atrium with ceilings that soared to thirty feet. Inside and out of the rain, the noise from the crowd thankfully drowned out any more questions from Kate.

"I didn't know this would be such a big deal," Hester shouted.

Banners fell from the ceiling announcing "Boston's Thirty Under 30 in Graphic Design" while servers in black ties circulated among a crowd of young women in cocktail dresses and men in fashionable glasses. One of their friends, Jamie Williams, a tenant in their house, was one of the thirty being honored tonight.

Kate took a step away into the throngs. Hester grabbed her hand. "Stick with me," she said.

Morgan checked their coats and offered an arm. "Should we dive in?"

Hester smoothed the fabric on her black cocktail dress and put a hand to her hair, which she'd tied into a bun. She'd even dug out makeup for this event. She occasionally attended cocktail parties at Harvard, where she worked at Widener Library, but most nights, the three of them stayed at home with their dog Waffles, or with a small, tight-knit group of friends. Tonight, she recognized familiar faces from TV, local newscasters and politicians, even a state senator. On the other side of the room, she saw Wendy Richards, a well-known socialite who Hester had met a few years earlier and formed a brief but intense friendship. The season of that friendship had passed, but Hester still hoped she'd get to say hello tonight.

"You made it!"

Hester turned to her friend, Angela White. Angela was a detective with the Boston police, and she usually wore tailored suits and practical shoes that made it easy to move. Tonight, she'd opted for a multicolored caftan and tied a scarf over her thick, natural hair. Heels added three inches to her six feet. "I went for artistic," Angela said, when she caught Hester eyeing her getup. "Don't get used to it. These shoes are killing me."

Hester brushed a few dog hairs from Angela's dress. "George travels with you, even when you leave him home."

"Damn dog," Angela said, shooting Morgan a glare. "I still blame you for foisting that creature on us, Mr. Maguire."

Angela's wife Cary handed her a plastic cup filled with white wine. "You love George," Cary said, in her soft, therapeutic voice. "Even when he slobbers."

"He's a pain in my ass."

Isaiah, Cary's seven-year-old son, tugged at Hester's sleeve. Unlike Kate, Isaiah was shy, and would usually only speak when Hester crouched so that he could whisper in her ear. "I won the hundred-meter butterfly," he whispered now.

"A blue ribbon?" Hester whispered back. "Make sure to show me next time I'm over."

Just as Angela hated most dogs, Hester, as a rule, hated kids. She made a few, rare exceptions.

Morgan sidled up to her. "Don't you want to know more about my high school?" he asked.

A server came by with a tray of hors d'oeuvres. "Lobster and corn empanada?" she asked.

"I'll take one of those," Hester said, shoving the whole thing into her mouth to keep from answering.

Morgan took one, too, but waited for Hester to finish chewing.

"You're very restrained," she said.

He tilted his head at her and raised an eyebrow.

"You look like Waffles waiting for a treat?" Hester said, and when he still wouldn't let it go, she added, "You know I'll look it up when I get to work tomorrow. I'll figure out what Jamaica Plain schools were demolished, then I'll read everything I can about it, find your yearbook, and then not tell you anything I learned. Happy?"

He grinned and ate the empanada in a single bite. "Where'd the kids go?" he asked a second later.

Hester turned in the crowded room, but Kate had managed to slip away. So had Isaiah, though Hester was certain Kate had led the escape. Since she'd begun kindergarten, Kate had shown an independent spirit that Hester constantly reminded herself to foster. "I'll find her," she said. "Get me a ginger ale and rye."

Morgan saluted and headed toward the bar.

"You go that way," Angela said. "I'll go this way."

"Text if you find them."

Hester pushed herself into the crowd. She also pushed down that shadow of fear that still gripped her heart whenever Kate was out of her sight. They couldn't have gone far.

Not in thirty seconds.

Connect with Us

Visit us online at
KensingtonBooks.com
to read more from your favorite authors, see books
by series, view reading group guides, and more.

Join us on social media

for sneak peeks, chances to win books and prize packs,
and to share your thoughts with other readers.

facebook.com/kensingtonpublishing
twitter.com/kensingtonbooks

Tell us what you think!

To share your thoughts, submit a review,
or sign up for our eNewsletters, please visit:
KensingtonBooks.com/TellUs.